PRAISE FOR POP!

"*POP!* is a stunning exploration of ambition and drive... in the capable hands of Angel Luis Colón, it becomes an existential journey not to be missed."

—**S.A. Cosby**, bestselling author of *King of Ashes*

"*POP!* brings Colón back to his roots, crackling with sharp noir energy and the grit and laughs folks have come to expect from him. *POP!* is twisted, fun, dark, and loaded with heart."

—**Alex Segura**, bestselling author of *Daredevil: Enemy of My Enemy*, *Alter Ego*, and *Secret Identity*

"As witty as it is vicious, *POP!* reads like *The Devil Wears Prada* and *Layer Cake* got into a gunfight that left them both too bloody to be distinguishable from each other. This is a grimly fun and uncompromising crime thriller."

—**Johnny Compton**, Bram Stoker Award-nominated author of *The Spite House* and *Dead First*

"*POP!* Is Angel Luis Colón at his best—sparse, noir-infused prose that lingers long after it's been read, an atmospheric New York City that's lovingly told even as Colón strips it of its illusion, and entirely unpredictable characters. Poppy, his latest protagonist, is a wonderful creation—jaded, hard, and ambitious, and yet somehow endearing. This is a book no other writer could create, and nobody writes like Angel Luis Colón."

—**E.A. Aymar**, author of *When She Left*

"I would do anything for Poppy Leathers. I would die for her. I would read a thousand books about her and still beg for more."

—**Libby Cudmore**, award-winning author of *Negative Girl* and *The Big Rewind*

"*POP!* is the kind of crime novel you didn't know you need: a hot blend of imagination and suspense, all led by a protagonist with an unhinged passion for winning at whatever she puts her mind to. This time it's crime."

—**Errick Nunnally**, author of *The Queen of Saturn and the Prince In Exile*, and the Alexander Smith series

"From the face slap of the very first line, Colón hooks you into a masterclass of pacing and snappy, often hilarious dialogue. Poppy Leathers isn't exactly a nice person, but she's one hell of a ride in this gritty story that features Brooklyn as you've (hopefully) never experienced it before."

—**Jeff Somers**, author of *Five Funerals: Choose Your Own Perilous Path* and the Avery Cates series

POP!

ANGEL LUIS COLÓN

RUADÁN
BOOKS

Boston, MA

POP!

ISBN 978-1-968143-08-4 (trade paperback)
ISBN 978-1-968143-09-1 (ebook)
ISBN 978-1-968143-10-7 (audiobook)
Library of Congress Control Number: 9781968143084

Edited by R.B. Wood
Design/Formatting by Leah Donell

First Edition

RuadanBooks.com

To all of you doing more for less

—your time will come.

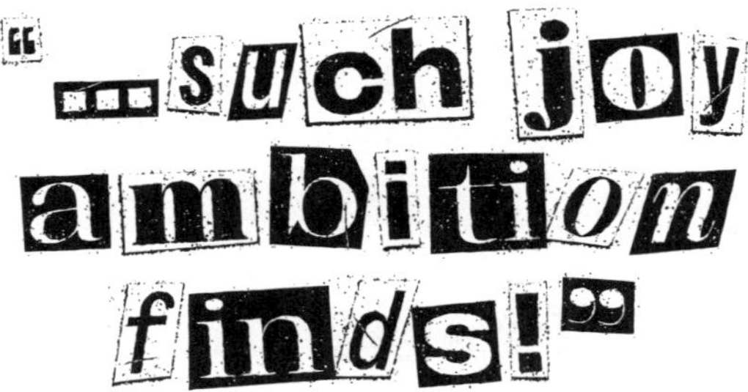

—John Milton

TABLE OF CONTENTS

WAIT…

I need you to understand something very clearly: I regret nothing.

Not one word. Not one lie.
Not one action. Not one bullet.
Not one body.

This is for your benefit, not mine.
I don't care what you think.

I've already made peace with me.

CHAPTER ONE

I sold my baby for fifteen thousand dollars back in the aughts—I think it was the aughts. Hard to remember. It always feels like we're ten years out from the '90s.

Anyway, there were people ready to care for that baby, and I needed money for grad school. I wasn't going to let all the hard work go down the drain that way. The nights studying pages of nonsense I would never bring up outside of an alumni reunion, cost-cutting my groceries down to $21 worth of rice cakes a week, the complete fucking lack of social life. No disrespect to the kid inside me, but I figured if I was going to give them life, they could at least do me a favor and make it worth my while.

I never let the two-pump chump of a TA know about his contribution to this. Didn't need another dude in a long line of dudes explaining how my decisions affected them for the millionth fucking time.

After I delivered the baby, the doctors offered me a free hysterectomy. I took them up on it. My plans did not have room for future babies. My goals were not in line with those of my reproductive organs. I had a Master of Fine Arts to wrap up. I had a career to look forward to—a path straight to the Metropolitan Museum of Art in New York City. Everything else after would be a run downhill.

The whole selling my baby experience was shockingly professional and, honestly, easier than I imagined. After they took the baby and stitched me up, I was visited by a woman wearing a bone white pantsuit and a gorgeous bolo tie inlaid with gemstones I didn't know the names of. She had a pleasant smile and an even sweeter voice, laced with Alabama honey.

"How are you, darling?" she asked.

"Tired," I said. "Relieved." Then, "Thinking."

The woman smiled and offered me a clipboard, sheets of paper in one hand and a pen in the other. "Sounds like it all went well, then. Other girls in your place have said the same thing." The corners of her lips straightened. "If you're in need of any emotional support—"

"Emotional? No. I'm fine. Won't count out that it might hit me in a day or two, but I'm feeling very detached."

"Ah, well then." Waved the clipboard in front of me. I could tell she wanted this over with.

I signed what she offered. Didn't bother reading it. They'd mentioned NDAs and other paperwork when I agreed to do this—when I signed the first set of contracts. It all felt so streamlined. Like getting a new cell phone or buying something at a fancy store. I was immediately obsessed, honestly, and when I found obsession, I had to find out *everything* about it. I had to understand it temples to ankles or it would drive me crazy the rest of my life. I mean, the whole selling off my baby thing was something I couldn't believe existed to begin with. How could I possibly walk away satisfied if I didn't know more?

Forget know more. Another thought snuck into my brain. It seeded itself firm in my frontal lobe, and I felt its roots entrench themselves. It was more than obsession: it was a goal.

"Hey," I said in between sheets, "I have a question for you."

"If it's about the stay, you're welcome to rest here for as long as you need. This isn't a traditional facility."

I shook my head and checked my penmanship. I didn't want to be sloppy. It's important, how you present yourself in moments like these. "No. Something else." I laughed a little. "I sort of think too much when I'm stressed out, and I started thinking about how—"

"Did you need transportation?"

"Uh, no."

"Would you prefer cash instead of a check?"

I wasn't a fan of how she was trying to get ahead of me. Any other time, I would have made that known. But this lady seemed like someone you didn't want to upset. I needed something, and her general good mood relied on that.

"I have a checking account, thank you," I said. "But

what I was hoping to know is. Well. Are you hiring?" I knew better than to leave off there. "I'm a fantastic notetaker. Not too bad with Excel. Fast learner. Incredibly observant and discreet." I smiled as best as a woman could after hours of Pitocin, childbirth, and recovery. Professional, a hint of teeth, including the eyes—my mother always told me people could tell you were faking when the eyes didn't match the lips.

The woman scoffed but collected herself quickly, cheeks flushing. I'd caught her off guard. Good. "You want a job?"

A single nod. The question was asked; I didn't need to come off desperate. "I'm an unemployed grad student. The money you're paying me is going to help me in the short term, but I'm a bit of a long-term thinker."

Alabama cleared her throat. "Well..."

"I know, I'm sure it's not normal for a freelancer to ask for something a little more permanent."

When these folks recruited me through my OB-GYN, I'd planned on traditional adoption. The kid deserved more than an asshole like me, and I was smart enough to realize that was the right path. That said, cash was an extraordinarily strong motivator. And the six months between recruitment and delivery had me thinking ridiculously hard about this operation. There was more to be gained than a one-time payment, and I was not about to be another asshole taking a slice when the whole pie was attainable. Fifteen grand wasn't about to get me through a Master's program debt-free. Steady income? Step it back: tax-free steady income? That was a goal.

The blank stare I received, though. I knew that look—the one folks gave when they didn't want to see you on their level. When you interrupted their very stable view of you—which was below them. I walked into this place, and she thought she knew who I was. I went and made it a big fat lie. The fucking nerve of me.

"Maybe there's someone else to talk to." I decided to go dismissive, reinforce what she thought she knew, make her feel better. "Or maybe I should just shut my mouth. Sorry. Has to be the drugs."

It was very much not the drugs.

"There is no 'someone else,'" Alabama lied. "We're happy to give you your payment and ensure your safety. Beyond that, I'm afraid we're not hiring."

"I'm happy to sweep the floor for a few bucks if it's a question of budget. Prove myself. Work my way up."

Canned laughter this time. "Aren't you a character." Not a question.

The smack I'd have given her if I could stand up. "Nah. I'm chock full of potential and I'm paying attention."

I worried, for a minute, that had sounded like a threat—which it was, but I wasn't stupid enough to want it to *sound* like a threat. Alabama collected my papers and went through them. It didn't seem to register. "They'll give you your cash once you're ready to check out. Since it seems you're feeling… energetic, maybe you can make it home sooner than we both thought."

I was getting to her. Good. She'd remember me. "Maybe."

Alabama left the room, I got my cash a few minutes later, and then was "gently" watched by a man a little too large for me to call an orderly—clear bias on my part—for the better part of the three hours it took me to feel awkward enough to limp out of the clinic. There was a car waiting for me out front that took me to my apartment—I hadn't told anyone where I lived, although I'd just assumed that they'd gotten the information from my shady OB-GYN at some point—and I slept for three days straight.

A week later, I went back to that unmarked clinic. Surprise, surprise: nobody was home. Maybe I'd spooked them. Maybe they were leaving either way. I remember standing out front of the vacant building and feeling so *angry*. Alabama could have given me a chance. She could have listened to me. We could have built something even better than what they already had. I had felt ownership, just for a little moment, as I lay in that shoddy hospital bed. And now, with the loss of that ownership, there was grief. Just a little bit. But it was there.

And it was enough to promise myself that I wasn't going to let that happen again.

If they wouldn't give it to me, I'd take it.

CHAPTER two

Whenever there was a stopgap—a stutter in the plan—my mother always taught me to take a step back and reevaluate. She told me to visualize my plan, and the very first step in doing that was to place it in front of me physically. To make the goal concrete, the plan had to be concrete, as well. Nobody got to where they were going with their eyes closed and a smile on their face. So, I got to work.

Poster board. Glitter. Large, scented markers. Lots of pictures from random magazines.

MY BIG PLAN.

I stared at my old board with its antiquated path to success. School. Grad school. The Met. Quick interruption by pregnancy. Utter derailment by "the incident" five months into my tenure at the museum. Wasn't my fault.

I stared at the new board: a clean slate. Only problem was, I didn't have a clue what I *really* wanted. I'd spent so long focused on the old goals, I didn't know where to restart. I mean, I was damn good at what I did. Graduated Summa Cum Laude. High recognition from my programs and professors. People literally threw letters of recommendation at me. The idea I'd have to start again? It made me feel so fucking small. And there was a voice in the back of my head that scoffed at that feeling. How could I possibly feel unprepared? I'd worked so fucking hard. Built a strong foundation. Before the incident, I felt on top of the world. I had confidence that my next 5, 10, 15 years were set for me.

I didn't have that stability anymore. I couldn't see hours ahead, let alone months or years.

Christ, I didn't have anything. Before the Met, that was all I wanted. I worked hard like everyone told me to. I paid my dues. I did all the right things, even when I made mistakes. All it led me to was a job I hated and allegedly breaking my boss' hand with a rubber mallet—which was only mostly true—it wasn't rubber. Plus, she started it with her bullshit better-than-everyone attitude. As if she hadn't gotten her job because her mothball smelling grandmother was a Vanderbilt or a Roosevelt or whatever other fancy-sounding white people last name existed in New York City with ancient money.

Without that job, who the fuck was I? I'd given up every part of myself in order to make it in a world I thought was meant to be mine, and I'd let a moment of weakness shatter that forever. My navel-gazing left me blaming myself. Had I sabotaged things on purpose? Did I question whether I deserved the payoff after all the work? Or were things far worse than that? Did I sabotage myself because I knew, deep down, that I'd never actually wanted it in the first place?

I didn't know what to do if that last part was true. What the hell did I want, if I could spend so much time lying to myself about who I wanted to be and not even know it?

Nope. Not worth worrying about. What's done was done, past is past. I had a brand-new board just waiting for some scented marker.

I started from the bottom; wrote "The Incident" in pink magic marker. It smelled like berries, but no berry I'd ever ingested before. Figured I had to address it somehow. Only way to go from there was up, right? But what was up? I had no idea where to go next. Nobody in my field was going to hire me, and I sure as hell couldn't see myself in an office gritting my teeth among white men with more daddy issues than brain cells.

What the fuck was it I wanted? What other ways could I use my degree? I knew a few gallery owners in Chelsea. Maybe I could investigate light work at a trendy spot. Do a little networking. Ingratiate myself to the little snobs who oohed and ahhed at trash art being sold by the sons and daughters of idiots who couldn't be bothered to let their kids fail the right way. Plenty of opportunities to make money that way. Even under the table opportunities, if the gallery worked with the right kind of people.

Great. A path to the middle manager section of New York City's art world. I could live with that—mostly. It was just for the cash, anyway—something to live off of while I worked on the other branch.

But that other branch. What would that be? I decided to be unrealistic for a change. If I could do anything, resolve any regrets. What was the glitteriest path to my still very undefined goal?

I thought about the baby then. No, that's not true. I didn't think about the baby—not sentimentally, at least. I thought about Alabama. The way she looked at me. The way she assumed who I was. Wasn't sure if it was a wounded ego or something more, but I kept coming back to her and her assumptions. Was it weird for me to ask for a job in what was clearly a criminal—or criminal adjacent—enterprise? Sure. Was I probably qualified for *something* within that organization? Fuck yes. I was overqualified if anything. But the stuck-up butthole had told me no.

And that crawled straight up my ass.

I used a fine-detail pencil for this branch. Made it as fancy as a fantasy like that demanded, a path through a criminal enterprise. A pink-frilled rise to the top of whatever that was. It was fun. Start at the bottom as a gopher, or some kind of go-between for nobodies within the business. Rise to the top as the person who pushed Alabama aside and did that business right. No assumptions. No bullshit. I knew how to run shit.

I just needed a shot.

When I finished, I realized that, at some point, my branches had converged. I knew I could leverage the galleries towards something a little more fabulous on the wrong side of the path. It would all lead to the same place. Not a job. Not a rank. That was baby stuff.

I realized my problem: I wasn't the person I wanted to be. And that was the person on top. So, no, these branches weren't right, after all. But they'd led me to what was. To a woman who was the embodiment of her dreams. Someone who played the part to be the part. Someone new.

I had a new goal, then. Two words: Poppy Leathers. *That* was what I was going to reach for. A new me. A woman in control. A woman who got shit done on her own terms. Poppy Leathers didn't live to follow the breadcrumbs.

Poppy Leathers lived to set the goddamn rules herself.

ONE YEAR LATER

"Do you like frittatas?" Atticus Garcia stood in front of his stove with an easy smile, his eyes locked on the eggs he was preparing, spatula held an inch over the pan as a promise and a threat.

Atticus was tall—strikingly so. Shaved head. Strong features—handsome—a little Middle-American darling, but with a gentle tan and a pair of lilac Warby Parkers perched on his nose. His beard touched the center of his chest. Handlebar mustache to boot. Impeccably dressed would be an understatement: lilac vest, white button-down with glossy green buttons, gray chinos, matching lilac loafers—no socks—as if it had all been sewn onto him. Whatever skin was exposed bore vibrant tattoos with no connected theme.

Atticus Garcia: what if the entire borough of Brooklyn was distilled down into a man-shaped mold that killed people for a living?

I loved it.

We'd met at a low-rent gallery that ran photo and art shows for college freshmen. I was just starting to manage a local artist, Jason Tasker. Jason was an extremely happy accident, since I was affordable and he was stupendously poor at the time. Besides, he hit all the right marks on my vision board.

Jason's star was rising, and Atticus was clued into what was what. He offered a stupid amount of cash for a Tasker piece and our conversation went from there. I knew who he was. Everyone did. The whisper networks were all aflutter over Atticus Garcia, the artist of violence. He worked for Silo Jotter, a man feared and respected for obsessively working to keep Brooklyn, well, Brooklyn. I realized that if I got in with a man like Atticus, getting in with a man like Silo Jotter was possible. I would be in that rarified position where the branches in my path converged. I would be that much closer to who I knew I could be.

But how did I get to having this strapping bastard asking how I liked my eggs prepared?

I asked for the job. How could I not? The entire point of getting myself muddled in the slums of gallery art was to have a happy networking accident, and there was Atticus on a platter. There was no other choice. I had to reach for that brass ring, and there was no way I would have let him leave that gallery without trying.

So, I offered him my services for exactly zero fucking

dollars, because—holy shit—this was my in. Art paid bills, but the world Atticus lived in? That ran on far more than a weekly paycheck.

"I'm going to admit surprise that you know who I am, because I usually know who knows me." Atticus smiled, easy but on guard. Still dangerous, even when making frittatas. Maybe especially when making frittatas. "But I won't lie: I am a little perturbed that I never heard of Poppy Leathers."

"Nothing complicated," I said, "I'm an art manager and, if you'll have me, your personal assistant."

"And that's all? Nothing else? No old vendettas? No connections to someone whose doorway I may have darkened in the past?" Atticus went back to focusing on the task. He held a hand up and continued staring at the eggs. "Before you answer, give me one second. This requires perfect timing, and I can't stand serving a guest less-than-perfect eggs."

"I can appreciate that," I said, watching as he finished his business before I continued. "I'd heard about you, and then there you were at the same art show as I was. I figured my interests aligned with a lot of the business you delve in, so I decided being direct was the best approach."

I wasn't lying. I did appreciate Atticus' eye for detail, his aura of get-shit-done. The man seemed impeccably capable. He was like my dream board brought to life, just with less glitter. What made it worse is the ease I felt around him. I knew his reputation, I knew he killed, but

I wasn't afraid. It was dumb, but the way I felt drawn to him was uncontrollable. It wasn't lust, just… fascination. How could I be the kind of person Atticus was? I needed to figure that part out. And that meant I needed to be with him; to be a part of his life in a way that went well past friends or lovers.

I needed to be a part of him. Like a limb he never knew he needed.

Atticus canted his head to the side and pursed his lips. "Okay. That sounds logical. Though, you understand what I do, don't you?"

"You kill people for money."

"It's a little more complicated than that."

"You kill people for money for a guy who has complicated reasons for killing those people."

"That's closer to it."

"I heard about the water sommelier thing. That was actually justified." I pinched my fingers and gave them a chef's kiss. "And drowning him in his own swill? Art, my man. Art."

Atticus nodded enthusiastically. "Immensely justified."

See, Atticus was the man Silo Jotter sent when things went wrong—when money went dry or, worse, missing. He was the last man Adelaide Delgado, the renowned spring water sommelier drowned in his own product, saw after a harsh controversy in which he had served Silo what was supposed to be verified spring water from the Yucatán but was, in fact, tap water from the slop sink of a dive bar in Mexico City. Adelaide was taken for a fool by cartel thugs looking for a laugh and a dollar. It cost the poor bastard his life.

That Atticus was a free man despite so many people like me knowing the details of his little escapades? Fear. We gossiped, but ain't a damn soul was going to have the audacity to tattle. Flapping one's gums would end badly, and Silo probably owned the cops in four out of five boroughs—not like he was going to throw money into the toilet that was Staten Island.

"So, I'm an admirer of sorts," I said. "And I'm interested in helping you while getting a little real, uh, underworld experience I guess is what I'm going for."

Atticus plated two equal portions of sweet potato, watercress, and feta cheese frittata with three slices of sourdough toast each. He poured fresh coffee from a French press and walked the food over to the table. "Grab the coffee, please. You'll find some fresh butter next to the sink. I believe it's been left out long enough to spread without issue." He sat down and folded his hands in front of him.

I did as I was told and sat down in front of my plate. It looked like the motherfucker pulled it out of a magazine spread. I was afraid it was fake, and even more afraid to allow my fork to sully what he had created.

"So, you want to learn how to hit?" His brows arched up. "I'll admit, most people in this field sort of fall into it."

I struggled with that one. "I'm not entirely sure I want

to run around killing people. But I know I do want to understand everything else."

"Everything else?"

"The background stuff. How you learn about targets or how you clean your guns. The boring parts."

Atticus seemed surprised. "The boring parts," he repeated. "Why?"

"Because that makes me indispensable."

"Huh. That's an interesting take." Atticus smiled softly and shook his head. "You're interesting, Pop." He motioned to the food. "Dig in."

"Poppy." I corrected him. I felt a familiar rush—anger. I didn't like it when people shortened my name. It was more familiar than anyone deserved to be with me. I introduced myself as Poppy and that was what people should call me.

"Oh, sorry." He watched me then. Not dispassionately, but with interest. I intrigued him—good.

I brushed off the awkward moment and looked at my plate. "It looks amazing."

"It's all fresh. Eggs from a reputable vendor, watercress from my garden. The feta is from Silo, though." Atticus spread a napkin over his left thigh. "He actually made it from capybara milk."

I glanced at the eggs again and back at Atticus. "The fuck is a capybara?"

"Eat it first. It sells for $4.50 a pound and I'd be crushed if knowing the animal made you averse to at least trying it."

I was hungry as fuck. Whatever the hell a capybara was would not have kept me from shoving this into my food hole. I licked my lips. Looked down at the coffee. "The coffee smells amazing. Another treat?"

Atticus took a sip from his own mug. He swallowed and smacked his lips. "A variation of kopi luwak. I used to have a civet at home. Fed it beans from my own trees. Sifting through its feces was unpleasant, but the taste of this brew becomes addictive." He placed his coffee cup down and frowned. "Poor thing got into my medicine cabinet and ate half its body weight in organic toothpaste."

"Is a civet like a capybara?"

"Sort of."

"Are there places to buy these things?"

Atticus nodded. "Silo Jotter has his ways."

Silo Jotter had his ways. The man controlled all artisanal pursuits in Brooklyn. You wanted to sell handmade furniture or sausages made of extremely exotic meats? This was the man you had to pay fealty to. You worked well with him and your life was going to be perfect. You'd build a reputation, make money, and have a legacy in this place. Silo built cultural institutions—even in failure. Restaurants spoken of like gospel passages; trendsetters long gone that still got name-called when people wore anything even hinting a connection—that was all Silo Jotter. He was *the* man.

That man, though, was a monster. He had to be. Who

else could leash a hitman like Atticus and demand his eternal respect like that? I mean, Atticus was clearly the kind of guy who changed his brand allegiances multiple times a month. His favorite butters. His designer jeans. His sandals. All of them were victims of a toddler-like ability to immediately hate and shun them forever. But not Silo. That was power, wasn't it? To demand loyalty like that and wield power unquestioned.

That was what I wanted.

Even Atticus. In a normal world, he should have been rotting in a prison. Not with Silo supporting him. No, Atticus was a free man living a good life admired by anyone who knew what it was to know. Atticus was a person people aspired to. *I* was one of those people. And if I made the right moves—if I ate a little shit for a few months and played the networking game—maybe I could benefit from Silo Jotter's "ways."

Atticus smiled at me and shrugged. "You know what, Poppy? Sure, why not? I could certainly use the extra help and honestly, I just can't see myself letting you walk out of here without seeing you again." He raised his coffee mug up. "To a new partnership."

I raised my mug of the rodent shit coffee in turn. "To a new partnership."

The coffee was too hot but I swallowed it anyway, feeling it burn every glorious inch down.

FIVE YEARS LATER

CHAPTER four

I liked taking long walks past the Gowanus to work. After five years as the personal assistant of the legendary gentleman hitman of Park Slope, it was one of the only bright spots of my day. I liked taking in the smells: the canal, the joggers going by, the occasional junkie passed out in their own sick. It was life and it was beautiful, and it was overwhelming, but it cleared my head something fierce, and for that I'd take in all the worst smells, tastes, and feels my mind could handle. It was a reminder of all the things I didn't want—of what life could be like if I didn't find the strength to keep walking towards a place I grew to loathe.

I stopped and stared at the brackish water in the canal and wondered what it would be like to jump on in. Wouldn't it be fun to go for it, to take the plunge? To taste the essence of the city and let it swallow me whole from the outside, filling me up throat to gut? I wondered if it would be cold, or if the sensations would fade away while my brain died—the sound of Rice Krispies in milk between my ears. I wondered if anyone else wanted to feel that way. It was probably more peaceful than people thought. Hell, I personally knew a few dozen people who probably deserved to get swallowed up by the waters of New York City. To literally be flushed out its system—a binge and purge for the asphalt jungle.

Damn pesky survival instinct kept me from taking the running leap. Besides, some well-intentioned passerby would probably jump in to save me, and then the whole thing would be more trouble than it was worth. I imagined the scenario. I'd jump in and someone would rescue me. We'd have a connection, maybe exchange numbers after the fact. There'd be a thank-you dinner where we found out we had all the same interests and—surprise—our mothers fucked us up for almost all the same reasons. We'd fuck like animals then lose touch for a few months only to bump into each other at a gallery show or some rathole bar band gig. Maybe a wacky misunderstanding would happen, and they'd chase me in the rain to apologize for said misunderstanding and cue whatever hokey romantic music was the flavor of the day.

I snorted. Like I had time for that shit. Like I'd run in the rain for anyone. Fuck that. My cardio sucked and I couldn't stand getting wet—the chafing alone.

I passed another junkie laid out on the concrete. His situation wasn't much concern to me, but his blazer sure as hell caught my eye. It was this sky-blue linen number.

William Westmancott. Bespoke. Expensive. I knew this because I'd bought it, and I knew it was the specific blazer I bought because it had the initials "A.G." hand-stitched over the front pocket.

The fuck was that about?

Plenty of people in the neighborhood copied Atticus. That was normal—and annoying. But this was someone with clothing I had personally bought less than a year ago.

I gave the guy a gentle kick to the ribs. "Hey."

No response.

I crouched down and gave him a little smack on the cheek. Still nothing. Okay, then, a little more pepper. I kept smacking—with growing viciousness—until the man, a little welt blossoming under his left eye, woke up with a slurred groan. He blinked and stared at me as if he'd never seen another human in his lifetime.

"What do you want?" he croaked.

"Where did you get that blazer?" I asked, trying to keep a smile on.

"Blazer?" He scooted into a sitting position and looked at his clothes. Straightened the lapels of the stained jacket with a small smile. "It was in the box this week. Nice find, right?"

I nodded. "Very nice find. What's the box? What does that mean?"

"The clothing collection box on Dekalb."

"Dekalb," I said. "Okay. And were there other nice finds?"

"Not as nice as this, but it was a good haul." He fingered the lapels of the blazer. "Guess one of the trusties got tired of their wardrobe this week, eh?"

I stood up. Fetched a twenty from my wallet and tossed it at him. "Sounds like it. Thanks."

I got to stepping. Not sure why it pissed me off to see him wearing that blazer, but it did. There was work behind those clothes—behind everything Atticus had in his closet. I understood being tired of an outfit, but we had a rotation agreement: if he wanted a change, he would let me know and I would be the one to divvy up what got sent to charities, what got sent to consignment, and what I kept to sell to rag factories or rubes. It was one of the many little avenues I had to make revenue out of this five-year internship. My Tasker money was solid, but I preferred the hustle money. Gave it a little extra zing.

And now my hustle money was being fucked with.

God damn it, Atticus. There were enough things to worry about: keeping him stylish, fed, out of jail. Making sure he was prepared for his jobs—which I did more and more research for lately, since he'd decided he could use more time to devote himself to whatever new hobby he desperately hoped he could master.

I was two blocks away from work and I knew I couldn't walk in angry. Never angry. Angry wasn't going to do me favors. I swallowed it as best I could. Found my center—my inner Poppy—the fun, silly side of me. I slapped a silly smile on my face and left it there until I could feel people staring, then let their stares turn it into a real smile. That's right, motherfuckers. Eat it up. You're looking at the one and only Poppy Leathers here.

The reminder helped. The hurt feelings faded by the time I got to my block and were left on the ground floor as I rode the elevator up to our office space. I would be alright. I would make the best of the day. And I would find a way to get closer to where I wanted to be.

Atticus, Jason, and charity boxes be damned.

"I cannot explain how badly I needed tapas today." I eyed my many plates. There was fried quail egg on a tiny piece of toast, octopus drowned in olive oil, these little cod fish croquettes that I was completely certain contained crack cocaine because I could eat an entire bucket of the fucking things at each meal for the rest of my life and feel no shame. "The Spanish have their food figured the fuck out. If it weren't for all the colonization and global genocide, they'd be respectable."

Atticus sipped from his hip flask. "I guess." He was in a state. Either mad at me for some perceived slight or back in his whole "woe is me and my ennui" mode. He wasn't eating because he'd ordered the house special, a whole fucking lamb, which took the whole damn day to prep—even having ordered it a month in advance. Someone was hangry.

"You sure you don't want any of this?" I asked. "I mean, I know you're gearing up to eat an entire baby, but if you're feeling peckish, have at it." I took a sip of wine. A favorite: vinho verde. Yeah, it was Portuguese, but that was close to Spain. Fuck it, I liked the stuff. And you could get it cheap at Trader Joe's, too. Better than what you paid $50 a bottle for here, to be honest, but I wasn't paying.

Atticus took another sip of rye and shook his head. "Nothing. Just another long day."

Great. This again. The last couple of jobs had been this way. Atticus got the job done, but the post-work routine for me had gone from cleaning up and assurance of execution to full-blown therapy sessions. He said he was feeling "less than alive" these days, or whatever midlife crisis privileged dudes give themselves to make them more interesting. That put-together demigod I'd met only a few years ago was fading before my eyes and turning into a shell of himself. He wasn't quite as focused as he used to be. He slipped on his skincare regimen and I often saw him indulging in those low-calorie sparkling waters. I wondered how long it'd be before he told me he wanted to leave Brooklyn for the Hudson Valley to buy an antique shop at Sugar Loaf. It scared the shit out of me. That after five years of service, after five fucking years of getting closer and closer to Silo Jotter, this shit stain could pull the rug out from under me just because he was feeling down in the dumps or whatever.

Boo fucking hoo. We all had bad days, but this man baby's little crisis was going to impact my long-term plans, and it drove me crazy.

I took a bite of that toast and egg thing. The crunch of the bread—just a tease of char—followed by silky egg yolk flowing over my tongue. Pure tongue seduction. I wanted to marry that bite. "Fuckballs, Atticus, you need to try this. It's out of hand. It tastes the way you imagined a fried egg would taste when you saw it in a cartoon as a kid." I relished the cloying aftertaste of egg and spices. Maybe I should have conned my way into food criticism. Free meals. Nice experiences. Opportunities to make someone in a funny hat cry. That would have been fun.

Atticus smirked. "Is it really that good, or are you trying to distract me?"

"Is it working?"

"No."

I leaned back and winced when a small, jagged piece of metal met the space between my shoulders. This restaurant—if that was the best thing to call it—LLL was an exclusive spot serving delicious food, but the aesthetic was beyond rustic. Well, and rustic was a weak word for a restaurant located in a topless water tower wasting away on an open tract of land nobody wanted to develop. We were protected from the elements by a tarp supported with rusted poles and sat on hand-me-down furniture donated by the five patrons allowed to frequent the space—Atticus having provided the table. It was strange, filthy, and probably a source of tetanus. The food was

God-tier, though.

The only real downer about this place—other than getting some extreme stomach distress—were the rich idiot gatecrashers all lined up in a row and ready to yelp their demands to the owner. The owner of LLL, a mysterious Spaniard who rarely spoke, ignored them, for the most part. When anyone got loud, he'd point at the large barcode posted at the bottom of the tower that linked to lengthy instructions on how to apply for a spot, with the warning that the current waitlist had a minimum of seven hundred names on it. This was usually enough to shut up the wannabe power brokers and tastemakers, but there was always one socialite who didn't understand their true place in the real Brooklyn hierarchy.

Thank God Atticus was one of the first investors. We had run of the place, and I loved that we could come here unannounced if we wanted—though we never did. We were people of fucking etiquette. I relished these weekly dinners too. It was a bright spot in what felt like a dimming business arrangement.

But those looky-loos. I had a feeling the most recent entitled idiot was staring at us from the fence—a slight twig of a man in a rust-colored suit rocking the glare of a toddler stripped of his third cupcake. Even though we were a few feet above the crowd, I kept seeing him shuffle from the corner of my eye and got the same feeling as if I was on a subway car alone on Wednesday night: trouble.

"You ever think of ordering something that doesn't

take ten years to prepare?" I asked, surveying my empire of emptied plates. "It's like you ordered a fucking student film. Everything's happening off screen."

"Señor," Atticus called out, "¿Cuando será la comida preparada?" His accent was stiff, like a robot.

The Spaniard raised a hand with four fingers up; his thumb tucked into his palm.

Atticus nodded. "I have no idea what that meant, but I think it should be soon."

"Yo!" One of the many poor little rich boys waiting below us finally lost his patience. "You guys aren't even eating anymore. You done yet?"

Atticus rolled his eyes. "So, Silo gave me new work. I'm going to need your help with organizing a few bits. Some idiot chocolatier in Canarsie. Started cutting his product."

"I got you," I said. "Just email the template I set up for you and I can fill in the blanks."

Atticus grimaced and ran a finger along the rim of the empty wine glass in front of him. "As always, the help's appreciated." He did that forlorn sigh thing men like him did when they were sad and thinking. "Maybe it's an age thing, but I can never quite focus on the pre-work anymore, you know? The wet work, I've been fine with. But I don't know what I'd do without you to handle the stuff I can't be bothered with."

Maybe that was a compliment? It didn't *feel* like a compliment.

I moved past it. "It's my job, right?"

"Do I detect a little hostility?" Atticus asked. "You never complained before. Is this about compensation?"

Guess my bitterness came out to play. Whoops. "No." I raised my hands. "I make my money off Jason. It's just. Well. For as much as you find the pre-work to be a time sink... I do, too." I stared at my plates again. I missed the codfish the way married couples missed sloppy hand stuff. "Anyway, don't worry. I had a crummy day."

Atticus stared at me the way he did whenever he was going to impart a "life lesson." "Listen, Pop. You said this partnership was intended to usher you towards opportunities in my world, right?"

I took a moment to collect myself. We talked about the "Pop" thing last week for the millionth time. I didn't want another argument, so I let it go. I was letting a lot go lately. "Yes, I did."

"Well, a part of that is taking your lumps. I took mine. Even Silo took his. You'll get there."

"And who tells me when I'm there?"

"That's up to you."

What a line of bullshit. He knew I was ready to do more. He knew I was ready to meet with Silo and pitch him my ideas. I had a whole PowerPoint deck on starting my own adoption racket. With an investor like Silo, I could get a solid foundation and be in the black within three years. It was all that bullshit I'd heard office jobs complaining about doing the job above you to prove you deserve the promotion. No. If you know I'm ready, you give me the fucking promotion.

I closed my eyes for a moment, took a big bite of food, and drowned it in wine. I told myself to work through it. I wanted to have a nice night and not fight with a man who could put a hole in my head as easily as he would adjust his shirt collar.

The Spaniard walked over with Atticus' lamb. He placed the platter on our table and pulled a mean-looking blade from his belt. He plunged the blade into the lamb's neck and deftly removed the head from the rest of the body. The smell of the meat enveloped me. As the Spaniard danced his blade around the lamb, a variety of liquids spilled onto the serving tray. I watched the steam rise from a pool of fat and blood. This shit was holy. The lamb was the Lord made flesh, and all those drippings sacramental wine. I could tell the Spaniard revered the work he was doing and so did Atticus. That had to be the appeal of it to him: the ceremony.

Atticus selected his preferred cuts of meat. The rest would go to the nearby soup kitchen—Atticus' way of squashing the guilt of wasting time and animal parts. I figured he was being smart when he did. I mean, why waste the meat you spent good money on? I also wondered, now, if that was the beginning of this great crisis of conscience he was in the middle of. If I remembered right, the soup kitchen thing started maybe two years back.

"Give me a fucking break." Rich boy was mouthing off again. He paced back and forth while a young woman tried to console him. She was dressed in a pleather getup that looked like it was designed by a six-year-old riding the Pixi Stix sugar dragon. Together, the couple looked like a pair of Eastern European vampires from a bad action movie.

Atticus ignored the whining and placed a napkin over his lap before digging into his dinner. I watched him sift through the meat and hot grease. I wasn't a vegan, but the sound alone had me thinking about a conversion.

"You're gross," I said.

Atticus nearly choked. "You wanted to watch it get slaughtered. You were upset we got here too late."

"Yeah, but not eat it so soon after. I was simply curious about process."

"I wonder about you sometimes." Atticus went back to eating. He took short sips from his flask between bites. He was satisfied with his meal. Had that afterglow look on his face a normal person would have with a lover.

He wondered about me. Cute. I wondered about me, too.

I wondered why I was sitting here with this fading star. Why this man ever made it as far as he did. What was the purpose of his work anymore but to maintain the status quo? He was a regulator, a bureaucrat with a gun. If Atticus in his prime had been an artist at his peak, the Atticus of today was a former soap opera star shilling a salad chopper in a late-night infomercial. What this town needed was new perspective. Silo needed someone like me, who could help him shake things up—help him walk into brand new ventures. Hell, his reach was borough-wide, but was it locked in? After I built a strong business with Silo, what if he had a person like me to run things in the Bronx? Or even stretch their legs into Queens while dipping their toes into Long Island?

One of my many—and newer—problems with Atticus, beyond his shitty attitude: he was satisfied. And that, I knew, was the crux of this newfound dissatisfaction. And it drove me crazy because I still held this strange mix of fear and guilt and admiration when it came to Atticus. I had a lot to be grateful for because of him, but the man felt like a sweater I wore in high school before I filled out. I was too much woman for him now, but I didn't know how to move forward without either getting myself killed or, worse, getting myself blacklisted from this world.

The rich boy finally snapped and walked over to the base of the tower. He looked up and cupped his hands around his mouth. "Hey, there looks to be room for two more. I don't mind sharing the table."

I wasn't in the mood for a second asshole to sour my night. "He's rude." I leaned over and called out. "Dude, ain't no meal gonna make that frigid piece of ass over there any more pliable."

"Fuck you, bitch. I wasn't talking to you."

Atticus sighed and rolled his eyes, but continued eating.

Nuh-uh. No. I stood and snatched a lamb shank with the bone in and tore the meat away. If Atticus wasn't going to shut this idiot up, I would.

Atticus remained in his seat. A man who hurt people for a living, and he didn't give enough of a shit to say something to the man screaming at me, a person he had just admitted made his life easier. Because *I was his fucking assistant for free.* I didn't need a white knight, but fucking hell, maybe a little respect? Was this what five years earned me? Being this man's insanely overqualified assistant? I had a fucking Master's, for God's sake.

I walked to the ladder and descended. At the bottom, I realized how greasy my hand was from the shank and frowned. I should have brought a napkin. There was no way in hell I was getting that stink on this dress—and probably no way I'd make it back up the ladder. More reasons to be mad.

Rich Boy sneered. "I'm not impressed with the bravado, honey." He looked up to Atticus. "Like I said, I'm more than happy to share the table."

Atticus cleared his throat. Adjusted his bolo tie. He plucked a piece of meat from his plate and bit into it. Adorable.

"My money's as good as your hipster cunt money, you know. Just because you dress like low rent clowns and brood all the fucking time doesn't mean you're special."

I sauntered over to Rich Boy. My heart rate going up with every step. "The mouth on you. All that projection—

says a lot about where your head is at. Says a lot about what you probably shoved up your nose, too." It was corny as hell, but all I saw was another adult child dressed like he was going to a kindergartner's birthday party.

Rich Boy met me halfway. "You're being disrespectful."

"Disrespectful is interrupting a dinner and accosting patrons and a business owner all over your baby ego," I said, almost affecting Atticus' tone of speech. "Me refusing to accommodate your temper tantrum is merely being a normal human with a spine."

Rich Boy turned to his date, raising his hands in that "can you believe this" way, and spun back around. "Talk to your friend. I'll pay triple what he paid for the table."

"No," I said, "but I've got a better offer. You leave now, and I won't ruin your chances of ever jerking off again."

Rich Boy laughed. "Are you kidding?"

"You want to find out?"

Rich Boy gripped my arm: a control maneuver, a date rapist's go-to. He wanted to show me his strength. He wanted to show me he could control me, like Atticus or Jason. But this was my free time. I wasn't working, and I wasn't beholden to yet another man who couldn't dress himself if his life depended on it.

I looked at his hand. I felt my lips quiver and the space under my left eye twitch. It felt like fireworks were going off in my chest. Like I'd swallowed smoke and needed to breathe it all out at once. It was the Met again. Another person who believed they were better than me placing their hands on me, making me the object. Trying to take away who I was to suit their own petty fucking needs.

"Why do people always feel the need to learn the hard way with me?" I spread my feet shoulder-width apart. Found my center.

"What?"

I pointed the sharp end of the shank bone at Rich Boy's offending hand. I imagined the damage I could do if I really dug this into the meat between his thumb and his pointer finger. If I severed the ligaments and blood vessels. It wouldn't be much different to how Atticus was tearing that lamb apart at the table, would it?

I tapped the sharp end of the bone against that space and smiled. "That one your second girlfriend?"

Rich Boy sneered. "Hollow threats aren't going to make me change my mind."

"That's probably true." I stepped forward, grabbing rich boy by the right wrist with my left hand. Atticus taught me this early on, but this was the first time I'd used it on a live person. It was simple enough to twist until I heard the first pop. I pulled down as hard as I could, and the idiot folded like paper.

"Say sorry." I didn't mean that. I wanted him to fight back. I wanted to hear that sound again, to hear it over and over like I was crushing cellophane. Come on, I thought, fight me. Make me hurt you.

"Fuck you." Rich Boy gritted his teeth. His cocaine-fueled bravery was only as steady as his feet. He was all bluff, a breath of hot air.

"Pop, leave him alone," Atticus called out.

I breathed through my nose and turned my head to meet Atticus' gaze. "Give me two good reasons not to." Spit flew out of my mouth. I felt disconnected, but not in that out of body way. More like I was deeper in my own head than I'd ever been. Like I was watching everything through a peephole instead of my own eyes, from a remove. Like it was a movie. Except it was the greatest fucking movie I'd ever seen.

"Just the obvious one," Atticus said with a laconic smile. "Police."

"You know we'd be fine," I said. "We'd walk." I leaned in towards Rich Boy. "We'd walk and I could hurt you as bad as I fucking want." That was from my chest, and it felt exhilarating. I looked back to Atticus, fire in my eyes. He knew damn well there wasn't a fucking thing anyone could do against Silo Jotter's golden boy, but that warning made me wonder if that courtesy would be extended to me. Or would Atticus just sit there as I was carted away? Would he do that to me?

I didn't think so. But somewhere, not quite my heart but not quite my gut—maybe more like a hairball in the throat—I knew that the fact I'd asked the question at all was the start of something that wouldn't have a happy end.

"The badass routine is adorable," Rich Boy spat. He was still on his little bravado kick, even though the pain in his voice was palpable.

"Shut up," Atticus and I said in unison.

"Second reason." I held that glare.

"I'll treat you to the dairy free corn gelato from that Argentinean place."

He knew my weaknesses too well. "That place on Bleecker? Like, we could hit up the Village for a change?" That did even me out a little bit. That corn gelato was delicious enough to compromise some integrity. Not all, but some.

"Yes. How often do I do that?"

Atticus only took bed conquests for gelato in the Village. While I was pretty pissed at him, I also knew the value of free gelato over this little headache of an asshole. I looked over to Rich Boy. "You think it's worth it? Me hurting you versus gelato?" I felt giddy from the whiplash, anger to hunger. "I can do both, though."

Rich Boy looked between us. He tried to pull away from me and seemed surprised when I maintained my grip. "Fine. You're both fucking maniacs. I'm sorry."

I gave his wrist a gentle twist and pushed him away. "You're bottom of the food chain, motherfucker—a nobody. That man up there? That's almost the tippy top. My best buddy in the world, and look how he grants you compassion." All lies. But it was good to butter Atticus up. I leaned forward and brushed Rich Boy's ear with my lips. "I'll be there, too. One day."

That was almost as good as the thought of free gelato.

Let this pissant hear the truth. Let him be the first to know that Poppy Leathers was coming for him, for Atticus, and for the rest of the goddamn tri-state area to boot.

Rich Boy retreated as I straightened myself out. I accidentally wiped my greasy hand over the front of my dress and groaned at the result. That was going to cost me a shit ton at the organic dry cleaner. I wondered if they'd be upset to know this was lamb grease and then snorted. For the price we paid, they should look away even if it was human blood.

I called up to Atticus, who was no longer visible. "I want gelato, dude. Let's go."

He descended the ladder to join me. "You know what? I'm glad you insisted on LLL tonight."

I was already walking away. "Less thanking, more gelato." The violence and promise of free ice cream had certainly improved my mood, but I still wasn't ready to look him in the eyes.

Atticus followed. "Did you call the Uber?"

"No. Why don't you?"

Atticus scoffed. "Will do. Don't want to get on the bad side of you and a lamb bone." He scrolled on his mobile. "Speaking of, you realize we had plenty of knives you could have threatened our friend with, right?"

I rolled my eyes. Fuck him and his particulars. I was feeling high off the moment and didn't need Atticus crashing me down to earth. "I grabbed the first thing I saw."

"Interesting."

"How so?"

"Well, I mean, you grabbed what would have made the deed as messy as possible. As chaotic as possible."

"And?"

"If you want to do a job, you should choose the most efficient tool is all."

"What if the job was to leave an impression, Atticus? What then?"

"Then maybe you chose the perfect tool."

Damn right I did. Though, I had to wonder after the fact if that impression was meant for our little snobby asshole, or if I intended to leave that impression on Atticus—or even me.

Hell of a night, then.

It was the day after a hit, which meant office hours at a shared office space: a converted shipping container. Very exclusive. Very rustic. Sort of stupid.

"Would you be offended if I started a religion using you as its godhead?" I stared at my nails, each painted with a different portrait of Catriona MacColl screaming from Lucio Fulci's *The Beyond*. I'd forced my nail girl to watch the movie with me twice. Tipped her four times the cost of the project. It was a lot of needless effort, but it was fun to hang out with a new person, even if she was extremely skittish by the end of our time together.

"I think I can get people to buy into you as a Christ-like figure," I continued, "Like, fifty percent of this neighborhood already dresses like you. Not a stretch to get them to simply worship your ass and hand you the cash directly." I smiled nice and big to let him think I was busting his balls. Really, I just wanted him to know I'd seen yet another wandering junkie in clothes I bought for him last season. Not like it was my money, and it wasn't that I was mad that someone in need had nice clothes, but it would have been nice to be informed that something I'd invested time into was being given away. Acknowledgment could have moved mountains.

Getting into my feelings was never the answer with Atticus, so poking at the man was the best—and most fun—option. "You're Latino-adjacent so it might be tricky, but you're pasty, too, so. I think once people get over the hurdle of a Black woman running a cult, it'd be fine."

"So, you're feeling better after the other night?" Atticus asked.

"No idea what you're talking about." I waved the answer towards him. That was all he'd get. That little spurt of violence was for me and only me. He didn't need a denouement.

I thought back on that little moment where I nearly snapped that asshole's wrist. The feel of the tendon and bone beginning to give way. His scream. It was fucked up, but the violence, the chaos—it turned me on. Not in a basic way—that's what porn was for—it was more complicated than that. More intimate. Those thoughts gave me gooseflesh so bad, I worried my skin might split. Thankfully, it did not distract me from getting my work done. Atticus was prepared and able to compose yet another strongly worded message to the astray criminal community of Brooklyn: *love, Silo Jotter*.

There was a mirror at the far end of the office space,

and I gave myself the once over. I loved me today. I was rocking a patterned sweater from the late '70s, a poodle skirt with a crocheted piglet at the bottom, leggings with spacemen all over, and a pair of platform heels with sugar skulls lining the toes. The colors and garishness worked with my nondescript multi-ethnicity. I was, as Atticus often described me, his "Psycho Pixie Nightmare Woman." He believed it made him more of a presence in public. I was fine with playing the accessory so long as it afforded me a little extra notoriety that I could keep all to myself.

"I mean," I said, "I'd push myself as Park Slope's messiah, but ain't nobody cosplaying as me yet."

Atticus locked eyes with me. He was on the cusp of it. Edging towards self-realization. The vinegar strokes of awareness in those hazel eyes.

And then nothing. My digs weren't fucking registering with him.

Enveloped in himself, Atticus paced the tiny distance between the opening of the shipping container and its rear, gently stroking a fresh layer of wax into his beard. He was wearing a black button-down shirt with jade trim along the seams, tight tan slacks, and black leather loafers—lounge wear for him. We only had forty-five minutes left in our rental time, and I knew how anxious it made him to see the line of artists, writers, and other idiots waiting their turn across the rooftop of Castle Glenn—the apartment building he called home.

The passive aggressive comments from outside probably didn't help: "How did he even get this block? I swear I was the first to register!" "Dude, one of the maintenance guys told me he'd hook me up with the after-hours key for six hundred, but I'm cooked right now."

It was one of the only reasons I was content with my apartment in Astoria. This place was competitive about everything. The laundry room, the weight room, the pool, the smithery—even the glassblowing station. Atticus and his fellow tenants were always looking for ways to jump over one another in the strange and fluid hierarchy of Castle Glenn.

The office space was an incredibly popular amenity of the building. The roof wasn't large enough to accommodate more than one shipping container—hoisted on the roof years ago for other, more mysterious reasons—and nearly every resident was desperate for that short hour per week afforded to renters to use the 25-by-6-foot space. Lord knows a schedule would have been a more efficient way to manage this mess, but instead the tenants lined up on the roof, giving each other side-eyes like customers in a supermarket express line counting each other's items.

After all: if it was easily accessible to everyone, it wouldn't be worth it, right?

I couldn't really wrap my head around why we bothered to use the space at all. Maybe it was to keep up appearances, or maybe Atticus just hated conducting business in his apartment. I couldn't crack that nut. What I did know was this certainly didn't help his temperament—especially towards a building full of people who knew damn well who he was and what he did. If anything, I felt like he was a little over-reliant on Silo's reputation, especially when we did nonsense like this.

"Did you hear me?" I gently sanded the edge of a nail; Catriona MacColl's screaming face wore down on the left side a bit. Shit. I'd have to adjust the right side to keep things symmetrical.

"No, Pop, I just... I've been thinking." Atticus stared at his phone. He'd been on hold with Silo Jotter for nearly twenty minutes.

"Poppy..." I scolded.

"Yeah, yeah. Sorry, Poppy." He pointed at the desk. "Hey, could you burn the Hishiro file, please?"

"Will do," I said. "You know, I wonder if Jesus had good manners." This was my way of playing with him, of jostling the marbles in his head.

Atticus stopped pacing and scratched his chin. "I'm willing to believe Jesus had terrible manners. He ate with vagrants and turned over all those temples' money-lending tables. Imagine the mess. Their entire economy was based on metal pogs back then." He stared at his phone. "At least I'm not flipping things over because of a slight inconvenience."

"That's blasphemy. Being crucified isn't an inconvenience."

"I meant the money lending. If the man didn't like it, he could have ignored it." Atticus looked over to me. He gave my outfit a once-over and gave an imperceptible nod of approval, almost a chin wag. "Since when were you a church-goer?"

"Since forever." I snapped my fingers, remembering a conversation from a few days ago. "Hey, are we still going to South of the Border? I need a new sombrero."

Someone called out from outside, "Any chance you're cutting it short today? I'm willing to trade some time with you. I made some really good scones today."

"We hate scones," we said in harmony.

"Bootleg ass muffins," I muttered.

"Always dry," Atticus agreed. "Only ever had one good one. All the way in New Hampshire, of all places."

"A good scone is not worth spending a microsecond in New fucking Hampshire."

"You are not wrong."

The hold music broke off. Nobody spoke, but it was clear someone was listening.

Atticus took the phone off speaker and held the phone to his ear. "Yes, confirming that we're all clear on the Hershey highway."

I cackled. "I love it." With all this shit out in the open, it was demented to use code on the phone.

Atticus slipped a loafer off and threw it over my head. He missed by a mile and the shoe banged against the metal wall. A warning.

"There's my boy. More like Jesus already." I kept laughing.

"Yes. Yes..." Atticus paced again. "Are you sure? Okay, tonight. I've got it. Thank you." Atticus disconnected the call. He took a deep breath and rubbed the bridge of his nose. "I have to meet with him."

"In person?"

"Appears so."

I placed my nail file down and fished a pink clove out of my pocketbook. I lit it with a thin lighter on the table next to me. "Think you're in trouble?" Smoke spilled from my mouth, since I hadn't fully inhaled. It smelled like berries and cedar wood.

"No. I think whatever is next is much larger than I'd like it to be."

"And now that retirement spiel remains in the desk drawer."

"Indeed, it does." Atticus plopped down on the lawn chair across from me. "I should have said something before this. I was worried I'd upset Silo." He sighed. "This contract was a talker. I'm worried he's in my head."

The fucking talkers. Over the years, the talkers were becoming more and more common. I wasn't at the jobs, so I couldn't confirm, but I assumed it was because Atticus was too focused on the performance of his work, more than the actual work. He wanted all this ceremony: frittatas, streaming video options, long discussions, drama. He should have simply killed the losers where they stood.

Why even do that to yourself, I wondered. Silo gave the order. Go shoot the target and leave. No muss, no fuss. Why talk with them? Why build a connection that would be severed so soon? It didn't seem worth the anguish.

Take this chocolate guy: Benjamin Hishiro. He was selling shitty product while pretending he was on the level. He charged over 1000% more than he was spending and pretended life was difficult while driving a fucking Lamborghini in New York City. The man didn't need to be pampered in death; he was pampered in life. But Atticus, he had to play the greatest hits. Had to live up to his legend. That legend was becoming a hindrance, and now these chucklefucks were getting to him.

It really had a way of dimming a man's shine.

"You always get this way with the talkers," I said, "They say some sad words, insult your occupation, and then you come back all sad sack wondering if it's even worth the effort anymore." I waved that nonsense away. "Come on, man. You know better than to fall for that."

"Didn't I hire you to keep things organized?" Atticus snapped. "Instead, you're narrating my life."

I smiled. "You hired me because I was free, good at what I do, and make you infinitely cooler than you would be as a solo act." I pointed at him with a MacColl. "I'm reminding you that there was a time when you had an edge, and you keep letting schmucks wear you down. This is the third time you've sat here and started feeling sorry for them."

Atticus shook his head. "I don't feel sorry for them."

"Yourself?" That would almost be more dangerous.

"No," Atticus said with uncertainty. "Maybe. I don't know. I don't feel like I used to about all of this. I do my work and I maintain my reputation, but every day it feels less and less like there's a point to it all."

Oh, boy. We were getting philosophical. And that meant yet another round of avoiding Silo—which was very much against my goddamn best interests. I needed to find some time with that man to squeak my way through the door. But no, sad boy Atticus had to get in his feelings.

I checked my watch. It was time to go through inventory downstairs. "I need to take stock. Will you be headed down with me?"

Atticus waved me off. "Please be sure to wash my apron. I think I may have stained it with some hot sauce."

"Not blood?"

"No, not blood."

"What about dinner?" I grabbed my mobile device and opened our calendar. "Wanna do LLL again?"

"I was hoping we could go somewhere different. There's that new place that makes all their dishes into milkshakes. The hanger steak and potatoes are supposed to be incredible. They age the meat for a year."

I frowned. "You promised LLL whenever I wanted after the debacle that was Space Pizza."

"Space Pizza was interesting."

"It was dry crackers with ketchup, Atticus. Either way,

our last visit was marred. I'd like a second chance at enjoying tapas, wine, and an iota of non-business chat." I'd have added that my complete lack of a fucking social life and no pay meant I had to be friends with him to get free meals at trendy places, but I didn't want to fight.

And it wasn't like I was poor, but Tasker was in a small dip, which meant my commissions were lacking. I had to stir some shit up on that side of my life. Funding wasn't going to drop out of the fucking sky. Had to hustle.

Fuck, I was tired.

Atticus' shoulders drooped in defeat. "Fine. LLL it is."

That was alarmingly easy. "Awesome. See you in a couple of minutes." I grabbed my things and started to head out.

"Hey, did you get me that latest Tasker piece?"

I ignored that question. The new Tasker painting was on its way, and I was feeling more than a little annoyed about it. This man I'd seen as an institution was turning into a gigantic toddler. Incapable of taking care of himself and incapable of getting past this newfound sense of guilt that kept rearing its ugly little head every time we finished a new job. What was worse, I broke my fucking ass to get him ready. I cased the targets, I put together his dossiers, and prepped his equipment. I literally put the man's life in easy mode—all he had to do was pull a trigger—and the thanks I got were constant threats of retirement, of making all this work amount to nothing.

On the elevator, I watched the numbers count down.

And as I did, as I let my mind wander and follow those blinking red digits, a thought snuck into the back of my head. Just a small one. Small enough to shake away when the elevator doors dinged open. Almost.

With everything I knew. With all the time I spent learning the ins and outs of Atticus and his business.

Just how necessary was Atticus Garcia anymore?

CHAPTER SEVEN

Three times. I checked the bag three times. I checked the pantry, every single kitchen cabinet, and—even on the off chance a fucking cast iron pan would find its way there—I checked the gun closet.

Nothing.

Atticus arrived as I was on my fourth run through my cleaning process. Lay out tarp, empty bags, inspect fabrics, inspect utensils, take apart and clean the guns. I did this to the letter and tracked every item via a password protected and locally hosted spreadsheet that was on its fifteenth iteration. Nothing that left this house was unaccounted for and nothing that returned was unaccounted for. This was my way of taking my experience in museums and applying it to the world of crime, and it fucking worked.

"What's wrong?" he asked as he walked into the living room.

"I can't find your cast iron pan."

"The Griswold?"

Yep. The spider skillet. Made in 1891. Bought for $8,000 as a birthday gift the year Atticus hired me. I had to sell weed for the rest of the year to make up for the loss, but at the time I considered that to be an expense for my future.

I did not expect the return on that investment to be that it was missing after another one of Atticus' jobs where he had to make a dead person a delicious breakfast for "reasons."

"Atticus. Are you *sure* you packed it up?"

Atticus looked into the distance. He was thinking—maybe not as hard as I would have liked. "I pack up everything after a job, Pop. You know I'm good at that."

I jammed my arm into his duffel bag again, as if the skillet would magically appear. "It's not here, Atticus. I know you don't touch this stuff once you get it home, and I'm not that absent-minded that I would misplace something that heavy." I dropped the bag and turned to him. "Is there any chance whatsoever you left it behind? Maybe you wiped it clean and forgot to get it in the bag?"

Atticus stared at the ground and back to me. There was doubt in his eyes. I'd never seen that before. It fucking terrified me.

"Atticus, if you forgot it, that's fine," I lied, "but you have to tell me if I need to hoof it over to Hishiro's apartment right now." I checked my watch. "He's got his daily sales meeting in forty-five minutes and that would be when they find the body. But if there's a used skillet sitting on the stove with your fingerprints or even an eyelash on it… Listen, man, I'm not sure Silo's got that much power, and I'm not sure he's going to love that sloppiness enough to test whether he has that power."

Atticus shook his head with all the vigor of a child insisting that his mom really did say it was okay for him to have extra dessert. "We'd be fine. We're always fine."

"That a risk worth taking?"

I couldn't fucking believe this. He'd slipped. Atticus Garcia had slipped, like a rank fucking amateur. Even if the skillet was clean, its make and age made it easy to track down. Christ, I'd had it delivered to my apartment. It would lead right back to *my* naïve ass. I ran my hand over my face. Why oh why did I buy that stupid pan? He'd betrayed me—and he didn't even see it as a betrayal. What the fuck was wrong with him?

"I'm going to go over there," I said. Someone needed to make the fucking call. "I'll text if everything goes right." I pointed to the bedrooms. "In the meantime, I laid out your outfits for tonight. If things go right, I demand bottomless margaritas and fully expect you to carry me into my apartment and hold my hair back if I end up purging."

Atticus nodded, but haltingly, still unsure. "It's not going to be an issue, Pop. You'll be in and out."

Oh, wonderful. Assurance from the fuck up.

"Yeah, well. We'll see."

"Oh, I completely forgot why I came here." Atticus pointed towards a closet, all that concern evaporating from his body. "I've got a bag of stuff I was going to drag over to that thrift store up the street for donation. Mind bringing it over while you're on the way to Hishiro's? Two birds and all."

The scream that welled up inside me could have shattered glass throughout Brooklyn.

The apartment was bright, with natural light spilling in from the windows. The Brooklyn Bridge was in view, as were all the cars on their way between Manhattan and the outer boroughs. I eyed the people across the way in the neighboring hi-rise, toiling away in a row of treadmills, elliptical machines, and stair masters—all huffing, puffing, and completely oblivious to what was happening in this apartment.

And what was happening in this apartment was my dayglo-wearing ass running inside, nearly tripping over my own feet, in a complete wet panic. Thank God I'd had the presence of mind to put my gloves on in the elevator, because I touched at least three things on the way inside.

I saw it immediately: the skillet was right on the stove top, a tea towel crumpled next to it. I ran over and snatched them both. So, Atticus had washed it, dried it, and then completely forgotten it. Wonderful. I shoved the skillet into the oversized shoulder tote I brought along and went to leave before a chilling thought stopped me in my tracks.

Could this have been it? What if Atticus forgot something else?

I closed my eyes, took a deep breath, and checked my watch.

The meeting was in twenty minutes. I needed to get the hell out of here in less than five.

I jogged from the kitchen to the living room and to the bedrooms. I ignored Benjamin's corpse, still seated at the dining room table. Caught a glimpse of his face: jaw hanging open, dried blood caked around the little bullet hole in his forehead. The back of his head was clearly an entirely different party. There was a red mess on the back of the chair and the wall behind Benny boy. All that trouble to save some money on the overhead from chocolate making didn't seem worth it now, huh, buddy?

The bedrooms looked undisturbed. Nothing off with the bathroom, either. I didn't have a choice in checking the table where Benjamin remained the perfect host. Plates were cleared and cleaned. Even the garbage was empty. Atticus did everything but remember this goddamn skillet. Wasn't it weird that he forgot the one thing that wouldn't lead to him as much as it would lead directly to me? Everything else was done with precision, but I was supposed to believe he had a brain fart like that?

I was overthinking it.

And I kept overthinking it as I left the apartment, stood in the elevator, and especially on the subway. Lots of thinking on the subway—distracted from the smell.

Atticus forgot a traceable item—specifically, one that would land me, at least, in an interrogation room. Wouldn't that leave me as a loose end? Wouldn't that place a big, fat target on my front, back, neck, etc. from Silo? The man barely knew me. Why would he even consider letting me live in that scenario? After all this time, Atticus was willing to get me noticed by his boss in all the wrong ways.

Between stops, that thought came back up in my head. How much use was Atticus Garcia to me anymore? How much closer was he going to bring me to the life I wanted—to the end of my shitty art job and the beginning of my life as a member of this circle? And not someone on the side, not a background player, but an actual participant.

It was becoming clear how unnecessary Atticus Garcia was in my life. But the bigger question bloomed in my head at that moment. The real fucking conundrum: how was I going to get Silo Jotter to begin thinking the exact same thing?

CHAPTER Eight

Jason Tasker. Good fucking lord. Both the dumbest and luckiest white man I'd ever met in my life. A terrible artist, objectively, but so fucking good at making people pay attention to him that it never mattered. The man bled finesse.

Wasn't even the paintings that got us attention. Dude went viral with a thirty-two second video of him painting with his dick. That was all it took. Over 100 million views on Instagram and there we were: one of the hottest social media influencers of the arts. The pay went from bologna on hand to dinner at Shake Shack whenever the hell I felt like it overnight.

Problem was, when you go viral, you sort of need to keep the act up. So, Jason made a reputation as a sort of heir to G.G. Allin.

And therein lay the next and bigger problem: Jason and his partner Sara wanted to adopt a baby. And people with reputations like Jason Tasker did not get to adopt precious babies, because there were videos of people like Jason Tasker smacking men dressed as children with a dead salmon while singing Russian folk songs.

That meant that I, art manager extraordinaire Poppy Leathers, also wanted to adopt a baby.

The day job. The real day job: manager to a milquetoast asshole with more inspiration than common sense. This was where I had to know my place. Where I needed to be the professional Poppy: no cursing and no eccentricity. Eccentricity was for the creator.

The shit I had to do to pay the goddamn bills because I was too dumb to ask Atticus for a few dollars.

Tasker was my only client, and that was enough to fill the time when I wasn't working as a handler for a now-ineffective hitman. It gave me the ability to live on the periphery of the art world—a place so obsessed with staring up its own asshole that I may as well be invisible. Nobody gave a shit about the folks who greased the gears. They only cared that the clock struck midnight when it had to.

So, the gears that needed greasing: Jason and Sara Tasker.

Baby. How fucking perfect was that?

Lord knew I provided avenues to every option: sex therapists, in vitro, radical medical procedures, surrogacy. Nothing ever quite landed or lived up to the Taskers' demands. Ultimately, adoption was the only path left—not ideal for them, but the burden of creating a child they'd hyped up in their minds was alleviated by someone else doing the heavy lifting, at least. Unfortunately, even that path was riddled with bureaucratic nonsense and impossible fees. Jason's job as an artist compounded difficulties, since his work raised objection with every social worker they met.

Case in point: the last sit-down appointment had ended in disaster as Jason attempted to justify his last multimedia project involving simulated oral sex on a baboon dressed as Santa Claus. It was the last of a string of seventeen-second videos posted on social media to tear down the American holiday complex. Fans weren't necessarily thrilled with the project. They expected raunchy and dangerous, but felt the entire premise was tired; plenty of people had work that railed against the corporate exploitation of pagan rituals. As one user, ButtSachs420, put it, "THAT SHIT WAS WACK."

Sadly, I agreed. It was potentially wiggity whack—the worst possible kind of whack.

"My manager should have the foresight to know this could happen," Jason said to me.

"What, that you'd want to give up on having money, a life, and sleep?" I scoffed. "My job is to make opportunity that translates to a higher net worth. You need a wet nurse or a doula or whatever, may I turn your attention towards Craigslist?"

That was the play: desperation. I needed carte blanche from Jason to move towards my own goals. Manager of one of the hottest artists in the world is looking for a favor—something slightly under the table? A means to get a baby without stirring up any paperwork? What was it that Atticus once told me: Silo Jotter has his ways?

Jason opened the door nice and wide for me to find out exactly what Silo could do. I just needed to get past the threshold.

Until then, my morning would be planning for his next show: "Shattered Parabolic VII (of LV) aka DOLVIDA THE THIRTH." Some multimedia "experience" nonsense Jason insisted had to happen somewhere dark and dirty. Something about the soul of the city, or some white nonsense.

"He awakens," I called out as Jason emerged from his bedroom in the nude, scratching his ass like an ape.

Jason smiled weakly and waved to me. "We got a space?"

"Two choices," I said. "We could do something upstate, like some wilderness nonsense—and don't think I don't see your face I ain't done yet—or I might have a line with Jenna Fontana on a new tour she's setting up."

Jason made that face he made when a name didn't register at all in his brain. This was about 99% of names.

I sighed. "Jenna had you do that residency in the abandoned Bronx warehouse a year or two back. She's good at finding unused spaces and mentioned a sewer or subway station that was on her list that we might be able to use."

No sign of recognition at all in his eyes, but I could see something in my spiel interested him.

"Sewers?" Jason mulled that over. "Bullshit. No way she could get us a space like that."

"More like human shit, and Jenna's good for these kinds of things. We can get ourselves in there for a specific amount of time while the space is nice and dry, have your show, and get out before all the nasty stuff shows up. Adds an air of danger that I get the feeling folks will pay a lot of money to be a part of."

Jason nodded. He went to the fridge and returned with a carton of oat milk he took to the head for way too long. Thirst quenched, he burped, sighed, and smiled. Who needed a baby when you had an artist? "The ceilings high?"

"I have no idea. I'm waiting to see if my request for blueprints comes back from City Hall, and Jenna's still trying to convince her contact to allow me to have their number. Figured I would get ahead of things and assume the location was appealing to you."

"Then why even mention the woods?"

I shrugged. "To see you make that face you make before I defy your expectations, Jason."

"You're a fucking rock star, Pop." He used the oat milk to point at me. "Fucking rock star. You think we can get the ball moving for a Fall show?"

"Poppy; we talked about that, Jason." I laid that out easy and breezy. Didn't need new stress. "Also, it is very much Fall now."

Jason stared into space. "It's October."

"It is, in fact, October."

"So that's no?"

"It's a shaky maybe," I said. "It would be better to wait until it's warmer. Unless you're dying to add portable heaters to our budget."

"Why would we need heaters?" Jason smiled wildly and threw his hands into the air. "We make the discomfort a part of the show. It's a sensory thing, right? Watching me work in a place that's aesthetically insulting on multiple levels. In the underbelly of this cold and hard city." He clapped his hands. "Poetry."

Yeah. Poetry. Sure. I admired Jason's chutzpah for making the elite suffer to simply say they were there, but that also meant *I'd* have to suffer, and I'd very much prefer a night out at a dimly lit gallery where I could drink some cheap wine and enjoy lukewarm canapés. Comfort, man, that was the goal. Get enough clout to keep folks on their toes while you're really angling to have some fun and enjoy the occasional bubble bath on the down low.

I guess I wanted to be in the place where my hands stayed clean, too.

"Any news on the baby thing?" Jason asked.

I rifled through my notepad. "Getting closer. I've got a chance to poke my head into a meeting later today with someone who more than likely has the resources to get me a location or number of the place I heard about." I smiled to him. "We'll get there. Dolvida, new baby. Everything will come up Tasker."

Jason raised his arms in the air, his cock at half-mast. "Hell, yes, Pop! Uh, Poppy." Finger guns and a blink. "You're the best."

I shrugged. "Do me the favor of getting some pants on and then I'll take a compliment."

Chapter Nine

The rest of my day was calls, calls, calls. Confirmed reservations for my own dinner and the next six weeks of dinners for Jason and Atticus—separately, of course. Called City Hall—again—to check on the status of my request. Stonewalled. Called a guy I used to mess around with to get a bead on someone else I could bribe to get what I needed, which forced another call to someone I could use as a middleman because the skillet thing had a lot of shit fresh in my mind and I was jumping at the goddamn shadows after my third coffee. There was a line on some weirdo cokehead go-between, but my contact on that one set the expectation low that the guy would even return a call.

Four to five hours flew on by when you were attached to your phone while coordinating your legitimate boss' monthly art displays and worrying about your illegitimate boss' mental condition.

Quitting time came. Drank a smoothie when I remembered I never had breakfast or lunch. Used the bathroom for the first time as well because it was entirely possible to train your brain to completely ignore your bladder and colon for hours and hours and hours. I read some gossip news and laughed at blind items about rubber fists. Good stuff.

Checked my itinerary: pick up Atticus from Silo's and then dinner at LLL—this time without the violence. Hopefully.

I walked into Silo's penthouse apartment right in the middle of a toast. Adorable. Two big alpha boys raising a glass to each other over whatever the fuck they had a bonding moment about. I wondered if I should ask if it was over the sloppy nonsense from the morning, but I knew better than to stir shit up with my boss and his boss around.

Silo nodded to Atticus, tipping his glass towards him. "To the future."

Atticus toasted back. "To Red Lobster."

"Don't invoke that name without any cheddar biscuits available, gentlemen," I said.

Silo turned to me with a warm smile. He was wearing a blue porkpie hat, a pristine white guayabera shirt with ivory buttons, perfectly pleated black slacks, and blue flip flops. The man made the beach look work in October,

God bless him.

"Poppy Leathers, look at you." He came over to me and gave me a gentle kiss on the cheek. "You're looking well above cheddar biscuit pay grade."

I smiled back and gave him a little turn. I decided to go full flamenco for dinner, since LLL specialized in Basque cuisine. I even wore a cute rose-shaped brooch—extreme old white lady look—that put the outfit over the edge. "Pleasure to see you again, Mr. Jotter."

Silo's eyebrows raised.

I'd only been on "hello" terms with the man for a few years, but he hated when I called him "Mr. Jotter." I don't know if it was a front and he really enjoyed it, or if my formality made him feel uncomfortable.

"Silo," I said. "Sorry. Still in office formal mode up here." I poked my temple and looked at Atticus. "Are we ready?"

Atticus nodded and finished his drink. "Indeed." He gave Silo a pat on the shoulder and nodded. "I'll call once we've gone over the details for the job."

Silo smiled. "Take your time."

Atticus passed me. No hello. No mention of my outfit or how the get up I'd laid out for him matched it in subtle ways—his bolo tie had a rose on it and the pants I chose had embroidered hems that gave him a hint of a matador vibe. But fine.

"Let's go," he said. "That biscuit talk has me starving."

"Sure thing, boss." I walked a bit slower than Atticus.

Waited for him to pass the threshold before I stopped, turned, and put on that smile, eyes and all. I had to give in. If I walked out of the apartment, I was going to spend yet another night playing out all the fantasy scenarios in my head of what could have been if I just mustered the nut to make my move. “Oh, Silo. I’m sorry, I actually had a quick question for you.”

I could feel Atticus’ eyes on me then, but it was now or fucking never.

Silo nodded as he sipped his drink. “Ask away, Poppy.”

“Ah, well, I’m not sure if you knew, but I work as Jason Tasker’s manager during my off hours from Atticus. There’s a problem he has that I can’t quite solve without a little of your insight.”

“Pop, should I wait downstairs?” Atticus sounded sincere, but there was impatience in his voice. I knew him well enough.

Silo waved at Atticus. “Give her a minute. I’ll bring her down.”

“Sorry,” I said to Atticus, “I couldn’t think of anyone else who might be able to give me a lead on this. Won’t be more than ten minutes.”

Atticus left. He could go enjoy a cigar outside or whatever. Let him wait for me for a change.

“Sit.” Silo Jotter gestured to a beautiful, handmade rocking chair across from his own. There was a large pot on a portable camping stove near the chairs, inside of which a pink liquid bubbled and gave off a sour stench that reminded me of lemons and warm milk.

I sat down and looked at the stove. "Is that a new experiment?" I asked brightly. I had to be careful. The boss was the boss for a reason. Silo Jotter worked his way up and sat at the head of the table. I had to respect that to keep my skin in the game.

Silo sighed. "Yeah. This ruby chocolate thing is a pain in the ass. Every time I think I got the formula down, it ends up tasting like fucking floor cleaner. This time I'm trying to use fruits to temper down the sour." He stared at the pot and shrugged. "We'll crack it. I know we will."

Silo was not the figure of immediate authority—the beach bum wear didn't help, even if it worked. He was tall, thin, and never the first thing people laid eyes on when walking into a room. When Silo moved it was slowly, deliberately, and with a hint of a limp on his right side. I knew there was more to him than the Jimmy Buffet superfan look. I could see hints of the man's violence, of what bubbled so much within, it threatened to erupt out his eyes, nose, and ears. It was familiar to me.

"Speaking of chocolate, great work on the Hishiro job, by the way."

I felt my cheeks flush. "Oh, no big deal. I was able to get out of there with time to spare."

Silo looked surprised. "You were at the hit?" He shifted in his seat. As if he needed extra room.

Whoops—maybe. "Oh, no. I had to go back there to grab something. Not a big deal, I realized we were missing some field equipment and it turned up there." That felt like the right kind of answer. Enough to throw Atticus under the bus without saying his name outright.

"Left behind?" Silo asked.

"Little oversight. The place was spotless otherwise."

"Well, good work on that pickup and the reconnaissance. Atticus says your notes are indispensable."

I nodded. "That's the goal."

Silo crossed his legs. "So, what is this Tasker problem you have. Nothing personal, right?"

I shook my head vigorously. "Oh, no. Not at all. It's just, well, with his reputation, there's been issues with—sorry, this is a little TMI, but he and his wife have been trying to have a baby and literally every option's been a dead end."

Silo's eyes widened with understanding. "The artist discovers that filming himself shitting in the shark tank at Camden Aquarium might have impact on his real life."

"Exactly."

"This is why it's always better to do your thing away from everyone else's gaze," Silo said. "Let the reputation be a phantom instead of a cadaver."

I liked that. "Sounds about my speed."

"Yes, but you aspire. That's plain as day. Working for Atticus without pay, becoming… 'indispensable.'" Silo smiled wryly. "I've seen you before, Poppy. Not you, but many versions of you. So, allow me to give you a little advice before I assist you."

"I'd appreciate that, Silo, truly." This felt like a moment, right? Like a really important step forward. I laid my hands on my lap for fear I'd do anything else with them.

"You're going to need to decide whether the aspirations are a priority or if *you* are a priority. Those things are not one and the same." Silo raised a finger to prevent my obvious question. "You ever finish something? Like a project. You write a song or maybe you build a birdhouse. Something you have passion for?"

I didn't have hobbies. "Well, I usually pride myself on getting my itinerary sorted out in a day. It's rare, but it happens."

"How does it feel when that happens?"

"Good."

"But?"

I thought on that. "Well, I mean, I rarely repeat it. I'd like to."

"So, there's the new goal. It comes along and overshadows the accomplishment, doesn't it?"

"And you're saying that's dangerous?"

Silo laughed. "Oh, absolutely not. That's the secret, see. That's the difference between also-rans and the real deals, Poppy. The moment you allow satisfaction to trump aspiration, you fail." He leaned forward. "You can find satisfaction in finishing a day all clean, but you know repeating that's too much of a dice roll. You can be satisfied with one day. But if you weren't..."

"I'd work myself to the bone."

"Which it seems you already do. You're sitting here with me, of all people, taking initiative to ask for a favor that your boss can't. And for what? What does it really do for you?"

I rubbed my hands together. "I'm doing my job."

"Nah, you're working towards something. And may I add I admire that; I do." Silo pulled his phone from his pocket and handed it to me. "Give me your number. I'll text details on a few operations I'm aware of."

I dialed in my number and called myself. "And now I have yours."

"Don't be shy if you need anything else. Okay?"

"I'm a professional, Silo. I'm not the type to bother anyone unless it's necessary."

Silo grinned. "There's a second 'but' here."

I grinned and tried to make it look sheepish. "Well, between you and I?" I slipped a manila folder out of my bag. "All this work for my other boss and I realized there was an opportunity there, you know? A chance to build a business. A Silo Jotter kind of business."

Silo raised a brow. "I usually live in the culinary and textile world, Poppy. I've also found that unsolicited pitches tend to end badly." It was a warning.

The question was if I would bother to listen to that warning. "I understand your position, Silo, but a person like you has to understand that sometimes you need to shoot your shot. You know, aspiration and all that."

"Point taken," Silo said, "But I won't make any promises. I'll listen to what you have to say since you're a good employee."

"Absolutely understood, I appreciate your generosity," I said. "That said, would it hurt to diversify the portfolio a little?" I nodded at the folder. "Give it a read. I think you'll find I did my research and there's an opportunity there if you're willing to invest. Otherwise, if there are other entities you know of that I could do business with, I'll take that, too." I smiled. "Like I said, I'm professional. I won't speak of this again if you find it to be a bad fit for you."

"I believe that." Silo took his phone and dismissed me. "Enjoy your dinner. I know I said I'd walk you down, but I have a few calls to make." He didn't even pause, still looking down at his phone. But his voice had turned anything but casual. "Speaking of, Poppy. What did you have to pick up at Benjamin Hishiro's?"

I collected my things and stood. "Oh, uh, just a skillet. Cast iron. The one Atticus uses for his frittatas."

Silo nodded. "Big thing to forget."

"Well, physically, sure. Could happen to any of us, though, right?"

Silo nodded, sucking his teeth. "Any of us."

"Well, thanks again, Silo. Sorry for taking up your time."

"Not a problem, Poppy. Keep up the good work."

I didn't let myself smile until I was in the elevator. Even then, I kept it low key, knowing damn well a camera was watching. I got Silo Jotter's number! I'd even managed to plant a seed. Just a little seed of doubt in there. Was this what satisfaction felt like? My heart was racing, and I felt like I could damn well run right through a wall. I shot my shot. Sure, I didn't get an answer, but I got a reaction. Silo knew I had aspiration. Even if he gave me a no on the baby business, maybe he'd consider me for something else. What mattered is I took a step forward and it felt like I was sprinting.

And it was so easy. I just had to do it. Everything else followed, didn't it? That confidence made Silo see something else in me. It made him give me the time of day and hopefully that could grow into respect. That first step was closer to the full sprint than I ever believed, and I almost felt ashamed for not having done it sooner.

Where had this version of me gone? I hadn't felt this way since grad school. Why hadn't I made these moves years ago? I made a promise to myself right there: more initiative. Whatever it took to reach my goals. I wasn't some fucking dreamer; I was a doer.

Dinner was decidedly nonviolent. I went against the grain and had branzino in a locally-sourced wine sauce—di-fucking-vine and Atticus had a stew that he poked at. All my standard conversation starters were busts. No amount of ribbing, digressing, or cursing could get the usual rise out of the man. He was clearly upset with me, but didn't have the nuts to mention it. I'd be lying if that wasn't the cherry on top of my confidence sundae. Not only did I approach Silo independently of Atticus, but it got to the man. Mr. Unflappable. Mr. Cool. All up in his feelings because his lesser had the gall to talk above his head.

"What was up with that Red Lobster toast?" I asked.

Atticus side eyed me as he motioned for the check. "Nothing. Just something from back in the day. Old inside joke."

I nodded. "Is it explainable?"

There was an awkward pause that led into one of

those fake "I'm thinking" faces. "Sort of? I mean, it's corny, but you had to be there to fully get it, you know?"

"Sure, sure. I feel you."

Great. Sucked all the air out of our converted water tower space.

I got home at a reasonable hour and checked the inbox. Atticus had already sent me the latest work docket. Was it his passive aggressive way of reminding me my place? More than likely. For me, though, it was a great move. Something to pass the time before I got tired.

I had a little ceremony I followed whenever it was time to compile information on a new job for Atticus: turn the lights down low, fire up a few dozen scented candles, put on some bad '90s R&B, and drink my body weight in wine. The secret: the cheaper the wine, the better.

It was a guilty pleasure—screw cap wine. It made me feel normal, like maybe I was working middle management at the regional office for a fast-food chain or something. Anything to forget Jason and Atticus for a few hours and focus on this stranger who would be dead in a few days.

I fed a little bearded dragon I kept fat and happy with frozen crickets in a large glass aquarium that once held difficult-to-maintain tropical fish. Changed its water, too. The damn thing was left behind, a "gift" from one of Atticus' hits during my first year as his assistant. He brought it back with him, saying it was a refugee of hollowed establishment—whatever the fuck that meant—and then handed all responsibility to me. Instead of giving it a death sentence and keeping it at Castle Glen, I decided to take the damn thing home with me. Never even gave it a name, because I figured once I gave it a name, I'd give more of a fuck about it than I already did.

I got my notebooks, laptop, pens, and some cashews to nibble on.

Time to work.

Okay. The target was a cheesemaker out of Coney Island named Amityville Lee Gordon. Fake ass name. I made a note to check up on that later.

Some light Google-fu told me that she looked to be a mover and shaker. She was thirty, held an MBA, and apparently spent three years teaching the poetic Edda in Japan—sure, that made sense. Interesting bit: she'd inherited the cheese shop from her late grandfather, Pjetri Toska. Now, digging into him turned up a couple of hits. Lot of background site spam, but there were hints of an arrest under some entries. I was going to need to use my buddy Chuck's credentials to run a background check on this guy to see if there were any criminal affiliations to be worried about.

I decided to get ahead of myself and set up the database check while I dug into Amity's life a little more.

Within a year of reopening her cheese shop, Amity won multiple "best-of" awards, earned acclaim for pioneering a means of infusing jams into brie, and helped launch a cheese of the month club called Cheese as You Please.

Amityville's shop, Sweet Baby Cheesus, was named a "Notable Up and Comer" in multiple dairy industry magazines, including *Better Cheddars Monthly* and *Fight for Your Right to Havarti*.

She was obviously a threat to Silo's install base. The contract was a little cruel, but Silo had the gift of foresight and wasn't about to let a new business grow under his nose. I wondered if Amity had been approached and rejected any offers. Wasn't any of my business. Figuring out why Silo wanted her dead wasn't my job. My job was getting Atticus all the details he needed to end this girl as quickly and efficiently as possible.

Amity didn't have any real social media presence outside of business accounts—which she rarely posted under. There were plenty of pictures from her grand reopening and a few trade shows, but nothing very personal. I saw one or two pictures of her side profile, or from behind—she wore jeans well—but nothing that could nail down an exact description.

I couldn't find a trace of other staff associated with her shop on LinkedIn or under the cheese shop's social media accounts. Most followers looked to be from outside New York. By all accounts, Amity didn't come off like she had many friends. A quick check on Pjetri's name on a family tree site turned up her parents, and wow, okay, that was actually her real name. Her mother was Annette Toska, and her father John Gordon. Both lived in Brooklyn until their deaths five years back in what looked to be a robbery gone wrong.

That raised a few alarms, and those alarms were damn well founded when Pjetri's criminal background check came up: our friend was a cocaine dealer. Not on a cartel scale, but large enough to have been arrested a few times in the '70s and '80s for some larger-than-normal scores. Looked like he was good at doing time and staying quiet, because he spent the '90s in the dark and the aughts as a "legitimate" cheesemaker in a neighborhood that coincidentally saw a spike of cocaine arrests and use among youth.

"Damn, girl, you got a dark side, don't you?" I muttered, taking a sip of my perfectly disgusting boxed wine. The sweetness stuck to the back of my mouth like a cavity.

No friends. No family except an old man in an assisted living facility. A business. Connections to a tiny drug empire.

I checked the time. Four hours from when I'd sat down. I hated how that happened. I gathered all my information and created a nice document detailing the histories I found in chronological order, as well as, a brief character analysis of Amity. I assumed she was probably difficult to approach, since she seemed to be a loner. And if she inherited more than the shitty cheese job, she was probably savvy.

My initial recommendation: get her outside of the shop and make it look like a stray bullet. Maybe target some others, as well. Her parents' deaths seemed off, and I couldn't find any conclusions for that, so I wondered if a death that looked similar would spur media attention—which would most definitely increase scrutiny of the events surrounding her death. I also noted if it was worth looking into her grandfather's history, in case Amity was protected. If she were still playing into the cocaine trade, there might be people who would be super upset to see her dead. Never a good thing.

Which made me feel unsure about the recommendation based off a few Google and database searches. I could go to the shop and get a feel for the environment. Maybe strike up a conversation with Amity to understand her behavior a little better—which would be a new move. I never, ever engaged the targets. Last thing anyone needed was a survivor with the memory of a new face so close to their attempted murder.

That begged another set of questions. I mean, if I went over there myself, would it be so bad if I took initiative and did the job, too? I could show off this newfound confidence of mine. Let Silo and Atticus see a new side of me that was always there, always valuable. Which was, admittedly, insane. I could handle a gun, sure, but I wasn't a professional. I liked my violence with less gunfire and more broken limbs.

I was being stupid. Letting my thoughts get ahead of me. Atticus only needed information and my analysis. There was no telling how much trouble I could get into if I took things further. Shit, if I was smart, I wouldn't step foot on Coney Island for the rest of my natural life. Stepping past my boundaries wasn't going to help me. I'd taken enough initiative already. I mean, holy hell, I handed Silo Jotter a fucking business plan. What more did I need to do?

So why did I feel this need to immediately go against everything Atticus taught me? Why did I feel like I had to go to this stupid fucking cheese store? Was it the little rebellious phase I entered, or was it something else? Was it impatience? A sudden desire to prove myself? To whom, exactly? Or did I feel a connection with this girl? Something about Amity was gripping. She was working with a legacy and trying to get past its shadow, wasn't she? Her aspirations were valid, exactly like mine. But they also called Silo's attention, and that attention wasn't like what he had provided me. Why? Was that what happened to people who accomplished something on their own terms? Were they torn down by people terrified to concede that others could succeed despite them?

That shit crawled into my brain and I couldn't get it out. I had to understand why Silo wanted this girl dead. I had to know if it was more than the cheese. If she was a drug dealer, too—if she was encroaching on Silo's claims in Brooklyn—I could understand why she needed to go. If she were simply guilty of being a hard ass working her best to make a name for herself, well, there wasn't much I could really do, was there? And if she deserved it, maybe I could be the one to take her off the charcuterie board. It would mean more that way: not an impersonal act by some bearded stranger, but a mercy from one aspiring woman to another.

I checked my calendar for the next day. Light load for my giant-sized toddlers. Just had to set up a few meetings for Jason and make sure Atticus was all set for some physical therapy on Friday. I could do all of that by phone. I had my own private time in the afternoon, but I could use the early evening to make a stop in Coney Island.

Worst case: I try out some shitty cheese and get to tell Atticus exactly how to end this lady.

Best case: I had no fucking idea.

CHAPTER Eleven

Sweet Baby Cheesus was, bravely, located near the Brighton Bazaar on Coney Island Avenue. It was a small space, but the signage made it stand out. Beneath the big red letters spelling out the store name were crude drawings tracing the life and times of the mouse Cheesus Christ, from sweet, pink baby in a manger to the tiny prophet with long flowing hair and a crown of mouse traps wearing cheese cloth over his mousey privates. The final drawing showed Cheesus nailed to a cross made of Popsicle sticks. There was a wooden plaque with the word "YUMMY" written in paint above the dying mouse-Christ's head. Right below the crucifixion scene was a cat in Roman soldier regalia holding a toothpick with a wedge of cheddar at its tip, a word balloon erupting from its maw as it screamed, "Truly, he is the Lord… of flavor!"

It was an image that intended extreme offense to most any passerby. I found it hilarious, an amusement which continued when I walked into the store. Cheesus Christ, the store's mascot, appeared everywhere and at different points in his life, detailing facts about the available cheeses. The adult Cheesus' stigmata were reminiscent of the holes in Swiss cheese, hollow with an inside that was textured the same as the mouse's skin. In other drawings, Baby Cheesus rose above the store's prices, a large wheel of cheddar in place of a halo over his head. In some, he was draped in cheese cloth, praising the price of sampler platters or the collection of worldly crackers. I scoured a few of the signs and was disappointed in the lack of Eucharist and sacramental wine jokes.

Not gonna lie: I fucking loved this shit. None of this signage was here when I'd taken the food tour way back when. If it had been, I'd have asked this girl to fucking marry me. Who doesn't love a ludicrous amount of cheese puns and blasphemous cartoons? Like chocolate and peanut butter, those were.

Sadly, all those clever displays left little room to traverse—or, presumably, successfully kill someone in cold blood. There were four stands, stocked with crackers and local wines. The main counter held the cheese and Cheesus art, behind which was a door that led to the back. There was nothing in the immediate area that signified a connecting staircase that led to the building's upper levels, and it didn't look like there was space behind any of the refrigerated displays lining the far wall. I pounded my feet against the floorboards gently. The give felt like there might be a basement, but I couldn't tell for sure. I eyed the ceilings and corners for any cameras and found none. There was a strong possibility this would be easier than I anticipated. Atticus wouldn't have an issue coming in here, giving her the quick double tap, and getting out without anyone noticing.

I continued to survey the lay of the land. A little sign with a graphic of mice angels all trumpeting a single letter to advertise the store's "Three-Time Award-Winning" Golgoth-zola cheese caught my eye. I wondered if I should buy some of it before finishing my dossier work. It would be a real waste to leave such an acclaimed product to rot.

"What can I do you for?" The voice was behind me—unexpected.

I turned to find Amityville Lee Gordon in real life. She was the same height as I was. Wore her hair short—a wedged pixie cut that looked like it was done with the assistance of a hand mirror. She had the requisite number of piercings and tattoos an owner of a blasphemous cheese shop should have, but dressed like the grandmothers wandering the street outside with children in tow. There was a little flair on the collar of her pullover: a golden wedge of Swiss cheese, its holes forming the number 17. The pin looked cheap, like something from the bottom of a cereal box.

I felt winded. Had to remind myself why I was there. This was a woman meant to die, not to admire. I blinked and thought about the work; about another recommendation I could make in the dossier or something I could do right there. I traveled all that way; didn't I have a right to do the job? Save us all the heartache of taking the fucking subway for so long—so fucking long.

An accident—I reminded myself as I stared into her stupendously huge eyes. An accident that ensured Amity could have an open casket funeral. I saw a row of cheese knives to my right. It wouldn't be difficult to stage a dramatic suicide: knock her out and slit her wrists. Good enough staging, and anybody would assume the poor business owner had buckled under the pressure. This was New York City, after all. The rents and expectations always took their toll. That was a good note to add: make it look like she tripped, fell, and cheese-knifed herself into oblivion. That was a believable cheese-related accident if I ever thought of one—and this was the only one I ever thought of.

But the knives were maybe too much. Amity looked like the type who wore wounds grievously. A long look at her told me that. She was a woman who deserved something better, more dignified.

She deserved to live, even. Another gut check. I knew that the moment I looked her up. The moment I saw what she was trying to do for herself. Amity was working towards her goals like I was. We were kindred fucking spirits—weren't we?

So, I did exactly what I was never supposed to do:

I spoke. "Um, yes. I'm looking for really nice gouda. Something for entertaining? Maybe smoked?" It was a jumble of cheese words I hoped made sense when strung together. Should have tossed in "charcuterie," but I had no idea how to pronounce that right.

Amityville smiled wide. "A woman of fine taste. How often do we get your type in here?" She seemed to sway over to a glass display with a small sign reading "THE ONE TRUE GOUDA." "I always feel like you need a nice spread. Really get the different flavors out there, you know? Like a mild to stinky rainbow."

I cleared my throat and shuffled my feet as I moved towards the display. Amity overwhelmed me. Her look. Her voice. The way she moved. This was some grade school level shit. Butterflies in the tummy and all. "I, uh, I'm not super knowledgeable. I mean, I've eaten a lot of different kinds, but I can barely remember what the names are. I remember someone giving me something called Brillat-Savarin. That was nice." I think that was nice. I couldn't remember the taste, just the stupid name. Why the hell was I acting this way? I hated people. What was this person doing any different than all the other ones that drove me insane? Like, she was just standing there existing.

"Oh, we're going deep cut, huh?" Amity laughed. "A person of many cheeses would be more cultured, no?" She jabbed an elbow into my side as she walked past. "Know what I mean?"

That was fucking charming even if it careened past the dad joke boundary so hard it came back around to pass it three more times. "I like to think I know feta." I nearly covered my mouth with both hands. It simply came out. What power did this lady have over me?

She was a cheese witch.

"Aw, snap," Amity said. "We're punning. We're punning." She grinned like a loon. Her cheeks flushed. "I get the feeling you're the regular type."

I felt suddenly aware of my surroundings. Kept turning to see if anyone else had walked into the store. This was a case job, and I had been in the store way too long. Amity knew my face now. If someone walked in, they would see us together. I was a memory now. I told myself to leave. I could simply excuse myself, be as flustered as I already was, and get the fuck out of there. There was emotion here. If I let it keep moving ahead, this was going to be a huge problem.

"I'm Amity, by the way." Amityville—now officially Amity—extended a hand. "I own the place. The big cheese, so to speak. Well, not bigger than our Lord Cheesus, but you get my drift."

"Poppy." I gestured to a picture of Cheesus splitting a wheel of cheese to feed dozens of tiny mice. "I take it you are also a devout Catholic?"

"Ha!" Amity's barked laugh was strong and aggressive in a way that sent a little tingle down my spine. "Indeed. Thirteen years of Catholic school sure sets the edge in."

"I was homeschooled, so I get the religious angle." Whoa. That was an honest answer. I never did that. And it slipped out so easily too. So much for professionalism. Poppy, be out. This had gone too far, I thought; this is going to get you fucking killed. This woman was a target—nothing more.

But she didn't have to be. That was what kept my feet rooted to the ground. What made it so wrong for Amity, this lively and corny-ass cheesemaker, to simply be left to her own aspirations? Why should she be punished? Why should any of us?

I followed for nearly twenty minutes as Amity explained each of the cheeses she sold, the process involved in making them, and her overall philosophy on dairy products—thirty-two different varieties of cheese or butters; she made them in the basement, and she may have had a small God-complex when it came to preparing them, especially when she used certain molds. I was engaged throughout. I laughed and asked questions. By the end, I'd bought each type of cheese and a brick of obscenely expensive French butter. Me, lactose intolerant as hell, bought almost a thousand fucking dollars' worth of cheese because of this lady's puns and eyes.

How the fuck could I let a hustler of this caliber be murdered?

Silo, though, was not the type to renegotiate a contract without a damn good reason. I knew that. And Atticus wasn't about to be lectured—or begged—by me to cut this girl loose. It was hysterically perfect coincidence, to find these feelings with the first person I'd met after deciding to work towards my ambitions without concession. But then, wasn't that why I was opened up to feeling this way? Amity was now an ambition of mine—she was something I wanted. Not like property—that's fucked up. I valued her, even if it were a beginning—I wasn't in love; that would take time. Though, I could see myself with this woman. I could see myself reaching my goals alongside her reaching her goals and becoming something more because of each other and despite each other.

There was poetry in that thought.

Amity rung me up and smiled. "I'll give you the friends and family discount."

I shook my head violently. No way could we get *that* familiar. "That's absolutely not necessary. I got cash and I intend to use it."

"Good, because I don't have that, and I was worried about what I was going to make up to look like I did." She laughed. "I have some family, but no friends. It probably wouldn't have been that much of a savings. Also, I suck at math, so I would have been all over the place with whatever discount I pulled out of my ass."

"Ah, well, is it a bad time to mention I only have Canadian dollars?"

"Bullshit. We all know Canada is a myth."

We both laughed, and easily.

Cheese witch!

I paid and made my way to the door. Amity opened it to let me out and I stepped back onto the street. It felt so empty and strange. A half hour in that store and I already missed its smells.

"Wait." I stopped and turned. I slipped my hand into my front jacket pocket, ready to do something stupid. "One more thing."

"I bought you a shit ton of new cheese to help ease that capybara smell you love so much," I said as I placed three—three fucking bags worth—of cheese on Atticus' kitchen counter. "Got stuck in a conversation and I didn't have a choice."

Atticus scratched his arm. "Did you use the petty cash?"

"Nope. I was hoping you'd cover the expense after the fact since it was a business transaction."

"Uh-huh." Atticus eyed me. "Did you get any good information out of this? Anything to make it a quick job? I feel like you may have spent too much time at this place."

"Well, it seems like she does have staff," I lied, "because I didn't see her. Just this know-it-all cheese head motherfucker who could not shut up about Havarti."

What was I doing? Why did I do that?

Atticus shook his head. "It was a mistake for you to go in there. We have her basics. I'll take care of her outside of her apartment." His eyes darted back and forth. "She's just a cheesemaker. I don't want you taking unneeded risks for something this low-hanging."

A flash of anger struck me. I did my best to ignore it; to keep Atticus from reading my eyes and seeing something that wasn't there before.

"Do you not agree?" he asked, letting me know I failed spectacularly.

I sighed. "I don't think she's just a cheesemaker. Cheesemonger? Cheesemaker or cheesemonger?" Once again, the attempt to act casual was… not going great.

"What did you find?"

"I don't have the dossier on hand, but some of my research showed her grandfather—from whom she inherited that shop—has a past moving cocaine. He hit it big in the eighties, but still, it's enough to get me thinking he might be protected."

"Do you think she's maintaining two family traditions?"

"Maybe. Like I said, I didn't get to meet her, so it didn't come off that way in the shop."

Atticus laid his hands on his marble counter and stared off in thought. "And now you've already been to the store, so a repeat visit to confirm puts us in a bad position."

"Yeah, man. Sorry. I feel like I fucked up today."

Atticus softened and gave me an incredibly patronizing smile. “Aw, Pop, you couldn’t control any of that. If anything, this might be for the better. Maybe I can go out and do some of the scouting myself. I can see if there’s anything else going on before we finish the job. If there’s a trafficking connection we’re unaware of, Silo should know.”

“Exactly what I thought.” I rubbed my eyes. “Do you need me to help with what’s next? Any research on cheese or the neighborhood?”

Atticus mulled on that. “No. No, I think I can go in with a small truth. Say my friend recommended the place without saying who. Move from there. If the opportunity comes along to stage an accident for the target, I’ll take it.”

“I noticed a lot of knives in the shop.”

“Trip, fall, stab?”

“Exactly.”

This didn’t feel the same as other breakdowns. I didn’t like opening the door for Atticus to move ahead either way, but there wasn’t any choice in the matter. Wasn’t much I could do to stop him outside of shooting him, and Atticus wasn’t an easy man to shoot—I’d seen enough proof over the years.

There I sat, broken-hearted. Surrounded by cheese I couldn’t eat, a boss I could no longer stand calling me by that fucking nickname again, and thinking about a woman who would no longer exist in a few days. At least I had my plans. I’d work on them that night. Set things up and get to work on making sure I never had to feel this way again.

One bright spot: I got her number. It would be a mistake to call her, though. Like, a massive, dumb mistake.

CHAPTER twelve

Never stared at my phone so hard as I did that next morning when I was supposed to be planning.

That's not to say I didn't start things off. I bought some new poster board for the occasion and set things up like a science fair presentation. "Poppy's Other Big Plan" in block letters, with glitter and everything. Never not glamming the planning. It's what kept me focused.

But the planning eluded me, despite how extra I'd gone with the glitter this time.

I wanted to know if Atticus had left his apartment yet. I wanted to see if Silo had that information for me. Maybe Amity called and I was on mute or she didn't pass the junk call filter. I had so many reasons to check the damn thing. But I also knew checking meant I was going to abandon this wonderful poster board with my name emblazoned on it.

So, planning.

The first step was to find a way to turn Atticus and Silo against each other. I had to show Silo that Atticus was no longer deserving of loyalty or protection. The goal wasn't to start a war or convince Silo that Atticus was his enemy—that had the potential to blow up in my face. What I needed to do was convince Silo that Atticus' time was up. That he was now a loose end—someone undeserving of the protections he enjoyed. Whether that led to sending him out to pasture with a bullet or in prison would be up to Silo. My job was just to cultivate that seed until it bloomed.

Then I'd step in and show Silo exactly how indispensable I was.

The skillet slip-up was a good start, but I needed something more. And, really, Amity was sitting right there. If I could find a way to make this job not happen—or at least happen in a way that made Atticus look like an idiot—that would be a big win. Though, the latter option wasn't very appealing. I wanted to have my cake, and I wanted to eat it with a tall fucking glass of cold milk—non-dairy since shitting my pants wouldn't be the best outcome.

I thought about the Mouse Jesus and smiled to myself. All that art and the puns were corny as hell, but it was cute to see how much effort Amity went through to make her store stand out. It made me wonder what else she did at home. Was she crafty? I didn't normally love craft people, but I bet Amity was good at something fun like cross-stitching or some other yarn-based bullshit.

I stopped myself. I was off track. The plan, Poppy—stick to the fucking plan.

So, my plan to screw over my boss.

The most immediate option: sabotage this hit. Problem was, how quickly could I pull that off? Atticus himself was going to the cheese shop tomorrow or the day after, and it wasn't like I could tell him not to. The only person with that power was Silo, and why would Silo bother to take Atticus off the hit if there wasn't a solid reason?

Unless he didn't know about the cocaine. Atticus sure acted that way, didn't he? And hell, Silo was an in-the-know kind of man. If he knew there was a drug connection, wouldn't he have made that plain?

That was a risk. I couldn't call Silo and rat all willy-nilly. That would be a major issue, and Atticus would have my head for going over his. Silo did make it sound like I could reach out to him, though... I grabbed my phone and pulled up his contact information. A text might be best, I thought, but not about the hit.

"Oh shit, oh shit, oh shit," I said as I typed.

> Silo – sorry this is Poppy. Checking in about adoption info. Boss is asking I don't mean to bother

I debated adding an emoji, but would an emoji be an appropriate punctuation mark when texting a crime lord? Nobody covered this kind of shit in school.

I checked my phone after trying to ignore it for five seconds.

Three dots…

Oh, shit. Three dots…

I stared at my screen, willing Silo to stop typing and simply hit send.

Hi Poppy. Sorry. Will send first thing in morning. Thanks for reminder.

Okay. Not bad.

Three dots again.

Holy shit. There was a follow up.

How is new job going? Does A have everything he needs?

No way he made it that easy. Unless the skillet thing had him feeling uneasy and hoping I was the type to spill a little tea over text. If that was the case, my instincts were good, right? That little seed was blooming.

I answered back:

Oh gr8. need to clear up some stuff with this girl's gpa

Gpa?

Oh, her grandfather, sorry. He had some weird info in the background check that didn't sit well with me. Priors. Drug trafficking. Doesn't look like it stopped.

Three dots…

Nothing.

Dots again…

Name?

Fuck yes, he bit. I pumped my fist into the air.

Pjetri Toska

ty good nite

How was that so easy? It *was* easy, right? It didn't feel hard. I texted and he texted back. No harm, no foul. New information sent over. It took a minute for my brain to register how absolutely monumental that was, though. I'd had a thought and then I acted and it worked out in my favor. How and why did that feel so bafflingly foreign to me? I used to do that all the time. That was how I got my jobs with Atticus and Jason to begin with.

The feeling was almost orgasmic. Like, stop for a breath, slam back that warm glass of wine, and shove a cracker into my mouth like a hamster kind of good. I couldn't believe it. My fucking toes were tingling. Another big moment for Poppy! If things panned out, Silo would look that old man up and maybe grant us a pause. I could avoid this poor woman getting killed for nothing at all, and Atticus could go back to looking like a chump for leaving behind a fifteen-pound piece of traceable metal in the apartment of the man he'd murdered in cold blood.

But then what?

That was the next step of the plan I had to sort out. How did I go from assistant to, for lack of a better term, low rung management? I wondered if I should start getting friendly with the lower rank stooges who hung around Silo's establishments and popped by Atticus' apartment occasionally. Not so much to make new friends, but to plant a few other little flowers. It would help to have some people around who liked me in case things went sour with Atticus. Not that I saw violence between us happening—and while I knew how to use a gun (I mean, look who I worked for)—I wasn't about to match up with a fella who could field strip and reassemble multiple kinds of firearms blindfolded.

The Silo text chain was a good thing, though. He saw me as an asset. All I could hope was he underestimated me. That put me in a position to surprise him; to make him see something in me he wasn't seeing in Atticus. I was the next generation. The person Silo could trust to help further his agenda in a field of work that wasn't known for granting anyone involved a healthy run or a comfortable retirement. From there, I could move towards the other goals. Make that money. Gain that position. Branch out into other fields. I mean, guns and drugs and artisanal pursuits were adorable, but there were entire ventures out there left untouched by more nimble-minded people like me.

That baby business. Elaborate tourist traps in out of

the way places. Themed bakeries. *Fuck*, I had ideas, and for the first time in my life, it all felt within reach. All I had to do was keep stretching. And once I grabbed hold, I was going to hold on like a pit bull.

I was still holding my phone. Riding that high of accomplishment. Matter of fact, that high was so high that I pulled up Amity's contact info.

> Hey – it's Poppy! 😊

Three dots…

CHAPTER Thirteen

"Jason, we're close," I announced as I walked into Tasker's loft. "Should have a track on those adoptions before end of day today."

"Awesome, Pop, fucking awesome!" Jason winced. "Poppy, Poppy, Poppy. Sorry. I promise I will be better about that." He was busy painting a crappy mural depicting a line of gorillas waiting to partake in a bathroom glory hole. It would have been funny and shocking back in 2003, but now it was also-ran nonsense that wasn't even meme-worthy. "What do you think?" he asked.

"That one gorilla's dick is too small." I put my things down and went to the refrigerator. Hunted down a salad I'd left in there two days back and was thrilled to see it untouched. One less lunch to buy. "Needs to be girthier. Which ape is going to be on the other side?"

"I was thinking man."

"Nature's biggest whore."

"Do gorillas actually have big dicks?" Jason pondered.

"Would it be weird to Google that?"

"Only if you're worried about ending up on a new database, but I have a feeling you're already on a few."

"That stomping fetish thing was on the up and up. I needed to find models."

I didn't need to hear any of that this early in the morning. Better to let him make his statement and stew in his own shame than have me validate any of that nonsense. "Uh-huh," I said. "Listen, you got that college appearance later today. Shouldn't be hard; it's a virtual meet and I already set up your laptop with reminders, the link, and all that good stuff. You click one thing and you're good to go."

"Aw, shit. That's right. How long is that again?"

"Little under an hour." I wandered over to the coffee pot and poured three cups. Finished as Sara Tasker walked into the room. "Morning," I said.

"Good morning, Poppy," Sara said groggily. She grabbed a mug of coffee and took a deep sip. "Oh, God, I'm going to need a gallon of this today."

"Busy?"

Sara nodded. "I'm behind. Trying to get a few pitches out to food mags. Running out of ideas."

Another opportunity. "You should do a profile on this spot I went to the other day, Sweet Baby Cheesus. That place is a fucking trip."

Sara perked up. "Is it good?"

"I spent a fucking fortune there and regret not a bit

of it, if that's what you're asking."

"Ooh, I'll do some poking around then. Thanks!" Sara topped off her coffee, grabbed a pack of cookies from the countertop, and disappeared.

Jason went back to his painting and I sat watching. "You got anything else happening today?" Jason asked as he checked his phone and went to increase the size of the gorilla's dick as per my recommendation.

I looked at my phone. No new notifications. My little text-a-text with Amity had gone well. All the standard first-time messages that ended with "lol" or smiley faces. Standard banter, but fun. I debated sending her a message about Sara but decided that was an afternoon kind of text. Sending a message at 7:30 AM was just plain weird.

Atticus, on the other hand, I wanted to hear from. I texted him as soon as I woke up, and it was worrying to not have any replies. He wasn't a big sleeper and was always prompt with his answers.

"Poppy, you there?" Jason was in front of me, a small smile on his face. "Drink a little more coffee, you're spacing out."

I shook my head. "Sorry, yeah, got lost. Uh, if you're all set the day, then I think I'm off to sort out a few errands. I still need to talk to a friend about getting you that space for the show, but word of warning: expect us to get next year at the earliest."

Jason shrugged. "I know you'll work your magic. I'm

not worried."

Work my magic. Sure. Yeah. I was a regular fucking miracle worker. I should have had stigmata I was such a fucking divine being. I was often stymied by the ability of the rich to completely ignore effort. They were always focused on the ask and the result but never what came in between. Like getting the space for this show. The fucking favors I had to call in. The walkthroughs. The permit research. *Actually* getting those permits. Hiring staff like servers or models—even the ringers who were there solely to inflate bids on pieces that weren't well-received. This wasn't magic, motherfuckers, it was hard work, and I was a beast of immense burden. None of that stuff was real to these people because they never lifted a goddamn finger. Of course they'd label it as magic. It was easy to do that when the whole world was Disney-fied for you; when the sausage was made far, far away from prying ears and eyes.

What was worse: all this effort didn't earn me a quarter of what Jason earned. All my work made him rich. All my work made Atticus the scariest man in Brooklyn. Why did these people deserve to have me be the updraft that held them aloft when they could barely appreciate the level of logistics behind even giving them the wings to begin with?

And that killed me because deep down, I knew my impatience was irrational—but to take steps forward and then come back here to gorilla dicks, adoptions, and sewer art show planning made all the momentum with Amity and Silo feel fake. Like I was convincing myself an elevator was moving but it turned out I hadn't pressed the goddamn button.

I finished my coffee. I had a sewer appointment to get to—lord fucking help me—and I needed to check in on Atticus. I sent him another text asking if he wanted me to pick up some breakfast pastries, maybe even a cronut or two. Pastries always made people kind, at least in my experience.

Honestly, I think I just wanted some pastry.

I chewed on a chocolate croissant as I emerged from the subway. Birds were singing. Kids were laughing. That nagging monster of doubt and poor self-esteem was more quiet than normal.

"Poppy?"

The voice jolted me out of my buttery chocolate hypnosis.

"Oh, shit. Amity?" There she was. Big as life. Right in front of me in a neighborhood that was supposed to be my stomping grounds, not a place I'd bump into a person like her.

We gave each other an awkward hug.

"What are you doing around these parts?" I asked.

"Oh. Uh. Visiting with a friend for breakfast," Amity

said. “I never get a chance to hang out like a normal person, so I decided to go for it.”

“Cool, cool.” I motioned towards Castle Glenn. “I’m off to job number two before I have to run some errands. Never fucking ends.”

“No shit. I’m late to open the shop and I’ve got some private clients coming in today.”

“Fancy! Anything interesting?” I grinned. “You selling some black-market cheeses?”

Amity laughed. “Something like that.”

That pause came in. Mega pregnant. Teen pregnant.

“Well,” Amity swung a leg back and forth and pointed to the subway with her thumbs. “Guess I’m off.”

“Oh, yeah, right. Not a short trip down to Coney, right?”

“Nope.”

“Well, um, it was fun texting. I was going to shoot you a message to see if you wanted to grab a coffee or something later.”

“Oh, yeah, well, of course. I’d love to.” She snapped her fingers. “You know what? There’s an awesome spot I know we can go to. Would tomorrow be okay? I’ve got work stuff and I know I’m going to need to lay down tonight, but I’ll bug you later. Sound good?”

“Sounds perfect,” I said. “Have a great rest of day.”

“You too.”

I watched Amity leave. Kicked myself for sending her off with that corporate jargon. “Have a great rest of day"—the fuck was wrong with me? She made me nervous, though. Stupid, even. I felt like the words dumped out of my mouth like rocks. I had no game. Zero. My ability to connect with a person I was genuinely attracted to was immediately demolished by years of ignoring myself and catering to the whims of everyone else.

So, I texted her. Not even a minute after saying goodbye.

Hey – weird question. Did we just make a date?

Worth asking. There wasn't a point in drawing things out.

Three dots.

Not a weird question. Toes a date…

Totes, not toes. Atocorrect.

Fuck damn it

I laughed. This was good. Maybe even great. I turned back to the building. Shook off my happiness and let the gray cloud of miserable employment come on back. It was what it was. At least I had something to look forward to later.

The to-do list: Atticus. Sewers. Food—maybe, depending on if the sewer thing involved smells—and then Amity.

Never so excited about a cup of coffee in my entire life.

CHAPTER Fourteen

Atticus was drying himself off when I got into the apartment. This was a new look for him: unkempt. There were bags under his eyes, too.

It took a minute for the realization to hit me, but when it did, I stopped mid-stride. "Hold up." I leaned in. "Oh, shit. You had company."

Atticus rolled his eyes.

"Overnight company at that." I laughed. "Look at you. It's been, like, three years, hasn't it?"

"Four."

"Feel better?"

"I'm not sure that's the right word for it." Atticus sat on one of the high stools near the kitchen counter eating area. He leaned on his elbow and took a long, deep breath. "I think I made a mistake, Pop."

"Pop," always with "Pop." For the love of fucking—no, no, it was fine. He was in afterglow. Let him have it. I'd correct him if he said it again.

"What, you fuck a friend's sister or something?" I asked.

The look he gave me. Like a little kid that had to tell a parent about being in trouble at school: a mix of innocent terror and shame. That look made me do the math. I'd bumped into Amity not two blocks from here. Atticus said he would case her store himself. Now he sat here in less clothes than he'd ever worn around me with *that* look on his face. The reverse walk of shame.

"Atticus, no," I said. Seriously, no. No. No. No. Of all the possible boneheaded, selfish, absolutely unprofessional things to do. He did the same damn thing I did. The idiot fell for the cheese witch's spell, and while I knew I was a blazing hypocrite to find myself thinking so low of him to fall for her dairy-based tricks, I wasn't the professional murderer here. I was the assistant. I was allowed a handicap when it came to this kind of stuff.

"I didn't expect things would escalate that way." Atticus shrugged. "I even brought my favorite PDP Compact along in case the opportunity to end the job arose. But here we are."

"Uh-huh. Sounds like what 'arose' was something entirely different." "Here we are." I couldn't believe he wasn't more panicked by the thought of what he'd done. He slept with a target. There were like a million movies and stories where the explicit problem was a bad guy's change of heart because of a target's ability to become an emotional anchor. I was totally onboard with sabotaging this entire job because Amity left me weak at my idiot knees. Now I had to worry about Atticus doing the same.

"We talked. We hit it off. And the next thing I knew, we came here for Chinese and..." Atticus grimaced. "She seems to really like me."

I felt a pang of jealousy, despite knowing that was idiotic and not helpful for the very dangerous issue right in front of my face. I couldn't help it, though. The idea that Atticus one-upped me right when I was experiencing a little momentum got to me. That Amity would choose him made it a little worse. She had met me first and went for him either way. That felt like judgment.

Then again, Amity was her own person. I hadn't made my feelings known until just a few minutes ago, and it wasn't like she could read my mind. She was a grown ass woman, and she could mess around with whatever sad sack middle-aged killers she wanted to. Besides, she'd had no way of knowing what my relationship with said sad sack middle-aged killer was.

But Atticus. Oh, man. If anything, my respect—despite the personal grievances—for Atticus took more of a hit. He should have known better. Now he was standing there, just... not caring. I'd have preferred if he'd at least reveled in the sexual conquest of a contract, or if he had some dewy, fresh-faced glint in his eyes. Fuck, even a half chub in his towel like fucking Tasker. *Something*. But nope—just as aloof as ever. Like she'd meant nothing to him.

And that—*that*, started to make me angry.

"What are you going to do?" I asked. I was, to be fair, genuinely curious.

"I know what I should do. I could have done it here."

"But you didn't."

"No." Atticus laughed. "I asked her when we could see each other again."

"Because you like her, too?" I asked.

"I'm not sure." Atticus gave it thought. "I think I'm just going to enjoy where it goes, you know?"

"Enjoy" where it went. I didn't have the words. I fought the urge to blurt it all out there and then. To tell him I also asked Amity out *and* she said yes—a little clapback for this crap—but I couldn't find it in myself to do it. What if that confession sent Atticus to finish the job? What if it turned his violence my way? There were too many potentials and I wasn't prepared to work them out. Stick to the plan, I thought.

I had to make him see the potentials here. Get it in his head that this was a bigger mistake than the damn pan. "You realize that none of that is going to make Silo change his mind if he decides this girl needs killing, right? You're going to have to choose between her and your continued employment." I stepped closer to Atticus. "Silo will fucking kill you."

"No. He wouldn't do that to me," Atticus said, quickly and self-assured. It was as if the thought genuinely had not occurred to him.

"Why, because you've done so much work for him?" I rolled my eyes. "Yeah, throughout history employers have been awesome at not turning on their employees when they had the choice." I sighed. "You need to make peace with the fact that it's either you that finishes her, or someone else who finishes both of you." That was good. Turn all my inside thoughts out and project them onto him.

But Atticus just shook his head again like a confused buffalo, shuffling his feet back and forth. "No, no. He wouldn't. Look, I need to get out of here. Go for a walk." He started to walk towards his bedroom. There was concern in his eyes. I'd struck a nerve—thank God.

"I don't like this sudden wild card role reversal we have going here. *You're* the one who lectures me for being impulsive, man. You should have waited a day or two before going over there."

Atticus stopped dead in his tracks. "Who the fuck are you to lecture me?" He eyed me. "You're not mad about this for non-professional reasons, are you?"

Crap. Was he realizing? "No," I lied.

The air between us felt hot. Atticus clenched his jaw and eyed me. His posture was stiff. He seemed to inflate to twice his size in that moment. A flash of the man I always heard whispers about. The kind of man that, despite my disapproval of him, was very much capable of ending me where I stood in a thousand ways I couldn't imagine. It was intimidating, but it was a reminder that this man was never my friend. Maybe that was my real mistake with him—thinking we were anything more than employer and employee. There was a time I genuinely liked Atticus—maybe even loved him as a good friend. For fuck's sake, this man was more a part of my life than anyone else in the world.

I couldn't lie: it hurt a little to see I didn't mean anything to him. And yeah, I was plotting against him, but still, we'd spent enough time together that my scheming left me with, like, a *little* guilt. Maybe guilt was a strong word. More of a sparkling shame?

Atticus shook his head. "I'm *your* boss, you know. The way you're questioning me—"

This lashing out didn't hurt for long, though. It focused me. He wanted me to bend the knee and no, I wasn't going to. He hired Poppy and he was going to get Poppy, not Pop. "I wouldn't question you if you were doing the right thing, Atticus. I wouldn't question you if you'd decided not to get your dick wet with the person your boss is invested in seeing dead and buried."

"It wasn't a big deal."

"Then why didn't you do it?"

"Why didn't I kill her?"

"That's the fucking job, Atticus. Silo points you at a problem and you magic erase that shit from the planet. Amity is the problem and all you've done is make that problem bigger."

"I didn't—"

"Why didn't you just finish the job? Admit it."

Atticus deflated. "I don't know. I'm not in love or anything, but… it felt like I could at least do someone the courtesy of enjoying a few moments after a decent night before ending her life."

Wow. What an asshole. "Atticus, what the hell is going on with you?" I stepped closer to him. "What is it that you need to get out of this—I don't know what else to call it but a funk—you're in?"

A wall closed over Atticus' face, like no emotion had or would ever cross it again. He'd stone-walled me. "Take the rest of the day off, Pop. I don't need you in my face right now." He turned and left the room.

So, there it was. Maybe he didn't quite catch feelings, but the beginnings of something… I'd been around enough lovestruck dipshits—myself included—that I knew the seed was there, whether he wanted to admit it or not.

It was with his absence and the calm it brought that I realized something: this was a fantastic opportunity. For me, but for Amity, too. I could keep her alive and, in keeping her alive, ruin Atticus Garcia.

"Call if you need me," I yelled as I left his apartment. My phone chirped. A text from Jenna Fontana about the sewer space—yay, Jason Tasker work to get my mind off this nonsense.

As I left, that sense of not guilt/obligation kicked in and I put in a lunch order for Atticus as I waited for the elevator, in case he forgot to eat. Fancy poultry salad with all sorts of locally sourced goodness on some roasted garlic sourdough he had a small obsession over a year or two ago. It was like a fancy lunch for a kindergartner, and I figured that would bring him some form of comfort.

The very least I could do was feed him as I plotted his downfall.

CHAPTER Fifteen

"Elton, right?" I asked for the third time.

"Alton," he said. He was not pleased with me.

I felt bad I kept forgetting this cat's name. It wasn't even intentional. "Sorry. Jenna could tell you what a scatter-brained asshole I am. I don't mean any disrespect."

"None taken, Miss Leathers."

"Poppy, please. Miss Leathers is for people I don't like."

"Very well."

Alton was a collector of city artifacts. He specialized in blueprints and old planning documents, and was especially well-versed in the forgotten hubs of New York City. He was considered one of the best urban explorers on the scene—the kind of man who rubbed elbows with rats, roaches, and mole people alike. What I was hoping for from Alton was a little insight into making one of Jason's requests come true.

I clapped my hands together as Alton unrolled a map

across his desk. "So, where can we throw a party in the literal underbelly of this city?"

Alton shook his head. "Honestly? This is a first. I've seen people hold shindigs at superfund sites or near the waste treatment plant over in Red Hook. But in the actual sewer?" He studied the map. "How many people are you people looking to accommodate?"

"The less the better, in my opinion. My client's an artist. The more exclusive this show comes off, the more money we make."

"Well," he turned the map so it was right-side up for me. "See here, near the Fourth Street Basin? There are some tunnels that aren't entirely flooded in this area. Well, most of the time. Maybe even closer to the bridge up north. I still think people would need waders at minimum to head down there, but I'd recommend goggles and masks, as well. A lot of the waste coming through here is nasty."

I looked at the map, pretending I knew what I was looking at. "Danger ups the price, my friend." I pointed at where I thought a bridge was. "How does this all work, though? Are there places where the water goes out into the canal?"

"Certain places, yes. But they were working until recently to create new sewer tunnels to divert excess flood water from the older ones."

"Are the newer tunnels being used?"

"I think the ones south of Douglass Street are, but to

the north? Maybe not. They were supposed to be finished by now, but there's always delays. I can make a few calls if you'd like."

"I'd love that." I smiled. "Alton, I thought this was entirely implausible, but this is sounding pretty frigging optimistic."

Alton cleared his throat. "Well, there are still other logistical issues to bear in mind."

I lost a little of my smile. "Shoot."

"Well, police, for one. You've got presence from city workers and conservationists as well. And, even if the newer tunnels aren't being used full time, there is the danger they'll be used part time."

"Would it be safer to find something abandoned? How about train tunnels? I'm always hearing about old train tunnels under the city. They even had that in the *Ninja Turtle* movies."

"Those are movies."

I stared at Alton. "And your point?"

Alton stared at the map and let out a long sigh. "I'm not supposed to tell people about this, but Jenna said you're good, and I trust her." He eyed me. "And your enthusiasm for the danger of a sewer party worries me."

This sounded like it was going to be good. "Go on, my friend."

"You'll have to double what was offered."

"Done."

"Fine." Alton pointed to a space on the east side of

the canal. “There’s a service station near here that was never completed. There are rails connected to nothing, and a single service train car. It was popular with street artists in the ’90s, but the MTA sealed it shut.”

“Until...”

“Until a group of us found it. It’s not easy to get into, and it’s certainly not safe, but it is definitely safer than the sewers.”

“Why was it never finished?” I asked.

“No idea. I think the people who planned it didn’t account for the fact that water could completely fill the tunnels if anything ever came down. Once they did come to the realization, they abandoned the project. It wasn’t worth the price building the supports it would take to keep the whole thing from collapsing and drowning train cars full of commuters.”

“So, there’s a whole space down there we could use. Would we have to access it through the sewer? Any chance you can take me down there before I commit to anything?”

“I’d have to check with Jenna. She has the only copy of the map and it’s a bit of a walk. Like I mentioned before, we’ll need waders and thick clothes. There are some tight spaces on the way.”

“So, the element of danger still exists.” I grinned. “What’s the name of the station?”

Alton shrugged. “I never found anything definite. We took to calling it Station Zero.”

“That name is marketable as all fuck.” I grabbed Alton by the sides of his head and planted a massive kiss on his nose. “You are a fucking lifesaver, man.”

“Bring me the money and we’ll schedule a walk-through. If you have any smell sensitivities, I’d recommend buying a gas mask. It can be pretty bad down there.”

“I wouldn’t expect any less. This city’s sewers? It’s like the clogged subconscious of every single person living here, ain’t it? All trash and shit. The very worst parts of us.” I traced my finger along the lines on the map. Lines stacked on lines. The convoluted body of a convoluted city. I saw why Alton was fascinated by these things.

“It’s a poetic way of looking at things,” Alton admitted. “It does feel like it’s a vault of history we want to ignore. All the work and ingenuity to transport waste. We rarely think about it. If at all.”

“I could run our little shit symposium here all day, man. Alas…” I sighed. “I have had a fucking day and need to lie down something fierce. Venmo you the money?”

Alton nodded. “Label it something inconspicuous.”

“I like tagging these things as specialty porn, so gird your loins.”

Alton winced. “You don’t have to do that.”

“I know. But I want to do that, Alton. I want to give you money for specialty videos of naked women in ketchup baths.”

CHAPTER Sixteen

Amity wore an oversized Legendary Pink Dots T-shirt as a dress, leggings covered in pulp novel covers from the 1930s, and a pair of bright red vintage Doc Martens with blue- and purple-striped shoe-laces. She wore a little makeup, but not much, and kept her hair tied back in a tight ponytail. There was a thick silver chain around her neck, a gaudy bauble hanging from it. It was a Lucite piece—a tiny freak show mer-maid's corpse trapped within, eyes closed tight as if in thought.

I was a bit stunned to see her. This was supposed to be a coffee meet, nothing extravagant or special. And there was still something otherworldly about seeing her outside of Sweet Baby Cheesus. If I had my druthers, I'd have asked her to stand in front of me for the rest of the day and take her in. Fucking hell. I had a total high school crush on this relative stranger, and it was way too obvious. How embarrassing.

"You're all dressed to the nines," Amity said.

Not really. The entire outfit was a slapdash mess of hand-me-down items I'd taken from Atticus and Jason's closets and had resized. Tonight's look was a light blue suit heavy on the straight cuts and stitching, black boots I'd found at a thrift store that were too good to be true, and a sharp-looking trilby I stole from Jason.

"All of this stuff is repurposed, but thanks." I tipped my hat. "Going full milady tonight."

We both laughed.

"You mentioned a place you knew?" I asked. "I'm excited to be in the Village. I rarely get to spend time out here."

Amity grinned and turned. "Awesome. Let's move. I'm hungry. The place I was telling you about is a block away." She stopped and cringed a little. "I feel like an ass for not asking when I texted. You like crêpes, right? No food allergies or anything?"

"I would not say no to a crêpe. And I'm only allergic to penicillin."

"Double awesome." Amity motioned for me to follow her. "Well, not the penicillin thing. That sort of sucks."

We stopped on the corner across the street. Amity raised her arms and slapped her sides in defeat. "Well… *shit*! Not even the takeout window is open." She turned, exaggeratedly puffing out her cheeks in a display of exasperation. "And I was all aboard the crêpe train today."

"If only we lived in a city where there was another

place to eat or drink a few doors down." I grinned, nudging her in the side. I felt a little kindle of electricity where our bodies met. "Let's call a rain check on the crêpes and find something else."

Amity leaned into me, just a bit, before pulling back, clearly weighing the options in her head. Her eyes shifted side-to-side, scanning the storefronts. "Fair point."

I pulled my phone from my pocket. "Do you want me to find another place for crêpes? I mean, if you had your heart set."

Amity shook her head. "I don't want to settle for second place crêpes now. Maybe a burger—something greasy. A real kind of 'fuck it' meal."

Damn, from crêpes to burgers. I was okay with that. Skipped lunch thanks to burying myself in more Jason work, so I could stand to overdo it for dinner. Problem was, I didn't really want a burger. "I got an idea. No burgers, but just as greasy. Is beer a part of that 'fuck it' equation? Because I could go for a few beers, too."

"Always beer."

And just like that, we were going to have ourselves a full-on meal. I didn't have much time for dating, but you couldn't tell me I wasn't smooth as shit. "You worried about highbrow? 'Cause this place is sub brow, but worth it."

"I'm usually chained to the highbrow, Poppy, but in this one instance, I'll deal with low."

I scratched the back of my head. "If you're willing to

take a trip, I know a place Uptown. I've been there with my boss a few times. It's pretty damn spectacular."

"The train?"

I'd had enough of the subway today. "You mind if we cab it? I'd like to see something more than a train tunnel after the day I've had."

Amity smiled. "I think I can live with that. I'd rather risk an Uber. Or whatever the kids are using these days."

"Really? Ride sharing? I'd have taken you for the type that prefers a yellow cab."

Amity eyed me and laughed. "That was totally disdain in your voice."

"No, no, no. Not like that." I held my hands up. "I figured with the cheesemaking you were the type to hold the old school stuff close to you. No judgments, though. I'm a fan of the future and the past both. Just depends on the product, you know?"

"You took me for a nostalgic."

"Absolutely. I mean, I've been in New York my whole life, and I miss the old skin. The projects, the old dive bars." I motioned to a yellow taxi as it drove by. "The yellow taxi cabs. At the same time, there's value in change, isn't there? I mean, look at your industry. I'm sure there are tools you use that weren't even invented a few decades ago, right?"

Amity laughed. "You have no idea what cheesemaking tools are, do you?"

I returned the smile and shook my head. "Not a fucking clue."

She kept the smile as she considered my question. "Mixing the new and old is what makes things fun. Hell, I'm mixing fruit into some of my cheeses. It works." Amity raised a hand and waved. Another yellow taxi drove on by. "Right now, that gig industry sounds awesome to me, though."

I held up my phone. "They'll be here in five minutes."

"Oh, look at you with the surreptitious rideshare order while we debated its merits." She gave my arm a gentle slap. "I dig the initiative."

I doffed my hat to her. "That's my style."

"Where are we going, Miss Leathers?" Amity smirked at me playfully.

I leaned towards her. "116th Street, the cuchifrito."

The driver snorted.

Amity blinked. "Harlem?"

"You're making a face like you've never been."

"Furthest uptown I've been is the 50s."

I stared at her, aghast. Shock and disgust mixing. "How long have you lived in New York?"

"Most of my life. I don't really do much traveling outside my circle. I have family in the Bronx, but last time I visited was before my grandma passed, so like... ten years? I guess that counts as going uptown, maybe?

I never actually went above ground from the subway, though, so I guess I've never been further uptown in Manhattan than the mid-50s."

"How does that work? We've got trains and buses. You mean to tell me you've locked yourself into the Coney area like that? Just living that carny life forever?"

Amity shrugged. "We've got everything available to us already. I mean, after Sandy, all the rebuilding going on? Shit, we've got fancy restaurants, old school grocery stores, plenty of places like mine that cater to the hipsters and the old ladies both." She smiled. "It's weird. I'm like a townie, I guess. I'm happy staying close to home." She turned to me. "You said you're local. Where are you originally from?"

Normally, I'd shut down a question like that. I didn't like talking parents. "I was a city kid. My parents did okay for themselves. We lived on Riverside Drive." All lies. I grew up with just my dad. Bowery. He worked three jobs and I was a latchkey kid. I didn't enjoy my childhood.

"Wow, Riverside Drive. That's unexpected. You don't strike me as a fancy city kid."

"Well, I mean, fancy or not, there's a level of independence you get out here that you wouldn't if you were from the suburbs. Rich city kids can hang; they're just assholes." I laughed. "Doesn't really matter, though. I left home early."

"What drove you out?"

"I just couldn't live in that place anymore. I felt like..."

I motioned with a hand, as if cueing her. "I don't have the right word. A prisoner, I guess? I don't know. I went through the whole rebellion thing. Smoking, drinking. Got knocked up. Gave it away." I blinked in surprise. How the hell did I let honesty slip into this?

Amity placed a hand on my shoulder. "I get it. I do."

I stiffened, embarrassed of the half-truth origin. "Yeah, TMI, though. Sorry."

Amity smacked my arm again. "Whatever. You need an ear; I'm a captive audience. There's no time for dancing around interaction, you know? Sometimes we need to talk to each other. Don't go getting uptight on me." She pointed a finger at me with a mock stern look on her face. "I demand the baggage, Poppy, demand it." She smiled easily. "Or not. Whatever works for you."

"Uptight isn't really my thing," I said. "Really, I'm a habitual line stepper. Truth is, I feel a little nervous around you."

"Oh, please. I'm the last person you should feel nervous around. I permanently smell like cheese, for fuck's sake."

We laughed again.

Amity watched the streets go by. We were making impressive time, already in Midtown. "I think we should all make it a practice to step over the lines people set for us. When we don't, we rot away, don't we?"

"I'd like to say that was overdramatic, but I feel the same way. You'd think it would be more obvious to people, right?"

"Nothing is obvious until it's out in the cold screaming for its life." Amity smiled to her reflection. "My grandfather always says that."

"Do you live with him?"

Amity shook her head quickly. "Oh, no. I think I mentioned that I inherited the shop from him." She turned back to me. "It's nice, but it's also a pain in the ass. I'm still sort of married to things he did. Taking care of his old regulars. And it shouldn't annoy me, but it really does. I hate feeling chained to this thing I didn't build for myself."

That was interesting. "I feel that," I said, cautiously. "Are the regulars assholes or something?"

"Not really? I set up bags for them, so the entire interaction lasts little to no time, but these women are fucking miserable, and I don't have time to try and build a rapport with them. I tried hard enough when I first opened the store and that was a disaster. Lots of cold stares and lengthy apologies on my part. Chalk it up to getting sick of hearing myself say sorry a million times every other Wednesday." Amity rolled her eyes. "They've been coming to the store since my grandfather ran things, and I don't have the heart to shut it down. Sort of his legacy, you know? Dependable income, too, so it lets me be a weirdo with the other cheeses."

"Like a real artist."

Amity grimaced. "I sometimes wonder if it's proximity more than loyalty. If there was a better deal available, they'd take it. I just happen to be downstairs for them."

"So why try? You've got a reputation now. Maybe you can go to another borough. Expansion north could be a really big deal for you, with all the thirty-something Brooklynites heading into Westchester to spawn like the saddest of salmon."

Amity laughed. "No way. Coney is where my family have their roots—whether I love it or not. I couldn't live knowing I separated that history from the store."

"No, that makes sense," I said. "Did grandpa teach you all his tricks?" Time to move the subject towards something that seemed happier for her. And maybe find out a little information in the meantime. I really didn't mean to work her on a date, but she'd gotten into good old grandpappy and his traditions...

"For the most part," Amity said. "My parents weren't thrilled about me getting into the old business. They both worked for Wells Fargo—still do. That life really didn't turn out to be what I wanted, even with a CPA. Cheese was my rebellion."

Interesting. Failure led her to the cheese shop. Failure led me to Jason. We really had so much in common, in the strangest ways. Nothing necessarily one-to-one, but hearing her speak just felt so fucking familiar.

"Well, the CPA has to be helpful for running a business," I said.

"Immensely." Amity shifted in her seat. A glimmer

of a frown flashed across her face. "I don't want to talk business, if you don't mind. What's your job like?"

"I've got two."

"Oh, wow, a workaholic. Then what are your *jobs* like?"

"Truthfully? Terrible. Life feels like it's in slow motion lately." I thought for a moment. "I'm finding myself feeling that rebellious streak again. But as an adult, I'm not sure how to tackle it. It's funny, but when I was younger, I thought I had no control. I realize now I had more control then than I have now."

"But how do you get that back when you have bills to pay?"

"Exactly!" I straightened up in my seat. "I've convinced myself I need to go out on my own. Be my own boss. But even that's so fucking hard. I have to consider so many things or else it all falls apart, and then it's my ass."

"I'm comfortable. I think that's all that matters to me." Amity leaned back. "I don't like the idea of having to throw my world into disarray because I need to live a certain way. I want to do what I enjoy and get paid for it. Simple as that. Though, my boss is me, so it's probably why I can say that."

"I used to feel the same way about my job."

"What do you do, exactly?"

"I manage the lives of two very different types of man babies."

"Ah, okay. I get it. I can see why that would have you

climbing the walls. You have to be responsible for yourself and then for others who take you for granted."

I looked out the window and saw we were nearing our destination. "And it's getting worse, that feeling."

"Then you do need the change. You need to cut them out of your life."

"I was always gung-ho about it. I figured my actions sort of balanced the world out a bit, you know? That there was almost an art to it—like, this was my craft. To make these people accomplish great things."

"What changed?"

I scratched the bridge of my nose. "These men are not the people I started working for anymore. I think I've begun to hate them. Like, really hate them." It felt good to finally say that. I'd let myself believe that my connection with these men who were my "betters" was on equal footing. I was lying to myself and they—whether they really knew it or not—took advantage of that. All that anger in me, all that black tar, was beginning to spill out of me, and I knew damn well where to direct it. The silver lining was that it made me feel better. It made me feel grounded and focused on attaining my goals.

Amity stewed on that. "Hate's a strong word, but if it's how you feel, then you need to make the break, Poppy. If only for your mental health. Before things get worse."

"Yeah," I repeated. "Before things get worse."

Amity chewed and rolled her eyes back like a stroke victim. “Jesus Christ, I would murder a family member to eat one of these every day.” She held up a half-eaten, deep-fried roll of yuca and pork. “What was this again?”

I wiped the corner of my mouth with a napkin after the cheese-splosion from the empanada I’d stupidly shoved into my gullet before allowing it time to cool. *“Alcapurria,”* I said slowly. “Yours is yuca. They make it with plantain sometimes. Legit, right?”

Amity took another bite. “How many years off my life is this thing with the unpronounceable name taking from me with each bite?”

I made a show of counting my fingers. “Math is fucked. You’re already dead.” Not the best joke, but it wasn’t like she knew about the hit out on her.

“And you grew up eating this stuff?”

“No, no, no. I had a shitty palate as a kid. Macaroni

with chopped up hot dogs was all I ever ate. I got introduced to this stuff through my boss, Atticus. He's always dragging me around to new places to eat. Took damn near a decade to enhance my boring sense of taste."

It took me a minute to realize why Amity had just pulled a face like the yuca was spoiled. Aw, shit. I said his name. I said his name like a supreme dumbass. That's what I got for feeling that comfortable with her.

I grabbed the Heineken near me and took a long sip. If I was lucky, the beer would drown me, and I wouldn't have to take part in the next segment of this conversation.

"Atticus... Garcia?"

"Uh, yeah," I said casually. "You know him?"

"He's your boss?" Amity leaned back let out a soft laugh. "Jesus, this is why we bumped into each other this morning. Did you know?" She put her hands over her face. "Please tell me you didn't know when you saw me."

I suddenly felt the weight of all that food in my stomach. "I did not know when I saw you."

"But you knew before we met up."

"I knew before we met up."

"Does that make this weird?"

I shrugged. "Not really. Oddly hot, maybe? Like I'm getting one over on him." Another lie. This time, so much more obvious. I went back to drinking my beer, but the bastard had the audacity to be empty. I motioned to our waiter for another one and was ignored. Awesome.

“I am so embarrassed.” Amity stared out the restaurant window. “Not like super messed up about it, but good lord, I thought I’d dodged a bullet when I bumped into you. No way she’d know I was on a walk of shame, I thought.”

“But I didn’t,” I said. “And, honestly, I don’t care either. You’re human. You did a human thing. Not like we’re married. Though, knowing Atticus, I do reserve the right to not only question your judgment but also do some soul searching if you’re attracted to both of us.”

Amity chuckled and shook her head. “Did your boss—uh, did Atticus—say anything, or did you figure it out?”

“A bit of column A and a bit of column B.”

“And he’s your boss?” Amity asked incredulously.

I laughed. Had to put together a story on the spot. “Well,” I said, “it probably had a lot to do with me raving about your cheese?”

Amity laughed out loud.

“You’re embarrassed and now I don’t know if I should feel bad or good about being the one who unknowingly made the hookup happen.”

“In your words: column A and column B.”

That was tempting bait, and it got me. “You saying it was a bad time?” Damn me and my desire to know if my employer sucked in bed.

Amity cringed. “Ah, no. No, it wasn’t like that. I just.” She sighed. “Look, this was the first person who showed any overt physical interest in me in, like, a year. I figured

I was owed a little fun. I don't know, I thought I was on a roll from earlier."

"A roll?"

"Well, you and I hit it off. And I'm not normally so social."

Wasn't in love with how casually this date became all about my boss, but fine, Amity, if you needed low-hanging fruit, Atticus was an inch off the ground. "You decided to take a little more initiative." I smiled. "I completely understand. I'm in the same place. I've been trying to grab at the opportunities put in front of me more often—stop being so scared of doing the things that will get me to what I want."

"Exactly," Amity said as she slapped the table. "I'm so fucking tired of being worried. Like, I take it back from before; I'm exhausted of being beholden to my grandfather's business. It's not disrespect, but how long do I have to toe the line before it's finally *my* turn?"

I nodded in agreement. "We should go for what we want. Whether it's business opportunities or more intimate ones," I said, knowing damn well I couldn't make my move. I didn't have many doubts that Amity still had interest in me, but this little love triangle didn't seem very appealing. Maybe things would change, but I got the impression that charging headfirst at that moment wasn't the best idea.

"So, yeah, I mean, Atticus. It isn't that serious. I'm not sure I'd want to hang out with him in a normal setting.

Fucking around is fine, but he seems a little…"

"Uptight."

"Yeah. And maybe in that whole midlife crisis thing, too. He kept going on about being bored, and I get the feeling he's trying to avoid some truths. I'm not about to sign up for that. Not my circus, not my monkey." She took a sip of soda. "What's his deal? He's totally not a local, right?"

I shook my head. "Broken family. Moved out here from Ohio. Real fucking weirdo sometimes, but he's an okay boss." I took a bite of another empanada. No more molten cheese. "Honestly? I'm not down to talk about him anymore. I spend way too much time with that man."

"I understand. I wouldn't want to spend an entire date talking about my boss either." Amity thought for a little while, eating and drinking in silence. "You ever wonder how we can take these risks we're talking about without hurting ourselves or others?"

That was a damn good question. And more on the nose than she knew. "I don't know. Part of me thinks you need to stop caring. Nobody who's successful—and I mean *successful*—gives a shit about anything but what they're trying to accomplish. You look at guys like Musk or Bezos, they only care about the mission. Everything else is tangential at best or solved when it needs to get solved." I took a sip of tap water, wishing I could Jesus it up into more alcohol. "I know this is probably a lot, and I'm not necessarily inspiring faith in me, but at this moment, it's how I'm feeling."

"I'm not bothered. We're all messes." Amity jabbed a thumb at her chest. "I don't think I blame you for feeling that way." She snickered. "Aren't I a great conversationalist? One-night stands and existential questions that only serve to make us sad."

"Well, I'm happy to be eating this delicious, greasy food and enjoying great company." That was the nicest thing I think I'd said to anyone in years. Literally years.

Amity covered her mouth with her hand mid-chew. "It is indeed greasy food," she said. "And don't think I didn't notice the compliment. I'm just trying to play it cool since I'm the idiot that probably made your working day awkward as hell."

"That's fine. Cool is fine. Awkward is fine, too. If anything, you gave me a kick out of watching that man squirm a little—and let me tell you, he rarely does."

"So, he won't be calling back."

We laughed. I did have a little doubt crawling around my skull, though. Amity wasn't outright stating she was more interested in me than Atticus. If anything, she wasn't really planting a flag at all. While that should have left me feeling a little confident, it still nagged at me and I was too worried to bring that up. That was a fourth or fifth date discussion.

My phone made a happy little noise. I checked it. Silo. All the info I requested and more. Six different "discreet" venues.

Then another message:

> Calling Atticus. Tlk w/ him tmrw. Change in cheese job.

"Oh, shit," I said.

Amity winced. "Is it Atticus? Please tell me it isn't him."

"Oh, man. Nah. Just a text I was waiting on. Friend of a friend with some information I needed to get the ball rolling on my other boss' nonsense." This was amazing. Maybe things would start coming up Poppy for a change.

"Man, you really do move heaven and earth for them, huh?" Amity asked.

I shrugged. "You'd think, but it's really standard shit. All things a normal adult should be able to handle on their own."

"You know what's good about that?"

"What?"

"You become indispensable to people like that and you'll always have the reins."

"I guess you're right," I said.

Amity was wrong about that. I never felt in control of a damn thing. I forgot to take care of my simple biological functions more often than I forgot about Atticus' dry cleaning or Jason's paint inventory. Indispensable was an illusion—a word these people made up to build my worth to them with the potential to uplift someone willing to live with the veil over their eyes. But I'd pulled that veil off, hadn't I?

We split a cab home. Amity kissed me on the cheek as I left—that was good, I guess. I watched the cab disappear down the street and kicked myself for not saying something—anything—to force a direct answer. Would she see Atticus again? That was going to drive me crazy and I simply didn't have the balls to find out.

Sleep wasn't on deck since I was for damn sure going to research the shit out of the information Silo sent me. Didn't matter if it took all night, I'd find a connection to the people I met all that time ago. I'd find a way to get Jason wrapped up with them. And then… well, I wasn't sure what I was going to do then, exactly. But I was going to do something. Something big.

I got it on the first hit. New Beginnings, Inc. Terrible name. Located in Secaucus, New Jersey of all places. The tell? Right on the front page of their website, all smiles—the lady with the Alabama honey accent. A little older, but still rocking the sharp suit and tie combo that left burn marks on my memory so long ago.

"Why was that so easy?" I asked myself.

I wondered if life was easy for the sharks—the people who grabbed every opportunity they could—because the opportunities were always there. Our apprehension made things difficult. The constant need for more rationale—to be able to say we were still the good guys in this story, that was what left people wallowing in their own spiritual sick. But then, look: I ask and receive. I watch, and the people I need to fuck up simply fuck up.

I had a weird epiphany. Something obvious. *This* is what they meant by capitalism?

CHAPTER Eighteen

"I still can't believe you fucked her. Like, I've discussed it with you, and then I discussed it with *her*, and then I slept on it, and then I woke up still acknowledging it, but I am *still* in complete goddamn disbelief, man." I was making a grilled cheese on Atticus' stovetop, sourced from three Sweet Baby Cheesus bags on the counter, because fuck it: I didn't want to spend thirty bucks on lunch or let all this product go to waste. Full hour on the toilet for me. Plenty of time to be fucking stymied by my idiot boss's sex life. Scratch that. I think I was jealous. *Think*. Bullshit. I was seething. What made it worse was that I didn't want to treat Amity like a prize. I didn't want to believe my jealousy was rooted in the idea that Atticus got her first. It was driving me nuts.

Atticus stopped rowing on his Concept II. "Be a little tasteful." He wiped the sweat from his eyes. "I haven't even confirmed anything."

I rolled my eyes. "Well, she did." I groaned. "Atticus, you're slowly becoming as boring as a food stylist. Like, you visiting her was a surprise. But then *hooking up*?"

Atticus narrowed his eyes "My moment with Amity was fleeting and carnal. You said you went on a date with her. By your logic, aren't we both delving into places we shouldn't?"

"I'm still working towards the fucking dossier, man. And I'm not the one who's being paid to fucking kill her." I eyed my sandwich and frowned. "You know, since I'm not a fan of Silo Jotter being mad at me."

"I'm talking with Silo today. He texted me last night about an update to this job. Maybe it'll be good news. Or at the very least, it will stop your needless concern about all of this."

I scoffed. "I am at the edge of every seat waiting to hear how one of the most successful crime bosses in Brooklyn is going to change his mind and no longer want to kill a person he was very adamant we murder just a few days ago."

"Snarky."

"Sorry. I'm getting antsy. Sure. Maybe after you talk with Silo things will be better. But until then, your dick is public enemy number one."

Atticus grunted. "Crude."

I shredded aged parmesan over my sandwich and slipped it from the pan to a paper plate. I stood back a second, eyed it like it was threatening me, picked that sloppy motherfucker up, and took a huge bite. I chewed for a while and finally drank a sip of red wine. That was really fucking delicious. "Sorry... wait..." I chewed some more and swallowed; felt my eyes drift a moment. Were those my arteries clogging in real time or were my guts already seizing? So be it, I figured, the tongue loves what the stomach fears.

I stopped eating so I could breathe like a normal person. "What would you have done if she didn't come home with you?"

"I have no idea. I guess I would have done the job if the opportunity presented itself."

I didn't like that "I guess" nonsense. That was the entire fucking problem. Amity wasn't an aberration for him the way she was for me. The problem with Atticus was, well, Atticus. He'd lost his edge, and that he couldn't admit to not doing the job because he found Amity attractive or worth his mercy for other reasons was the tell. Also: sort of gross that of all the times he decided to spare someone, it had to align with sex. But that was maybe a me thing.

No. Fuck that. It *was* gross.

"I don't know, man," I said. "Even if Silo pulls some never-before-seen forgiveness card—how does that not completely shatter your reputation? You still didn't do the job." I asked myself why I was pressing this. I didn't want Amity dead, and I didn't need Atticus to agree with me. I think I only wanted to fuck with him. To press him in ways I'd never pressed him before.

"What is wrong with you lately?" he spat.

Shit, he called my bluff. "Wrong with me? What do you mean?"

Atticus stood and toweled his forehead off. "Your attitude lately, Pop. You're meaner. Acting off-kilter—more than usual. The whole Silo aside? That never would have happened years—if not months—ago. Suddenly, you seem to be holding—I don't know—is this resentment? Are you angry with me? Why are you being this way?"

I shook my head. Play it off, Poppy. "I'm acting this way because I'm fucking insane and intensely power-hungry, Atticus. I don't see how I'm being anything but on-brand." I drank a little more wine.

"You say that, but we both know you're not as troubled as you say out loud. A funny person, sure. A diversion at times. But you're not in need of actual medical help." Atticus pointed at me. "If you're feeling like you're stuck, you can talk to me. I could find something for you with Silo or at another business he's running."

This motherfucker, offering me a booby prize. Atticus the savior, uplifting poor Poppy Leathers because she's in a rut. Fuck him even harder than I wanted him fucked before.

"You're being ridiculous. And as for my mental state, Atticus, Christ. Look at me." I stepped out from behind the counter. I was dressed in what would best be described as an outfit that belonged on a Barbie from the 1980s, but with more neon than should ever be consumed by human eyes. My shoulder pads were also obscenely large because the '80s taught me that shoulder pads were a sign of my complete and utter dominance. "Would a crazy person wear this?"

Atticus rolled his eyes. "Clothes aren't the best means of telling a person's mental state."

"I'd argue the opposite. A guy ain't walking around with a loaded diaper unless there's a screw loose—physically or mental."

"Fine. You know I can get you some medication—even some help."

"I look like I don't have access to mind-altering medication?"

"Helpful medication."

"Either or, man." I tossed the rest of that sandwich away because I wasn't gambling with my stomach any more than I needed to. I still had Jason errands to run, and it was feeling like I needed to get away from Atticus as soon as possible. He was making me itchy. "You need me to do anything before the Silo meeting? Get your clothes out? Powder your ass or something?"

"No," Atticus said, "I'm fine. I'm going to make a smoothie."

"Fun times." I collected my things.

"I'm thinking of calling her again," Atticus said.

That was a barely veiled attempt to get under my skin and I was not here to play that game, so I waved him off and started to leave. “My dude, you do whatever it is you feel like you need to. You always have.”

"What did I say?" I handed Jason my phone with the New Beginnings page open on the browser. "Don't ask how, who, or why. Just call and you'll get what you've been asking for." I couldn't look him in the eye. The money was all that kept me chained to this shit, but damn did abject poverty feel appealing these days.

"How did you even hear about this?" Jason asked as he scrolled through the page. "Is this like, illegal?"

I sighed, pinching the bridge of my nose like a first-year drama student. The drama is what got Jason's attention, more often than not. "What did I literally just say about asking questions, Jason? You know how networking events go. You always end up talking shit with people in business you have zero interest in and they're always the ones who give you way too much information about what they do and where they work. I can't necessarily vouch for it, but I do think it's worth a shot." I shrugged. “But think on this: when was the last time a hunch of mine ever led us astray?”

Jason leaped out of his seat and hugged me hard enough to make it uncomfortable—a rare feat. “You think you could make the call? In case it’s, um, you know—”

I sighed. Fine. No use. “I’ll keep that pointy nose clean, man. Even if you don’t deserve it.” I tried to lace a little joviality into that last bit. Not sure if it landed, but Jason was an idiot, so it probably flew over his head.

“Pay raise?” Jason asked.

“Massive pay raise.”

I didn’t hesitate to call the service later that day. A man picked up and remained monosyllabic throughout the phone call, avoiding all questions that required explanation in his strong New Jersey accent. He provided me with another number to call for further details, and the assurance that Jason’s information was logged and would be vetted in case they had reasons to completely sever any future communications—guess even when you’re operating illegally you need to be picky about the clientele. There were veiled threats behind every other word, and my eyes strained from all the rolling. I wanted to tell the guy I was hip to all the murky bullshit, but the last thing they needed was to know I was on their level. Nope, simply a sweet assistant calling for her rich and stupid art boss.

After that was sorted, I gave Jason a call. "Looks like we are officially in the pseudo-illegal baby adoption game," I said. "Excited?"

"Crazy excited," Jason said. "It all feels so cloak-and-dagger, you know?"

"Oh, yeah. James Bond-level shit." I made a jerk off motion.

"You know, this is something any young Brooklynite would adore. Whisper phone calls with suspicious dudes? Theoretical physical harm? This would kill as a performance piece thing." He went silent the way he always did when he was making notes.

I groaned—internally—at what I'd have to set up next.

"If this all pans out, we should see if we can do a LARP group with people out here. It's fucking invigorating," Jason said. "We can set up a spy story, hire some people to play it all out. I can see it taking off as a bit of tourist-trap performance art. How much do you think I'd have to offer someone to let me stab them as part of the tension building?"

"A stabbing? Speaking for myself, I wouldn't let a stranger hug me for less than a grand, so work from there."

Jason cackled. "Hey, by the way, Sara had a few questions." Of course, Sara the smart one had questions. "She's a little worried that this isn't a shell game. Thinks we should try a few more offices—legit ones—before we go all-in."

"And what, wait months for the glimmer of a chance? If—and I qualify that 'if' with authority, Jason—you're lucky?" I snorted. "Look, this gets you to a place where you're helping people in real need out there. Think about it: you'll be saving these children from hell. Christ, remember that documentary you and Sara told me about Sri Lanka? You'd be doing a public service." I walked to my fridge and fetched a beer. Bought some on a whim. Strong shit. Something new for the new Poppy. "Besides, no red tape. You scoop these kids up no problem and you're on your way to becoming the multi-ethnic, modern, city-living family you always wanted."

"That's a strong argument. Last item. What's up with that check we're waiting on? From the Mockingbird dude?"

"Atticus Garcia? That should come through soon." I'd completely blanked on writing a check in Atticus' name earlier in the day. I needed to remedy that. I wasn't keeping notes the same way anymore. And *that* reminder reminded me to check and see if the art even arrived at Atticus'. He hadn't mentioned it, but his whole erotic travail with Amity was distracting him either way.

This was why I needed to make the three jobs I had—working for Atticus, working for Jason, working for me—into a single job. After all, by my last check, my favorite boss was me. And I didn't think that would change any time soon.

It took seven more phone conversations that day, but I finally secured Jason a meet-and-greet with a man who was supposed to be the financial liaison of the organization promising to secure them a baby and/or babies. The group didn't share a name, and while I pressed that issue, I also really didn't give a shit, since this was on the boss and out of my hands. What mattered is we had to do the meet on the same day. No delays. No second chances. This was our only shot.

Obviously, Jason begged me to join him. There was no other choice.

Jason was to meet the man on the Upper West Side, in a small park frequented by older women and a few junkies. He sat on a bench, arriving an hour early for fear he'd be late and ruin the entire deal. Over the course of the hour, Jason had to switch his seat four times whenever someone sat next to him who clearly intended to use the bench as a bed.

I watched him from the window of a coffee shop with a perfect view of his idiot ass fidgeting and wandering around like a lost old man.

"For fuck's sake," I said as I sipped my coffee. "Grow some balls. This isn't even that illegal."

Fifteen minutes later than the agreed upon time, a skittish man sat next to Jason. He wiped his nose and cracked his neck. The man was dressed well—a sharp blue suit, rings, a gaudy watch on his right wrist. He spoke staring straight ahead.

Jason fetched an envelope from his jacket pocket.

The man said something that made Jason stop.

Jason nodded and slipped the envelope between them.

The man scratched at his neck and began talking again. Jason nodded like an idiot and said some words that seemed to annoy the other man.

Wonderful, I thought, he'll blow this and we'll have to start over again. I should have made the drop myself. Hell, even posed as Jason's wife. Hindsight and all that bullshit. It was too late to call for a do-over, so I had to depend on one of the world's greatest idiots to help me get a little further toward my own goals. Wonderful.

The man stood up and subtly took the envelope with him. I felt a tinge of annoyance I even had to take the time out of my day to address any of this. I kept myself busy running a few email and text errands that had piled up. Shot Amity a message to see what she was doing tonight or tomorrow. If there was anything that could bring me a little happiness, it was seeing her. Especially before things got any more serious with Atticus. I had a feeling if that did blossom, I wasn't going to enjoy being exposed to that nonsense—and certainly wasn't ready to be around for any potential fallout.

Anyway, back to Jason.

I watched him look around awkwardly. He lifted his

hands and gently slapped his thighs. Looked directly towards me and waved with a huge smile on his face.

I waved back with a tight smile. "Yeah, keep smiling, asshole. This is how we get arrested."

My phone chirped. A text.

Whoa, Atticus. Hadn't received a text from him in a long ass time. He normally liked to call.

Cheese job off. Silo OK.

Wait, what?

I wrote back.

He cool w u seeing her????

No. Will talk later.

Fine. Fuck it. Don't offer me an explanation. What mattered was, the job was off. That was good, I guess? I wasn't sure how I felt about that. It was sudden and it was easy and it was convenient because I did not want Amity to die. But was it what I really needed to happen?

Jason walked into the coffee shop and sat in front of me. "Holy shit." He held a hand to his chest. "That was so insane. I'm all amped up." He smiled wide. "I'd do that every fucking day for that high."

"Like jumping off a plane?" I asked.

Jason blinked. "I don't know," he said breathlessly. "Maybe I should do that next."

Fuck me. Nothing was ever fun if there wasn't a chance what you were doing was wrong. Silo killing the job? That opened the door for a lot of potential obstacles—most of them stupendously boring.

No. I wasn't going to have that.

"I need to run," I said, standing and rushing out the door.

I had a bad idea.

CHAPTER Twenty

I watched as Silo grabbed a chicken to break its neck—efficiently, with the flick of his wrist. The bird went limp, and Silo passed it over to a woman who quickly cut off the head, dunked the bird in scalding hot water, plucked its feathers, and gutted the animal. Her hands were fast, and the process was hypnotizing. She was like a machine. I envied that—the skill level of brutality that was probably banality to her. I wished I could find my Zen that way.

Silo being an unnecessary actor in the assembly line was the unsettling bit. This woman could clearly snap the necks with ease, but Silo was intent to be a part of the show. It was a show of power. His way of letting anyone seeking audience know that he wasn't afraid to get his hands dirty. Which was interesting, though. I couldn't remember hearing about Silo actually laying hands on anyone since he'd installed himself as the artisan kingpin of Brooklyn crime. I wondered if that was by design.

I mean, he worked his way up, right? Couldn't keep doing the same stuff that got him to the top, but he couldn't let people know he wasn't willing to. Seemed like a tricky balance.

I walked on into what was effectively a gussied-up slaughterhouse; Silo's restaurant, ¡Viva La Viveria!, was licensed to bring in live animals and prepare them in-house thanks to standard and imaginative political and industry maneuvering. The only caveat: the killing floor couldn't be within 100 feet of the dining area, and nothing larger than a goat could be slaughtered. That kept things somewhat clean, but Silo was a cunning man. He quickly worked out that calves were within their size limits and exploited that fact to serve up some of the most expensive veal in all of Brooklyn.

I wasn't big into veal, but how the fuck could I not respect that level of swagger? The ability to take what he wanted, find the backdoors and hoops that needed jumping through, and execute to success. It was invigorating to stand there. Even more so than walking in completely uninvited.

Of course, the veal meant there was an almost ever-present protest occurring outside, but it only served to make the location even more of a hot spot for the glitterati—whether they were protesting along with the vegans or overpaying to eat a meal they could get for pennies in a similar location. To Brooklynites, it wasn't always about the quality as it was the ability to brag about eating or protesting at such a famed hotspot.

Genius level branding.

It wasn't until I was further into the space that I noticed a young man to my right struggling to do push-ups. Silo craned his head from his chicken killing position, his brows arching. "What number we up to, Bobby?"

Bobby—kid couldn't be older than 22 or 23—found the strength to complete another rep and let out a curt, "One hundred thirteen."

Silo smirked. "Well, shit, just three hundred and eighty-seven left, big shot. Keep going." He then turned his attention to me. "I'm never unhappy to see you, Poppy, but I will say this is a little off protocol." Silo snapped another bird's neck. He maintained eye contact with me the entire time. "Is this an emergency?"

I kept my distance. "I wouldn't classify it as an emergency, but there is a high level of concern."

"The cheese job?"

"The cheese job."

"I spoke with Atticus today. We're cooling it off for the time being, thanks to your information. I don't exactly have confirmation of her connections, but some chatter from that area clued me in to some old school presence. I want to assess before we do anything, but I have a feeling it shouldn't be too much trouble." He snapped another chicken's neck and smiled at me. "Though, this feels like something more than the cheese job or your adoption woes."

There was no chance Silo was ignorant to what was going on. He knew I was up to something, and he knew damn well that Atticus and I had become personal with the target in our own ways. He had eyes all over. It was obvious. The chicken killing, the line of questioning—Silo knew, and he wanted me to know.

"You're right," I said.

"So, what is it?" Silo continued snapping but maintained eye contact with me. It felt silly and terrifying at the same time. I fought the urge to laugh.

I gave thought before speaking. "I think Atticus doesn't want to do this anymore." It was truth, at least to me.

"And?"

This was a fucking razor's edge. No choice but to keep moving forward, though. The trip back wasn't possible. "And I think it's placing him, me, and you in a bad position. I told you about the skillet."

Silo chuckled. "You sure did."

"And now the cheese job. He didn't listen to me when I mentioned the cocaine thing."

Silo nodded. "Obviously, he was too busy wooing her."

"I don't think he's looking for anything serious, though."

Silo shook his head. "Atticus will do whatever he wants as it strikes his fancy. With the job held off, he will absolutely continue his pursuit. There will be a glimmer of hope I might go back on the decision. And then he will be tested."

"Not a healthy way to live."

"None of this is a healthy way to live." Silo sighed. "You understand that. You went off gallivanting with the cheesemonger as well." It wasn't a question. "And now you're trying to work out exactly how far this conversation should go. You're trying to figure out if you've gone too far since Atticus and I have history." He held the most recently perished chicken up and stared at it lovingly before placing it aside. "What's our count Bobby? I feel like I don't hear the heavy breathing I should expect at this point."

"One thirty-five, boss."

"Pick up the pace there, boy. Thought you was a Navy Seal."

I looked back over at Bobby. That kid was absolutely not built like a Navy Seal. Focus, Poppy. Back to the conversation. "Silo, it isn't like—"

"I'm not entirely concerned about what *you* think it's like, Poppy." Silo finally stopped killing chickens. He cleaned his hands off with a towel and motioned to me. "Walk with me."

I followed. "I'm not trying to cause trouble."

Silo laughed. Humorless. Dry. As if sand would pour from his mouth. "Poppy, let me explain something to you." He led me to a back office as large as my apartment. Inside was an oak desk and multiple matching chairs. There was a wall of TV monitors behind Silo's chair. Some of the screens showed the restaurant, but others showed Silo's businesses from all over. Poor Bobby was in the lower left-hand corner. His trembling visible on the 13-inch screen. There was even a feed showing the two tables at LLL. "Have a seat. You like bourbon?"

"I like whatever I'm offered. My father taught me to accept hospitality."

"You had a smart daddy." Silo poured us each three fingers of bourbon from a crystal bottle and slid the filled rocks glass over to me before sitting. He nodded at the chair across from him. "I've known a dozen versions of you, you know."

I sat and took the glass. Didn't drink. Not until he did. There was a knot in my stomach the size of my head either way. I worried I'd vomit right there if anything touched my throat. "What do you mean?"

"What we talked about before: a person with aspirations."

"You said that was important."

"And I believe that. But aspiration, deception, and manipulation?" Silo clicked his teeth. "Bad recipe, Poppy, bad recipe. Take the skillet thing."

"Which was a sign of sloppy work," I blurted out. I immediately took that feared sip just to shut up. It burned its way down and I fought not to cough.

"It is," Silo agreed. "And frankly, I'm thankful you pointed it out. If you hadn't, I wouldn't have made it a priority to keep an eye on things." He took a sip of bourbon, as well. "Imagine my shock seeing Atticus fraternizing with a target. All while his assistant is trying to make a power play off his fuck-up." He held his hand up as I tried to sputter something out. "Granted, I understand taking free opportunities. Atticus is literally setting these things up for you, and you're smart to capitalize on them.

"My concern, Poppy, is how this all falls down on me and my business. I respect hustle, and I respect people who go after what they want. But you must understand that, as a person who is also aspirational, I'm going to pay great attention to those around me when they start getting a little too close to my lane." Silo eyed his screens. "Did I tell you it was time to take a fucking rest period, Bobby?" His voice boomed.

Bobby continued to do his push-ups.

I looked down at my glass. "I'd never try to screw you over, Silo."

"Feelings change, Poppy. You see yourself outgrowing Atticus now. How long until you're ready to outgrow me? Five years? Ten?" He stared at me, or more like into me. "My question to you then: what is it that you want? Lay it out. Let me understand what I'm dealing with before we have to find out the ugly way."

We stared at each other for what felt like minutes. I took a deep sip of that liquid fire and swallowed hard. I couldn't tell if he was playing me. Trying to get me to let my guard down to trap me somehow. This man had history with my employer and here I was, an unproven greenhorn who was stirring shit up. For all I knew, he was setting me up for a fall, amusing himself with my naivete.

But success came with taking the jump, didn't it?

"I want power," I said. Another liberating moment. The honesty felt like it shouldn't work with a life of crime, but it was necessary. I had to bare my soul to myself if I was going to accomplish my goals.

"My power?"

"No. I want *my* power. I want to build something on my own without having to hijack someone like you. I see benefit in existing in parallel with people like Silo Jotter. I see that to maintain my honesty and keep my ass in line, I need to work with people who know what they're doing." I leaned forward. "What I want is a seat at the table. Not yours and not anyone else's. I just want my own damn seat. Honestly, Atticus doesn't even have to move out of my way. I already passed his ass years ago. I'm only just realizing that now."

Silo smiled softly. "Is it that you want to hit? Manage a business?"

"Whatever gets me at the table," I answered.

Silo grinned. "That's big talk. You ever actually hurt a person?"

"I've fought. Never did what Atticus did, but I'm an accessory a few dozen times over, so it isn't like I'm unfamiliar."

"I'd say it's very different to do the act than help, but

that's up to debate." Silo put his drink down and folded his hands on the desktop. "So, I got the what. I need the *why*."

I scrunched up my face. "Come on, man. I want to be my own boss. I wanna run shit."

"Bullshit. Those are perks." Silo pointed to himself. "My pops used to sell weed. He spent most of his life a low rank, do-nothing asshole. Died in prison because he rolled on a supplier. I saw that shit and told myself no way was I going that route. I saw the potential in those businesses. By the time I was out of college, I was supplying 95% of the weed going from New York City into Westchester. Made my money off all those white boys who couldn't tell the difference between skunk and oregano. I was the motherfucker people thought twice to roll on.

"Then I moved up. Started growing. Got interested in the finer aspects. And here we are now. I became the kind of man that had a Midas touch. If I wanted to make a new success, I could." He pointed at me. "Now you."

I drank the rest of my bourbon. Stared at the floor. Rode a wave of anger that threatened this delicate peace we had going here. I knew damn well if I overstepped, it was going to be right into the path of a bullet, but fuck me if I didn't want to smack the fucking taste out of his mouth for putting me in this position.

So, I found a better way to frame it. "This. This is why."

He sat back in his chair, eyebrows raised. "I'm confused."

"My entire life, I've been placed into certain positions because of what I needed. I needed money, so I sold off the only kid I'd ever have. I met Atticus, and I sacrificed everything to take one step forward and two back. I come to you to move ahead, and now I need to say these things." I breathed deep. "I'm tired of having to explain and rationalize what I do and what I want. I want to be in a position where I open my mouth and nobody asks me why. They only ask me what and how."

"You're pissed off."

"Always."

"You think that wouldn't be a hindrance?"

"Every damn thing I've done for myself that's paid off has been done with anger, Silo. Not a damn moment where I cater to myself isn't clouded with fury. Whether that's healthy is an opinion I'm not interested in hearing right now. I just want my seat at the table, and I'm sitting here asking for it because you're right, politicking my way there isn't the best way to respect you. And while I might be an angry person, I can be rational, too."

Silo nodded slowly. "The adoption business. Is the story about your other boss true?"

"It is."

"Huh. Hell of an opportunity for you to track down that baby, isn't it?"

More soul baring. Silo was giving me the opportunities nobody had ever given me before, but I knew it wasn't for my benefit. He was playing the game as much as I was.

This was his means of compiling a little mental folder on me. Digging in and figuring out what made me tick. Somewhere in this conversation, I was either leaving him at ease or raising a dozen alarms in his head that ended in bloody tragedy for me.

I was in too deep, though. I couldn't tell him to go fuck himself and walk out of there. Nope. Had to keep chugging along and let this man watch me tear away at the skin until he was satisfied.

He wanted the truth, and I decided to let him have it all. "That baby is living its best life and I give no shits about finding out what happened to it. I never wanted it, and I'm content not knowing a damn thing about its life. I wish nothing but good things for them, and I'm thankful they helped me finish grad school." I raised a hand slowly. "And before you tell me that's cold-blooded, it isn't. It's just truth."

"Okay. Fair enough." Silo spun in his chair and opened a drawer behind him. He turned back around and tossed my manila envelope in front of me. "Your research was helpful. While this is entirely new waters for a man like me, I can't help but admit I am enticed by the potential here."

I straightened up. Go time. "I am hoping that with your help, Silo, I can start this from the ground up. Or we can go after this company I'm working with for Tasker. Doesn't matter to me. What matters is where it goes and how it grows."

"Entrepreneurship." Silo bit his lip and began to laugh. "Poppy fucking Leathers. You have issues, girl. And, despite your promises, I do think you're dangerous. But despite myself, I think your ideas could be profitable."

"So work with me, Silo. Give me a chance on my own and I can show you exactly what I can do." There was my moment. Now he had the decision to make. Give me a chance or reach into a drawer and end this entire conversation with the ultimate punctuation mark. The fear didn't matter anymore. What was the point?

Silo sat back and thought. He placed his drink down and ran his fingers along the top of his desk. "This kind of shit is tricky. Requires guarantees and some sweat equity. That said, I have an idea." He stood up. "Let's have some more bourbon. This is going to be a long talk. But first..." Silo opened a desk drawer and pulled out a shiny revolver. "That kid doing the push-ups in there?"

"Bobby?" I looked at the screen. Poor Bobby was washed. He lay on his back breathing hard and sweating all over Silo's nice throw rug.

"Yeah, Bobby was light on this week's earnings. I had a feeling, but a few fellas confirmed he was skimming. Not a crazy amount, but enough for me to know if I let it keep going, he's only going to get bolder, you know?"

I nodded.

"I was going to embarrass him with these push-ups since he talked shit with friends about his military service, but looking at him now..." Silo sighed and pointed at the screen with his gun. "Poppy, what I'm hoping is for you *not* to be a Bobby. Do you think I can trust that to be the case?"

"I've only ever been Poppy." I eyed that gun long and hard. Its threat lingered like a fart in a small elevator.

Silo nodded. "Good... good." He walked out of the office, leaving me to watch the screens. He appeared in the lower-left hand screen in seconds, gun held out. Bobby scrambled backwards, his face contorting as he opened his mouth. Silo didn't hesitate, though. Two pops. We'd never know if Bobby was going to beg or argue, but that throw rug was more than ruined then.

Poor Bobby was a sacrifice. A messenger. I understood exactly what Silo was telling me, loud and clear.

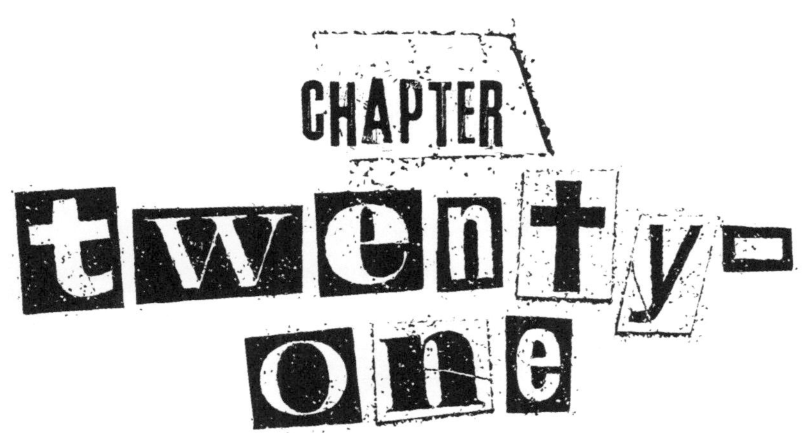

In the two hours that I tailed him, I learned that Gregory Chen was a skittish, phony, psychotic weakling of a man. He didn't stop moving, and when he wasn't moving, he was in a men's room refueling—so to speak. He had the gait of a man gripped with fear or anger, the kind of walk you saw when someone mustered the nut to face off against a rival as if they'd had enough of someone's crap. In Greg's case, whoever it was he finally decided to no longer tolerate didn't exist. It was if he was geared up to fight a ghost.

My new friend Greg was the one who'd met with Jason and took that down payment on the adoption. My new friend Greg had a massive cocaine habit and had all the livelong day to wander around the West Village, sniffing and stepping.

I did not like Greg.

“The man you saw with Jason. He’s the key,” Silo said. “The first person you meet is the lowest on the totem pole and usually the most likely to talk.” He pointed to me. “So, what you need to do is find him, corner him, and exploit whatever weaknesses he may have.”

“Doesn’t that expose me?” I asked.

“Maybe. Maybe not. Either way, the higher-ups are going to have a choice. Either they panic and make stupid moves, or they batten down the hatches. Either way, you weaken them. What you’re hoping for is a little bit of both. Ideally, your move makes them prepare to go underground for a while, but also forces them to rush any current business. Which means you continue to travel down the path with Jason.”

“I feel like I should be taking notes.”

Silo smirked. “You ever watch *The Wire*?”

“No.”

“Then take *that* note: watch *The Wire*. Everything else? Plant that shit in your head.”

Greg’s overall sense of style opposed his thuggish nature: he cleaned up nice, as some would say. Sharp suit, nice shoes, some scattered but tasteful jewelry. I noticed there was even a little jewelry on his lapel. That uniform gave Greg the look of a man with business to attend to, a far cry from the belligerent loiterer vibe he projected in spades otherwise. Shit, even with the suit, Greg looked like he smelled like pee.

My man's propensity for being outside at all hours holding court at random West Village pseudo-institutions was concerning. Visiting the odd bartender or store owner, talking about football, then disappearing into the back room made me think Greg was doing a little more than taking the drugs. He was, all signs indicated, potentially selling said cocaine. Not sure how I was going to corner and scare a power walking cokehead, but we'd cross that bridge when we got to it. The other issue: it was broad daylight. Gregory went home at night—which was, honestly, impressive for a guy like him—so whatever I came up with had to happen either in the open or at one of these bars during off peak hours. Which meant I was going to be noticed.

"I'm complicating my life," I muttered as I walked across the street from Greg, maintaining multiple car lengths between us to avoid detection. It was easy tailing on foot, and I was glad that cars or mass transit weren't involved. That would have been a supreme pain in the ass. Greg was also not an observant man. He had a habit of drifting off, almost losing his own trail as his legs carried him towards a subconscious goal. There were a handful of times I had to stop and wait a few minutes when Greg would make it look like he'd turn left but suddenly stopped, faltered, and turned right.

Gregory's next stop was on Sullivan Street, a small

wine bar called Shade. They advertised crêpes to go via a side window. I remembered this place from before: it was the spot Amity loved, and it gave me a little thought rabbit.

I rushed past the bar to order something savory and complicated to keep the kitchen staff busy—two goat cheese, smoked salmon, and veggie buckwheat crêpes, left in a refrigerator for exactly three minutes after preparation—and walked back around to the bar entrance. After this was all done, I figured I could shoot over to Amity's with a nice surprise. Look at me mixing business and pleasure.

The place was empty except the bartender, a young woman covered in tattoos, wearing a T-shirt displaying a giant kitten's head exploding Tokyo with eye lasers. I loved her the moment I saw her and felt sad I wouldn't be able to make a new friend today.

"Hi. There a bathroom I can use?" I asked.

"Only for customers," she said.

I pointed to the kitchen. "Put in an order and nature called." I pulled twenty bucks from my pocket. "I'm happy to pay now."

"Go ahead." She walked out from behind the bar. "Behind the curtain. There are two doors. One's occupied." And off for a cigarette she went.

"Much obliged." I walked towards the curtains and pushed them aside. There were two doors facing each other, both closed and only one bleeding light around its edges. There was the sound of water running and someone sniffing. I stopped before opening the door where my good friend Greg was busy shredding his nostrils.

No. I wasn't prepared to do this bare handed—and, frankly, that would be insane. I turned and went back to the bar. Grabbed the biggest bottle I could find—champagne, fancy—and took a moment to get familiar with its weight.

"I beat him up?" I asked skeptically. "Little old me?"

"Bring a weapon. Something with heft. You corner a person and aim for the head? Nine times out ten, they ain't fighting back as much as they're scratching at air. Never underestimate panic, Poppy. That's your real weapon."

"What's even the point of that?"

"Oh, please. You know exactly where we're going with this."

What was it Atticus taught me? Kick where the lock was. Never use my shoulders because that was a quick path to an injury.

I leaned back, picked my right leg up—thank the lord above I was wearing flats today—and put some of that high school Tae Bo obsession to good work. The door swung open with ease.

The bathroom was small, and the door swung hard enough to shove Gregory against the sink. He screamed, and a small vial fell from his hands. I ducked to build a little momentum and swung the bottle bottom side up, exploding out of my squat with as much force possible. The blow connected with Gregory's gut hard enough to take all the wind—and, thank God, noise—from him. I shoved Gregory into a seated position on the toilet. Took the bottle in both hands and let his face become acquainted with that thick glass bottom two times. Once for the shock and twice to put a period on the end of that sentence. I donkey-kicked the door shut to give us a little more privacy.

"Stay the fuck down," I said. My voice felt different.

It felt strong.

With my victim stunned and suffering from the world's worst case of the sniffles, I straddled him and held the bottle to his temple. Those butterflies I felt when I met Amity were in overdrive. Maybe this was love. Maybe it was a sudden rush of chemicals bathing my insides with pure bliss. What I knew for sure: I didn't want this to end.

"You Greg Chen?" I asked and pressed the bottle against his head as hard as I could.

"Ye... yes," Greg stammered. He snorted and leaned his head back. "What the fuck is this?"

"Fan-fucking-tastic, Greg. You think you got a clue or two about why we are sitting here in this very strange and precarious position? Or do you need an explanation?"

Greg sniffed again. He blinked, his eyes darting back and forth.

"This ain't a timed question, Greg. You have an answer or not?"

"I… I don't know." He licked his lips. "I do a lot of things for a lot of people."

Interesting. "Well, fine. I get it. You stick your dick in enough hornets' nests and it gets hard to figure out where the first boil is. I'll narrow it down for you: babies."

Greg rolled his eyes and smiled tightly. Had a look on his face that felt dismissive. Like, this was it? "Come on. I wasn't even skimming much. Tell Frankie I'll have her money by the end of the week."

Frankie. I tossed that into the vault. "Nah, I'm an outside party. But if you got a line on this Frankie, maybe you could do me a favor."

"I fuck him up. I send a message." I sipped my drink. The bourbon was starting to set in. "I got nothing, though. No real info that I can hang over them."

"Lie your ass off. I know you know how to do that," Silo said.

"And what if he can fight? What if he calls my bluff? I've picked shit up from Atticus, but I ain't a one-woman army."

Silo smiled. "I got you covered there."

"You tell Frankie we know and that we're coming. That's what you tell her." I pulled the bottle back and hopped back onto my feet. "Come here."

I pulled Greg by his collar and onto his feet, backed us up just past the bathroom threshold, and pulled back the curtain separating the little alcove from the bar. The waitress was still outside talking to two large friends of mine: the backup.

"See those two moose-sized motherfuckers in the sharp blue suits?"

Greg nodded slowly.

"I'm the nice one. You don't get that message out? You fuck up again and you're getting double teamed in a much more uncomfortable place next time. You feel me?"

Greg raised his hands up and gave me a wide smile. He licked the blood off his lips. "Look, I get you, but I think you got the wrong guy here. I'm a nobody, you know? Plenty of other guys in the city that mean more than me."

I pushed Greg away and he almost fell over, catching himself against the bathroom sink. I spotted his coke vial and crouched down to pick it up. The vial had a sticker of a cartoon cheese wheel on it. Awfully familiar.

"Empty your pockets," I said.

Greg did as he was told. I held a hand out and he gave me his phone, wallet, and money clip. I took the cash out of the clip and tossed it back to him. Pulled his license from the wallet and looked it over. "You live on Staten Island?" I asked in disgust. "Weird." I tossed the wallet on the floor and checked if the phone had the lock engaged. I held it back out to him. "Unlock this and pull up the numbers associated with Frankie."

"Numbers." Greg chocked back a laugh. "I ain't got no numbers. I told you; I'm a nobody. You know, there's one guy in the Bowery. Eddie Tegan. He's more wrapped up in shit than I am. I'm, uh, I'm like a hobbyist."

"What if he lies?" I asked.

Silo smirked. "They always lie. That's why you don't let up. You keep pushing."

I grabbed the bottle again and gave Greg another gut check. "The fuckin' numbers, now."

Greg dry heaved, struggling to straighten up. "Come on, fuck..." He coughed. "That hurts."

"It can always get worse."

Greg twisted in place and tapped on his phone screen. He thrust the device at me. "Fucking take it. Stop fucking hitting me."

I grabbed the phone and exported his entire contact list to a burner device I kept at home.

I had other questions, though. That cheese logo was bothering me. I pump faked with the bottle to shake Greg up. "Where'd you get this coke?"

Greg flinched and held his hand up over his face. "Fuck, come on, enough. Got a guy in Washington Square who hooks me up. He scores that shit out of Brooklyn. That's all I know, I swear."

"You sure about that?"

"I swear to fucking God. I'm just a courier and middleman."

"Sounds like a great career track, Gregory." I pointed back towards the bar. "Give me a few minutes before you come traipsing out there. My buddies are going to stick around and enjoy a beer. They'll watch you a while. Maybe even accompany you home if they don't feel very satisfied. You feel that?"

Greg nodded enthusiastically. "Yes. Everything is very felt."

"And I'm assuming you know damn well to forget this face." I smiled. "As hard as that will be."

Greg continued the nodding. I could see he was desperate for me to leave.

"I'm keeping the coke," I said before heading back to the bar.

The bartender was back at her station. "Were you taking your order to go?"

"Yes, ma'am," I said, and peeled off a fat wad of Greg's money to lay down on the bar.

"How will we know it worked?" I asked.

Silo shrugged. "I'd give it a day or two. You go on with your life, and if these people are half as inexperienced as I believe they are, they will let you know exactly how desperate they are and in as direct a way as possible."

"What if they're more put together than we assume?"

"Then they'll know you're associated with Atticus and, therefore, with me. And they won't do a thing."

Silo Jotter had his fucking ways.

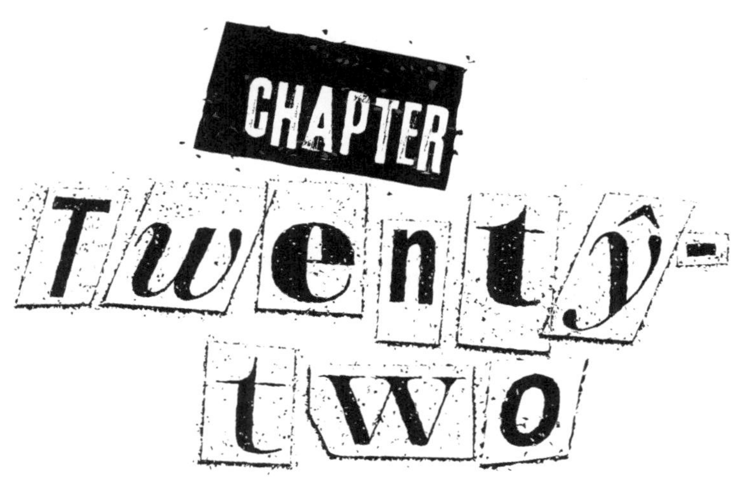

CHAPTER Twenty-two

"You are a fucking superstar," Amity said as I handed her the crêpes from Shade. "I can't believe you remembered the place."

I shrugged. "I was in the neighborhood and figured, fuck it. Gave me a good excuse to take the long-ass trip out here."

Amity smirked. "Oh, how you suffer."

"I do."

"Yeah, whatever. I have a little convection oven in the back. I'll get these warmed up in no time." She placed the bag aside. "But let me finish what I was doing first." She motioned behind the counter. "Come on, you're allowed. The manager isn't that much of an asshole."

"Here's hoping," I said. "Not sure about the company they keep." I walked behind the counter and followed her to an out of the way spot where she had a little cheese station set up."

"You'll never guess what happened," Amity said.

I had a sick feeling of what was about to come. "What happened?" Why did I ask? What was the point of letting the discussion go this way again? This power she had over me. It made me feel weak and strong at the same time. Happy and sad too.

"Atticus called me." Amity smiled softly.

She was way too happy about that.

"We talked for fucking hours, like more than I ever thought he was capable of." Amity wrapped a wheel of bright orange cheddar in wine-steeped twine. Every three rotations, she sprinkled what looked to be sawdust over the wheel, flipped it over, and started the wrapping all over again. She saw me watching her work—doing my best to work out a way to turn the conversation off of Atticus. "I call it pixie dust. Enhances the overall flavor."

I rocked on my heels. Relief washed over me. "You need me to do anything? I feel weird just watching you work." I was surprised to make the offer, but the silence was driving me insane, and I didn't want to keep pushing the conversation towards Atticus. There was a reprieve on the job, no need to be an active participant in that bullshit.

Amity stared at the wheel of cheese and frowned. "Thanks. Know what?" She grabbed a bucket of that pixie dust and handed it to me. "Come here and sprinkle while I turn this bad boy."

"Got it. Should I be generous?"

"Go fucking crazy." Amity focused on her cheese.

I grabbed a handful of the dust and sprinkled as she

turned the wheel over. Once the layer was applied, Amity wrapped more string and brushed a liquid over the layer. "Okay. One more time." She smiled. "So how are things going for you, Pop? Your plans moving ahead?"

I winced at her calling me "Pop"—she'd never done that before—but it felt nice to be asked about my situation. "Yeah," I said, "this week's been pretty good. Lots of great things planned and other things happening. I actually think I might be in a hugely different place before too long."

Amity sighed. "I'm jealous. I'd kill to be somewhere else today."

"Any particular reason?"

Amity craned her neck to check the time on the large clock overhead. "You're about to find out."

The store's front door opened, and an older woman sauntered in. She wore an old track suit and a baseball cap. She gave me a look I'd seen a million times before: disdain wrapped in antipathy. Do not engage, lady. I got that message fucking clear.

The woman walked to the counter and rapped her knuckles against it three times. She said something in a gruff smoker's voice. The language was indecipherable. Sounded like a joke, honestly.

"Gimme a sec." Amity walked away from her cheese and crouched behind the counter, then came back up with a bag and placed it in front of the rude woman. The woman handed Amity some money and walked out as briskly as she walked in.

"What was that?" I asked as the door closed.

"One of the regulars I told you about before. The days they pop by sort of drain me, you know?"

No way in hell that was *just* cheese in those bags. Between the vial from before and the creepy old Baba Yaga collecting half her body weight in merch, I was beginning to wonder if Amity was a bigger mover than I had anticipated. She kept going on about carrying on her grandfather's legacy. I had to wonder if the cheese was more her thing than the old man's.

"They love the old-style cheese that much?" I asked. "My girl looked like she was going to make it maybe a quarter block out of here with the size of that bag."

Amity laughed. "Those ladies are stronger than you think. They project something. I can never put my finger on it, but I find it pants-shittingly scary."

"Is that the smell? Or is it that new blue cheese I saw when I walked in?"

Amity barked a bright laugh before giving me a light elbow to the gut. "Asshole. Come to the back. We'll heat up that food, drink some expensive wine I should be selling, and I can tell you embarrassing shit about your boss from our phone call."

"You mind if I ask an awkward question first?" I stared at my feet, feeling like a damn middle-schooler.

Amity stopped cold and frowned. "Shit."

"It isn't like that, it's just—"

“No, I’m being shitty.” Amity took my hands in hers and dipped her head a little to meet my gaze. “I’m really sorry, Pop. The past couple of days have been wild, and I made a decision without giving everything the thought I should have.”

“Poppy. Not a fan of ‘Pop.’”

Amity’s eyes widened. “Oh, sorry. Just came out like that.”

I waved it off. “No problem.” And of course, I felt bad lying to her. I didn’t have to feel bad, but I did. I needed to leave. Simply walk out. Let this nonsense run its course. Focus on what mattered: my goals. I was getting in good with Silo. Why should it have mattered if Amity and Atticus got together? It simply set Atticus firmly where I needed him.

“I understand if you’re mad at me or if you felt led on.”

I shook my head. “Nah, we didn’t even get started. I understand that.” I hated myself for not being open with her. I wanted to admit this hurt, even if we only had one date, but I couldn’t find it in me.

Amity pulled me towards the back. “Crêpes will fix everything,” she insisted.

I went along. Hearing more about Atticus wasn’t appealing, but the company more than made up for it. Besides, I knew with everything happening, I probably wouldn’t see her for a few weeks.

What was the harm in hanging out for a little while longer?

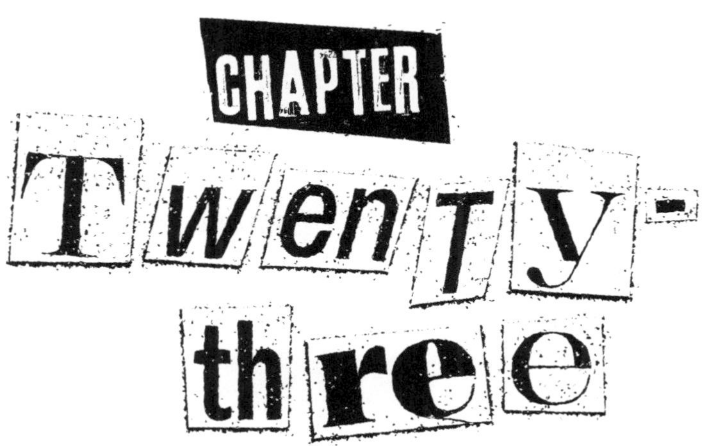

CHAPTER Twenty-three

"It wasn't our fault that the money went missing. Please, you need to understand what happened." Jason Tasker was manic. "I gave your man the amount requested, and he left. It wasn't my fault if he didn't give it to you when he was supposed to." He turned to me with a desperate look in his eye. "How is it my concern if he claims to have been robbed?" Jason gave me a "what the fuck" face. "Couldn't he be lying to you?"

Fuck me. Greg still had Jason's money? Why would he still have that money? Shouldn't he have passed it off? Goddamn cokeheads.

I snatched the phone away and took a deep breath. Business Poppy. Business Poppy was going to speak. Business Poppy paid the bills. That's what mattered. Not the agonizing pain of being around this idiocy. "I'm sorry," I said, "Mr. Tasker is a little too emotional and I felt it would be prudent to take over for him. This is

Poppy Leathers, his business manager."

"Good afternoon, Miss Leathers." The woman had a pleasant voice, but firm. Not Alabama. "As I told your client, we're invested in helping resolve this issue. The problem we're facing is in dealing with our partners. Frankly, they do not care what happened to the money. They only care that their fees are taken care of—no exceptions."

"Uh-huh. Sure." I nodded, for Jason's benefit. "I understand that. My issue here, and bear with me as I just walked into the apartment, is that it sounds like your employee was given the money and was allegedly robbed. Isn't confirmation of payment enough? I'd imagine once it was out of Mister Tasker's hands, it was no longer his responsibility." I gently laughed, real friendly. "I mean, that would be like me being responsible for the money taken in a bank robbery after I deposited my paycheck."

I wondered if I should throw Silo's name around but knew it would be a mistake. Nobody name dropped Silo Jotter unless they were looking to meet a bullet mid-flight. Business Poppy did not have those kinds of overt connections. Business Poppy was the one who worked hard and stumbled onto opportunity.

Business Poppy was no fun.

"I cannot speak to the events which occurred, but in short: yes," the woman said.

They wanted their money. It was like Silo said: Greg took a beating and seemingly disappeared, but not before telling someone at least a little about what happened. Now the company was shook at being noticed, and they were going to pull all resources and hunker down for a while to avoid heat. To demand cash from Jason was some bush-league shit, though. Made me wonder if this nice lady wasn't so much of a third party as someone sitting near or right next to whoever Frankie was.

Jason paced on the other side of the room. "Can we pay over a set period? I've got checks coming in—you're getting me those checks." He motioned to me. "Tell them. Tell them money's coming. We can work out installments. Whatever they want." He was near tears, the poor bastard.

I nodded. "Would there be a way to finance what's due?

"Like we're a store?"

"Is it something to be considered? Look my client up, Jason Tasker. He's well-known in his field. I can assure you we'll pull in more than enough from our upcoming installation piece."

The woman on the phone cleared her throat. "I'd have to check. Can I call you back once I've discussed with management? Do you have a direct line?"

"Certainly. Thanks so much for having an open mind. I'll add, though, that these events are a bit unsettling. We've provided the first half of payment, but as we've yet to get any return on this, I'm not necessarily confident we could work with the initially provided estimate for services. If you could communicate with management that we feel something is also due to us, that would be appreciated." I provided my cell number and disconnected the call.

Fucking amateurs. All of them, Jason included. If I hadn't walked in, he would have agreed to pay double because a schmuck was going to fucking schmuck.

Jason sat down and heaved out a sigh from the very depths of his being. "Oh, God. Thank you, Pop. I told Sara things were going perfect—fucking perfect. And then this mess." He covered his face with his hands. "Between this and the show, my brains were going to start pouring out my nose."

"Yeah, well, I still have to take a tour of the venue. I'm wiring money to a contact later this week to get the ball rolling there. The good news is if this Station Zero place pans out, we can probably do your show exactly when you wanted."

"You think the same can be said for the baby business?"

"I think they were trying to grift you out of extra cash by acting like it's your fault their man got robbed like a dumbass days after he should have given them the money." I shook my head. "I'll work it out when they call back. We're not doubling our payment to them for sloppy work. They wanna play the cloak and dagger shit, then they better get good at it."

"See? I told you there was opportunity in that kind of

stuff! I'm scared and excited."

"It's my job to make sure you do not take unnecessary hits to the financial scrotum, Jason, but I can only do so much. So next time, send them my way."

"I'm so fucking glad one of us can be the professional," Jason said.

"It is a bad time for you to want me to be the only professional in the room." I couldn't hide the exhaustion in my voice. Truth was: I was fucking tired.

Atticus, Amity, Silo, Jason, these babies, the beating I gave Greg—my hands hurt like hell—it all came crashing down on me after a night of zero sleep. Just tossing and turning. All thinking. What would be next? What would I do if x and y happened but z didn't? Was this what going crazy was like?

"Why's that?" Jason asked.

"Nothing. A silly little joke." I handed the phone back. "When they call back—and they will—we'll have leverage," I said.

"This whole baby thing is driving me insane," Jason said, "I mean, what the fuck am I going to do if this happens again? What if they're playing me?"

I hushed him gently. "No extra money. It will work out, Jason. Relax, okay? These guys aren't above board and they have a lot to lose if they fuck with us." I walked over and gripped him by the shoulders. "I'm going to help you, Jason. Then I'm going to take three Ambien and pass the fuck out. But before I do that, I am going to get us past the line and a little closer to your hopes and dreams of never doing anything by yourself again."

Jason laughed, and the lightness of it almost drove me fucking crazy. "Thanks, Pop."

"Thank me by calling me my actual name." I motioned to Jason's dining room, jammed with whiteboards and hundreds of sketches, plans, and flowcharts. "How's the show looking? Take our minds off that one problem and focus on the other, more interesting problem." Maybe this would calm him down.

Jason walked over to the materials. He stared at plans for the live action portion of his show. "I printed out what you sent me before. The specs are rough, but it looks like the ceilings are high enough for me to try to do a Sistine Chapel kind of deal with pulleys. I can paint the ceiling while the guests look over the installations below." He made his problem face.

"But?"

"Well, I need to know how slack I need to make the cables to let me paint unencumbered, but I'm not 100% on whether the brush is going to be too heavy to tape to my dick." He motioned to a drawing of his member with a medium-sized brush taped to it. "See, ideally, I'll be flaccid for this whole thing, but what if I get an erection? Will this be heavy enough to prevent that? Will it be too heavy? How much momentum will I need to build up with my hips to get a good brushstroke? It's hard to crack."

"The struggle of an artist is indeed real," I deadpanned. It was adorable how much extra width he gave himself in the rendering, too. That man was nude to a fault whenever I was around. He needed a reality check.

“Well, this is the go big or go home show,” Jason said. “I’m bleeding Instagram and Twitter followers. If I don’t outdo the last show, what happens to the whole art influencer thing?”

“A valid cause for concern. Not sure if it’s a break-your-dick kind of concern, but I can see where you’re coming from.” I winced. “Sorry. I mean that I get it. Life without risk is life wasted, right?”

“Right.” Jason shuffled through a few papers and pulled out a larger brush than the one in the sketch. “What do you think of this one?”

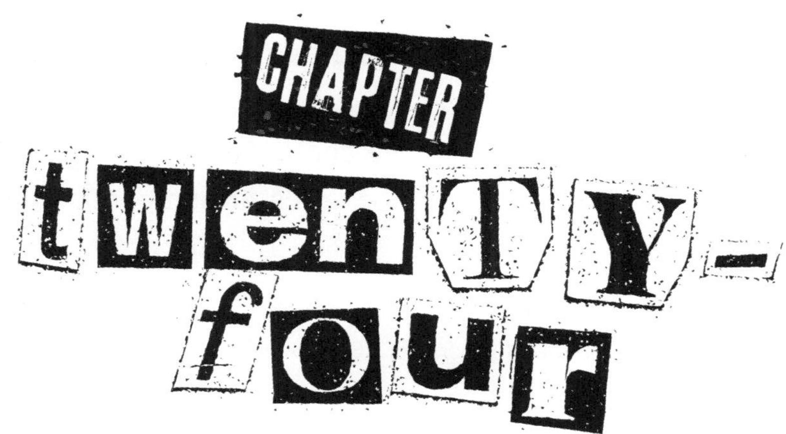

CHAPTER twenty-four

The safety chain stopped me from walking into Atticus' apartment for the morning brief and wardrobe spread.

"The fuck," I muttered. "Atticus. Hey, Atticus. Your employee is here."

Five fucking minutes of waiting—there went being early—and Atticus turned up in a terrycloth robe and the look of a man who'd shat his pants in public. I rubbed my temples. It was too early for this shit, and while I knew that I had endorsed this nonsense, it was already getting in the way of the work I still had to do.

"Oh, hey," Atticus said, almost a whisper. "I'm sorry. Uh…"

The choice was made. I shouldn't have been angry to be out of the loop. Amity told me about the phone call, but a text would have been nice. Just an update, "Hey, I'm fully in the bone zone with your boss now, winky-face emoji," something.

I leaned against the door frame. "Dude, I know Amity is here. You could have at least adjusted the calendar like I taught you."

Atticus didn't remove the chain. He peered through the crack in the door as if he were a prisoner. "Could we get a later start today?"

I checked my phone. "We had some work to do with some bank transfers we're getting close to overdue on. I was hoping to dovetail that into some financial discussion, since it might be high time to start transferring some of your liquidity to cryptocurrency." I sighed. "Not much else. If you want to call today a wash, I'm fine with that. My afternoon's going to be spent in Jersey, so no matter how I look at any of this, I'm plain fucked."

Atticus' eyes brightened and he nodded eagerly. "OK, cool. Go take the day to handle that and text me later. I'll be better next time. Sorry about that." He closed the door.

Well, shit. I knew I wanted this business relationship to die on the vine, but I didn't have a clue how quickly it would happen if this asshole simply found someone else to glom onto. I almost texted Amity something cheeky, but even that wasn't appealing. Amity had set her line with me; it hurt a little, and that annoyed me. I didn't like that she could make me feel vulnerable and grumpy. I didn't like that anyone could make me feel this way. I think the only thing that kept me from getting angry about it was how genuine she was. It made her different—worth having around even.

Oh well. I had shit to do, and I didn't have time to feel sorry for myself because someone I had a little crush on—okay, fine, it was totally more than that—didn't feel the same way.

Fuck it. I texted her.

> Thanks for getting me a day off :P

No point in waiting for an answer.

Outside, I was greeted by the two mooks who'd backed me up with the Gregory beating.

"Oh, hey boys," I said with a wave. "Atticus is a little, um, indisposed."

The larger one, Eddie—I think—shook his head. "No, Miss Leathers. We're here for you."

I took a step back. Shit. "What I do?"

"Nothing," Eddie said. "Mister Jotter asked that we begin accompanying you if needed."

"Like bodyguards?" I have to be honest; I was confused as hell.

Both men shrugged. "Or if you need help with an errand. Or anything else." He motioned to a Town Car a few feet away. "We can even drive you anywhere you need to go."

Oh. Were these… *holy shit*. Did Silo gift me henchmen? Driving henchmen? In this economy?

I stood still, waiting for the punchline: "Ha ha, dummy, we're here to shoot you and bury you in the deepest, smelliest part of the Meadowlands." But no, this was legit. I pointed at Eddie. "Okay. Eddie, right?"

A nod.

I turned to the other one. They were both clean shaven—faces and heads—and wore similar suits. I was not having that. "And you?"

"William, but people call me Bill." He smiled, professional but not unkindly.

For such tall motherfuckers, these guys gave off pleasant vibes. I liked that. What I did not like was the fashion sense. If these boys were going to be around me, they needed to brighten up. My path to villainy was not going to be banal, and we needed some high camp.

"Sorry, lost in my head." I gave a little curtsy, miming my skirt lift since I was wearing capris. "I actually could use a ride for a few errands. First and foremost," I said as I pointed to my new friends, "is getting you boys looking pretty." I headed over to the town car. "Let's go, sweethearts. We got ourselves a forty-minute drive to somewhere it would take fifteen minutes to get to by subway."

We had ourselves a makeover montage that morning. Well, half of one. I could tell Eddie wasn't loving the constant changing, but we did progress from ludicrous Steve Harvey suits to golf fashion and over to a few perennial outfits I liked picking for Atticus. Nice, pleated slacks, smart dress shirts, thin ties, and vests—vests as far as the eye could see. I wasn't a blazer girl. Blazers were for old white men trying to look like they were fancy. But a sharp vest? That was sex on a platter.

I had Eddie in a matching salmon vest and slacks set and Bill in a dark green number that worked with his complexion.

"You both look like the back cover of a '90s R&B album cover," I said, looking my new creations over with no small amount of satisfaction.

"Is..." Eddie looked at his outfit. "Is that good or bad?"

I grinned. "Right now, we're at a Bel Biv Davoe, so we're good. We hit Color Me Badd or All 4 One and then we have a problem."

Bill blinked. "I have no idea what those are."

"Good. Don't Google them. It might upset you." I snapped my fingers. "We're all paid up and ready to go. Y'all prepared to drive out to New Jersey?" I leaned forward. "I understand if that worries you."

"I'm from Morristown," Eddie said.

"Wonderful. You'll understand the jug handles." I stood up. "We need to pick up my other boss Jason." I checked my phone. "And then go to. I don't know how to pronounce this." I held out my phone to Eddie.

"Secaucus."

I arched a brow and looked at Will. "Seriously? See-caucus? Not Seh-caucus?"

"That's how my parents always said it."

I shrugged. Fine. Whatever. Maybe his parents were

bad readers, I don't know. "See-caucus it is." I walked to the store's exit. "Off to the Dirty Jerz."

Goddamn I felt like a certified badass with these gorgeous bastards in tow.

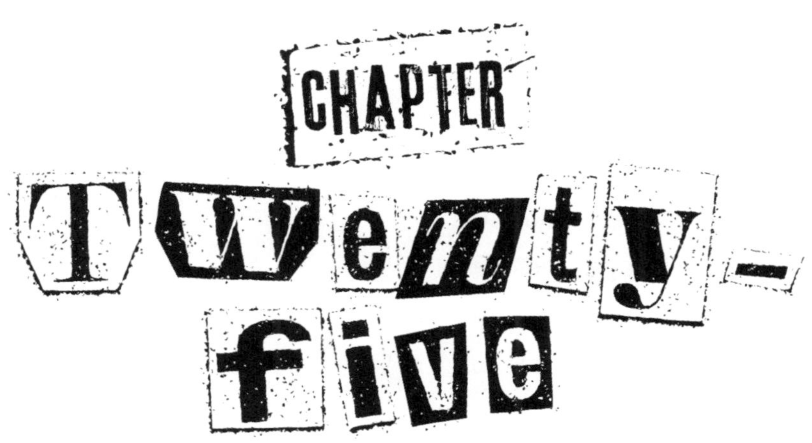

Chapter Twenty-five

"I'm sorry, your name?" Jason Tasker held a hand to the gentlemen who approached us outside of Secaucus Junction.

I was tired of feeling like a goddamn nanny. Jason begged me to accompany him to this meeting. Begged me to make all the calls. Every step of this supposedly deep, desperate need to be a parent was entirely fucking supported by my actions, while he sat around whining about how hard things were for him. If none of this was useful, I'd have quit or simply refused to help. For that moment, I needed to bite my tongue and live with the taste of blood in my mouth.

At least I was able to secure a ride. Worried about that before. The fuck were we going to do, Uber our way to a semi-illegal transaction?

The man waved Jason's hand away. "No formalities. The money?" He looked at me for a beat too long. "Do I know you?"

I stared back. “You go to Marist College?”

“No.”

“Well, shit. Thought you were my old Spanish professor.”

The man sneered. “Cute.”

Jason stepped between us with a tight smile. “I think it may be easier on me if I could confirm you were the man I was sent to meet. Mr. Villalobos, right?”

“Who are those two and why are they dressed like wedding wait staff?” Villalobos nodded at the car with my handsome boys seated, waiting for us.

“Those are my drivers. Nothing to be concerned about. They do what I say, and I said to sit still and wait for us to get back.”

It clicked in my head then. This asshole did indeed know me. I’d forgotten him until that very moment—right when we locked eyes. His grouchy ass was in the clinic the day I gave away my little bundle of joy. Shit, was he the one who drove me home? No way for me to fully remember. I was high as fuck that day off whatever they dumped into me and hormones. I’m lucky I remembered my fucking name, all things considered.

The man motioned for us to walk with him. “Villalobos. Next time say it a little louder, those transit cops couldn’t hear you.” Villalobos was built broad and wide, like an old bodybuilding ad from the back of a comic book. “You two mind taking a ride? If the money’s squared off, I can take you to the right guy to sort out the paperwork.” He scratched the hairy knuckles of his right hand. "Your handsome boys can follow us, if that helps."

Jason nodded enthusiastically. "Of course. Is that okay, Pop? Sorry, Poppy."

I nodded. Not like I had much choice.

Villalobos pointed to the briefcase Jason was carrying with him. "I take it that's the money? You do subtlety like a fucking gas station fire. Famous guy like you running around like a shivering dog with a fucking briefcase filled with money." He pointed at me with his thumb. "That outfit's worse. That's a school bus fire."

I looked down at my bright yellow dress and candy apple red pumps. "It's laundry day."

Jason lifted the briefcase and frowned. "I didn't know how else to transport it."

"Well, they've got this thing called internet banking these days. It's fucking magical."

"Wouldn't that leave a trail?"

Villalobos shrugged. "Shit's above my pay grade, son." We approached an SUV parked at a handicapped space nearest the entrance to the train station. "You two eat yet?"

"Um, no. No, I have not," Jason said.

I texted Eddie to follow us and to keep eyes open in case I needed saving.

He replied with a thumbs up emoji, and I knew then I loved my two big, burly vest boys forever.

"If it's a free meal, I can and will eat whatever's most

expensive," I offered. I knew I was being an ass, and frankly, I gave no fucks. I was tired. Tired of needing to baby idiot one and then drive however many miles to babysit idiot two, only to get ninety more phone calls from the initial idiot because something, something, "mah arts."

One of those rare moments I regretted my aspirations. God, it would be so much easier to have no goals in life.

Villalobos opened the car with his alarm dongle. "Let's get some food. I'm craving Portuguese. Then I'll take you where you need to go. Heads up, I can't stick around for the whole thing. So maybe it's a good thing you've got your chauffeurs following us." He looked at me. "I take it those boys are discreet? Barring their outfits."

"Silent as a church fart."

"The hell does that mean?"

"She's a joker, right, Poppy?" Jason looked at me meaningfully. "Big jokes."

"I'm a walking clown car of hilarity."

"I ain't laughing," Villalobos said.

"I'll have to try harder." I smiled sweetly.

The drive was short. I wasn't familiar with the area, but it looked nice enough. At least, the portion of the neighborhood we were in did. A block or two down were stop signs blacked out with spray paint, two triangles with a line joining them. Maybe gang signs? Or maybe just some jerk off tweens acting like they were cool.

Villalobos parked in front of a small café. "We're here.

Order the fish; it's a Tuesday, so it's fresh."

Jason looked at me and mouthed, "But I'm vegan."

"Then eat bread," I muttered.

"You can leave the case." Villalobos continued walking into the café.

Jason stutter stepped, turning and staring at the SUV. "Are you sure?"

"Ain't nobody going to touch my car, trust me." Villalobos lumbered into the café and found a seat. "You have your babysitters across the street too."

"Oh, that's right. I keep forgetting them. Poppy, how much is the tip going to be for that? I thought rideshare drivers had to keep working." Jason stepped back and sighed. "I think I'm going to hold onto this. You know, in case. The world is crazy. Anything can happen."

I opted to keep my mouth shut. I could easily point out that this restaurant had massive windows and a free table with a clear view of the large SUV that anyone would need to have a head injury to try to steal or break into, or that our drivers were very much not obviously affiliated with any rideshare app he'd ever heard of. But I saw that Jason was in that anti-Zen state he entered when he was freaked out. No amount of logic was going to save this white boy from making an ass out of himself now.

Jason wandered in behind us. He tried to make the briefcase come off as a normal accessory, but the juxtaposition of his ratty T-shirt and frayed jeans made it look more like he'd stolen the stupid thing.

"Sit the fuck down and put the case under the table if you're so fucking scared." Villalobos was already drinking tap water out of a cloudy glass. "Not like you're buying crack. This is charity work." He smiled at me. "Maybe you should have your manager work this gig. She's got the right attitude to work discreetly, despite her choice of attire."

"Well, what we're doing *is* illegal." Jason sat down and edged as far down the booth as he could. He wedged the briefcase between him and the wall. "I mean, I have so many questions."

"And I ain't the information booth." Villalobos picked up his menu and scanned it. "You ever eat this stuff?"

"Um, there's a Brazilian/Mongolian fusion place near my house. That's about as close to Portugal as I've been. Food-wise."

I read my menu. "Never traveled in my life." Partial lie. I'd been to New Rochelle. And this place too.

Villalobos raised an eyebrow. "Really? No traveling? You both come off like the type to have traveled a little."

Jason laid the briefcase on his lap and picked up his menu. "I've done a little traveling." He seemed annoyed. "So where do we go from here?"

"A little further south. Near the airport."

"Is there like a baby warehouse there or something?" Jason asked.

Villalobos raised his eyebrows and sniffed. "Something

like that."

I decided to order the tilapia before slipping my phone out of my pocket and turning on the audio recorder. I had a feeling I'd need to remember a few things.

"Oh, hey," I said to the waiter, "can you set up two more orders of the tilapia to go? I have two friends who haven't had lunch yet and I'd hate to screw them over."

Villalobos dropped us off in front of what appeared to be an abandoned factory. The SUV pulled away before Jason could formally complain. I took the time to examine the lot. It was funny: this felt sketchy. It looked sketchy. Exactly the kind of feel a black-market operation should have. But maybe that was the point—obvious to the point of camouflage.

I spotted Eddie and Bill parked near an auto repair shop across the way. I gave a little wave and a thumbs up. Checked my phone—no signal. The lot was filthy with broken glass, old beer cans, and syringes, all glinting in the sun dipping behind the main building in the lot. I noticed another blacked-out stop sign at the end of the block. If there was trouble, I'd have to depend on Jason's child-like screams to get us through the danger.

A door slammed shut in the distance, soon followed by footsteps. A woman emerged from behind a shipping container. She was dressed in a pristine, powder blue suit with a matching trilby and shoes. She held a cane in her right hand, but clearly didn't require it to walk.

I nearly squealed. It was her. Alabama honey lady herself.

"Oh, fuck me," Jason said.

"What?" I watched Alabama approach. I bristled with nervous energy. Would she recognize me? No way she could. It was way too long since we last saw one another.

"I forgot the briefcase in the SUV." Jason was a master at shattering the calm. A real fucking genius with a metaphorical hammer to my temples.

"Are you fucking kidding me?"

Alabama closed the distance between us. I gave Jason a stare and a nod as a sign for him to shut up and let me handle things.

Obviously, he did not pick up what I put down. "I am so sorry," he said. "I left the money with Mr. Villalobos."

Alabama smirked. "Ah, well, we can fix that." She fetched her phone and swiped a moment. Held up the phone to her ear. "Stan? Sorry, Frankie here." She laughed. "You saw it before I said it. Great, see you in a few." She disconnected her phone. "He's on the way."

Jason sighed in relief. "Oh, thank God." He leaned over and shook his head. "I was ready to have another panic attack."

"Oh, sweetheart, no more worries." Frankie motioned to the building. "How about we take a walk and see if we can find you both a momma that aligns with your aesthetic."

Aesthetic? I fucking loved it. Wasn't about to argue about whether I was Jason's partner either. I figured I'd hold off on speaking for a little while longer. Frankie didn't recognize me, but she might recognize my voice.

I watched her. Not sure I ever wanted to be Frankie—maybe once upon a time—but at that moment, all I could see was a crown perched precariously on her head. All I had to do was reach out and grab it.

Chapter Twenty-six

The facility: holy shit. It was like an Apple Store for baby shopping. All white. Screens every-fucking-where. Readouts on the prospective mothers and how their babies were doing. Whatever money these people made went right back into the business.

Frankie walked us over to a desk and sat down. She motioned for us to sit across, and she swung a monitor around for us to see while she logged into a terminal attached to a small monitor facing her.

"So, if I remember right, you guys were looking for something multi-ethnic? Potentially twins?"

Jason sat and smiled. "Yes, yes. We were hoping for kids that could use the love. So many of our peers are adopting out of the third world, but when we heard you focused on stateside mothers in need, I think that really put things in perspective, you know?"

"Absolutely, Mister Tasker." Frankie looked to me. "Now, Mrs. Tasker..."

I raised my hands to stop her. "Nope. Not the wife. I just manage him."

"My wife is busy with some work," Jason added, "But I assure you, not *too* busy for kids." He laughed awkwardly.

Frankie nodded and maintained eye contact with me. "Oh, my mistake. Miss Leathers, right?"

The name wouldn't be an issue. She knew me by an old name that wasn't worth saying anymore. That girl died a long fucking time ago. "Correct," I said. "I think I spoke with one of your reps a few days back. I wanted to say, aside from that robbery issue, this has been a great experience for my client so far." I looked at Jason. "Even if his nerves have been shot over all of this."

"Oh, I can understand," Frankie said smoothly. "And we do apologize for what happened. Now, onto happier subjects. The babies." A few keystrokes followed. "Here we go. I think one of our mothers-to-be, Valencia, is perfect for you."

A kind-eyed young Afro-Latina, like me—the profile said that first bit—came up on screen. There were vitals that flashes under her picture. Her criminal and toxicology history. Education. Where she lived in the past ten years. Number of sexual partners.

This was far more involved than what I remembered, but still as impersonal. This was intrusive. Over glossy. What was wrong with simply helping two sets of folks out with different needs that happened to intersect?

This was some sellout shit.

Jason fawned over the profile. "And she's expecting twins?"

"In three weeks. We usually do C-Section on premises. We have topflight staff; all nurses and doctors are licensed professionals we pay competitive fees to. We like to do three to four days of observation to make sure mothers and children are healthy and ready to go, and then..." Frankie snapped her fingers. "All yours. We handle credentials. Birth certificates and all that are handled here. All you need is a car and car seats."

"Perfect," Jason said. "Poppy, she's perfect, isn't she?"

"Looks it," I answered. "Any way we can meet her?" I felt that sting of light regret. I knew I shouldn't push it, but I was going to. I didn't like how this was panning out. How sterile it felt.

This was not the business I wanted to be a part of, and certainly not what I wanted to take over. This enterprise required a soul, something more tactile than screens and profiles. Actually speaking to this girl would help. Getting to know her, matching her to the prospective parents. Real assurance everything was going to be okay. That was my way of making this business better. Aim for the bespoke. Make it a boutique experience and there would be more opportunity to make money.

Frankie smiled and blinked slowly. "The girls don't live here, Miss Leathers."

That felt like a lie. "Would we be able to set up a video call? Something for Jason and his wife—who again, we're sorry couldn't join us—to get a sense of the mother's personality. I understand if it isn't. Simply wondering, given the amount of money we've put down already."

Frankie nodded. "Well, we can certainly try. Mister Tasker, would that work for you?"

Jason looked to me. "Well, I mean, I'm raring to go." He laughed. "But Poppy's got a point. Related question: would we be able to provide her updates on the baby if she wanted? I wasn't sure how that all worked."

"We normally ask that separation is complete," Frankie said, "but once our business is concluded, that would be up to the parents. I'd remind you of the contracts you'll be signing. At no point will we be connected to this transaction on paper and we would not be able to support any further once the it is complete."

Which meant fuck-all if this was all under the table. A scare tactic. We were doing illegal shit; the motivation to shut the fuck up was already there. NDAs and contracts were theater at best and a way to slap Jason's name on paperwork in case he did decide to pursue legal options at worst. But people like Jason and Sara didn't give a fuck about that. They only cared about what they wanted, and sometimes that desire had a habit of fading. That girl onscreen, Valencia—maybe she was cool with all this. Maybe she was cool with being treated like a can of soda in a vending machine. But she deserved to know where her kids were going and with who. Even if it didn't matter.

That process. All of it. Once I had my hands on this operation, once I reminded Frankie just who she'd barred from the door? All of that was going to change.

Frankie smiled as she looked at her phone. "It sounds like the money has been returned safely, Mister Tasker. Do you think you want to see anyone else, or is my recommendation to your liking?"

Jason sat a moment in thought. I could see the look in his eyes. This was a big boy decision, and he knew there was nobody else in the room that could answer for him. Another beat. I felt near ready to choke the words out of him, but he finally said it: "Yes. Let's do it."

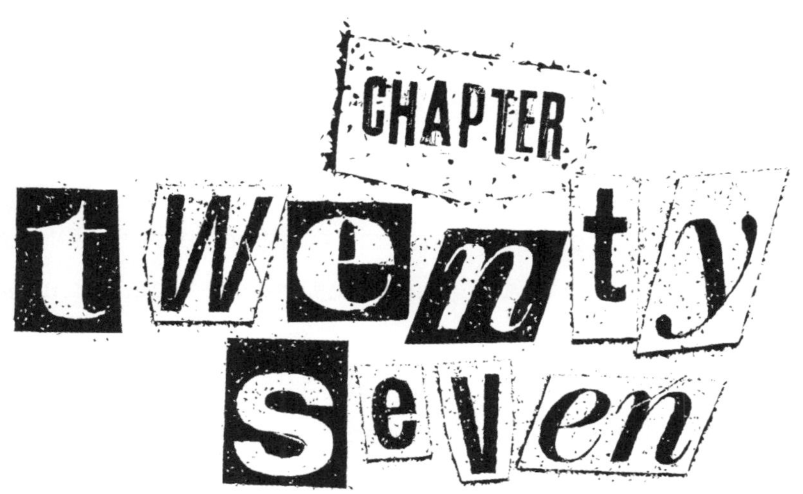

Chapter Twenty Seven

"Hey, Poppy?" Bill gently nudged my left shoulder.

I shot up, wide-eyed, lips curled in a sneer. "Would love to know what part of my whole 'please let me power nap' speech did not register with you. I was almost at the best part of my Patrick Swayze-possessed Whoopi Goldberg sex dream." My eyes ached; head felt like it weighed twenty pounds. The exhaustion was familiar—but under the circumstances, completely unwelcome. Worse yet: I had an appointment to go night spelunking in the sewers. More Jason work. Annoying, with Atticus knee deep in that girlfriend life, that Jason was suddenly more a priority than he'd been in years. If he wasn't, I could have taken a fucking day off.

Bill pulled away. "Apologies. Just, um, Mr. Jotter is here?" Bill walked over to the giant red door I'd installed for my apartment office space—I had them upholster it because it looked really fucking cool. The walls of the room were covered in vintage posters of 1990s heart-throbs—Jonathan Taylor Thomas, Joey Lawrence, at least four of the New Kids on The Block. Lots of hyper color and Zubaz pants. I wanted anyone that walked into this room to understand me at age fifteen. That was important to me: chaos and sexual awakening. It threw people off balance.

I stretched my arms over my head, acutely aware I was only wearing a T-shirt and a pair of cartoon character underwear with the galoshes I had Eddie buy me for the sewer trawling. My hair was tied back tight—no coloring or product.

"Fine," I said. "Let him in."

It was a display of power, clearly. A sudden visit to remind me that there may be a business relationship between us—still on the low—but Silo Jotter was, would always be, the boss. I watched it happen to Atticus constantly but experiencing the power play firsthand certainly gave me some perspective. I was wrong to assume Atticus was spineless when it came to Silo. No, spineless was the wrong word—the man was cautious.

Not my style. I understood that focus and discipline made for fine leaders, but I needed a little room for a storm in a teacup.

Silo walked into the office and sniffed, wearing a frown that looked stitched on. He sat across from me in complete silence: no greeting, no conversation. Silo removed his pea coat and tossed it to me. "Cover up."

I caught the coat and draped it over my lap. "I think it's weird you're a prude."

"You want to shift to pleasure after the business and I'm an open book, Poppy. This, right now, is a meeting between employer and employee. Which requires a little formality."

I fought back a yawn. "So, what *business* brings you to the butthole of Astoria?"

Silo narrowed his eyes. Displeased with the state of me, obviously. "I received a call yesterday. Troubled me greatly."

"Tends to happen with sudden phone calls these days," I said. "People only ever text good news now. Phone calls are always a sales pitch. I mean, hell, I keep getting these Chinese robocalls and I'm fit to go insane."

Silo cleared his throat. "It appears that Atticus has not only slept with his former target but is clearly in a relationship with her." He held a finger up. "And it sounds like perhaps the two of you seem to be forging a friendship as well. Not that I find that to be a problem, since you're the type to be working an angle. But I am not pleased to know that Atticus is still working this out of his system."

The man still had eyes and ears everywhere. I knew this was going to come bite everyone on the ass—hard, too. "I thought she was in the clear. Is it a problem we're all interacting?"

"All things considered, she is not 'in the clear.' I was

reassessing before engaging again."

That was troubling. I may have been less than thrilled with Amity, but my assumption was she'd be safe. This little game I was playing was entirely about burying Atticus.

I frowned. "Well, Atticus is your man. I'm sure he'll flip the switch as needed. Though, you could have brought this up the last time we discussed it. I'd have stayed on top of him." I straightened up and dragged my fingers along the lapel of Silo's jacket. "Unless there's something else." It took a second to register what I was doing. Touching him. I knew this was a boundary crossed, and frankly, I didn't give a shit. I considered this was another bout of self-sabotage, but no, it was something more. I wasn't feeling as frightened of this man anymore. That aura of Silo's didn't land quite the way it did when he was in his element.

If anything, he felt smaller here? This could have been a phone call, but he felt the need to make it something bigger—something scary. I could sense that and it gave me a pleasant case of the belly tremors.

Silo stiffened. He was uncomfortable, not angry.

"You're finally beginning to doubt as much as I do," I said. This was the time to take control of the narrative. Even if just a little.

"Maybe," Silo conceded.

Holy shit. I had him. I couldn't pull back this time. Every moment with this man gave me opening after opening. I was either a manipulative genius or my friend Silo was a little more Wizard of Oz than he was Keyser Söze.

"Not to give you unsolicited advice, boss man, but in my experience, these moments call for an extreme solution—no bandage, no lubrication." I mimed sawing through my forearm. "Sever the limb. And any other appropriate medical and/or rough sex metaphors."

Silo narrowed his eyes at me. "I am not going to kill Atticus," he said. "I've had my suspicions that you were hoping—" He clenched his fists. "Poppy, I have had people killed for less than this. Your appearance. The state of this place." Silo adjusted his stance. His voice threatened to become something more than a smidge over indoor volume. "I am your employer, and this is not how I expect you to behave under the circumstances."

That *felt* weak sauce, but the gamble was beginning to get wobbly. Should I push shit further? He came all the way over here for what? To berate me? To explain his plan with Atticus? Why not simply do it? Silo was clearly doubting more than Atticus' intentions. This change unsettled him, which could explain why he felt less than himself.

So, throw the dog a bone. "I apologize Silo, but you are wrong about my motives. I have my problems with Mister Garcia, but I think a dead Atticus is a wasted opportunity." I pointed at myself. "Me? I see the solution being more about Amity."

"So, get someone else to kill her?"

"Not that, either."

"Then what do you propose?" Silo snapped. He was getting impatient. Not necessarily good, but I was interested in figuring out where his buttons were and how I could push them.

"Tell her."

"Tell her what?"

"Tell her the truth. Who Atticus is. Why he's in her life. You snatch it away to show him that this mess isn't to your fucking specifications." I was surprised to say that out loud, and even more surprised I hadn't thought of it before. Sure, exposing Atticus exposed me, but who looked worse: the woman protecting her or the asshole who was supposed to put a bullet in her brain but was laying the pipe to her instead?

Silo pulled a small chair over and sat down. He sat at the edge and leaned forward, as if any moment he'd leap at me, teeth bared. "Have you ever heard of the Rudaj?"

I nodded. "Albanian mob from the Bronx. Outstanding fashion sense."

"Yes. And our target seems to be tightly connected to them." Silo allowed his eyebrows to rise in surprise, delicately. He leaned back, crossed his legs, and watched me cautiously. "Where are you from again?"

"Does that matter?"

Fucking Wikipedia. I wasn't going into a life of crime without reading up on all the scumbags I might surround myself with. Wasn't about to admit that out loud. Amity's connection to the Albanian mob was surprising. I assumed that, if she was operating, it was on a little more of an independent level. But if she was working with organized motherfuckers, I understood Silo's apprehension. Killing her could be the first domino in what led to an all-out war.

Silo leaned back. "Thinking on it, Poppy Leathers doesn't come off like a real name."

"And yet here you are, calling me that." I stood up. "Atticus is still valuable alive. We both know that. If exposure is what's needed to shake him out of this little midlife crisis of his, I say go for it, Rudaj or not."

"An army of Albanians is not the kind of thing we treat like a minor inconvenience. An army of Albanians limits my ability to do business, Poppy. For *you* to do business."

OK. There he was. A threat against the plan. That was my other stake, wasn't it? Not just my idiot life; Silo knew I had plans in my plans and for the first time it dawned on him he held that card. He puffed up a little.

Fuck me, so I was on defense. I had a little fun here, but I couldn't risk everything blowing up so soon. "Look, I'm not trying to discount the need for calm in both of our endeavors; especially yours," I said. "But I am thinking of the long term. You had to research Amity's connection to this group, which means it isn't commonly known. Even if she's out there carrying on her grandpa's old business, from what I've seen, it's small scale. None of this drama was ever necessary, but..." I watched Silo, hoping this wasn't just riling him up further. "I do have a little something nagging at me now that I'm stepping through this: if the cocaine wasn't a factor... were you really going to kill this girl over the cheese?" I wanted to physically pull away after asking the question, but it had to come out.

"I feel that was obvious," Silo said.

Wow. Okay. He was legit scared of her skills. That's something. Go Amity. "And was there never a chance of a partnership? Maybe a way to get her to carry your product or consult on what you're making. She seems to be fairly good at what she does."

"I don't order these things indiscriminately. She had three opportunities to join up with one of my shells and took none of them. After everything we've dug up, my assumption is her side hustle keeps her afraid of pursuing the legitimate business."

That was something to work with. "Then we expose the hit and say it's because of the drugs. Scare her towards where she needs to be. Make her profitable to you instead of simply a box to check off."

"And trade off the reputation of my best hitter?" Silo motioned to me with both hands.

"Who is aging out and is proving repeatedly that he's lost his edge. Sooner or later, he was going to fuck up enough to organically shatter your relationship. You know, take control of the narrative."

"This is an amazing amount of insight for a woman who likes to pretend she's certifiable."

I laughed. "I'm not sure what the fuck I'm doing, to be honest. And don't even get me started on the sex dreams."

"This is almost a good idea." Silo stood up. "But this places me in a position where people will see me as weak for simply not killing everyone involved."

"You keep missing the part where I say 'control the narrative.'" This idea that was brewing. It was a big one. Unwieldy, but it might just work. Maybe. "I'm not about to delve into your feelings over Atticus and why you won't simply put him out to pasture."

"My reasons are my own."

"I can respect that, Silo, I really do. I just hope you respect that I am the way I am. It ain't personal."

I stood and slipped on a pair of pants. I clumsily buckled my belt and wandered back over to my sofa to sit back down. One more overreach. "Give me a few more men—guys you know are faithful. Let me expose him, run him through the gauntlet, and then let him get one over on me. Blame it on my greenhorn sensibilities. You stay clean. Amity, hopefully, buys into working for you. We all end up happy." If I had a voice of reason in my head it would have been screaming into a megaphone.

Silo remained emotionless. He stared at me, stroking his beard, and biting his lower lip before nodding slowly.

And then—he extended a finger. "Oh."

I stared at the finger. "Kay?"

"You have feelings, too. For this cheese girl."

I couldn't help but appreciate how sharp Silo was. If he weren't so skinny, he'd be a catch. "Does it matter?"

"It matters in the case of Atticus. It matters that he is dating the cheese girl and you are attempting to convince me to run him out of town."

I spread my hands, disarmingly. "Fair play. Difference between him and me is, I know my place. No romantic entanglements are going to lose me what I've been working for. The opposite is true of him: he's trying to make up for all he's sacrificed."

"And you believe you're immune to that."

I shrugged. "Maybe. Maybe I'm just fresher and I'd become more like Atticus over time. I certainly like to think I'm immune. I like to believe I can equally value a life and my wallet without having to be dramatic about it. You know where my attention is." I waved my hands around. "All this static clears up and all I see is the business I want to build. With your help."

"All this to snatch up the baby business? I'd say it was less a goal and more of a light obsession." Silo grinned. "Fine. We can be creative about it. I'll send a few people to help out."

"And then what?" I asked.

"You get money for now. And I continue to consider your place within my organization or whether you are too much of a potential liability." There was weight in the words, but I knew I reached him more than he pretended.

"I can live with that." True enough. I didn't love it, but I'd take it. For now.

"When do you plan on playing out this little tragedy?"

"Soon as you get me the boys to work out the action."

"And what if Atticus resists? His feelings for this girl may inspire him to be the legend he used to be, rather than walk away."

"That's almost a best-case scenario," I said. "If he finds his mean streak again, then we can talk him down and get him to realize where he went wrong. You two have history. I don't need to know it to know that he will listen to you when he needs to."

"Well, there you are, Poppy Leathers," Silo said. "You're already performing above your station." He stopped one more time. "Oh, and Miss Leathers?"

"Yes?"

"You know that if this ends up on my doorstep—if this does not play out in a way that benefits me as you've described—it's over? And not over in the sense we no longer speak, Poppy. I will kill you; I will kill your little cheesemaker. I will burn down everything you associate with and wipe all record of you from the goddamn world." Silo pointed at me. "I'm putting an amount of faith in you, but I want you to remember that you have yet to make yourself indispensable to me."

"Can I ask why you're bothering with this if that's

the case?"

Silo snorted. "Potential. There's money to be made and if I turned up my nose at every eccentric I ever met, I'd be a very poor man. Just be clear on where we stand and things will be fine."

I could live with that. "Crystal. More than crystal—we're Cristal."

Silo walked out.

I kept my eyes on the ground. In my mind, I was the star act, the one who made the audience hold their breath—no time to concentrate on distractions. Silo, Jason, and Atticus: they only thought I was a supporting actor in their bullshit lives.

Silo was wrong about the baby business. That wasn't my obsession. It was just another rung in the ladder. Another step to realizing who Poppy Leathers was. It wasn't enough to give myself a cute name; I had to get to the top of that dream board—be the sparkle I was meant to be. It was unfortunate to see a little weakness in him. The way I acted wasn't much different from the way I was with Atticus or Jason, but Silo seemed almost hurt by my words. He wasn't used to being spoken to like a normal person, but he also couldn't handle it in stride. That felt strange. He had his own weaknesses too. All of them did. None of them could see it.

What fun it was going to be when they woke up to who the fuck they were really dealing with.

I met Jenna and Alton in a small patch of forest north of Atticus' apartment. It was cold. Not the typical New York City cold for the time of year. It was biting; a mean cold. Like it knew I was up to something and decided to punish me for my choice of activity—and fashion. I was not happy with the fit of the galoshes I bought, but the waders I found were hot pink and I fucking loved them, so, hey, fuck Mother Nature if she didn't have taste.

My urban explorer friends looked far more equipped than I was. Their bags had smaller bags attached to them. Accessories galore. Little gadgets hanging from straps. Hanging from their belts. Alton had not one, but *two* fanny packs. Who the fuck needed two fanny packs when all we had was one fanny? Their coats looked toastier than what I was wearing. I was willing to bet they sensibly layered their clothing too.

At least I didn't go commando. I doubled the undies up

for fear of sewer water.

"Should I have brought a backpack?" I asked. I didn't want *everything* I owned to smell like New York City's ruptured asshole, so I figured the clothes were enough. "Or an extra fanny pack?"

Alton smiled tightly. "No worries. We've got flash-lights, some food, and other emergency supplies in case anything goes wrong."

"What could go wrong?" I asked. Fun when I was blissfully ignorant of urban spelunking's very obvious dangers until someone drove that car right into me. "We aren't talking about mole people, are we? Oh, shit are Ninja Turtles real?"

"Well," Jenna said, "Not to freak you out, but sometimes water gets diverted to tunnels without warning—in emergencies only, but still, that's a potential danger."

"We're also crossing some subway tracks. Not publicly used, but MTA workers could be using them to transport materials. The third rails are active, so be aware of where you're standing at all times," Alton added.

"It's an adventure getting there, huh?" The fear subsided. I was about to go under New York City. I wasn't dumb enough believe there were alligators or mutant animals down there, but there had to be a zillion other interesting things. Lost bodies. Lost jewelry. Maybe even—gasp—treasure.

We were Goonies. The night was made right there. Didn't even matter if what we saw met Jason's requirements. I was a Goonie. End of fucking story.

Alton walked over to a patch of grass between dying trees and pulled a large, hooked tool from his belt. He plunged it into the ground and pulled up a manhole cover.

"Holy shit," I said. "They got manholes in the fucking forest?"

Jenna laughed. "Wild, right? The city's full of little secret places and entrances. It blows my mind more people aren't into this kind of stuff."

Alton slid the cover to the side. "To be fair, not a lot of people are fans of the dark, or rats, or human excrement." He frowned. "Ours is a rare and weird breed."

"You ask me, the world needs more of that," I said, genuinely. "Is this the only way to the station?"

"It's the easiest way without anyone noticing," Jenna said, "but yeah, I have a few other routes mapped. I wasn't in the mood for us to get arrested today."

Alton went down first, then me, then Jenna. The smell was immediate. There were obvious notes: piss, shit, and hot trash, but there were other odors. With each rung, I discovered something new that turned my stomach. There were smells that reminded me of dead flowers, spoiled milk, and lemon. Smells that brought back strange sensory memories—like the smell of a school cafeteria burger, rancid vinegar, and the occasional hint of hot dog water. I retched a few times headed down the ladder—thankfully, I knew well enough not to eat before coming on this little journey.

The ground at the bottom of the ladder was dark but illuminated by weak lights which lined the corridor we descended into. There was a narrow canal in the center of the room, an inch-deep trickle of water flowing towards a rusted grate. Alton and Jenna turned on their flashlights—crazy powerful little fuckers—and pointed them down the opposite end of the tunnel.

Jenna held up a paper map—delightfully insane—and scanned it with her light. "We're walking short of two miles. Doesn't seem like much, but we're also descending another hundred or so feet. Stay between us and do what we say when we say it, cool?"

I nodded. Wasn't about to argue with anyone that was between me living through this or dying in the accumulated toilet waste of a few hundred thousand people.

Walking a mile in a sewer isn't like walking a mile in the city. The tunnels are cramped and dirty. The smell is overwhelming—which, okay, can be said about aboveground NYC. The sounds, though. Low groans coming from nowhere. Skittering at my feet. Strange echoes coming from above. Couldn't tell if it was voices carrying through the grates on the street or from the train stations. It felt like being in a haunted house.

People were going to fucking love this. People were going to pay a fucking mint to be here just so they could tell their friends and enemies they did it—they ventured into the New York City sewer system.

When I was done with Jason, maybe I'd capitalize

on this place. Find a business opportunity of my own. Monthly parties or bougie orgies with lame themes like the '80s or vaguely racist nonsense. Whatever attracted that sweet, sweet transplant money. Locations like this were flypaper for newbie New Yorkers and I understood very well there was a mint to make among people like that; among people who couldn't forge an identity without being a receipt.

As we walked, I admired what little scenery there was: century-old masonry falling apart. Pools of greenish liquid that did not look at all appealing, unlike in cartoons or comics. Which was a bummer, because I would have loved to dip a toe in and see what nuclear superpowers might be bestowed upon me. There were occasional signs directing us towards maintenance hatches and exits. I even stopped short at an intersection between tunnels when I caught sight of a fucking rowboat in a dead-end area.

"The fuck is that for?" I asked.

"Remember what I said about water?" Jenna asked. "That's in case the tunnel floods and you're lucky enough to be down here and close enough to that boat to survive."

"What if there wasn't enough room to get on it?" I couldn't get over the sight of the boat on its own, bobbing gently while chained to the wall.

"If that's the case," Alton said, "you're probably done for if you can't swim to a ladder."

Fun times. "Is there much water here?"

"We're not far from a treatment station, and Station Zero is flanked on the west side by the Gowanus," Jenna said. "The walls are thick as fuck, though, so those aren't an immediate danger unless something breaks through." She laughed. "Or blows it all up like a Batman villain."

I couldn't stop examining the walls. The brickwork and the aging. "And you guys mentioned the trains? How's that work?"

"Good timing," Alton said as we walked through an alcove and emerged in a much taller set of tunnels.

The ground was littered in trash. Old glasses of Pepsi and Styrofoam takeout containers. Rats the size of, well, me. There were tracks, too. I looked down at my feet and realized that we were absolutely standing on them.

"Well, shit," I said.

"Nothing to worry about here. We need to get across and take a ladder down. Station Zero will be right there."

"Well, first is the hard part," Jenna said, a tinge of annoyance in her voice.

"Spill it," I said. "I don't like surprises."

Jenna sighed. "The way into the station was blocked off a long time ago, so there's an... alternate route."

"A foot-wide slit that goes for maybe two hundred feet. It's a tight fit," Alton said, "and sometimes. *Sometimes* it can flood. Only waist deep, though."

"So my naughty bits might get dipped in underground water is what you're saying?" I shivered. "Should've worn like a diaper or something."

“Wouldn’t do anything but get weighed down,” Alton said.

“Okay, expert,” I laughed, delighted.

Alton grunted. “I wasn’t talking from experience.”

“Sure,” I said. “No judgments here in the mole world, Al. Let that freak flag fly.”

We crossed the tracks. I wondered how true all that third rail talk was, but wasn’t about to test that theory. Always thought there was a bit of bullshit behind it, since there was a distinct lack of fried rat on subway tracks. Maybe the rats knew better, though. Maybe they felt that shit from far away. Who knew? They sure as hell didn’t seem to feel any imminent danger from us, given how many times I had to kick the poodle-sized motherfuckers away from me.

The wall at the other end of the tunnel was dangerously close to the tracks; we had to walk like tightrope artists towards a caged maintenance hatch. Alton took the lead and grumbled when he reached the cage.

“They fixed it,” he said.

“Did you bring the cutters?” Jenna asked.

“I learned my lesson last time.” Alton pulled his backpack off. “Give me some light.” He handed me his flashlight.

I held the light on the bag and Alton pulled out a small pair of wire cutters.

“We’re going to need to hide an extra pair near here, and your staff will need to carry them in case they fix this again before your show," he said.

"They really stay on top of this?" I asked.

"Not really. Last time we came here was a year ago. They probably ran a check to see if anyone was living down there. City's real fucking weird about the homeless. They don't want them on the street, but then they don't want them in the place nobody will see them." Alton shrugged. "In the meantime, nobody realizes the solution is to fucking help people."

"I appreciate your moral stance there, Alton. Balances out the diaper thing." I smiled but was sure he couldn't see it.

"We can always work out one of the alternate routes to the show as well," Jenna added, "Like I said, I wanted us to have privacy for this run, but we might be able to sort things out if we pay the right people."

Alton got to work cutting enough space off the cage to let us slip through. Once he was done, he went through and opened the hatch. "Thank God. I was worried they'd locked it with something difficult." He turned to me. "Might want to look into tools to break padlocks—strong ones. Just in case. Even the alternate routes might require them."

"Mental note taken," I said.

The next ladder was a lot longer than the first. Felt like I was climbing down a fucking building after a while. The depth of the city was surprising to me. As if they could fit all of it down there without much trouble, but the dark probably made things seem so much more expansive.

"Any chance we can have folks set up more lighting down here?" I asked.

"Depends on how much time you have between placing lighting and the show," Jenna said. "You go crazy and someone will notice. That said, I think you can buy those stick-on closet lights and go nuts. Those click on, so you won't lose battery if they stay off."

"Didn't Richie almost kill himself because of those things?" Alton asked.

Jenna snorted. "That was because he used wired lamps. Richie was always an idiot. Did you hear he lost his left hand?"

"How the hell did that happen?" Alton asked.

"Gender reveal party for his nephew. I heard it blinded his father-in-law, too," Jenna said. "I knew he was going to do something extra stupid once he left the city."

Whoever this Richie was sounded extremely uninteresting and not related to my problems—which were far more important. "We almost there?" I asked.

"Few more feet. I can see the bottom. There's a little water, so heads up."

A few more seconds and I heard Alton's feet splash below me. "Almost there. It's ankle deep, so it shouldn't be too bad," he said.

"Is it running?" Jenna asked.

"Nope."

I got to the bottom and the water was indeed standing.

The real hint was the dead and bloated something floating a few feet away. Fun.

Alton turned his flashlight on against the far wall of the chamber. There was a large crack at its center. Water dripped from greenish stalactites above. Smelled like motor oil and rotting garbage down there.

"We go through here and it leads to the top of Station Zero," Alton said. "There's a sturdy ramp leading down into the station, so it's a good entrance point even if the spacing is tight here."

The squeeze wasn't as bad as Alton said. It wasn't comfortable, though, and the concrete was wet—maybe sticky—with a very mysterious liquid. As we slowly slid through the crack, I thought about the requirements we'd need to list on the invites to the event. Rain gear was going to be a must. Masks and goggles. I wondered about the feasibility—or point—of having people install hand sanitizer kiosks throughout the space. Maybe at the crack itself?

This was going to be difficult to organize, but entirely possible, so. That was a win.

"You guys have extra maps and layout plans, right?" I asked. "Unless one of you wants to lead the staff down here as we prep."

"Does it pay?" Jenna asked.

"It does indeed pay." I stalled a second as my waders snagged on a little outcropping behind me. "Alton, we almost there?"

"Almost. I can see the walkway now. Nothing looks different. We're clear," he said as he stepped out into the open.

I followed. "Oh fuck."

Station Zero was immense. We had to be maybe thirty, forty feet off the main floor where the unfinished tracks were scattered throughout the tunnel. It was shockingly pristine in the station, as well. Dusty, sure. But no signs of water damage or rat nests. Above us, I heard an active train shuttling by. I turned in place. There was room enough for maybe three to four hundred people. Plenty of ceiling height for Jason to do his little Michelangelo impression, too.

"This is fucking amazing," I said. "How have you guys not made this into a party space before? The fucking money you'd make."

"We've been afraid of exposing it," Alton said. "And logistics planning with just the two of us wouldn't really work, you know?"

I nodded. "I feel that, but I also see a shit ton of potential here, folks." I pointed at Jenna. "When we negotiate your rate top side? We're gonna talk over what it'll take to set something up. This here's an egg that needs laying on."

Station Zero. An untouched place in this city. It could be mine to use, or it could be left to my two nerd friends to brag about with their other weirdo buddies, and I sure as shit wasn't having that. This here was yet another opportunity, and I wasn't going to ask or fret. I was going to snatch it up and make it something special. Something as special as me.

"And no chance this area floods?" I asked, spying a puddle just a little way from us.

"Probably some leaky areas above. The sewers beside us shouldn't be an issue, but like I said, the tunnels will get flooded sometimes. As far as we've seen, nothing makes it down here, though." Jenna cast her flashlight down towards the tracks and into a tunnel. "There's a maintenance hatch over there that might be a better entrance. We'll have to check and see where it leads since my maps are spotty."

"Cool. Cool. Cool," I said, "I'll see what palms we can grease. An easier entry will make folks happier to spend money."

I pulled my phone out—no signal, no surprise—and started taking photos.

We had a lot of planning to do, but this was going to be the motherfucking party of the year.

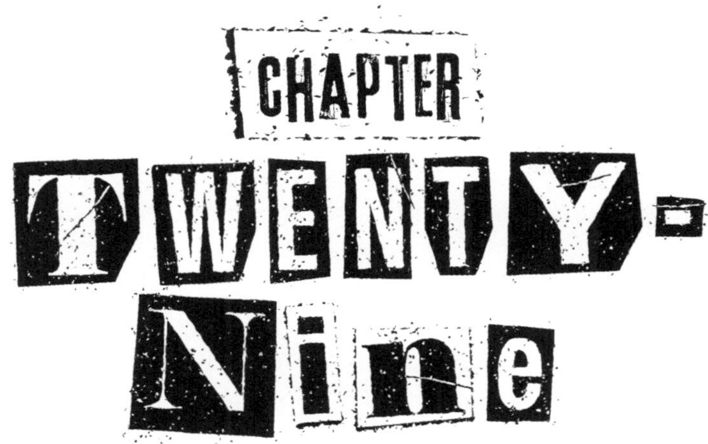

Atticus looked surprised to find me standing out front of Sweet Baby Cheesus. To be fair, I was wearing an outfit that was probably more appropriate for a Day of the Dead parade than a normal afternoon in Coney Island. I wore red and white makeup that gave me a freshly skinned look. It felt appropriate to look this way—dramatic, off-putting. It was going to be that kind of day.

"Is there a theme party in the neighborhood?" Atticus removed his sunglasses and gently placed them into his front shirt pocket. He was wearing a Canadian tuxedo, his denim jacket sleeves and jeans legs rolled up symmetrically. Gross. At least he was making it easier for me to do this.

I rocked back on my heels. "There's always a theme party somewhere. But no. I wanted to look special for your girlfriend."

"I wouldn't necessarily call her my girlfriend." Atticus

stroked his beard. "How did you know I'd be here?"

"I saw you get on the train. Took a cab here to beat you." I went up on my toes and peeked over Atticus' shoulder to make sure that the men Silo sent along were ducking between buildings as they should have been. The fix was in.

This was big. My first real moment in this business. I wondered how I'd report this out. Did the boys let Silo know that I did a good job? Did I give my own evaluation—that felt strangely disingenuous—at the end of the day? Did criminal enterprise even work like that? For the most part, this was all taking each other's word and providing the occasional photographic evidence. I debated launching the recorder app on my phone. Would have been weird to just video the whole thing from the jump.

I was overthinking things. There would be a ruckus and I'd either succeed or fail. That was it. The mark of failure would be obvious, really. If I showed my whole ass, Atticus would more than likely end me right in that cheese shop. I'd bleed out over a sign of Cheesus Christ himself—the viscera having no chance of being consecrated.

Oh, fuck me. Enough of my bullshit, it was time for the show to start.

Atticus sighed. "This is a little uncomfortable, Pop."

I breathed through the annoyance. Not today, Satan. "The fashion or my presence?" I smiled. "Sorry, not enough amphetamines in the coffee this morning. My brain keeps lagging behind my ears."

"Both. But your presence is teasing an alarm bell or twenty."

I smacked Atticus on the arm, not ungently. "I figured it's long overdue for me to third wheel my ass all up in your business, man."

Atticus grimaced. "You don't wear envy well."

"That you get to bone her? Possibly. That she gets to bone you? Mostly pity." I turned on a heel and opened the door. "Come on. We can buy a foolish amount of cheese to prove your love for her."

"It isn't like that." Atticus followed behind me.

"Do you smell burnt toast as well?" I walked into the store with a skip.

"Not since the next to last stop on my train."

"It was probably actual toast then."

The regulars—those older women I saw in the store weeks prior—were there. They stood in a circle, talking in harsh whispers, eyes darting back and forth while their hands danced to accentuate their emotions and punctuate their words. Amity stood holding a wheel of cheese, speaking back to them in broken Russian. She jerked her head up as Atticus and I walked into view, held a hand up, and gave a curt nod—her way of letting us know to avoid the space. The conversation continued. Amity frowned as she repeated several Russian phrases to the women, her tone and body language conciliatory.

"Oh, my, these ladies look amazing." I examined their clothes. "It's like a stage show." I lifted one woman's skirt at the edge. "Oh, dear Cheesus Christ on a cracker, this is completely hand-stitched." I squealed. "Atticus, these ladies are everything I've ever wanted to be: well-worn, potentially violent, and wearing clothes with super sketchy knit work."

The woman turned and spat at the floor in front of me.

Well, fine, asshole. I pay a compliment and that's what I get? Lucky I didn't smack her upside the fucking head.

Atticus pulled me away. "Why don't we give them a minute?" He edged me towards signage for Amity's latest work, Son of Manchego. "I like the little drawing of Lazarus on this one."

I rolled my eyes. "You're nervous. Also, Son of Manchego would have been a much better name for this place."

"Absolutely not to both of those assertions. I mean, if Amity was a man, sure. But for a woman, I think Sweet Baby Cheesus is much better."

"Find me a single stranger that knows what it's about and I'll agree with you."

"How do you hear that name and *not* know it's about cheese?"

The old ladies walked past, each woman with a bag in each hand, filing out without a word. I fought the urge to slap one of the bags out of the next lady's hand. Knew there was more than cheese in those things.

Amity walked over. “Sorry about that. Ladies around here are absolutely *thrilled* about an event I’m helping with.” She smiled at both of us. “Double visit, huh? And fuck, Pop, you’re looking amazing. What’s the occasion?”

Cute. She was calling me Pop now as well. I loved that for her, I really did.

I smiled back. “My emancipation.”

“Yeah, gonna shelve that topic of conversation for another time. But I think you look fucking fabulous.” Amity gave me a side eye. She knew something was up.

Atticus cleared his throat. “I decided—independently—to pop by for a quick visit since I was interested in roaming around and taking some pictures today.” He patted the little bag slung over his shoulder. I hadn’t even noticed it.

“Is that a film camera?” I asked incredulously.

“Yes,” Atticus said. “I wanted to do something different today.”

“Uh-huh. Different. Sure.” Nearly got a cramp holding the eye roll.

Amity pointed out of the shop. “If you know where to look, you can still find a few really weird spots. Old lots and places that used to have rides in them. Not as run down as things used to be, but that old school New York City is always hiding somewhere around here.”

“And I came by because it was my day off from my non-paying job.” I stuck my tongue out at Atticus, playfully.

"You told me you wanted to work for the experience," Atticus countered.

"Take it as light feedback, Atticus." I smirked.

Amity narrowed her eyes. "You don't pay her?"

The front door chime went off, but nobody walked in.

This was it. My time to shine. The moment all the scatter-brained planning and existential panic was leading to. A great betrayal. A moment where Atticus and I stood at opposite sides of a line I had the fucking gumption to finally draw in the sand. I felt dizzy from the terror of it. There was every equal chance this would happen exactly how I wanted or it would end in seconds with a bullet between the eyes and not a word out my mouth. This was nothing like the high from being assertive. I felt like I was swimming in ice water and my body was seconds from giving in—to letting me slip into its grip and dragging me into the ink, never to return again.

Or I had too much coffee that morning—three cups, couldn't sleep.

Still.

The door chimed again.

Atticus turned to look out the window, his hands at his waist. A beat. I saw the look in his eyes shift. Those instincts were still there. Silo was right, Atticus did still have the potential to be dangerous—but I had to count on the emotions to get us over the line. I knew I could do this. I knew I could convince him to walk away.

Atticus drew his pistol from his back holster. Glass

shattered and the display case behind him nearly exploded. I dove towards Amity, tackling her to the ground and pulling her closer to the nearest counter as far away from the front of the shop as possible. I worried she wasn't screaming but felt her breath against me.

"You okay?" I asked into her hair.

I got a quivering nod as a reply. Small win.

I turned myself onto my back as Atticus doubled back to check on us.

"Did they get you?" He stared at Amity. No acknowledgment of me or the fact that I clearly went to help her instead of clapping back like a fucking brute.

"Get going, dummy." I waved Atticus off. "We're fine."

Atticus stutter stepped a moment, doubt in his eyes, before he gave chase.

He was going to be busy. We had time now.

I stood up and painstakingly brushed the errant glass from my skirt until, finally, I sighed in satisfaction: work done. I didn't help Amity up. Instead, I traipsed behind the counter and fetched a cheese knife, selecting the closest wheel of cheese and slicing a thin piece off. "What was that all about?" I slipped the cheese into my mouth. It threatened to melt on my tongue. It was a little sweet. Very nutty. Amity was very good at this. Silo would be smart to keep her alive. He could dominate the NYC cheese industry. Give Velveeta a run for its money—and, fuck, Velveeta was some magical shit.

Amity stood up, red and out of breath. "What? The

gun?" She turned to me. "It was a fucking psycho with a gun. And, hey, did Atticus have a gun too?" She rubbed her temples. "They really couldn't have been that mad, could they?"

"Oh, that?" I snorted. We'd get to that in a minute. "I don't care about all that." I cut another piece of cheese. "I meant the golden oldie Bratva that was in here before. What's the deal? Why were they pissed off?"

Amity surveyed the damage to her store. "Jesus." She walked towards the front. "These windows were original to the fucking building. Fuck me."

"Amity." I said it with conviction—like a teacher at the end of the long day.

"What?"

"You didn't answer my question."

"I—" Amity exhaled. "There's a lot going on here all at once, and to be honest, you're being a little too fucking weird for me, dude. That get up alone. What the fuck is wrong with you? Why did Atticus have a gun?"

"I thought you liked the outfit."

"I liked it until it became a part of a pattern I'm incapable of understanding, Poppy." She raised her hands towards the front of the store. "Again, what the fuck? Why the fuck?" She let out a stressed laugh. "I don't know what I should be doing right now. Why am I even in here with you?"

I propped myself up onto the counter, wheel of cheese on my lap and the knife plunged into it. I used my thumb to dab at the corners of my mouth and pulled a compact out to inspect my makeup. I frowned: some of the shading that made my cheeks look sunken in had smudged. Goddammit. "Well, you're stuck with me, and I think you're going to want to answer my questions. Matter of fact," I said, "I know you are."

"Oh, yeah?" Amity asked. The sass on this one. "And why is that?"

I grinned. "Because, you big dummy, I'm here to save your life."

Amity grabbed a broom and began to sweep up the broken glass. Her eyes darted back and forth as her hands trembled. It was obvious she needed to busy herself with the mundane to keep from screaming.

I think I felt like that too, once. I think I even tried screaming a few times. When I saw all that got accomplished from that was a sore throat and the occasional noise complaint, I realized it wasn't worth letting it out. It was better to take all that anger—all that confusion and resentment and despair—and put it to good use. I wasn't a fan of bottling shit up—that was dumb—but a car wasn't going to move unless you filled the tank up some.

"You're not even gonna ask what I'm talking about?"

Amity stared at the ground. She'd swept the same place three times. "I need to clean up."

"Uh-huh. Clean up. Not call the cops. Not run out of here screaming murder." I crossed my legs. "I need clarification, then. Is it because of the cocaine you're selling or is it something else? Because you realize someone shot into your store and there's a damn good chance—" I checked my phone's clock— "that someone called the cops. Since this is, you know, a fucking city."

Amity dropped the broom. "Oh, fuck."

"Yep."

"Oh, fuck me, fuck me." Amity nearly sprinted at me. "You need to help me. You need to help me now, Poppy. You said you were saving my life, right?"

"Well, from entirely different things, but sure."

Amity closed her eyes and rubbed them with her right thumb and pointer finger. "We can get to your shit later. Right now, I've got twelve bags filled with drugs that need to disappear. Can you help me make them disappear?"

I was already texting Eddie and Bill. "On it. I got my boys outside. They can get your shit in the car." On cue, Eddie and Bill walked into the store. I nodded towards the back. "Bags are over there, right?"

Amity's eyes widened. "Um, yes?" She watched the boys walk into the back. "Who are they?"

"My boys," I said, as if that explained everything. Quite frankly, it explained everything that Amity needed to know.

Eddie and Bill got the product and walked back out. They both smiled kindly at Amity. My boys were good boys.

"They'll bring it to my apartment," I said. "And don't

worry, I don't fuck with coke. Got tired of that shit in my twenties."

Amity blinked. She turned in place, then back around.

"Remember to breathe, girl."

Amity took a deep breath. "Why do you have henchmen?"

I laughed. "Same reason why Atticus has a gun, Amity. Come on, you know you can put two and two together. I'd rather you say it before I do."

A tear finally rolled down her cheek—finally going through with the threat in her eyes the whole time. At some point, it would've broken my heart, but today was my day and nothing was going to stop my high.

"Why did he have a gun, Amity?"

"Fuck." Amity punched the counter. "Fuck. I didn't even fucking—it was a one-time thing. I needed extra money."

I had no idea what that was about, but I figured we "yes, and" this one. "Yeah, well, you fucked up and pissed the wrong people off. You pissed off the kind of people that employ men like Atticus to clean up the things they find distasteful."

"He was supposed to…" Amity pointed at me. "But *you* work for him."

Was this blonde cheese witch trying to turn all this around on me? The gall.

"I did." I frowned. "It was why I turned up originally. I didn't agree with the job. It wasn't fair. You were trying to do better for you, and I understood that because I've been trying to do better for myself for a long fucking time. I hated that there was an invisible line some asshole set without anyone else knowing that meant you—or anyone—deserved to get hurt or worse just for trying."

Amity's eyes were still wet, but there was anger there. "You didn't tell me."

"I figured I could get you out of trouble without anyone knowing. Then Atticus decided to make his own moves, and here we are."

"Was he trying to help me, too?"

I shrugged. "I want to say yes to make you feel better, but I don't think so. Atticus is in the middle of a moment right now. Maybe it's a midlife crisis. Maybe it's a crisis of conscience. I don't think what he's done is as much about you as it is about him."

Amity chewed her lip. She wiped her eyes and straightened her shoulders. I admired her in that moment, I really did. Her brain was probably going a million miles an hour, but she knew she had to keep her shit together. That was what I saw in her initially. That kinship. We were two people who had to keep running because if we stopped, we'd die.

"And what about you?" she asked. "Why did you decide to do this now?"

A moment of truth. Fuck it. Give it to her straight. "Because I do care about you. But also, because exposing Atticus serves my plans, as well. That's the long and short of it."

Amity turned and stared out the broken windows of her shop. "Do you know where he went?"

"I can find him." I hopped off the counter. "How come?"

"Because I want to kick his fucking ass."

We found Atticus sprawled out in a back alley behind an old bumper car attraction two blocks away. Was that Donna Summers I heard from inside? If shit wasn't so weird, I'd have run in to check. Maybe do a little dancing. I made a mental note to add her to my playlist. What a fucking crime I didn't already have her on there.

Atticus rolled over and, slowly, got onto his knees. He looked like he was in pain. Took him near a full minute to get onto his feet. I didn't have the empathy to call out a warning of the blonde hurricane behind me, though, so. Seeing him back on his ass was going to be entertaining.

"You piece of shit." Amity sprinted at him with her right hand aloft and came in with the tightest fucking hook I've ever seen outside of a boxing ring.

It sent Atticus reeling. On the ground, he lifted his hands in surrender. "Amity, please—"

Amity spit on him and turned. She ran off as fast as she ran in.

Me, I stood in this alley, dancing between pieces of junk. I felt like I was radiating pure fucking sunshine;

a child living in a dilapidated wonderland of glass and shredded paper. And there was the great Atticus Garcia, the gentleman hitman of Brooklyn, taken down a goddamn peg. Humility looked good on him.

"Why did you do this?" Atticus spit as he tried to roll over.

"You lost your edge, and you betrayed me more than once," I said. "So, yeah, Atticus. You lost my loyalty. Surprise."

"You're leaving me without many options here."

I hopped over a large pool of shattered glass. "Far as I see it, there's only one: you disappear. Go live the life you want to live. Open a bakery. Go groom cockatiels. I hear Silver City, New Mexico is fucking wonderful. They have a jazz festival and everything."

Atticus struggled to stand. "You've supplanted me."

"Not entirely, but enough." I stopped hopping and alternated leaning my head left, then right. "You made your choice the moment you decided getting your dick wet was a path to redemption. How am I supposed to work for a person like that? How could I possibly allow myself to stay in limbo to entertain your little bout of ennui?" I scoffed. "Nah, Atticus. You made the bed; you lie in it. I'm destined for much more than dressing and feeding you."

"I killed quite a few of those men. I take it they were yours?"

"Silo's."

"Jesus. I knew something was wrong that night you had that little sidebar with him." Atticus sat up, slowly. "After everything I've imparted to you. I taught you to use guns. Taught you to use knives. How to iron perfect pleats in any kind of pant." He pointed at me. "You're lucky I lost my piece."

Adorable. An empty threat. Like I didn't have my boys ready to come at the first signal. "Listen, man, I appreciate being the most lethal version of Mr. Belvedere that ever lived, but not once did you offer to upgrade me. Whether it was a networking opportunity or a stipend—you didn't offer it. Instead, you got everything you wanted from me without ever so much as an ounce of gratitude. Without ever checking in to see if *my* needs were being met."

"You offered your services for free," he barked, as if I needed reminding.

"Almost six fucking years ago, Atticus. I didn't expect to *still* be working for free while you were debating whether you should date a girl half your age or get dangly earrings."

The face he made.

"See? I knew you were thinking of piercings." I sighed. "Whatever. It's all done now. Doesn't matter."

"I have no idea what that means."

I skipped over to him. I wasn't falling into his bullshit sad sack trap. This wasn't a discussion on his terms. It was on mine. "This is my resignation, Atticus. Also, a one-time warning."

"Warning?" Atticus staggered up to his feet, gingerly stroking his side.

Fine. Serious for this part. "You went soft at some point. No idea how, no idea when. I am doing you the favor of a graceful exit that does not involve an exit wound. Get the fuck out of Brooklyn and nobody bothers you again. Stay, and I can't guarantee a fucking thing." I gave him a level stare.

Atticus shook his head. He moved quickly—even in his injured state—and had a hand around my neck in the blink of an eye. "Say that again?"

I frowned. He was so predictable. So, honestly, disappointing. "I was really hoping this would be a conscious uncoupling, Atticus." Cool. Plan B it was. I whistled between my teeth.

Almost all the doors in the alley opened at once. Behind each, a man with a large gun.

B was for Big Fucking Guns.

"You were a fun side hustle, Atticus. An alternate angle. And, yeah, it worked out at the start." I was calm, even with his hand around my throat. I knew he wouldn't do a damn thing. I knew him. "Truthfully? I didn't owe you shit, and you were too fucking blind to see me for what I was and what I am. You're the dishonest one here. Not me."

Atticus let out a long hiss of air through his nostrils. "Silo really signed off on this? Because I'm wondering if that's another line of your bullshit."

"You willing to take that chance?" Bluff, Poppy, bluff because I didn't have anything left to work with.

Atticus loosened his grip and looked around, seemingly taking in the scenery. The boy was despondent—like someone who got told his crush wasn't going to prom with them. "I fucked up. I really fucked up."

I watched him and backed away, slowly, so as not to trigger anything rash. "You are an amazing man, Atticus Garcia, but you aren't meant to continue this way. Neither am I. I'm meant for something better. You're meant to take the L and retire."

"I still had more left in the tank."

"We both know that's not true. The minute you left that skillet behind, we both knew you were done."

Atticus stared at the ground and stroked his beard. "That was the moment?"

"It was the moment for *you*. You're the pro, man; you knew damn well that was weakness. Nobody worth a shit in this business would fuck up like that. But let me add, you did it with something that was traceable to *my* ass."

"If you're trying to say I betrayed you first—"

"Trying? Motherfucker, I'm being blatant about it. I fucking catered to your every whim, and the very least you could do was *pack up that fucking pan*. But you didn't. You didn't because deep down in that pea brain, the one that chose murder as a living instead of doing anything with a point, you see me as someone who's not worth the consideration." I had heat. No way of holding it back. I wanted to pull back because he didn't deserve this. He didn't deserve to know how much he hurt me, how much he let me down, but I needed to air it out. I needed to say these things because it was fucking exhausting to carry the baggage around on my back day in and day out. "You are not the first or last to do that but fuck me if I was going to keep taking it on the chin, Atticus. Not anymore. I'm taking what's due to me because I worked for it. Not because I found an easy route or because I fell ass backwards into it thanks to my connections. You slipped. I'm just sliding into your space." I closed my hands into fists and stared at them. I relished the feeling of my nails as they dug into my palms.

I should have told the boys to shoot him right where he stood. To let bullets and fire replace my words, let them be a surrogate of all this toxic waste that had been sitting in my belly for so many years. And while I knew all of it wasn't Atticus—that was impossible—he was the right shape to dump it into. He was the willing receptacle of my rage and I wanted to fill it in every possible way.

But I didn't. I was still more afraid than I was angry, and I wish I fucking knew why.

"Fine." Atticus raised his hands. "Can I leave now?"

Cute. I knew he'd play apathy. Didn't matter. What mattered was it was all out in the open. He'd lost. I'd won. "That look in your eyes—I'd go to a hospital if I was you. But yeah, Atticus. You can leave."

Three straight nights of knocking. Only for fifteen minutes at a time. Only right after dinner. Didn't want to be a fucking stalker about it.

Finally, Amity opened her apartment door.

She stared at me in silence.

I'd decided to go full neutral. Wore a simple black T-shirt, jeans, and a cute pair of old school Pumas I'd copped years back but never wore. I wanted her to know this wasn't the typical Poppy Leathers visit. This was something more heartfelt.

I clapped my hands together. "Hi."

Amity stifled a laugh. "Jesus, that's what you got?"

"I have no idea what else to say."

"You've knocked on my door the better part of the week and all you had when I opened it up was 'hi.' Jesus, all of you are fucking morons."

"Can I come in, at least? We can order Chinese? Talk it over?"

"Talk it over? Talk what over, Pop, the contract on my life?"

"Poppy."

Amity scoffed. "I think I deserve to be a little disrespectful here." She eyed me. "Are you ready to tell me how much you're ransoming off my product for?"

Amity looked at me like I was a stranger. Gone was that familiarity, that way she made me feel like we'd known each other forever. I realized that was bullshit just from that look. That I had no idea what hate looked like on Amity, but this felt pretty close to it.

Her product? The cocaine? Was that the problem? Not Atticus, but the drugs. "Whoa, whoa, whoa. That stuff is still where it was brought, under my protection. Nobody knows I have that shit. It's yours if you want it." I pulled out my phone. "I can have it all here within the hour." I failed at hiding the anger in my voice. The fucking nerve of her to accuse me of ransoming her product. As if I ever gave the impression that I was the type to be that kind of sleazy.

"Dude, I'm not about to hold that much product in my own house." Amity turned. "Fuck it. Come inside before a neighbor sees. Word of warning: I have a gun."

There was no way she had a gun. And even if she did, I knew damn well she wouldn't know how to use the stupid thing. I walked in but kept close to the door when I closed it.

Amity sat down in her living room and tucked her

legs up to her chest. “Three fucking days straight,” she said, holding up a copy of a book called *Razorblade Tears*, “trying to distract myself. I can’t keep my focus for more than two or three pages at a time. And I’ve been wanting to read this book for fucking ever.” She sighed, staring at the cover. “But I guess having a hit out on me is a bit distracting, isn’t it?

“I knew it was stupid to trust Atticus. He was strange. Stiff. Sure, cute as hell, but there was something about him that always made the hairs stand up at the back of my neck, you know? Whenever it felt like a wall was coming down, there was always an immediate retreat that followed. It felt like I was dating a cat sometimes. Affection came sporadically. The feeling I was being hunted was always there.”

“I’m sorry, Amity. I wanted…”

“I’m not done talking,” Amity snapped.

I nodded apologetically. Let her get it out, I figured. The more she railed against Atticus, the less poison she could send my way—hopefully.

“The man is a goddamn predator, and it pisses me off that not only have I locked myself away in my apartment—which I fucking hate—but that I have to sit here with you talking about him like he should matter this much. It’s… it’s sticking to my ribs, this feeling, like I’m burning up.” She stared at me. “Can you begin to understand that? It’s like I’m on fire and drowning at the same time, Pop. And some of this is your fault, too.” A finger drifted my way. “You could have warned me off. It didn’t have to be, ‘Oh, hey, by the way, this dude might kill you.’ It could have just been a lie. Fuck, you could have told me he had herpes or something.”

I didn’t know what to say. That I hadn’t thought of the impact on her was obvious, and frankly, that didn’t even make me feel all that bad. My best skill was reacting. I knew that—I’d known that from the beginning. I planned, sure, but plans rarely fell in place perfectly. No amount of preparation left a person ready to handle the hiccups that demanded improvisation. Did I plan to use Atticus’ feelings for Amity against him? Yes. Did I give thought to what that would do to her, even if she’d survived? Yes. But I didn’t really care.

Which landed on my shoulders like bird shit. I didn’t really care, did I? I couldn’t figure that part out. It could have been the moment. A tinge of guilt, or shame. The anger being directed at me. I couldn’t figure out if my feelings were rooted in real compassion for Amity or if I was just a six-year-old upset at the fact that I’d gotten caught.

“You talk now,” Amity said. “Or I’ll scream.”

I didn’t know what I wanted to say, but: reacting. This was my chance to do what I do best. To feel my way through. “I don’t have a word for whatever it is you’re feeling, but you’re right to feel it,” I said carefully. “I also can’t stand here and apologize like that’s going to fix everything, or like it’s going to be entirely true. I didn’t want things to be this way." I smiled. "I wanted to have something with you. You know that. Something more than what we had."

"Are you trying to say that none of this would have happened if I'd chosen you instead of Atticus?"

"Holy shit, no. Not at all."

"Then why are you here, Pop?"

Something bubbled in my guts. I knew she was right to be mad, but she kept calling me "Pop," and honestly, it was worse coming out of her mouth than anyone else's. Like being slapped extra hard. It felt like any respect from her was gone and now I was just this *thing* in her life. An impediment. Something she wanted to go away.

"I don't know," I said.

I really didn't. Part of me thought I could salvage things with Amity, that I could make things better. And it wasn't being lovesick that made me want that. I knew Amity was a thread, and it worried me that leaving her like this would come back to me—or worse, Silo. I didn't want to end up at square one with her.

Amity stood and walked closer to me. She watched me and shook her head. "You used me, didn't you? For whatever it is you wanted. To get Atticus out of your way. No big deal however it worked out, right? I'm just some idiot, cheesemaking, drug dealing asshole."

"It's not like that. Amity, I really think that—"

"But it is. Since we met, it's only been a few weeks, but I've seen the change in your demeanor. I've seen how your clothes are a little flashier. The guys you can call to get things. You were politicking. This entire fucking mess was a power move for you."

I dropped my hands to my side. "Amity, I… it's not a personal thing. It wasn't supposed to be like that. I've got plans, and I needed to make the move now. It was either that or—"

"Or let me die? Are you going to play like putting me through this is better than the alternative? Dude, absolutely none of the options are good. Nobody comes out on top in any scenario here." Her eyes watered, reddened. "But I liked you. I thought we were friends. I told you I didn't have any friends. I didn't have time for that, but you… made me want to make the time." Amity struck her thigh with the bottom of her fist. "Goddammit, I fucked up. I should have kept the course, like you." She scoffed. "I wish I could do that, Pop. I really do."

"I wasn't going to let anything happen to you," I insisted. "I had contingencies. I had ideas. Ways to work out an escape. And it *did* work out. Atticus is gone. My boss isn't willing to do this job right now, and I know I can push him to squash it entirely. I've got my hands on the wheel and I promise you I can get us through this."

Amity stared past me and blinked. "There's no us anymore, Pop. You risked my life, maybe even my grandfather's. You risked my business. I've been gone three days, and there are people who are probably getting ready to kill me either way, thinking I ran off with their product." Amity turned and started to pace. "You've made shit worse. Shit's out of control, and I'm the one who needs to take it all back."

"Amity, listen—" I blinked back tears. "I don't know if the right word is love, but what I felt for you, what I *feel* right now? I think it's as close to love as anything can be." Tears? Why the fuck was I crying? Why was I telling her these things? It was driving me insane. The emotions, this feeling of weakness that didn't feel quite right. Was Amity really what I wanted or...

Or did I simply want to control the narrative?

"Fuck you." She came back at me with a sneer. She saw right through me. "I want my coke back and then I want you to tell your boss that you fucked up royally. That you not only poked an Albanian mob, but that the cops are going to be involved, too. I'm not letting this shit stand." Amity went back to pacing. "No. Fuck this. I'm blowing it all wide open, Pop. You wanted to stir things up? Fine. Now you and Atticus can run off and hide forever in some bumblefuck town. I worked too fucking hard to be where I am to let you decide to walk all over that work, for what, to play crime boss? Someone like you? You're a fucking glorified executive assistant, Pop. You're not a boss. You're a fucking likable weirdo with delusions of grandeur.

"And love? Jesus. We've had enough time together to check each other out, maybe want to fuck around. But love? You're out of your fucking mind. I thought we could be friends, Pop. And yeah, I thought you were hot. But you want to know why I chose Atticus, in the end? Because I could see all of your red flags from a fucking mile away, and nobody with an ounce of sanity would have chosen differently."

I took a long breath at that one. She was mad at me. It made sense. She was allowed the low blows. I still needed to turn this around. It was what was best for both of us. But how could I convince her I cared if she was very aware that I was in this for myself?

"I mean, you're the fucking *help*," Amity snapped. She was still going. "You're a fucking servant who decided to play the game and went way over her head because she didn't have the fucking range for it. I mean, what have you built, Pop? What have you ever made? I made my business. I made my side hustle. I worked on making it into what it is now and will be. And you, a glorified babysitter, think you can do better? You know what my grandfather taught me about people like you? That you were like, like..." She threw her hands in the air. "Like single serve utensils. Good for the moment, but meant for the trash."

Amity was too close now and way too fucking personal. I held my hands up. "Amity, I get that you're mad. I do. But you need to tone it down."

"Tone it down? Tone it fucking down?" Amity hit me. A punch to the chest.

I was surprised she hadn't hit me sooner, honestly. I

let it pass. It almost felt good, the physical contact, knowing that she wanted to be close to me, to touch me, even if she'd chosen violence. I let the next dozen punches pass, as well. By then, I was angry, sure. I'd thought she was better than her words. But I watched her face crumple as her weak little fists made contact, watched as her lips twitched, watched her mean every single word she'd just said.

No: even with anger as her excuse, I could see the look in her eye. That look was something I always got, sooner or later. Just wasn't expecting it from her. Disdain. Disgust. Something with a "d." And while I knew this was a special case—I knew my actions were awful and even dangerous—I couldn't get that look out of my head.

This was who Amity was—her anger justified, but opening the door to the person who she'd been inside the whole damn time. She didn't respect me—she never did. Amity saw in me a friend. But like she said, she had no friends. There had to be a reason for that. I knew that from the start. Maybe I deluded myself a little to find some kinship with her, but that was stupid of me.

"Get me my drugs," Amity spat, "and then you need to disappear, because they're all coming, and I don't give a shit what happens to you when they do. I fucking swear to God, Pop. I have something I want done, just like you, and I don't care who ends up underfoot."

"I told you it wasn't like that." I couldn't stop fucking lying. It was totally like that now. It was like hearing myself. I wanted all the things Amity wanted and more. I wanted to achieve, to control, and be more than I ever was. I wanted the things that stood in my way to either clear a path or deal with the weight of my stilettos—because fuck them, I was going to do exactly what I set out to do. "Or maybe it is." I sighed. It was exhausting lying to her and lying to myself. "But when we first met—"

"Oh, fuck you, 'when we first met'—please, it was always like that. Maybe you're just too craven or stupid to realize that. You can't keep trying to pretend that you're innocent when you've done all the work. You aren't the passive party here, Pop."

I closed my eyes. She needed to stop calling me that. It wasn't helping. "Just breathe and think about this, Amity."

"*Think?*" Amity began to hit me again.

I moved in closer and grabbed her by the shoulders. "Stop it."

Amity tried to pull away. "Fuck you."

I pulled her in closer. My hands drifted to the sides of her head. I touched my forehead to hers. "Amity, please."

"You fucked up so bad," she muttered. "So fucking bad."

"I know. I know that now."

I felt her breath against my face. Hot, wet. There was a hint of raspberry lip balm. It was nice. She sniffed. Tears fells from her eyes and down her face. We remained quiet. I closed my eyes and tried to imagine a better set of choices. A way to please her and move on with my life. We could do that. We could live in a world without acknowledging one another, ever again. I could do my thing and she could do hers. I was a target for her anger, but Silo and Atticus were at fault, not me.

"I will not let you eat me alive," Amity said. "I've worked too hard."

"Listen," I said, still holding her close, "I'll get your product. I'll leave. We can all go back to what we were doing before things went south. Back to the worlds we had set up for ourselves before Atticus."

Amity shook her head gently. "That can't happen, Pop. Not anymore. If I don't do something, I die either way. I don't have a choice anymore. You made this happen."

No choice. There was always a choice. Always a solution.

I pulled away from her to look into her eyes. My hands drifted to her cheeks and I wiped them clean with my thumbs. I really liked her face. Her big eyes. Her slightly crooked nose. Her lips.

I kissed her. Pulled her right in and kissed her. Snotty nose and all. It didn't matter. I wanted to feel this.

Amity didn't respond with surprise, just fell right into the rhythm. Her arms wrapped around me and it was primal. A raw moment that had festered between us for so long. A release we both needed. All that emotion. The chaos. The threats. It built up, just to this quiet moment between us, and I felt this tremendous pressure begin to release from my chest and through my shoulders, down my arms to my hands. My eyes were clenched shut so hard they burned. My teeth trembled from how hard my jaw was clenched. My knuckles began to hurt from the pressure of my hands.

My hands.

My hands around her neck.

I opened my eyes. Amity's face was ever so slightly blue, her hands gently slapping at me. My grip loosened a little at the realization. What was I doing? How could I be doing this? But then Amity's own words came back to me. What had I built? What would place me above my station, for once? Wouldn't doing what Silo originally intended bring me there?

She'd wanted to judge me, to act like she was better than I was just because she inherited a business and some money and had the luxury to pretend she did it all herself. I was self-made. I was the person building something from nothing. I wasn't the impediment, *she* was. All her threats, all her yelling. She was right, we couldn't go on as if nothing happened, but I could go on. I could move forward and build what I was meant to build.

I tightened my grip. Once more, with feeling.

I couldn't stop. Nothing in the universe could stop me at that moment. I stared at my hands and the words were in my head, "stop," but nothing happened. Every time I thought to pull away, I just tightened the grip, as if they were operating completely separately from my mind. Blood began to pool around my fingernails, the chipped face of Catriona MacColl slowly being overtaken by the red.

Amity's tongue rolled out of her mouth. The tongue I'd felt against mine seconds ago. The mouth I so desperately wanted to taste. The life in her wet eyes gone.

I made my choice.

And then, when it was done, when I could feel the slackening of life underneath my hands, I finally let go and Amity dropped to the ground. I stared at her body. She lay there in a clumsy position, one arm above her head and her legs tucked under her. The loose end was loose, undone. That was what she always was: a loose end. Silo understood that. Atticus and I didn't. That was my mistake. I never needed her for anything more than moving Atticus out of my way and once that was done, all those feelings I convinced myself were there melted away. She was right, I had wanted innocence in this. I wanted her to force my hand so I could blame her, but that was wrong. If I wanted to be something more than I was, I needed to accept that this was my goal.

A lot to think about whenever I was alone, I guessed.

I scanned the apartment for anything that could help build the story of her suicide. Had to be a hanging. Maybe in the shower. The recent fracas at her shop. The disappeared boyfriend. It all lined up. Even if the cops thought her end was sketchy, none of it would fall on me. Atticus would need to deal with that.

A parting gift to him from me. A lot bigger than a forgotten skillet.

CHAPTER thirty-two

Silo Jotter stood overseeing a row of capybaras as thoroughly vetted, small-handed women milked the massive rodents. The milkmaids' thin fingers were nimble, more capable of coaxing the precious fluids from the capybaras' teats.

Any normal day, the view would have been classified as completely fucked up.

This was not a normal day.

I was wearing a ratty tank top as a dress with superhero leggings and a pair of platform boots that gave me an easy seven inches of extra height. I needed a distraction, and the capybaras looked eager to provide that. I dawdled by one of the animals. It was docile—happy enough to be there. "I think I understand the appeal of these little bastards." I crouched and scratched the capybara behind the ear. "I want a chariot drawn by them. I'd be the Rat Queen of Bushwick Fuck-All." It felt nice to be "me" for a minute before that would all need to tumble down.

There were more than a dozen young men in the room. They all came off as twitchy—overly nervous. I figured recent events with Atticus didn't help matters. I wondered how many of these guys were rookie wannabes more invested in the appearance of looking prepared and tough than being a fraction of either.

That was a good thing. It meant I was still winning—even if Silo was putting on appearances to convince me otherwise, or if I wasn't feeling particularly like a winner, at that. There was a time I thought all of this would be easy.

I think I may have been wrong.

Silo smiled widely at me. "Capybara milk sells for $36 a gallon."

I gawked. "Fuck your mother. What psycho would drink rat milk?"

"A few thousand psychos, in fact. They swear it provides an immunity boost, that capybara milk has properties better than mother's milk," Silo said. "You'd be amazed how many pediatricians swear by it. Convinced it will prevent allergies and make their babies into the next great Olympians."

I raised a brow. "That sounds like the kind of bullshit that magically appears online when some asshole about to lose his shirt to a malpractice suit starts squawking about Vaseline giving you diabetes."

Silo crouched and petted a capybara at his feet. "Amazing how studies are timed."

"Isn't it?" I sat and continued ogling the capybara. The animals were oddly soothing. Petting them made the feeling of Amity's neck fade away from my tactile memory. The smell of raspberry still lingered in the air.

Or maybe I was a step away from having a stroke. "So, about current events."

"You mean the events where my former best employee killed four of my men, disappeared, and my newest employee killed a target despite being told we were freezing that contract?"

I pointed at Silo. "Those. Definitely not the voicemail I left asking about the market on used panties." I couldn't help it. I had to divert the mood. Couldn't allow things to get morose. Melancholy was like mold. The moment it started to grow, it was a bitch to get rid of.

Silo turned. "I know a guy in Queens. The reselling market on panties is lucrative in Staten Island especially."

Silo gave as good as he took, though. Sucked some of the fun out of fucking with his balance. "Amity couldn't be helped. She started to threaten me—you, too. She was going to call the Albanian mob, the cops, anyone who would give her a measure of revenge."

Silo stopped his work and walked over to me. "And you made a decision."

"I certainly did."

"First time?"

I hadn't thought of that. Well, in the past hour. "Yes. First time."

"Not your first violent outburst, though," Silo said. "I heard about LLL. I also did some fascinating reading about an incident at the Metropolitan Museum of Art where a new registrar broke twenty-two bones in a sixty-six-year-old administrator's hand."

"My history of violence is, at best, a footnote."

"Murder's a chapter, Poppy. Don't pretend it's a paragraph. It ain't." Silo crouched down to my level. Studying me. I wanted to know what he saw in me, now—if he could tell the difference. I wanted to know how it had changed me. If it made me more the woman I'd been trying to become. I didn't dare ask him. "You did right, though. I've got men ensuring it all goes over the way it should. Got that cocaine back in the cheese shop, too. If the cops find it before those old ladies, fine with me."

"And Atticus?" I needed to know if he was still an active threat or a potential threat. Did I need to press Silo to handle things? Would it be better for me to track the man down with my own boys? Maybe clean that board with bleach. There was some annoyance that Silo wouldn't have squashed things himself—it felt like the boss's responsibility—and I was apprehensive to take the full initiative. Though, if Silo was dragging his feet on that, should I have been worried?

"In the wind. We're being watchful."

"You think he's going to pop back up?"

Silo sighed. “Not sure. He and I have history. I’m hoping that keeps him away. Maybe we can reconcile once things have cooled off.”

I knew there was more to their relationship, but that was as close as Silo ever got to being open with me about his own life. I wondered what their history was like. Should have asked when I could find a fuck to give. That he was hopeful of reconciliation was worrying. What if a part of that reunion meant an end for me?

“I guess I have some reservations about his status, if I think long enough about it,” I said.

“Yet you jumped head-first into whatever it is you two had. What? An internship? You knew who and what Atticus was, and you chose to become his assistant.”

“You telling me you wouldn’t launch yourself at a networking opportunity like that? To get myself in front of a man like Silo Jotter?”

Silo scratched his nose. “That you knew who we were worried me. Maybe it still does.”

I was annoying him. I could see how stiff he stood, how his eyes were just a little narrowed. I was a little more careful before when Atticus was an actual factor, but with his absence and the change in my status, I felt better being me around Silo. It was a gamble; I could still draw his ire at any moment, but with every dip of my toe in that piranha-infested pool, I kept finding that nothing was willing to nibble. Had to wonder if that meant Silo liked me or if there was anything more to that. Maybe he felt exposed without Atticus around. Could I have accidentally stumbled onto something with that? Made the emperor aware of his lack of clothes? That would have been fun, no?

I continued, "Y'all are far from fucking discreet. Biggest open secret in all of Brooklyn. And Brooklyn is fucking weird, even when it comes to its criminal element."

Silo pointed to himself and then back to me. "And what about us? Aren't we weird?"

"We wear the skins, but you sure as hell don't fall in line with the rest of these people. Admit it: the hit was about the cocaine, wasn't it? I saw some of Amity's product in the Village, for fuck's sake. That had to be an issue."

Silo choked back a laugh. "The cocaine? Look, I still do some dabbling in the drug trade, but I never gave a damn who was selling where. Cut my teeth on weed, but I got the hell out of that dead end job as soon as I could. My money is invested in more niche markets, Poppy. That girl threatened one of them, so I made my move."

"Oh." It really was all over cheese. Fucking cheese.

"You're making a face that leads me to believe you're having a hard time understanding my motivation. Think less of the product and more of the long-term earnings. I have goals, Poppy, and those goals were at risk." Silo stood up and groaned as his knees made a sound like cellophane. "Just like your baby business thing. There's potential, right?"

"Well, yeah."

"And you see profit in the future for you if you simply grab it. But the impediments need clearing." Silo walked over to a backpack sitting on a bench near a little pack of capybara snuggled up in a pile. He fished out some paperwork and walked it over to me. "Speaking of," he said. "Got the lowdown on your little endeavor. With everything mostly cleared up, I decided it was time to state my terms and formalize this little relationship of ours."

I took the paperwork. All the info on Frankie's set up. Home addresses. Satellite locations she had set up for the work. Lots of info on that Stanley guy that treated us to lunch. Looked like he wasn't only a middleman, but quite the enforcer. He kept things clean for Frankie. Made the problems magically go away.

Silo bit his lower lip. "I need to confirm what you think this partnership will be, Poppy. I believe the angst between you and Atticus was derived entirely from your belief that there was equality between the two of you."

I shook my head. "No. I know where we stand, Silo. I don't take the knee as easily as other people, but I'm not fucking blind. That said, you endorsed my aspirational, eh—zeal? That a good word for it?"

"You make me money, Miss Leathers. You back up this attitude? You and I can work together without issue. But if all this talk is bluster, you disappear into the goddamn Gowanus. Aspiration is admirable, but there's a fine line between aspiration and being a bullshit artist."

"Cool. Happy we can start off with honesty." Yeah, we could swing this for as long as needed. But the cracks were showing already. I wasn't going to ignore those signs again so I could find myself underfoot for another five—or worse—ten years. So long as Silo let me run things how I saw fit, we'd be in a good situation. Unfortunately, the pessimist in me didn't see that lasting awfully long. I made a mental note: plan for the removal of Silo Jotter. A back pocket project. Something to use if there was an emergency. Big fucking gamble. Insane gamble, really. Silo was still obscured in lots of smoke and there was always a chance that once it cleared, the hype was true. There was also the simple answer: that Silo was as much of a punk as Atticus, and maybe even more so without his number one hitter.

It was terrifying to think about those next steps, but I had to. If Amity taught me anything, it was that I couldn't afford to entertain anything beyond business if my intent was to stand at the head of this handmade table.

Silo turned back to surveying his capybaras. "Wonderful. Handle your hostile takeover. We'll discuss the profit split when things pan out."

"Cool. One last question. Let's say our man Atticus Garcia decided to come after me and only me, considering… you know."

"Handle it," Silo said. "If you're in need of help, holler."

"And no static from you if it ends bloody?"

Silo chuckled. "Should I expect something low key

from you?"

"Oh, love, I'm only gearing up." I eyed a smaller capybara and scooped it up into my arms. The animal offered no objection. If anything, it was elated to get a cuddle. "I'm taking this now—we'll call it part of my retainer." I nuzzled the top of the capybara's fuzzy head. It smelled like pine chips. "What does this thing eat, by the way?"

I stared at the baby's big eyes. *This* was the kind of love I was equipped for. That lizard back home lost the competition before it even started. Shame.

CHAPTER thirty-three

"Hey, where the fuck are you?" I didn't hide the disdain in my voice. Jason was a no-show to what was supposed to be a very big day for him, and instead, my ass was his surrogate at a time where a) I was done with his bullshit, and b) not in the goddamn mood to lay eyes on a baby. I mean, what the fuck was I even doing there? The muscle memory was hard to kick. I woke up, went through my routine and there I was: back at the job I had left that was doomed to bear all my anger and resentment.

Dumb move, Poppy.

I stood outside the warehouse Villalobos had taken us to a few weeks prior. Things still seemed normal, by all accounts. Folks milled around. The building's lights were on. Maybe the beating I gave poor Gregory was seen as a blip on the radar instead of a full DEFCON kind of mess. Their mistake.

"Hey, Pop. A little busy right now with the show. Can

I call back?"

Busy? This motherfucker. "The show? You mean the show I've been managing while also managing the adoption that is happening right the fuck now—and all I see from where I'm standing—" I waved to Sara Tasker, who was sitting in the passenger seat of a rented Nissan Sentra a few yards away with her ever-punchable face "—is your wife in the car I had to rent and get insurance on when I mentioned the baby seats that you also did not buy?"

A smarter person would have walked away. I could order an Uber, get a ride to a bar, and drink the rest of my day away. I owed Jason nothing, and in my current mental state, I was probably more of a liability than ever. Only problem was I couldn't find it in me to walk away. It wasn't fear or obligation, though—no, I had started this ball rolling, and I wanted to see it finish. Not for Jason's sake, but for mine. I was charging headfirst into the business, having been on one side of it—and there I was on the opposite side. I almost needed to see it to completion, because then I would know all of this was possible—and maybe I would know I could pull this shit off too.

Unfortunately, it had to be all me or nothing. I couldn't count on my boys for this one. They were busy keeping eyes open for any sign of Atticus and/or the Albanians. So far, not a sign of either. Hell, keeping them at arm's length was healthy for me too. I still didn't have any guarantees these boys were totally loyal to me—though

I had my suspicions they were happy with a boss who let them be a little more themselves. Even if they were loyal, I still felt paranoid. My neck hurt from all the looking over my shoulder. All my moves got me attention, and none of that attention was positive.

"Pop, you there? I know how quiet you get when I make you grumpy." Jason chuckled, and it pissed me right the fuck off. "Look, I'm sorry. I totally understand. Problem is, one of us needs to keep an eye on the cash flow, right?"

Grumpy. He was acting like I was a toddler and not a grown-ass woman—not someone to consider when he played at being the star of his dimwitted fucking life. I rubbed an eye with my thumb. I wanted to gouge it out. Maybe pain would take my mind off murder. "You realize that I'm now babysitting? That was very much not a part of our deal, Jason. None of this was. I find you the venues. I check the contracts. I make you the money. I do not play mommy."

Jason disconnected the call.

Oh, so that's what it felt like to have my face go so hot the flesh threatened to melt. I paced back and forth. Reminded myself that there would be babies and that those babies did nothing wrong to deserve my ire—though, what they did to deserve the Taskers as parents had to be karmic.

I turned back to Sara waiting in the car. Another wave. Another tight, joyless smile. Sara hated me, but the bitch would need to hold that inside if she wanted the day to end well.

Thankfully, Frankie—according to the file Silo provided, Frankie Dionysus—was the consummate professional, a sort of buoy in the choppy waters that made up my life lately. Frankie was genuinely concerned with improving our overall experience, especially considering the attack on Gregory and other "strange turns of events," as she put it. I shifted the parcel under my arm, oversized and unwieldy, but way too important to put on the ground. The discomfort would only be temporary.

Frankie emerged in a bright peach suit with matching tie, kerchief, and bowler hat. She walked to me as she adjusted her cufflinks—diamond-studded baby bottles. "Ms. Leathers. You look radiant." She waved to Sara. "Apologies to Mrs. Tasker, but we prefer someone who was earlier vetted be here for this." She sighed. "Could be worse, really. We're standing here under God's bright sun and open sky. A small blessing indeed."

I half-curtsied—my Chanel dress limited knee flexibility. "I'm certainly happy we can finally finish our business on good terms, Ms. Dionysus. Apologies Jason couldn't join us, but he's busy with his show—has to feed these new kids, right?"

"I totally understand that need." Frankie grimaced. "It seems you'll be our last visitor at this location."

I feigned surprise. "Do you need to move?" So, they wanted to finish up before clearing out. Made sense. Also made my schedule tight. I needed to make sure whatever I did happened soon, because I wasn't sure if I could convince Silo to help me track these folks down again.

"Unfortunately." Frankie sighed. "I liked it here. Fairly remote. Not much like where we'll be headed next, though that'll be temporary." She clapped her hands together like a nursery school teacher. "Ready to meet the kids?"

I felt like I could use a dose of cute on a shitty day, so why not? "Sure."

Frankie began walking towards the warehouse. "No time to waste, Miss Leathers. Come along."

I followed, simultaneously hating and loving this endlessly fascinating woman. If things panned out, I hoped to find a way to keep her on my payroll—but I had a feeling she wasn't the type to bend the knee to anyone but herself. Probably why I liked her so damn much. Reminded me a little of myself. "Do you have any kids of your own?" I turned back to see if Sara was still watching, but the new mother was on her mobile device.

"Nieces and nephews—" Frankie slid open a large door leading inside "—all blessings."

There was an unsettling quiet in the baby office. Like we were there on an off day. In the center of the large space were two car seats—in each seat, a sleeping little bundle of vaguely ethnic joy. Exactly the kind of babies a rich, pseudo-liberal couple dreamed of parading around brunch meetings and themed barbecues.

"Want me to get that off your hands?" Frankie offered

to take the parcel from me.

I looked to my right and realized I was still holding onto it. Jason's final payment: art. "Oh, absolutely. This should cover the money lost. Appraisal papers are inside." I handed the work over. A few bidders were thoroughly miffed at losing the painting after Jason's latest auction, but were mollified when we offered custom NFTs in their stead. I was masterful in negotiation—another feather in my cap that he ignored. I mean, I'd sold the motherfuckers receipts for digital art. Literally nothing.

Frankie returned with a double stroller and helped me get the kids set up.

"Have they decided on names yet?" Frankie asked. "Once they have, tell them to email this address." She handed me a card. "They'll sort out the SSIDs, birth certificates, and other important forms. Far as anyone will ever know, you got these boys from Florida. Their mom was at her wit's end and had to give them up to make ends meet. She up and overdosed on whatever chemicals she could get her hands on—a true American tragedy."

Sure she did, I thought. Wondered where that girl was now. If she was sitting home nursing a fresh C-section scar and dealing with that anesthesia hangover. I looked the card over. No physical locations. Emails and a website. I was willing to bet these were tied to any number of addresses and P.O. Boxes on the file Silo provided me.

"That's tragic," I said as I placed my hands on each child's head. One was asleep and the other was getting there. They were cuties. Made me feel bad they'd be shackled with idiots for parents, but I had a feeling they wouldn't want for anything if my plans worked out. "Almost too real."

Frankie frowned a little. "It's believable and sexy. Trust me, the social mileage here is huge. Seen it a million times."

The Taskers would be thrilled about that, I guessed.

Frankie accompanied me back outside before saying her goodbyes and closing the doors behind them. Sara helped situate the boys, and I jumped back into the car.

Sara huffed. "I can't." She unbuckled her seatbelt and climbed into the backseat. "I need to watch them. Are you okay with me back here?" Her legs swung upwards and smacked me on the right side of my head. "Crap. Sorry. Oh-em-gee they are so fucking cute."

I rubbed my head and frowned. "Don't wake them up. You'll regret that."

"I'm trying. Way too excited to be a mommy." Sara sighed happily. "Are they loud?"

"No idea. I didn't ask them."

"Did you or Jason hear back from the nanny?" Sara asked, completely oblivious to the fact that I was not in the fucking mood to deal with her shit.

Another task that was very much not in the job description. "She's moving in tomorrow."

"Oh, thank God. We're going to need the help. Jason and I need our sleep. There's no way we'd survive more than a night without it."

Poor fucking babies, I thought.

No poster boards. No glitter, scented markers, or fancy pens. A notebook, a pencil—for erasing—and an entire French press filled to the brim.

It was time to work out Plan B.

The very first thing I had to work out was what would have to happen for Plan B to be a "thing," and whether I needed to have everything in place for said Plan B to be executable at any given moment. Runway would be nice, but a Plan B didn't feel like it should be something for the long term—that felt more like Plans C–Z—and I figured shit was going to go sideways at some point or another. That meant it had to be immediate. Something I could pull off tonight, if I needed to.

God, what I would give to have a spa night.

So, the bad scenarios:

Atticus came back for my head and/or

Silo decided I needed dying and/or

Frankie was a lot savvier than I gave her credit for

and/or

Some other asshole turned up to ruin my life

All of these were entirely rational. Fuck, all of these could happen all at once. This meant my escape plan had to be as dramatic as I could possibly make it. Only problem was, a plan like that wasn't a plan I could carry with me. I had to keep my eyes open all the fucking time, unless I forced it to happen when I wanted it to. Which would really make it Plan A.

Maybe I was being paranoid. I had Silo on my side. He'd have my back for as long as I was useful to him, and I planned on being really useful. Then again—was I signing myself up for another version of what I'd just dealt with over the years? Was this really a promotion, or just a lateral move?

The coffee didn't help. It made the paranoia and over-thinking speed up. Switched to wine. Not the best choice either. That made the worrying more creative. When I tried to stop thinking, I could feel my hands tense. I opened and closed them over and over, the tendons almost creaking, my fingernails digging into my palms until they were numb. "In over my head" was a mantra I had to repeatedly shove out of my brain.

I was not "in over my head." That was bullshit. Other people dealt with more stress. More obstacles. Look at Silo. Look at Frankie. Look at—okay, Amity wasn't a great example.

I was going to figure out a way to get out on top.

Back to square one, then. If people were coming to get me, well, they'd have to know where I was going to be. If I were smart, I'd let them come to me, wouldn't I? I'd let them know damn well where I was before shit went down so I could bring *them* to whatever little plan I'd hatched.

Station Zero.

Oh, holy shit. That was perfect. I was a fucking genius. There were tunnels everywhere down there. I lead someone like Atticus the wrong way and he's gone forever. The rats or the fucking trains would take him off to cold case land. Even if someone made it to the show, there'd be too many people down there to fuck around without exposing themselves.

Then again, would someone like Atticus give a damn at this point?

Would Silo?

So, two plans: something to throw someone off I knew was coming and something to have on hand in case I didn't know they were coming. Bottom line, though: I had to let them know where I was for that to work. Considering I wasn't working against idiots, they'd see right through anything obvious. I closed my eyes and thought on that.

Staging. Atticus loved staging. The domino effect of one bad move.

I had to make one bad move and hope for the worst, right?

I grabbed my phone and texted Jason.

Re: guest list for show. any new? Or use newletter subs?

Left on read. Not surprising.

Which meant I was going to use the email list I had on hand, with a handful of extra folks added on for good measure. I wasn't dumb enough to add Atticus directly, but I was dumb enough to forget to remove a few of his dummy emails he liked using for the auctions he participated in. I added Frankie's contact information and the email address for Silo's business fronts, as well.

Let that be the first of the dominoes, and I could plan out the rest in the coming days, parallel to Jason's show. If that was going to be his last gasp at maintaining social media relevance, I figured it was my chance to throw a bit of a coming out party. The drama alone: a violent event at the year's hottest art show? That was fucking genius, I convinced myself. It was almost art. A meta-performance piece!

I set up the distribution list—went over the invites as well. I'd send them by the end of the week—still had some more logistical items to work through. I grabbed my phone again and jumped into my group text with Eddie and Bill.

Hey – qq: u or any of your buddies former military?

Bill: I was in USMC

Eddie: Oh, shit, really?

Bill: yeah, 10 fucking years, man. I told you about that.

Have frnds with…exotic material connections?

Eddie: …

Bill: Maybe not in text?

K thx bye.

They were right. What I had in mind required materials I couldn't order or find at a specialty boutique. We couldn't leave a paper trail, though. I'd talk it over with them live. I didn't have doubts they could find me that needed hook up. Eddie and Bill always entertained my questions and off-color demands with aplomb. I was grateful Silo provided me with two solid henchmen.

I could use a few more for what I had in mind, though.

I continued sketching out the now-hybrid Plan B/DOLVIDA Station Zero event. It felt good to have some motivation, even if my overall direction felt a little murky. That was art, right? Sometimes a masterpiece didn't quite feel like a masterpiece at the start. I figured I could revise and improvise to get to the finish line. I didn't have to have all the answers. It was a good feeling

I knew wouldn't last, but I rode that wave for a few more hours. Didn't need coffee or wine, either—big win.

At 3:00 AM my phone rang. Silo.

Why the hell would Silo call me at that hour of regret?

I connected. "Hello?"

"Poppy. Apologies for calling at an ungodly hour like this, but there's something we need to discuss."

Shit. I went through an inventory of potential transgressions, but none lined up with anything Silo would be this concerned about. I turned my head. Unless he was watching me. I stared at my computer screen. Or watching my screen. Could he do that? Was this the moment he decided to show me what he could do? Why else call me at a ridiculous time like this if it wasn't to swing his member around to let me know how big of a man he was?

Honestly, it made sense. I knew I was lippy and a little annoying—a lot—and it would make sense for Silo to finally put his foot down to set the real tone of our relationship. I mean, it's what I would do in his shoes with a pain in the ass like me on the pay roll.

"Are you there?" Silo asked.

"Oh, sorry. You woke me up. Still a little off." I told myself to keep it simple. No Poppy-isms in the middle of the night. If this was a little test, it might have been worth showing the man that I was a dependable pain in the ass.

"I need to see you. Now."

"*Now*, now?" I bit my lip. "I'll see if I can get a ride

over now."

"I've got a car coming for you. Should be there in five minutes." Silo disconnected.

I put the phone down and nearly deflated. No sleep. Had to pee from all that coffee and wine. I needed to get dressed, too. Couldn't even plan a potential double cross against my employer like a normal person.

This was the start, though. I knew that I wouldn't sit on my ass waiting for the next big thing to happen to me this time, but I needed to remember Silo probably wasn't the type to wait either. I rushed to dress myself and grabbed a notepad. I had to jot down some instructions for the boys. Hopefully, I'd leave Silo's place in the condition to provide it to them.

At the very least, this shit wasn't going to be boring.

"You sent someone after Atticus?" I was at a loss. Things were quiet, and sure I was fighting my own paranoid delusions, but surely this motherfucker couldn't be worse than me? "Why would you do that?" I couldn't help myself.

This all felt strange. I'd just seen Silo and he was cool as a cucumber, but now, all of a sudden, the man was having some sort of paranoia-induced meeting with me after he made a move on Atticus. And for what? Hadn't he told me he believed Atticus wouldn't come for him? Like, I thought Silo was smarter than that—or at least more collected. Why the sudden change of heart?

Silo sat in a large wicker chair nursing a half a coconut with a tiny blue umbrella poking out of it. "I got tired of waiting for the worm to turn. Figured proactive measures would be suitable." He pointed a finger at me. "And please, I understand you're probably still a little tired, but I don't appreciate the tone."

I shook my head. "You're right, I'm sorry." I sighed. "With respect, you could have let me know to pick up the pace. I would have handled this within a reasonable amount of time." The respect was minimal. His rationale didn't hold up.

The face he made.

Fuck me.

Fuck him.

"I realized it was foolish to think Atticus would provide us a 'reasonable' amount of time." Silo drank from his fancy drink and straightened his shirt collar. "The decision was mine to make, and I made it."

Uh-huh, sure, I thought. That hubris fit the man like a dollar-store suit. Unless he was bullshitting me and was trying to lure Atticus back to his turf just like I was—which was pretty fucked up, since he could have simply ended Atticus whenever he felt like it, unlike me. Instead, he waited, sent someone after him—who'd fucking failed, smart—and this was the panic, wasn't it?

Fuck me. He called me here to be a human shield.

Maybe my problem was that everyone I assumed was competent because they had rank was, in fact, not competent at all. Shit, did that make me incompetent for falling for the grift? Was it as easy as "fake it till you make it," or was that something only men got away with? Everything I ever knew about Silo Jotter came from Atticus—his employee, his sharp instrument. It was in everyone's best interest that the myth be maintained, wasn't it? That nobody could know that men like Silo and Atticus got lucky once and did everything they possibly could to hold onto that little moment.

I hated them for it, and I hated myself for falling for their bullshit. Look how easy it was for me to pull at the little thread that was unraveling around us at lightspeed. It was a disaster and that was because it had always been a disaster. A pig in lipstick.

I couldn't let that be what happened to me.

"The Tasker show," I said, giving up all secrecy with my Plan B. Fuck it. Silo thought he was untouchable, which meant he was just as inept as Atticus. "I was thinking of drawing everyone and their mother there for a big old fashioned clusterfuck." I rubbed my temples. "That was why I was dragging my feet."

Silo sighed. "We're past time to play games or hatch elaborate schemes."

"Well, yes and—I'm confused. Because you want him taken care of now, but you also seem fairly nonplussed about that," I said, and shout out to my word-a-day calendar for bringing nonplussed into my life. "I'm struggling to nail down the new level of urgency here."

Silo's laughter erupted like a pipe bomb. "I suppose I am being contradictory." He took a long breath. "Simply put, Poppy: I want him dead. The idea of a loose end, while initially appealing because of my relationship with him, is no longer tenable. I'm feeling skittish at the idea of someone so knowledgeable of my own operations existing outside of them. Does that make sense?"

"Sometimes. Look, whatever. I can either handle him in two weeks or you can handle him now. No skin off my balls."

"This is the last time I'm going to ignore your attitude, especially with you lying to my face like that," Silo said. "I can understand your worries. I'm bouncing between worry and joy myself. That said, you need to learn what I say goes or I can easily see you to an early grave right here." He grimaced.

Yeah, he was probably high off that rat milk. I wondered if that was what was in the coconut. The erratic tone. His decision to make with the threats. It didn't feel like the big-time criminal mastermind was at work here. This was a man that was afraid and filled with regret. He knew he fucked up betraying Atticus and he was probably not thrilled with me as the booby prize. That said, if this was all the act of a man slowly becoming more desperate and worried, then should I have been scared? Was he baiting me to keep poking? To keep testing? Or was Silo a man so used to being untested that he lost his edge?

Something to mull over.

Silo's gaze drifted off. "How are things with the adoption takeover?"

What in the living fuck was this nonsense?

"Silo, it's four in the morning and my poor brain isn't equipped—" A noise. A loud noise. "The fuck was that?"

Again. A clap. A familiar clap. A lot more followed—too

many. I narrowed my eyes. That was an M&P 40—Atticus' preferred gun. Heard the sound of that thing in my fucking dreams the number of times I field tested that piece.

Silo leaned back and drew a breath. "He's really doing it." All that power he had only a few days ago seemed to be gone. Made me think of an air mattress with the air plug out—just a little squeeze and the air was going to come out of him.

I felt my heart about leap out of my chest. No. This was not ending this way. Absolutely not. "You have an escape hatch or something? An alternate route out of your high-rise death trap?" I did not want this. If I had to tear Silo's throat open as a means of placating Atticus, so be it. No way in hell was I dying at four in the fucking morning. Only common criminals died at four in the fucking morning. I was a primetime kind of criminal. If I was going to die it was going to be at 8 PM Eastern like a proper bad ass.

"I have a panic room." Silo pointed behind him. "Code is 1385. Go open it and wait inside."

A weird offer, but I wasn't about to turn my nose up at safety. Still, I had concerns at the act of charity. "I'm having a hard time believing Atticus don't know that code, Silo."

"You enter the code again inside and the keypad out front is a dud," Silo said. "Just go on inside and I'll let you know when to come out." He waved me off. "Go. He'll only be angrier if he sees you."

I made a beeline to the keypad but stopped short when Silo's words caught up to me. I turned. "The fuck you mean 'when he sees you'?"

"He knows about Amity," Silo said.

"How does he know about Amity?"

"It came up."

Aghast. That was the word. Fucking aghast. The motherfucker sold me out. He sent people after a professional killer, failed at that, seemingly had a têt-a-têt with the murderous psychopath, and then told him I'd murdered the girl he liked.

More gunfire. "We'll talk about that later," I said. I went to the keypad, dialed in the code, and the wall panel slid open.

"You have nothing to worry about with that room," Silo said. "It is very safe."

"And if it's so safe, then why aren't you going in with me?"

Silo licked his lips. "Because I can salvage this."

The naïveté of the man did not match his reputation or station. "Salvage this"? He sounded more like a heartbroken teenager than a crime boss. Wait.

"Silo, I used to think I knew there were no friends or love in this business, but Amity certainly taught me how wrong I was. Don't let Atticus be your lesson." I don't know why I bothered to say it. Atticus yanking Silo out like the fat tick he was would be useful, but I couldn't help but feel a small link when I looked into the man's eyes. This falling out had hurt him, and there was the wound, plain as day.

"Just go inside," Silo said.

"One more chance, man."

"Don't presume to understand my motivations, Poppy."

Fine, fine, whatever, I thought. Maybe that three feet of steel was enough to keep the heat of my goddamn rage from scalding the duplicitous butthole. I walked into the shockingly large panic room and found another keypad. I dialed in the same code and the door closed behind me. Lights flickered on and a bank of screens came to life. Each showed me a different view of Silo's apartment and the view outside.

On camera 17 I saw Atticus aerating the back of someone's head as he approached a door. He was wearing all black—a terrible look on him—and he had shaved his beard off. He was limping, his shirt stained with blood—couldn't tell if it was his own or the blood of others. He reloaded his gun and then appeared on camera 18, ducking behind a couch as two of Silo's men fired at his general direction with all the finesse of a three-year-old playing with a water gun. Atticus fired back, but there was none of that flair to his movements. He was just as scattershot as they were.

"Oh, look at you," I said. "You all look like you're playing at recess."

I lit a yellow clove and exhaled. Found the comfiest

chair in the room and watched Atticus make his way to Silo's apartment. It was the first time I really saw Atticus in action and it was... underwhelming. He moved clumsily from cover to cover and when he did aim true, it was either a flesh wound or a grazing shot, forcing Atticus to expend clip after clip just to see a little momentum towards the double doors that led to Silo's main chamber. He was out of breath and moving sluggishly as one of the last members of Silo's guard slide tackled him against the wall. The men struggled awkwardly, like first time lovers, until Atticus managed to overpower the other and shoot him in the throat.

"Headshots, dude," I critiqued from the comfort of my seat.

I noticed a keyboard near the bank of screens and pulled it onto my lap. I found the volume button for Silo's little surveillance set up and took it off mute. Not the greatest quality, but the cacophony of screams and gunfire were a lot more manageable in the panic room. I checked on Silo. He remained seated in his wicker chair, drinking his little cocktail. He had a capybara on his lap. Looked like a bootleg Bond villain.

The fuck did I see in these men? Nothing about this chaos proved any of their reputations as true. I sighed and rubbed my temples. Took another drag of my clove. I'd stretched myself thin; I knew this. Atticus and his crisis of amorality, Tasker and his babies, Silo and his idiotic hubris. They led me here. They led me to Amity and the mess that came from that. To spinning my wheels with plans of iterative gains. I was insane to think iteration was the key to my goals. I had to take a running fucking leap, not a hop. I mean, look at the state of these people: they were idiots.

If I made it out of this alive, I was going to go ahead with Plan B. It would all come together at that damn art show—hopefully. All the preparation, all the moving parts. None of this was even slightly predictable, and I needed peace: a moment of quiet to finally gain a semblance of real control. Until then, I was constantly changing plans, switching gears, watching all of them for their reactions, and taking the opportunities that fell from the table like a dog desperate for scraps. Nothing ever came easy, but hell, was this run a hard one.

I closed my eyes. I remembered a little something my mother used to tell me: "It isn't worth doing if you can't do it with your own hands."

I held my hands up, palms facing me. That lingering feeling still there. As if Amity had burned me. That's what it felt like—scarred skin, a callous that wasn't going away.

"Got more work to do," I whispered. And I watched him come.

I watched Atticus scavenge for guns. He moved as quickly as he could, his injuries severely diminishing his pace—good, I figured. That would make it easy to run away from him if I had to.

I didn't count the bodies Atticus dropped to get into Silo's apartment, but it had to be in the range of a dozen—maybe a baker's dozen. It was impressive despite the sloppiness of it all. The man was clearly on a mission; I'd have to give him that. Was it weird that this was all a little more Three Stooges than it was John Wick? It was easy to think that way when I was sitting in a locked room and out of the danger zone—for the time being.

Atticus kicked open the front door to Silo's penthouse apartment and walked in. I turned up the volume on the console of the screen bank and held my breath. Would this be quick? Would they actually have a little dialogue? Crap, what if that dialogue made Silo change his mind yet again? He was fickle, wasn't he? What was to stop him from hanging me out to dry to make peace with Atticus?

"That was a little unnecessary." Silo shifted in his seat. He placed his drink in a cup holder and continued petting his capybara. "I would have taken a call."

Atticus limped into the room and sat across from Silo in the same chair I'd been seated. I wondered if he could still feel my warmth on it. It felt almost intimate—almost like old times. He stared at the piece he'd pilfered and his shoulders sunk. "Yeah, well. Things have been weird. Felt I owed you a personal visit."

"You look pretty awful."

"I feel twice as awful as that. Gorgeously awful."

Silo raised his eyebrows and raised his hands up. "What did it? The contract on you or the death of the girl?"

Atticus looked down at the ground and frowned. He shook his head. "You know it took me so much longer to realize I wanted out of this than everyone else?" He laughed. "I wanted to believe leaving the stupid pan behind was the moment, but that's a lie. I've been feeling like this for years. I've been looking for a way out of a place I never fucking belonged. This all grew out of our control."

"Out of *our* control?" Silo asked.

Atticus straightened. "Silo, we were fucking cellmates. You were a shit tier weed dealer, and I was in for aggravated assault. We weren't built for this. We fell ass backwards into it and we've been building this little house of cards." He mimed stacking objects. "I don't know when we convinced ourselves we were these titans of crime, but we're not. We're lucky. That's all. Lucky idiots who started killing people to keep the lie up. To make sure nobody realized we're a pair of loser cowards."

Silo watched him. "Feeling a little personal here. It was never supposed to be personal. That was our first rule."

"You fucking made it personal. You tried to kill me. You let that power-hungry moron kill Amity, too." Atticus placed his gun on his lap, the barrel facing Silo. "You knew damn well Amity had connections. You knew damn well we kept the hits to the low-level targets, but you decided to flex."

Wait, what? That couldn't be true. I'd been there for dozens of contracts. Was Atticus saying they *only* went after nobodies? Like, they were goosing their numbers to build the legend, but not really grow power?

Silo leaned forward and motioned to Atticus. "I canceled the contract, Atticus. It wasn't my fault the two of you continued to engage."

Atticus shook his head. "You know it would have been a fling. You got caught up with your ego and you know it. She beat you on the cheese scene and then she was in my bedroom."

"Why would I care—" Silo cleared his throat and composed himself. "She was a danger to my business model and a potential competitor elsewhere. It made sense to be cautious, but I never fully squashed the contract. We were in a holding pattern. Yes, Poppy made a big move, but it was probably a foregone conclusion."

They both remained silent. Still as stone. I wondered who was going to make the first move. Who was going to decide that violence was the only way out of the apartment?

"I didn't come here to take your life," Atticus said. "I came here to make a point and I came here to find out where you hid her."

"Poppy? Why would I hide her?"

Oh boy. Here it was. The moment of truth. Either he was gearing up to tell Atticus exactly where I was and how to filet me, or he was going to cover for me. That made me more nervous than a nasty end. All the work. All the advantages taken. And there I was, once again without an ounce of control. There was nothing I could do to snatch the ball away from these testosterone-drunk assholes.

"Clearly you were angling for her to replace me," Atticus said. "You even gave her a few men to help out. I even heard rumors of an angle you were working with her. Using her to get your hooks into new business."

"'Using' is a strong word. We're partnering. It's good business to grow new relationships and network with others. At least she understands that." Silo placed the capybara down. "In what world was this business going to end with you, Atticus? Where did you see things going as you decided you no longer wanted in? Did you believe I'd offer you a retirement package? That I'd be content to rely on our friendship as the only thing keeping you from walking to the nearest police station or field office and dumping my business out in the open? After all we've been through? We built ourselves an empire and you clearly stopped having the stomach for it."

"So, you admit paranoia beat you?"

"Beat me? Atticus, paranoia is the rule of the day. Someone is always out to take your slot. I mean, look at what happened to you."

I held my head in my hands. This was fucking torture. Talking about me and talking about their precious feelings. I slapped the desk. "Fucking shoot each other already." The control console shifted, and I noticed there was a big button with a picture of a microphone on it. "Oh, word?" I nearly squealed. This was like *The Warriors*.

Oh my God. I snatched my phone and Googled choice quotes. No way in hell I wasn't going to butt in on this conversation without saying something very cool and very much from *The Warriors*. I scanned a few sources to make sure I wasn't about to say the wrong thing and pressed the mic button. It lit up for me to give me the knowledge that I was now the voice of God.

"Hey boppers, your girl Poppy Leathers here." I said it with that velvet smooth tone—or so I imagined. Who knew how it sounded in the room?

Atticus stared upwards and rolled his eyes. "She's in

your panic room."

Silo shifted in his seat again. "I wasn't about to tee her up for you," he said.

Atticus ignored him and looked towards camera 13. He gave me a wave. "Hey, Pop."

I sneered. "Could you stop calling me that?"

Atticus feigned surprise. "Oh, that bothers you?"

"Real cute, asshole," I answered.

Silo said. "See, that's the difference—"

"Shut the fuck up, Silo." Atticus and I spoke at the same time.

"Jinx," I said. "Gotta let me live, Atticus."

Silo frowned. "Are you parlaying, Poppy?"

"Depends," I said. "How open is your guest to speaking?"

"Can't say I'm in a talking mood knowing you're this close, Pop."

What an asshole. Still, I could see his perspective, I guessed. He was mad for a lot of reasons. Amity was at the front of his mind—and not really the root of his issue—and that made me a perfect target for his grief or anger. I got it; I just wasn't going to give him a free pass for it.

"I can see why you're pissed, Atticus, but you need to understand where I'm coming from. Wheels were spinning for way too long, and I had to make my move."

"By killing Amity?" he asked.

"That was something else," I said.

Atticus scoffed and leveled his gun at Silo. "I'm not doing this back and forth. How do I get into the panic room?"

Silo shifted again. He placed his hands neatly on his lap. His right hand was edged towards his waist—he was armed. "And now we're back to threats. How many times are we going to shift our motivations and intentions here, Atticus?"

"I could ask the same of you, Silo. You're just as fucking scatter-brained," I said.

Silo stared at camera 21. "Says the woman sealed behind steel and concrete thanks to me."

"Oh, am I supposed to let you both talk it out without having a say? Am I supposed to pretend like I'm not the one with the advantage right now? You woke my ass up at 3 AM to let me know you tried to kill the man currently aiming a gun at you because of your idiotic power move and now you're telling me when and where to make *my* power move?" Silo was right. The room was safe as fuck, and that safety gave me courage.

"I could make all of our lives very easy right now," Atticus said to Silo. "Tell me the code and I get what I want. I'll walk out and you'll never hear from me again."

"If I had known revenge would give you your murder boner back, Atticus, I'd have told Amity to make fun of your sweater collection," I said. "You fucked around with her for what, a few weeks, and now you're acting like the hero of the story? How much goddamn blood do you have on your hands to sit there and pretend like anyone in the room or out is even close to being as vile as you?" I laughed. "Oh, you have a few eccentric hobbies. Adorable, baby, very adorable. You're still as bad as me or Silo or anyone else."

"I don't abide by conventional philosophies of morality," Atticus said, "You know I've always been more of a practitioner of Zoroastrianism."

Silo chortled. "I'm sorry to inform you, Atticus, but I've yet to really witness anything that would lead me to believe you adhere to any good thoughts, good words, or good deeds."

Look at that. Atticus once again spilling a bunch of barely informed nonsense to make himself feel better for being a complete fucking waste of space. He was over-privileged and deluded. Same as almost any of us. Problem was, he didn't have the self-awareness anymore. It had faded over time as he kept crawling through the mud convincing himself that he, the victimizer, was a victim. That somehow, in his seven-figure life, he was being held down by an invisible force that existed simply to advance the idea that he was normal. It was bullshit, ingested day in and day out to rationalize and excuse every awful fucking choice he ever made.

I understood that, and it made me hate him more for it. I knew what I was, and I knew why. I didn't need excuses or deep, dark reasons. I was a shit heel, and you know what? I enjoyed it.

Atticus made his argument face—this weird scowl he had whenever you called him out on his bullshit. "I've always taken responsibility for my actions. There's never been another person to blame for the wrong I've done or the lives I've taken. I made the decision to do what I did. I may be on the wrong end of the moral spectrum, but I have zero desire to rationalize a single damn thing I've done."

"That makes you either a narcissist or a sociopath. Or plain old insane," I said.

"*You* feel guilty?" Atticus asked.

"I can't speak for Poppy, but I tend to." Silo scratched the side of his face. "How could I not?" He rubbed his beard. "There's still the matter of all this ugliness. And being I have you here..." Silo snapped his fingers.

A few men entered the room. None with weapons at the ready, but the bulges at their waists hinted that violence was certainly plausible. They stood in a ring around Atticus and Silo, waiting for the first sign of conflict. A few twitched, the muscle fibers used to dole out harm ready to be used.

Not going to lie: the finger snapping thing was cool.

Atticus stayed as still as possible. "Does this mean you're going to take years of friendship and flush them down the toilet for my fucking assistant?"

"Former assistant," I added. "And fuck you too, sweetheart."

Silo shifted in his seat again. "I've half a mind to end

both of you, but if revenge is what you want, I don't think it's something I can offer you. It isn't because I'm protecting Poppy as much as I'm protecting a future investment. Had you stayed on course, maybe we'd be discussing the opportunities together right now. But you made up your mind about what it was you wanted a long, long time ago."

Atticus shook his head. "I was never sure what it was I wanted, Silo. That's sort of what got us here."

"I firmly disagree," Silo said.

"Then here we are."

Silo nodded slowly. "Here we are."

"You two are such fucking drama queens," I said.

Atticus stood up and strafed to his right, firing wildly—his movement leading him away from Silo and towards a particularly sturdy marble bar. This was a smart choice, considering everyone opened fire at the same time—two guys actually tagged each other in the chaos.

Atticus leapt over the bar and landed on his ass. I muted the volume on the console as the gunfire intensified. No use listening in when I could faintly hear the chaos through the walls. I stood up and inspected the rest of the room. It was spacious. Had a few comfy chairs, a refrigerator, a sink, and a few cabinets. At the opposite end was an alcove that led into a pantry filled with jarred foods and bottled water.

I ran over to the cabinets to find something—anything—to protect myself with. All the cutlery was made of recycled paper, so the knives were of no fucking use. The other cabinets held bins marked for compost, trash, and "human waste"—gross. Jesus, Silo, you couldn't spring for a toilet in your fortified hidey hole? The last cabinet was a pantry-style piece. Around my height. There were cleaning supplies inside. A mop and a broom. I pushed them aside and the cheap plywood paneling that lined the inside nearly buckled into what should have been a very flat and very hard wall behind the cabinet.

"The fuck is this?" I grabbed a broom and jammed the top against the wood. It gave in again. I reached up to a corner and I was able to dig my nails behind the cheap barrier. It pulled away and, lord, the sigh of relief at what lay behind the façade.

Guns. Plural. Many pistols. A few rifles. Ammunition, too.

The man had Senatorial-tier hubris, but he wasn't so stupid as to assume this room was impenetrable. I grabbed a rifle, since I needed something with a lot more stopping power, and went through inspection, loading, and safety check the way Atticus taught me. I had the basics, and I wasn't a terrible shot, but I was bush league compared to him. That door slid open, and I knew I had to hold the trigger down until the clip was empty if I was going to have my breath by the time the sun came up.

Back on the screens, Atticus edged towards the far side of the bar and was surprised as a henchman jumped out in front of him. Both men fired their guns, and both found their target. It looked like Atticus took a bullet to the left arm as the henchman's right eye exploded. Atticus pushed the fresh corpse away from him and leaned back against the bar as he checked his arm. Satisfied with whatever he saw, he went back to creeping as others in the room held their fire as they reloaded.

Mistake. That moment of peace gave Atticus the cue to break cover.

Atticus managed to tag the guy closest to him in the leg. The poor bastard fell over awkwardly and as he slammed into the ground, managed to have his own gun go off in his face. I yelped out loud. How did he even manage to do that, and where the hell had Silo found these absolute tools?

Atticus then crossed the foyer towards where Silo was seated, but was shot at from behind. Running like a roach under fluorescent light, He flipped the wicker chair and took cover again.

"That shit's made of wicker, not metal, you dumbass," I muttered.

I saw Silo pop his head out and fire another round. He called out. I checked all the other camera feeds, and it looked like my guys were still outside—thankfully. I checked my phone to see if I had a signal. Just a bar. I shot a text off, hoping they'd see it, and watched their feed. Eddie looked down and fished his phone from his jacket pocket. He read and turned to Bobby to say something. They then went back inside the SUV and left. Nice.

They'd follow the next step of the plan.

Back here, it was a standoff. Fun. The chaos abated; I turned the sound back on. Needed to make sure I knew if and when Atticus got access to that door. Silo said it was only able to open from the inside once someone locked it, but that was a tough sell. A guy like Silo had to have a way around that protocol in the event—very much like this one—where he let someone else in the room first.

The conversation came in mid-way.

"...me and then what? Take over? Hand the keys to that psycho as a peace treaty?" Silo laughed. "I would have considered an offer to kill her, you know."

"That's a lie."

"Maybe." Silo made a few blind shots over his cover. "Atticus. Step out. Let me end this for you kindly and cleanly. I've played for too long."

On camera feed 4, Silo's capybara appeared and settled next to Atticus. It was completely ignorant to all the carnage, opting instead to find a warm body to huddle up against for comfort.

"Sure. Okay." Atticus scooped the capybara up with his wounded arm and stood up. He pointed the gun to the animal's head, but it turned to stare at the barrel.

"Not cool," I said.

Silo shared my sentiment. "That's low."

Atticus shrugged. "Opportunity presented itself." He pointed the gun where Silo was crouched. The cover was serviceable, but from the angle I saw, it looked like Atticus could manage a messy shot if he went for broke.

"Last chance," Atticus said. "Just tell me how to open that door and you can leave. No hard feelings. No follow up. I finish this and we're all good, okay?"

"I could make the same offer, Atticus. Do you think you'd believe me?"

"Fair point." Atticus raised his gun, took a bead, and pulled the trigger.

Nothing. It was empty.

Silo took the opportunity to stand then and aimed his gun at Atticus to give the kill shot.

Nothing. He was empty too.

Both men stared at each other then. Atticus made the first move, dropping the capybara and scrambling for the nearest gun as Silo did the same. They both found pistols on the bodies of the thug nearest to them and sprung back up, emptying their clips as they struck nothing but the walls behind them. Silo was the first to finish his clip and he quickly moved to grab another gun. Atticus was smart enough to maintain composure this time and finally aimed down sight. Pulling the trigger one last time.

It took a moment for the blossoming hole in Silo Jotter's forehead to release an egregiously small amount of blood, considering the caliber of the pistol. The man's tongue slowly lolled from his mouth and he leaned back dramatically, taking what felt like eons to give up the ghost. When he did, he collapsed onto the floor hard, the lapels of his jacket flapping dramatically before settling back on his chest.

My breath felt stuck in my chest.

Silo's capybara padded over to its dead master, walked to the open wound in his forehead, and lapped at the blood with its little pink tongue. After spending way too much time watching, Atticus craned his neck backwards and motioned at the nearest camera.

"Hey, Poppy," he said. "We need to talk."

"Am I next?"

I waited for Atticus to answer, but there was no response.

Fine. He wanted me to talk. "I imagined you'd have so much more to say, what with you murdering the guy running the show and all." I set my rifle down and paced near the cabinets. Opened one up and found some gum. I unwrapped and slipped a stick into my mouth. I chewed fast. Felt like I was going to choke. "Pretty badass move, man." I paused to pull myself together. Be normal Poppy, be unflappable Poppy: the mantra in my head. I re-approached the screen bank and console. Sat down and rotated the feeds until Atticus was on the largest screen.

"None of this was the plan," Atticus said, "until you did what you did."

"I finished what you wouldn't. The target was going to be a problem, like Silo said." I leaned on my elbows and lowered my head. That was the truth. I was afraid of it before. I tried to turn it around at first, tried to protect Amity, but I knew what the result was supposed to be. "This was the same as any other hit. The water sommelier. That glassblower with the sex toy side hustle. That one dude with the hemp bracelet thing. They tried elbowing in on Silo's business and your job was to prevent their upward mobility."

"My job was to murder people trying to make dollars out of thin air. It was unfair."

"It was capitalism." I sighed. "And motherfucker, what are you wearing? All that time and you never learned how to dress yourself without my help. You let that girl break you."

"I'm not broken. I have no idea what this is. Not anymore." Atticus shifted his weight. "And stop doing that."

"Doing what?"

"You're avoiding Amity's name like you don't care."

"We knew her for a few weeks, Atticus. Stop playing like this was life changing."

"Pop, I—"

"Stop calling me that!" I screamed and slammed a fist against the console desk.

"Fine. Poppy." Atticus looked towards the panic room door. "You know we're both in over our heads here. I just killed the only man protecting you and honestly," he chortled sarcastically, "I just opened the door for the next idiot to saunter on in and playact at being a big deal." Atticus motioned to the door. "Open up and let's finish this. You don't have to let any of this weigh on you anymore."

I nearly lost it. Was this son of a bitch acting like he was bringing me mercy? For what? For doing exactly what he would have done a few months ago? "Atticus, let me say this slowly. Fuck. You."

"Poppy. It doesn't have to get any worse than this."

This piece of shit acting like he was here to save me with that bullet. As if Silo's end meant that was that. Mission accomplished for our little hero. All it took was a dose of inspiration from a dead girl, and he came in to end the evils that took her away from him. Like Amity was his, like she was a possession. Amity had passion and goals. She aspired—like me. What she wasn't was a prop for this murderer to use to gain his deluded sense of redemption. Amity was supposed to be honored, and the only way I could think to honor her right was to take the goddamn reins and show this toolbag exactly who the fuck I was.

I snatched my phone from the desk to text Bill and Eddie the news: Atticus Garcia had just killed Silo Jotter. He was coming for me. I needed them to send everyone here now, but keep to their work. It was a gamble, but I had to take it. Silo was dead. Atticus was the enemy. I was standing right here. There was always a chance someone would voice a complaint, but if I handled the next couple of minutes the right way, I had a bigger opportunity than I ever did before.

Lemonade, right?

"I'm still here," I said, "and I don't plan on going anywhere. My original message stands: Fuck and you. Two words. Very clear."

"You really think you're going to get out of that panic room alive?" Atticus asked. He looked as incredulous as anyone ever did at the suggestion of my success. My confidence—a joke to people like Atticus. Something to roll their eyes at, to look down on me for. But over time, I'd learned that incredulousness—that doubt—was all a smokescreen for their own issues. When you're the tallest tree, people always try to cut you down. Problem was, I never quite understood how tall I was until that moment. I had the power. These fools only ever had their violence. I had a plan.

I could win this. Go with my gut, I thought. Power through. Plan B the shit out of this bastard.

I sat up. "Look, whatever. I'm texting you info. Check your email. Tasker show—the big one. You show up and you're protected. You made my Christmas come early, and I owe you something for the work done."

Atticus made a face like someone farted. I threw him off with that one. Good. "Work?"

"Oh, sweet summer child. Silo Jotter, the Luddite Kingpin of Brooklyn, is dead," I said. "Nature abhors a vacuum, and I'm more than willing to be the idiot that 'saunters' in." I pulled a length of gum from my mouth. "You come down to the show and I'll even explain it all to you—every bit, all James Bond-style and shit." I spied a caravan of Town Cars pulling up in front of the building. "That said, Atticus, there's about two dozen terribly upset humans outside the building armed to the goddamn teeth and headed your way. So now, you are faced with a choice: pretend you are in the condition to kill anyone—even as poorly trained as these boys seem to be—or you get the fuck out of here."

Atticus pursed his lips and holstered his gun. He looked back at the camera. "This isn't over."

"No shit, I just fucking said that," I said. "Now run."

For once, Atticus did as he was told.

I sat at the console. Clenched my fists so hard my hands shook. That anger was so raw. Worse than it had ever been. Worse than it was at the museum. Worse than it was with Amity. I wanted so much to open that door and call Atticus back. I wanted to empty every gun in this room into his body. I wanted to make him pulp. I should have opened that door and emptied the rifle clip into his face.

I closed my eyes. That anger wasn't going to help me yet. Save it. Hold onto it for later. Just a few more days. I was going to wipe the slate clean. Take what Silo built and tear it down to the foundation to make something new and stronger than what was there before. The artisan products, the drugs—even the fucking cheese. I was going to show this town exactly who I was and how I deserved what all these idiots had spent so much time squandering. I wasn't going to fall backwards into this—no, I was going to snatch it and hold onto it until my palms were raw.

Until then, there were loose ends to consider, and I needed a new outfit for the festivities. Something bright and airy, but with a hint of authoritarianism. I needed to be someone's favorite fascist.

The thought came to me at once, Atticus all but forgotten: Mary Poppins. How in the hell had I never tried that look out?

I watched as reinforcements poured into the apartment. They were all holding their guns wrong, like kids at play. That was something we needed to fucking rectify once I sorted things out. We were done with boys pretending to know what they were doing here. This shit was going to be a professional outfit.

"One second, boys," I said into the microphone. "In the panic room. Door's opening now. Please don't shoot me."

I entered the code into the little keypad to my right and the door hissed before sliding back open. I emerged from the room holding my rifle. I made a beeline to that little capybara still seated on Silo's dead chest and picked it up.

"King's dead," I said. "Long live the queen." I took a long look at the men in the room with their dark suits. "First thing's first. Clean this shit up." I walked towards the exit. "Then go buy some new clothes. Also, please call anyone on Silo's payroll and inform them that I know where all the money is and I'm willing to give anyone that sticks with me a nice little raise. Maybe we'll throw in dental or something." I smiled. "As a treat."

One of the boys raised a brow. "What if they say no?"

"Then tell the faithful about the bonus I'll offer for retiring anyone who thinks so low of me as to refuse my initial offer. Tell them that Poppy Leathers ain't looking for change but expansion. And if that ain't enough, you end them yourselves. Unless..." I turned to see if anyone had objections.

Just a sea of blank faces with wide eyes. A group of nobodies with nowhere to go. They needed direction. Focus. They were open to being led by whoever had the biggest dick, and I was the one with the goddamn rifle while they were all waving around pistols.

"Good. Move on with the plan. We got a lot of ground to cover."

No more fucking around.

Loose end number one.

"You're gonna want to turn that ass around and head right back out." Stanley Villalobos stood behind the counter of his gun shop and counted off a medium-sized pile of $20 bills as he loaded them into a duffel bag. "You and I got nothing to talk about, and I got places to be."

I spun the umbrella I had perched on my shoulder. My outfit wasn't the same as the movie, but I felt I'd done a proper job modernizing it a bit. It was more "*Mary Poppins* by way of *A Boy and His Dog*." It felt appropriate.

"Oh, come now. Have I done anything to offend? I was simply hoping I could receive a little assistance with home protection." I smiled sweetly. "It seems you've had some problems with that."

Villalobos counted off the last few bills, zipped his bag closed, and sighed. "You think coming at someone while he's surrounded by guns is the smart move?" He pointed at me with a fist. "Word gets around. I don't need or want trouble like you in my store or even my fucking county. Last warning you're gonna get."

Whatever. He was puffing his chest out. Giving me a show. He was damn right word went around. Shit, I'd started the game of telephone that went from Atticus Garcia turning on his boss to Poppy Leathers committing a power grab and *getting* Atticus Garcia to turn on his boss. I was building my legend, and it took less than a week for that story to reach the far-flung reaches of Garfield, New Jersey. Now that's what I call power.

"Oh, sir, I don't fear upstanding men like you. You, so gruff and rough, are a good man. Not like—" I paused to look from side to side "—the *Mexicans*."

Villalobos stared at me, apparently unfazed with my attire, accent, and unsubtle—if sarcastic—xenophobia. "Look, I need to leave, and at this moment you're an obstacle in my way. I'll own up to being the fucking moron who didn't lock the door—that's on me—but I really don't need a body to my name tonight."

I ignored the fortieth tough guy warning and instead examined the wall behind Villalobos. I pointed at a gun over the man's head. "Pardon me for being all about looks, but what about that one? I like the aesthetic." The gun was displayed beneath a portrait of a family holding various armaments. The youngest in the photo—a boy maybe around eight years of age—was holding the largest gun while everyone else stared, mouths agape and wide-eyed at the child's girthy cock metaphor. Of course, they all wore different types of camouflage, too.

"I ain't turning around."

I walked to the counter and placed my parasol on it. I raised my hands. "I'm an eccentric—" I gave up on the accent "—but I assure you, I'm only interested in learning about that gun behind you. You feel threatened? Feel free to give me a more personal exhibition of its qualities."

A beat.

"Fine. We'll play your game." Villalobos turned around. "The M&P 9? You're probably drawn to it from watching a cop show or a movie."

No, it was my favorite gun, dummy. "Oh, I don't even own a TV, but I'll take your word for it." I held a hand daintily at my throat. "Is it any good? I mean, would it be in the category of 'no second chances,' as you described before?"

"It's about as good a beginner's piece as you're gonna get for the price, but it's a fucking gun. Guns kill people."

Cute with the little jab there: "beginner." Stanley made it easy to hate him. I thought it was charming when I first met him, but over time, I realized it made him annoying and a potential liability. I didn't need someone like him in my way as I made more moves. I could have sent Eddie or Bill or really anyone else out here to run this little errand, but goddamn, there was something about doing this myself. It felt necessary.

"I always assumed the person pulling the trigger did all the killing," I said. "May I see it? It might be exactly what I've been looking for."

Villalobos continued sorting the counter. "I played along." He motioned to the door. "Now I'm done. You want a taste of what I got in this bag, you lead the way and we walk out of here as friends. You can buy yourself a few more of those fancy dresses. You want to keep fucking with me, well, we can take a different route. An uglier one at that."

He thought he had my number, but I wondered if it was worth drawing this out any longer. Sure, I was having fun, but a man like Villalobos probably hit a silent alarm or had a sawed off at the ready to shear my pretty little head off my pretty little neck. That... would not be as fun.

"Le sigh." I reached into my petticoat and pulled a gun out with the speed dozens upon dozens of Atticus training sessions blessed me with—I hated those sessions. "My M&P 40 is a little better. Stopping power's a bit improved, and the clip's got greater capacity." I steadied my aim using both hands—no second chances here. This was the real shit.

Villalobos brought both hands up and held them in the air. He gritted his teeth as if he'd swallowed glass. "This right here? This is the mistake you're gonna remember on your final day. The moment you're going to regret before the bullet enters your hollow fucking head."

I licked my lips. Was this nervousness? Was I really going to get the prom willies during my second actual murder? Wonder why that was. Maybe I didn't give enough of a shit about Villalobos to push past the trepidation. There was no passion to this. It was part of a plan—and really, more of an excuse to get practice. To see if Amity was a fluke. I still wasn't sure I had the stones to really take a life without a care to give.

"Okay, here's what we're going to do," I said. "We're going to talk all about your work with Frankie. We're going to talk all about where the money is, too. And when we're done with that, Stanley, you're going to tell me exactly where you're keeping all those pregnant girls holed up. You dig? And I want receipts. All the proof you've got on hand, or those sweet babies of yours are gonna face consequences, too."

Stanley Villalobos narrowed his eyes and scanned my face. Gears turned in that bald head of his. A glimmer in his eye, a moment of clarity. He recognized me. Not Poppy Leathers. No, he recognized the other girl.

I kept my aim steady. "You look like you're getting close, sweetheart."

"Holy shit, I remember you."

"Obviously. You knew me when I walked in." What was the hurt in drawing it one second longer?

Stanley shook his head. "No, no, no. I thought I recognized you. It's you..." he blinked, the name on the tip of his tongue. "Gr—"

That was enough of that. Trigger pulled. Loose end sorted.

Next.

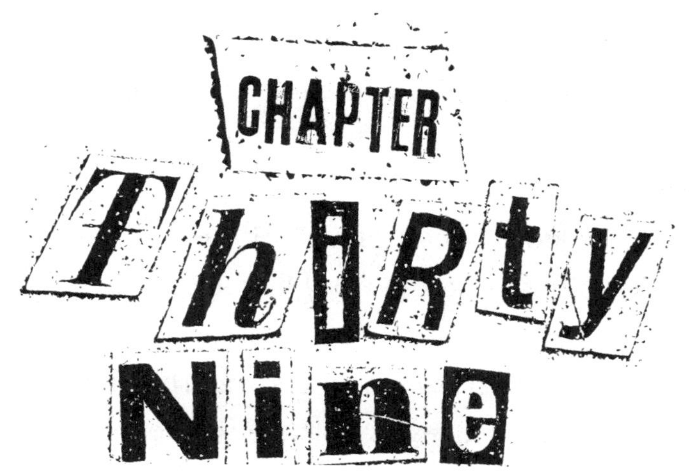

"You wouldn't believe how many air fresheners we left down here to make it smell this nice." I walked into the antechamber, my voice echoing against the corroded walls. I raised my hands and turned in place. Station Zero was repainted, outfitted with scaffolding, and an entire pulley system was created specifically for Jason to paint the ceiling.

Above and fucking beyond. I was amazing—as always.

We even widened that tight entranceway for fear somebody would get stuck—or worse.

You paid Poppy Leathers; you got Poppy Leathers quality. And this wasn't just for Jason anymore: this was my goddamn coming out party.

"You better have good feedback for me, homey," I said.

Honestly, it didn't matter. I felt like a million goddamn dollars. Things were moving along. Plans were in place. Even if Atticus turned up right then, it didn't matter. I was ready for the king of the midlife crisis.

"We're a day out." Jason smiled. "No more options." He looked around. "But you very much did outdo yourself, Pop."

"Poppy."

Jason nodded. "Yeah, sure." His eyes lit up. "Holy crap, you splurged on the Petzl harness?"

I shrugged. "I got whichever one the white guy at the white people sports store told me was the best one."

I went to sit but realized that I preferred my skirt not pick up venereal diseases from the 18th century. "I managed to get the planner's word that we're safe down here tomorrow night. 'Fairly safe,' he said. He did mention tying things up before midnight. That smell ain't going to get any better the longer we plug up the works, if you get me."

"I plan on finishing at ten. People need to get here by 2 PM sharp," Jason said. "No stragglers. I want asses in here and ready to watch by 2:30. It's going to take all that time to get the painting finished and to ensure the team constructs the other pieces for the walkthrough."

It was Jason's most intricate show. He'd be painting while a group of interns put together previously prepared found art pieces meant to be abandoned or broken on site. While that happened, a live brass band would play the soundtrack to one of his earliest films, *Fuck Your Fancy Nothings*—a six-hour treatise on multi-cultural capitalism and the process behind making chicken nuggets. The special part about the film, though, was that all dialogue would be performed by a theater troupe in a rare dialect of Romani slang.

The event would be filmed on seven different IMAX cameras as documentation, and to put together Jason's next film in his DOLVIDA cycle. Jason intended to create a sequence of multimedia explorations of society focused on the taboo and uncouth. The plan for his final production would be to have a readily available, forty-eight-hour version of DOLVIDA posted in fifteen second snippets on TikTok. After that, the account would be deleted, and the only way to access the work would be to sign up to view the show in an uninterruptable stream. People would also have to refer each other once the first twenty plays were sold. The hope was to give the entire experience a "club feel." It would be a reminder not only of Jason's work but, ultimately, the fragility of human existence—a work outliving him but utterly dependent on other humans to keep existing.

Despite my conflicting emotions, I was impressed with the entire affair. It was stupendously arrogant and pompous. Distracting and overindulgent. It was the kind of show that would attract the absolute worst people across all boroughs, the king- and queenmakers of the jet set. The heirs apparent of Silo Jotter and their hangers on. Literally dozens of potential and established enemies all in the same place.

It was perfect.

"I've got the interns rehearsing at your Brooklyn

space. What time do you need them here?" I lit a clove with a gun-shaped Zippo I stole from Villalobos' shop.

"Where'd you get that?" Jason asked.

"Found it at Goodwill," I said as I took a drag. "Too awesome not to pick it up." I exhaled and picked a spot of dried blood from the base of the lighter. "When do you need your art slaves to be down here, and do I have to be the one to Pied Piper them over?"

Jason walked past me and grabbed a stack of old metal folding chairs. "You can have them follow the directions we put up on the site." He took a moment to position the seats, erratically. "Or make them work for it. This endeavor isn't without effort from both sides."

I rubbed my eyes. "I'll be here doing finishing touches the night before and morning of. Not sure I'm sticking around for the whole show."

"No interest in staying for the long haul?"

"Sweetie, I've spent years seeing you make the sausage. I know better than to eat it. I trust in your ability to put on spectacular and well-earning theatrical feats of artistic merit. We'll see each other the day after and giggle over mimosas and frittatas like civilized motherfuckers," I said. "Besides, I've got a ton of other work to do."

Jason watched me. "You've got that tone you get when you're holding back something."

"I'm allowed to have a private life, Jason."

"No doubt. But whenever you talk like that something crazy happens."

I laughed, bright and happy, right from the gut. "Oh, sweetheart. You know me all too well." I walked over to a chair and shifted it over a few inches. That was working, right? "Is Sara coming?"

Jason shook his head and walked over to a projector. He slowly rotated its position, so it was facing a clean patch of wall. "No. She's busy with the kids and decided to go upstate for a little while. Her parents live in Rockland. Probably for the best."

"The best?"

"Things have been tense is all."

"Tense like nobody sleeping because the living poop machines you bought are difficult to handle or tense like explaining to those poop machines that they weren't why mommy and daddy stopped loving each other?"

Silence.

"Seriously, Jason?"

He rolled his eyes. "It's been coming for a while."

"Then why did we just spend an ungodly amount of money on gray market babies?"

"I thought it would make things better," Jason said. "But it made things worse. I couldn't live with her before, and the babies made me hate her even more. I never wanted them to begin with."

I felt a flare of anger there. "Hate's a strong word, my friend."

"Well, it's true. Listen. Pop, can we concentrate on getting this show set up? I'm not in the mood to discuss my domestic issues with the help, alright?"

I raised my brows as I watched Jason fiddle around with that projector. The chair in my hand begged to go for a direct flight to his fucking head, but now was not the time. I continued unfolding chairs and placing them wherever they made as little sense to place them. Once the anger subsided, I actually felt a little grateful. There'd been a twinge of guilt hanging around the periphery and Jason managed to wash it all away with a few words. I needed that, honestly.

Needed a lot of shit to wash away, really.

CHAPTER Forty

I picked up my phone. "What's going on, Eddie, my love?"

"He's here. Over by the Fourth Street Basin."

"Well shit. He really just turned up like that?"

"I guess he did. What should we do?"

I was sitting outside a spot called Bison & Bourbon enjoying a little meat and a gigantic cocktail. If things were going to go down, I reasoned a nice meal was a luxury I could afford myself. Didn't hurt the owner was on Silo's ledgers as a buyer of fancy cheeses—free meal for me. I really hadn't expected Atticus to be so obvious.

"He has to have something planned," I said.

"He's by himself. I've got six guys with me. We can roll up on him and bring him to the spot. Honestly, Miss Leathers, it is probably best to ambush him and end this."

I mulled that one over. Atticus was hurt. He couldn't possibly be a threat anymore, could he? I wasn't about to walk the two blocks to find out, but come on, they had to be able to get the job done.

"Ambush him, but don't end things without me there. Do whatever you need to do. Shoot him in the leg. Hit him with a car. Doesn't matter. Text me if it all goes well and I'll meet you in the service tunnels once I've made a walkthrough of the show and let Jason see my face."

"Got it, boss."

"Oh, and Eddie?"

"Yeah, boss?"

"We got everything else, right?"

"We set it all up." He cleared his throat. "I, uh, even got a whole thing ready in case you change your mind about any of it."

Eddie was a good guy, but his caution wasn't necessary. Not anymore. Had my mind made up and I wasn't going to go back on my decision. Atticus and Silo had done that and look where it got the both of them—they exposed themselves, and soon the both of them would be feeding worms, destined to be nutrients for the goddamn trees.

"Excellent. Make sure the boys we asked to camp out are where they need to be by..." I checked my phone's clock, "3:30 PM the latest, okay? That's super important."

"Will do. Anything else?"

"Ah," I took a bit of my sandwich. Finished my drink. "Try not dying when you go after him."

"I'll do what I can, boss." Eddie disconnected.

I liked Eddie. I needed to have more conversations with him when this was all over.

I lingered near the manhole entrance that led to Station Zero until three minutes before the show was set to start. Did I have other plans? Yes. Was I about to let this show start without doing a cursory quality check? Absolutely not. I'd spent way too much time coordinating to leave it *all* up to chance—even if I was exhausted of Jason and all his bullshit.

I lightly jogged over to a young woman dressed in skintight blue vinyl and a matching snorkeling mask. "Sorry, sorry. Am I too late? I was waiting for my date and he's like, five minutes away."

The girl slipped the mask off her face and lifted a laminated script to read. "Mr. Tasker is insistent that nobody enter the show after a specific time. If you don't go in now, there's no going in at all." She took a drawn-out breath. "We'd hate for your ticket to be null, but also remind you that there is a strict no-refund policy that you agreed to at the point of purchase. I'm happy to provide you with a paper copy of the disclaimer if you do not have one." The girl held up a small brochure as thick as the tip of my thumb in her other hand.

Wooden delivery, but she did what she was supposed

to do. "Fine," I said, "his loss. Anything else I should know about?"

The girl rolled her eyes in thought. "Um, oh, there's someone down there that should give you a poncho and a veil. If you want a hat, they should have extra fedoras—anyone identifying as a man is required to wear one."

Hey, look at that, she nailed it without using the job aid.

"Excellent, love. Thanks very much."

I approached the manhole and stopped for a moment. "So, do I sort of...?" I had not planned the descent via manhole in a tutu and platform shoes. What I got for trying to dress a little more formal for the occasion.

"Oh, it's weird, there's a rung maybe a foot down. Feel for it with your foot." The manhole girl approached and pointed into the darkness. "Maybe use your phone's flashlight for a second while you go down."

"With my third hand?"

Manhole girl only offered a shrug.

I crouched and turned on my phone's flashlight, noting the strange drop off in the weak light. "Guess breaking my neck's part of the immersion." I turned and lowered my legs down, my foot finding the rung before slipping.

"Be sure to use the hashtags for #DOLVIDA or #Jason-Tasker if you post on social media," the girl called down. "Please repost others under those tags to enhance the experience."

"Yeah, sure. Thanks." I continued down the ladder.

I reached the bottom of the ladder and stepped onto the old brick. It felt strange to enter the tunnels here. I'd grown so accustomed to the other entrance Alton and Jenna used that it was a little disorienting at first. It was a shame not to have them with me then, but I'd conveniently left them off the guest list, lying about the show's date to spare them the, um, indignity. I made it up to them with money and a few contacts in Prague that were willing to show them a hell of a time in their sewers.

The deodorizers were clearly ineffective at this point. There was something foul lingering, like standing where someone had farted minutes before. I followed the path—covered in glow in the dark arrows—towards a nude man holding two glow sticks in one hand and a large sign with the words, "I AM THE DIRECTION FUCKBOI," in the other.

Next quality check. I stepped towards the precious fuckboi and smiled. "Okay, directions." I leaned forward and saw a tunnel to the right, multiple work lamps rigged along the walls. There was a sealed grate at the end of the tunnel and a fancy canoe chained to it. Thank you very much, Eddie and the boys for moving that there.

"The canoe is not part of the show, so please do not begin your judgment until you are fully immersed in Mr. Tasker's interactive art experience." The fuckboi was British. He turned his head away from me and suggestively thrust his hips in the direction I needed to go.

"Make a left here, walk fifty-seven steps, turn right, and keep walking until you reach the cupcake kiosk." His thrusting increased in urgency. "Be sure to use the hashtags for #DOLVIDA or #JasonTasker if you post on social media." He moaned with all the sex appeal of an orphanage fire.

Eh, that was mixed. Credit for paying enough attention to the fact that I was staring at the boat and calling out that it was not worth my interest. Had to wonder if a lot more folks thought it was part of the installation and he had to ad lib that after the twentieth time it happened.

"Wonderful. Excellent." I turned left as told and entered a stunning double-arched brick channel, enough headroom for me to look up and examine the gorgeous construction. It was a surprising moment—to marvel at the brickwork for the first time even though I'd been down here so many times already—but it was nice to find something beautiful in such a dingy place.

There was so much attention to detail. The way the bricks seemed perfectly laid. The fact that the cement and grout all stood the test of time. Down in a place nobody bothered to look. This work wasn't for attention. It was for the city. The people who put this together had a purpose beyond social media clout or bragging rights among friends. I wondered what happened to people that they were so willing to let motivations like that simply fade away, but I also realized that the people who built this—who supported a city bursting with nonsense—

were filled with motivation and aspiration, weren't they? They willed this shit into existence with their blood and sweat.

Respect. There were lessons in every stone and every arch. I made a note to remember that. If I wanted a strong foundation, I had to put care into the work. Look at how easily Silo and Atticus' power simply faded away. They'd been reliant on aesthetic—the *idea* of their power holding people off—when the truth was that the power was an abstract. All it took was my chaotic ass pulling at a loose brick and everything began to fall apart.

Following the turn, I continued to notice new details. Names on bricks stood out: Abernathy, Tippets, Burnham. I noticed the small grooves along the bottom of the channels. It was fascinating, as if an entire secret world were buried beneath concrete and steel. I wondered what was going on above me, and I pitied the people walking around simply taking this place for granted—not a single one understanding how this entire city was a fucking miracle.

Then I got to the next checkpoint and all that miracle bullshit crashed down around me.

The cupcake kiosk was exactly that, a small hut housing a glass case with tiny, tiny cupcakes. There was an overeager woman in a bright pink shirt and an appalling lime green visor smiling like an idiot behind the case. "Welcome to DOLVIDA 3," she said slowly, as if the four words were rehearsed but not yet memorized.

I stopped and admired the ridiculous cupcakes. I trusted some of the support staff to order these things since I was busy with more important tasks, so it was my first time seeing them and I was a little underwhelmed, but I got what I paid for—nothing. I'd paid these people nothing.

"Are these for sale?" I asked.

"Oh, God no, miss. This is a reminder that you are officially putting aside the sentiment afforded to you by the beautiful and the addictive. Capitalism is no longer your savior here."

Not a bad line of bullshit, I thought, but if capitalism was no longer *our* savior down here, why did Jason happily charge those down here to enjoy his entire… thing?

I gave the girl a hearty thumbs up. "Well, sure. The teat is no longer there to suckle or whatever—great. So, do I go in behind you?"

"No, miss." The cupcake girl pointed behind me with her chin.

I turned and was greeted with another intricate brick archway. Down a tunnel lit with cheap citronella torches was a gaping hole. It was flanked with calcified stone and mold, erupting as if the entrance was forcibly pushing the substance out. It was the prolapsed rectum of urban New York—spewing waste out as a fossilized record.

I loved it so much.

"You'll need these." The cupcake girl walked back into my view and handed me a small package with a poncho, rain visor, and the biggest blunt I had ever seen.

"Is that actual weed in there?" That had to be a last-minute Jason addition. Just like him to add that extra bit of whimsy—if that was the right word—to go into overkill, but fuck it. Let folks enjoy whatever they could while standing ankle deep in toxic waste and staring at art they pretended to understand.

"Synthetic. We'd like to remind you that Jason Tasker is not responsible for any adverse reaction you may have in partaking in this complimentary item. It is, of course, completely optional to partake, and if you'd rather not smoke it, you are welcome to offer it to any of the other showgoers if they would like to have an extra. We will caution that side effects may include but are not limited to hallucinations, frequent vomiting, severe coughing, abdominal cramping, bloody stool, and night terrors."

"The blunt, you mean."

The woman blinked and stiffened. "Said object."

I enjoyed how uptight she was, and I found Jason providing these folks with synthetic weed hysterical.

I took the package. "Okey dokey." I walked towards the mouth of hell and tossed the care package to the side once cupcake girl was out of view.

Cupcake Girl's voice echoed down the tunnel. "Be sure to use the hashtags for #DOLVIDA or #JasonTasker if you post on social media."

Chapter Forty-one

I tried to assess what irritated me most about Jason's show. As I stood in front of a massive mural depicting '80s cartoon characters peeing against a brick wall covered in corporate logos—the least effective piece, in my opinion—I ran through the items that most incensed me:

A video playing on multiple screens of Tasker running a small assembly line manned by adult men dressed like children of the '80s. The "kids" were tasked with building meaningless bric-a-brac while Tasker ran around fully nude with a dead fish in each hand screaming, "Work, work, work for your nothing!" and stopping to smack someone across the face with a fish every thirty-two seconds—there was a timer. I wasn't sure how legal this video was.

Dancers dressed from the waist up in mascot outfits, but nude from the waist down. They shuffled around the room, always working to wave their genitals at patrons when they sat down. One or two people had already lodged complaints to a man wearing a suit who remained silent, aside from screaming a random racial epithet every three minutes—there was also a timer over this man's head. Jason liked timers.

Everyone—absolutely everyone—was staring at their phone. I saw multiple people watching the show on live stream, jamming their thumbs to litter the screen with a digital diarrhea stream of emojis, hearts, and idiotic memes. Others held their phones up at an angle while they blathered on and on to their pretend audiences about Jason's "vision."

Jason Tasker himself, lifted at least twenty-five feet above by a pulley. He was fully nude—this man sure loved nudity—and painting a surreal self-portrait with house paint using his penis as the brush. He grunted dramatically with every thrust and wiggle of his hips, making it appear as if he was trying to fuck the ceiling. People milled about and stepped around the growing puddles of paint below wherever Jason concentrated on his work.

Overall, the show felt completely devoid of real substance, a reminder that while the money was solid, there was not a damn moment I understood his point. Why was any of this even happening? The mood of the room matched mine. Nobody was happy or gazing at the work in wonder. They were simply here to say they were here. It was an awful reminder of the kinds of people that attached themselves to this city like parasites—taking everything and giving nothing.

I wasted some time and walked from installation to installation—live pieces with interns tasked to sculpt clay sculptures based on IKEA-style instructions written up by Tasker in fake languages, couples filling balloons with their own urine and playing the world's worst game of hot potato, an armless sword swallower with a sign around his neck asking who was strong enough to remove "Excalibur" from his gullet. I checked my phone for a text from Eddie. A sign that I could walk the hell out of this place.

It was the world's worst carnival, and every single attendee lost from the moment they paid for the privilege of descending into a New York City sewer to immerse themselves in an exercise of pretentious futility. As if this entire debacle couldn't be hosted in a warehouse or some tech bro's loft.

After five laps around the room, I stopped for lack of motivation to pretend I was a part of the crowd. I leaned back to watch Jason continue his grunting and thrusting. His project had no form. It was just a poor man's Pollack plastered on the ceiling of a forgotten subway station. Fuck me, my mind was going poetic I was so bored.

There was a moment I thought I saw Atticus, but it was only a different tattooed and lanky white guy. He was accompanied by a few other lanky, tattooed white men. One stopped in front of me and made a move to speak, but stopped, backing up with a flush in his cheeks.

"Pardon. Thought you were friend," he said. He had an accent. Strong. One I never really heard before.

"No worries," I said, and turned away from the group.

I ordered a drink at the only bar in the room that wasn't next to a pile of indistinguishable gray slush. I avoided the seats positioned in awkward spots and found a clean spot on a column to lean on. The column vibrated a moment, forcing me to stand straight. I went to take a sip of my drink, but that was ruined by a clump of rock—I hoped—falling into my cup. "Fucking trains."

Three women walked by and stared above me. "This is fucking ridiculous," a woman said. She was dressed head to toe in yellow vinyl. Her accent matched the guy from before.

One of her companions, in black vinyl, frowned. "I'm sort of sad we can't see his dick," she said with a weak, but noticeable accent. She looked at me for a fleeting moment. The way a person would try and catch a glimpse without getting caught, but they didn't know they sucked at being sneaky.

The women laughed, throwing their heads back and holding their chests like they were in a commercial for the latest antidepressant medication.

I slammed back my drink and placed the plastic cup on a chair. Something was really fucking wrong. I checked my phone.

One message. Eddie: *We got him.*

I heard a dozen little pings and chirps drowning in the music playing from the speakers nearby. I spotted a few groups of people checking their devices and looking at each other. A few stolen glances my way. Muttering. A few subtle nods of the chin and raised eyebrows.

I narrowed my eyes. No. This was wrong. Scanned the room. I didn't see any of the familiar faces that turned up to Jason Tasker shows. None of the art glitterati. None of the trust fund idiots barking about their latest investments. None of the sloppy drunks—the faded artists—swaying and muttering jealous incantations in hopes they get a little bit of the old rub back.

I was surrounded by strangers. Almost all white. Almost all in Atticus-lite clothing. Glowering. Less focused on the spectacle than they were on looking like they were focused on the spectacle. Hollow people, I realized. Just like Atticus and Silo and Jason. They all lacked substance, mimicking the way people were supposed to move through the world, but too up their own asses to even get that part right.

I texted Eddie back: *OMW* and turned towards the maintenance exit I marked as a restroom. The door was locked—I had one of two keys—so I knew nobody was going to surprise me there. The walk over was fucking rough. I felt eyes on my back. Felt like any moment someone was going to pounce. I turned slowly, watching as a small clutch of patrons pretended not to look my way while the vapider of the crowd continued staring at their phones. Something wasn't right, but I couldn't let that stop me. It was time to move. Time for all this shit to work itself out. Keep moving, Poppy, we were almost done.

Once I was past the threshold and locked the door behind me, I took a second to let my brain catch up with my heart.

"Were those guys Albanians?"

I waved to Eddie and Bill as I walked into the maintenance room. This was the one place I kept to myself as we planned the show. A little hideaway at first, but now a base of operations and a spot with access to the second fastest way out of this literal shit hole.

"Get everything set up and wait for me topside," I said. "Me and this motherfucker need to have some private time." I pointed to a tied up and blindfolded Atticus at the far side of the room.

Atticus sniffed and shook a chill out. "You would have made a half decent assassin, Pop. Seriously."

I waited for my boys to clear out and took my shoes off. I got undressed and dug into a duffel bag Eddie left behind. Inside: a powder blue wetsuit covered in yellow duckies, matching flippers, a pair of goggles, and a waterproof flashlight. I pulled the equipment out and laid it on a small cot we had in here in case I wanted to nap between planning meetings with organizers.

"'Half-decent'? I'm already better than you ever was," I said.

Atticus couldn't help but smile. "You're probably right."

"Oh, please, don't choose now to patronize me. You never took a word out of my mouth seriously until I strangled your girlfriend."

Atticus rolled his head side to side. "I'm not kidding. Maybe I acted aloof about your… eccentricities, but I think there was always that little instinct in my head screaming at me to turn you away the moment we met. My hubris won the debate."

I slipped on the wetsuit. It was tight. Felt like I was wearing a full body condom. "And now we're having our big conversation." I clapped my hands. "All cards on the table?"

Atticus nodded. "It appears that we are."

I finished dressing and dragged the cot across from Atticus before sitting down to figure out how to put on flippers. "I'll go first," I said. "Why didn't you kill her? And tell the truth."

"I told you: I liked her. Maybe not so much at first, but over time, things changed."

"Enough to gamble away everything you worked for? Even your life?"

"I think so. I liked her as a person, though. More than that… probably not? Things are complicated. Always were. I used Amity as an excuse. It wasn't fair to her, and it certainly wasn't fair to you or Silo. I think I understand that now."

I laughed joylessly. "I guess I saw her the same way. But then I was able to get past that and realize she was going to be another obstacle. No matter what happened."

"Yeah, you took initiative. Proved to Silo you were a legitimate talent."

"Man, that sarcasm is super subtle."

"She didn't deserve to die, Pop."

"Nobody you killed deserved to die either. You sit there acting like your dick somehow made that girl worth something more. The audacity, to believe she was special simply because you deemed her to be." I shook my head. "That's what separates us on that one. I knew she was special, but I also knew nobody is ever *that* special."

Atticus lowered his head. "You say I'm convinced I'm the hero here, but I say you're completely deluded into the belief you're the villain."

I stared at my hands. Gave that one some thought. He was wrong, but I wanted to give my brain time to let him know why instead of just lashing out. He *wanted* me to lash out. To be the impulsive Poppy he knew and loved.

"You know what? *That* right there? That's the problem I had with you and with Silo. Even with Jason, God bless his dick painting stupidity. All of you felt like you were able to—shit, maybe you even felt like it was a God-given obligation—to define me and anyone else you look down on."

"I never looked—"

"Shut the fuck up, I'm speaking."

"The balls you've grown." Atticus jerked his head backwards. "Can you take this stupid thing off?" He tried to swing his head a little to move the blindfold. "I'm working with the assumption this is sort of an ending, so I think it would be okay to look each other in the eye."

"Fine." I stood up and walked over to Atticus. Yanked the blindfold off and walked back to my seat and tried to figure out whether I could keep ballet slippers on under those flippers.

"That's a look," Atticus said.

"It's more about function than fashion today." I motioned to Atticus. "I miss the beard, by the way."

"You are so fucking smart, Pop. I mean that. Beyond anyone I've ever met. But you need to admit this is all too much. You need to admit you're in over your head here. A sewer art show? This many people who probably saw you come in here?"

The people. He was bringing that up on purpose. "You teamed up with the Albanians, didn't you?" I asked. "You went to Amity's grandpa and got the hook up? Probably told them my evil ass was the one who took poor old, coke dealing Amity out to infringe on their business, right?"

"See? Smart beyond your years." Atticus smiled wide. Never saw that level of joy on his face in all our years together. Helped to know that inflicting pain on me is what inspired it. Seriously. It meant I was important to him. Never believed that before.

"Wise beyond my years indeed," I said. "Bet you'd never guess my age."

"I thought you told me you were twenty-three?"

"Thirty-two."

"Lies." Atticus scoffed.

I stroked my cheeks. "Moisturizer and wide-brimmed hats, my love." I waved the banter off. "Anyway, you and I keep going off the rapport cliff before we get to the point. You seem to have a plan."

"I do indeed. See, you're going to have some great pain getting back out the way you came." He raised his brows. "Well, really, any exit's going to be a problem. Did you know Amity's family is beloved in New York? I was pleasantly surprised."

I snapped my fingers. "That's why you came at Silo the way you did. You had an army in your back pocket."

"I'm angry, Pop, not stupid." Atticus leaned forward and let his head hang down. "You all thought I was slipping. Honestly, I was. We can pretend Amity inspired me somehow. That you killing her is what brought back whatever this monster is inside of me. But that's bullshit. You all made it fun again."

"So, you're admitting this hero complex thing is bullshit."

He scoffed. "Of course it is. Like I said, you're deluded into believing you're the villain, Pop. The truth is, people like me. The people waiting outside that door? The ones who are probably killing your well-dressed crew? We're the bad guys. You're just some idiot off the street who decided to playact at being bad because you're mediocre."

Oh boy, there he was. There was Atticus Garcia. Mask off. Cock out. This was the man he pretended didn't exist all those years. All those Sunday brunches. The good manners. The impeccable clothing and accessory game—thanks, me. Here was the man who murdered for a living and flinched when he realized that maybe he wasn't as good as he used to be.

"The fucked-up part, Atticus, is that you're the only one who thought people didn't see that part of you." I stood and stretched. Had to be limber for what was next. "But the real problem wasn't whether I thought you were a homicidal maniac, an effete brat with a violence problem, or some loser felon with an anger management problem that decided to give into it at the first possible chance."

"What was it, then?"

"You lost your fucking edge." I went back to my bag and found the last gift Eddie left behind. It looked like a shitty remote for a shitty toy car. Little grip. Red button on the top. Such a small tool for such a big fucking problem I was about to cause. "Edge, Atticus, is being prepared for the worst with the worst possible option. You dig? Like in the '80s. The US and Russia had the whole mutually-assured destruction thing, right?"

"Right. Sure. I feel like it was a little more than that, but I get your comparison."

"There's always more."

"So, say it."

I didn't want to give him the satisfaction. His betrayals hurt me; it was that simple. Ignoring how I felt about Amity, ignoring my goals. I thought he cared about me at one time—that we were a great mentor and mentee—but that was a big lie. I was just a tool for him—something that came for free that he felt he could use forever and that he could cast off as soon as I wasn't important enough anymore.

Like that goddamn cast iron pan.

I decided to change the subject. Emotional was a bad place to be with what was coming. "What made you believe that I would trap myself underground with you—or even without you—and not bother to make damn sure that if shit hit the fan it blew both ways?"

"Is it wrong to say I'm excited to hear about this?" Atticus gave me a joyful grin, but the look in his eyes betrayed him. It was a good thing to take the blindfold off. To see that doubt there. Maybe even a little fear? It gave me a rush.

"I'd be doing a bad job if that wasn't the case," I said. "So, did you ever know there were streams and brooks down here? In the sewers, I mean."

Atticus shook his head. "Can't say I'm well versed in city planning."

"It's kind of amazing. There's almost an entire world locked away under the one we take for granted. It's like something out of a video game, you know? Down the pipe, and boom: secret level." I pointed above us. "There's a metric fuckton of water above us too. It dumps out into the Hudson, further north of here. I hadn't planned on Jason using the sewers as his theater for the show, but when he chose to, and I did my research... Christ. No better place to take care of all my bad business in one swell foop."

Atticus narrowed his eyes. Then they widened. He got it. "What about your boss? What about the people here legitimately?"

I stared back at the floor. "The biggest thing a person needs to accept about mutually assured destruction is that everyone's going to hurt. It's what makes people avoid pushing the shiny buttons. There's a part of our brain that realizes exactly what you're realizing right now. To use your teenage boy analogy, it's what separates the villains from the real fucking bastards."

Atticus straightened up. "You're bluffing."

"Nah, sweetheart. I'm taking initiative." I held up the remote, took a deep breath, locked eyes with my ex-boss, and pressed that shiny red button—not once, but twice. Throughout Station Zero and the tunnels surrounding us, two dozen little packages Eddie and the boys set up for me got the signal.

It was time for the real performance art to begin.

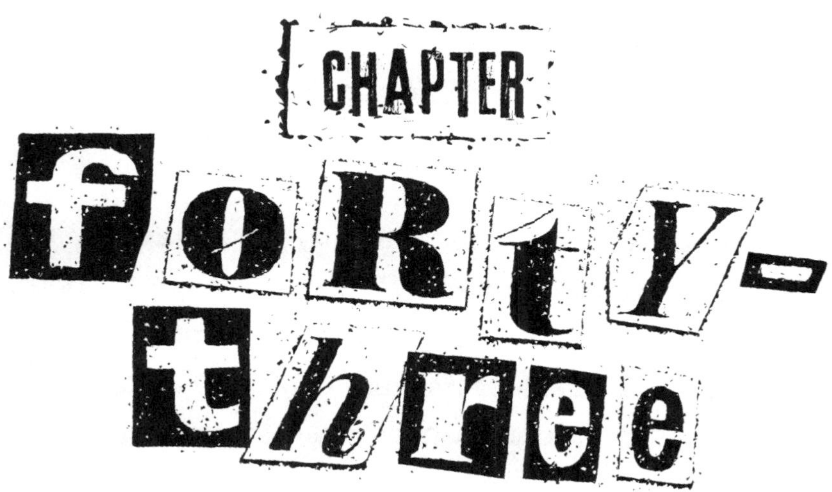

CHAPTER forty-three

I gasped as I broke the surface of the brackish water. Might have underestimated the impact of all those explosives. Overestimated my ability to make it out of there before getting swept away. I pressed that button and the next second: darkness. Only upside was knowing Atticus was still tied to that chair. I hoped the last sounds he heard were the churning water and his gurgled screams.

Speaking of screams. Jason Tasker was only a few feet above me, barking at people across the way with urgency, directing them towards items to use as flotation devices. My head hurt. And my arms. Also, my left leg. I wondered if the water had shoved me through that door like a blunt weapon. Only explanation for the pain and for being in an entirely different part of Station Zero.

I paddled my hands and feet, slowly at first, while I blinked hard, desperate to get my bearings. I found a wall and managed to brace against it for a moment before a coughing fit began and I swallowed more water. I wretched, the taste of metal, dirt, and what I distinctly remembered as the smell in the Penn Station bathrooms coating my tongue and lips.

Something wrapped around my upper arm and I pushed it away with a weak yelp. My eyes, ears, mouth, and chest all burned terribly. I wished I found more time to go to the gym before committing to flooding these tunnels. Didn't count on how much swimming took it out of me.

"Miss! Please, miss—we're trying to help." It was the woman who'd given me the poncho, perched on a filthy canoe—my canoe—with three other people. "We don't have much room, but we can get you over to an exit, I hope. Please calm down." The woman grabbed at my arm again.

Oh, she was helping. That made sense. Maybe. They pulled me onto the boat. The movement kicked up the nausea and I leaned over the side to vomit. My stomach seized so hard I cramped. "Oh, God," I slurred. "This was not how things were supposed to go."

"I think it's a terrorist thing." It was the sword swallower I saw earlier, sans sword. He was filthy, and there was dried blood caking the sides of his mouth. "I saw some skinhead pressing a remote or something before everything blew up."

That was a lie, but fuck it, maybe this was a chance to start a game of telephone. "You're right." There was a growing pain in my gut and the base of my skull. "I think I saw that, too." I wiped my mouth with the back of my hand. "Is anyone going to get Mr. Tasker off..."

Another loud boom and the room shook. Bricks and chunks of concrete fell from above. I gripped the side of the canoe so hard that splinters bit into my fingertips and palms. Another explosion rocked the room, and more people screamed. I turned to cling against the edge of the canoe when the final explosion went off a few hundred yards away, taking the entire wall down and bringing in a new torrent of water. I had time for one deep breath as the canoe flipped over, then I was under again. This time, the water did not mix well with the fresh wounds on my hands. Every paddle was a fresh slice of hell, but I was resigned to my choices—if I drowned, it was all my fault. I accepted that.

Breaking the surface again, I was shocked to see the ceiling of the room only a few feet above my head. Ahead, the shattered wall. And worse: the intricate pulley system Jason was still strapped to as more water filled the room.

Jason was nowhere to be seen. That meant he was under, tied up to the ridiculous contraption he used moments earlier to mark up the ceiling. Fresh paint was smeared along the bricks above, making it difficult for me to use the ceiling to push my way through the water and towards the submerged cables.

I felt a tinge of pity for the man. He was an idiot, completely inept in so many ways. I wouldn't mourn him, though, and I sure as hell wouldn't feel bad for the family I helped make stupid rich by drowning him during his biggest show. If anything, Jason got the most out of my scheme.

Which was typical of him. Still making bank off all my hard work.

"Hey!" Someone screamed out from across the room: a young man, bald and sporting tattoos all over. He clung to the wall and called out again, "Hey! Poppy Leathers, right?" He was too eager for someone who should fear drowning. That damn accent, too.

The call attracted the attention of a group who managed to turn over the canoe I'd hitched a three-minute ride on before. Of course they were fucking armed. And thanks to my loud friend, they also had something to aim those guns at.

I dove back under the water, this time bumping into the naked corpse of my former employer. OK—I took back some of the hate; he finally showed up to do me a favor. I grabbed the back of Jason's harness—I think that's what it was—and tucked my legs up to my chest, trying to cover as much of my body with his. Jason didn't resist. Couldn't imagine a worse fate than dying balls out in a sewer.

Lies. Dying while using a naked painter as a shield was probably much worse. I swore I felt the impact of bullets hitting Jason, but maybe I was hallucinating at that point. My arms were beginning to feel heavy, and my legs cramped up along with my midsection. Stars began to burst in my vision. Felt like my chest was filled with boiling oil. I couldn't see a damn thing, so there was no way of knowing if those assholes were still above me or even looking for me at all. The room was still flooding, and I couldn't have been so important they'd throw their own lives away for me, right?

I tried to adjust my legs, but a cramp of biblical proportions caused my right thigh to seize. I gasped out of instinct and swallowed water. I struggled to move, to hold the breath that wasn't there anymore. Down became up as panic set in, and I let go of Jason's body to try to find my bearings, unsure if I was reaching to the surface or to my end. Water rushed between my ears. I heard its lullaby, soft and strangely melodic. This was a hell of an ending, I thought, trying to ignore the icy needles pricking my neck and my arms. Yep, even if this was it, I left a mark, hadn't I? That made me feel a little better as the world began to darken and the sound in my head dulled.

It wasn't so cold anymore.

It wasn't so painful anymore.

CHAPTER FORTY-FOUR

It felt like waking up too early. The way it came in phases. The light different every time I opened my eyes. My position shifted. Head throbbing. Throat burning. Chest so tight I couldn't find a breath.

I opened my eyes fully. Felt like I was floating. I bobbed and stared at the ceiling only a foot away from my face. I heard my heart beating between my ears. Didn't want to move. It felt good to just stay still and let the water carry me wherever it would.

The water, apparently, wanted to take me to the wall. I knocked my head against brick face. Clearly, the water wasn't thrilled about my laziness.

"Fuck," I moaned, and turned slowly. I leaned against the wall to get my bearings. Looked like I had drifted out of Station Zero and into one of the tunnels that led there. No way to tell where I was exactly. The water had detritus strewn all over its surface. Decorations, TV monitors, and the occasional tray of cupcakes floated by.

Further down the tunnel, I thought I saw what looked like an empty canoe—*the* canoe?—bob past. I felt a vibration at my back—the trains above—and the water churned a little, pushing me away from the wall and towards the canoe. I tried to stay in place. Conserve energy and paddle my feet slowly so I could keep afloat.

It was a bad move to falter. The water didn't agree with me on that move, either, and pushed at me again. I slammed into the wall and lost my breath as fireworks went off behind my eyes. I scrambled to find my place as the torrent dragged me across the tunnel and towards the canoe—thank fucking God it was real. It was a last-ditch effort, but I found the strength to break the surface of the water and cling to the old boat, working through the almost excruciating pain—I'd clearly pulled or broke something in my midsection. I swung a leg over and screamed as I fell into the canoe.

Maybe I could ride this out—wait until things calmed down and navigate my way from this maze. This was karma. All those perfect opportunities gave me the ego to try to play the game, and this was my punishment: trapped in the sewer I'd exploded, waiting to drown or get shot. Maybe I did overdo it—a *little*. I didn't need to be so open about where I'd be. Certainly didn't need Eddie and the boys to set twelve charges. One would have been enough, really. I wanted to prove myself, though. Atticus had called me a villain, and that wasn't what I wanted to be. I wanted something more than that. I wanted to be the story people told to each other at night. To be a walking fucking warning.

Still, yeah, maybe a little too far there.

Another series of booms went off in the sewers, and the water level began to recede—drastically. Some of those charges were delayed. Not sure if that was something I'd asked for or a defect in the set up. Not that it mattered.

I rolled over and hung my head off the side of the canoe to see what had happened. It wasn't enough to drain the place completely, but the water stopped at about the depth where I could feasibly walk with my head and shoulders out of the water. I sat up slowly and, rummaging around, found a makeshift paddle to push this hunk of wood where I wanted it to go. See—still captain of my own ship. Or something like that.

I paddled—gingerly—towards the nearest turn in the tunnel. Something knocked the side of the canoe and nearly flipped it over. I found my balance. Grumbled from frustration and pain. I moved the paddle to push whatever it was that hit me out of the way and spied a shock of yellow. It was one of the women I saw in Station Zero earlier.

Another thump, another body. As I steered the canoe from the tunnel that housed it, more bodies hit the boat. I struggled to keep the canoe from capsizing and finally had to stop paddling, allowing the waters to dictate the direction while I used the paddle to brace for impact.

Soon enough, the canoe collided with a wall and was flanked by enough bodies to leave me stuck in a logjam of people.

Every face was a stranger's—not much of a relief—and already discolored. They must have drowned around the same time, but there were signs of other damage done: some sported fresh wounds. It was hard to tell if they'd suffered their injuries before or after death. I wondered how many of these people were there as backup for Atticus. Did he really bring a whole fucking army down here just for me? Under less stress, I would have been flattered.

Or maybe these were all those Tasker fans here for clout. It was strange to feel my disdain for them was gone. Not that I was guilty; well, maybe there was a twinge here and there as I saw certain faces. Was this numbness? Maybe I was in shock and this would all hit me later on—I really hoped not—but it was as if this whole mess was my own little disasterpiece. After all the time spent setting things up, after all the effort, well, here we were. I didn't feel quite like I'd accomplished anything, and I didn't feel like I'd really won.

If I was being honest, at that moment, it all felt so completely fucking pointless.

I stopped trying to paddle through the logjam and lay back on the canoe to stare at the old bricks lining the ceiling. It could all come down. Every bit of concrete and metal rushing to entomb my ass, and it was my fault, right? Right above me, everything I've been working towards. All I wanted: the control, the ability to make my own good luck, and the power to throw karma a big fucking middle finger—because when did being nice ever pay off for me?

Jesus, I wasn't satisfied because I wasn't fucking done.

And this, this wasn't karma. I caused this. I had explosives planted. I pressed the button. I set the players up. Maybe I could have waited to get topside before succumbing to my impulses, but I had to remember this was all me. This was me controlling the situation. It always was. I just made the choice to play victim, so I didn't need to ever point the finger my way. If I really wanted the things I felt I earned, then I needed to take every bit of that weight. The good and the bad.

Working for Atticus. Taking the indignities. The violence. The planning. For fuck's sake, I could still feel Amity's neck caving in under my grip, still remember the way her heat dissipated as I kept the very air she breathed from her lungs. Control. I had the capacity for great and horrible fucking things, and all I needed to do was get to the surface to take what was waiting for me. It was right there, and I was lying in a fucking crusty canoe feeling sorry for myself. I was speedrunning to the same destination as Silo and Atticus. I was being a fucking quitter. I was giving in to the part of me that hung out in the shadows, that little doubt beast that always wanted to remind me that for all my hard work, I didn't deserve the reward. Which was bullshit because I worked hard. I fucking earned what was ahead of me, and it was insane to let this shitty little boat be my coffin.

I sat up—slowly—and decided that if I was going to be a corpse, then I was going to be an ugly corpse. Motherfuckers were going to know I fought as hard as I could until the end.

"Fine," I said. "Fuck it."

I slowly dropped into the water from the edge of the canoe and waded towards a maintenance door at the end of the tunnel. I kept hold of the paddle to push the swollen, drowned corpses away from me. When I arrived at the small platform I had to climb—an easy thing any other day, but now I felt as if I was literally being broken in two—there was no choice but to use a corpse as leverage. It was painful, and morbid. A little squishy.

The body was a young man's, swollen already from the brackish sewer water flowing in through all his exposed orifices. I took care as I put my weight onto the body. It bobbed back and forth, bubbles rising from beneath it, gas expelling from his bowels. For one horrible moment, I met the corpse's gaze. His eyes looked fit to burst, his eyelids locked open, nostrils flared. His mouth hung slack—opening and closing each time I adjusted my weight. It was immense effort to move with the body and not to lose my lunch, but the effort paid off. Soon enough I was laid out with my back on solid ground, breathing heavily and fighting back tears.

I swore I heard voices in the distance. Whether it was in my head or not didn't matter. I couldn't risk the chance of someone finding me. Let them think I was dead. What mattered was getting out of here and finishing up the last little bit of work. I was still breathing. That meant I still had a chance to put the exclamation mark on all of this—seal my place in the hierarchy before it was too late.

I stood slowly, painfully, staggering, and surveyed the traffic jam of dead bodies, as if a child had overfilled their tub with action figures. It was horrible. But I'd told Atticus that this was the fallout of knowing what I had to do, and I accepted that. If I got out of this and into daylight, I knew it would be worth it. I owed it to myself to keep moving. I turned to the door and found myself face-to-face with the next obstacle.

The door leaked water from all four corners, and I was certain opening it would result in a cartoonish explosion of water and corpses. It was boarded over sloppily—I'd probably asked for the boys to do this as they set the charges—but it was easy to pull off the cheap wood. As I pried each board off the old metal door, the weight of the desperate, pent-up water caused it to quiver like a virgin. All hell reared to tear through as soon as it opened. I held off, wondered how best to approach the situation. Stared off down the tunnel I came from. Down that way were deeper waters, a shitty canoe, and a traffic jam of bodies. Not the best options.

Still: those bodies had to come from somewhere. Maybe if I walked opposite the current, I'd find my way back to Station Zero. That assumed a few things, though: for one, that the people who'd passed away in that specific wave were in the main presentation area, and that the area was in any way safe from water or the geniuses trying to kill me.

I wracked my broken brain. None of the options available to me were entirely pleasant. I was beginning to feel cold, and there was a taste that wouldn't leave my mouth no matter how many times I spit or forced myself to vomit. The chances of bacterial infection, toxic shock, or potential hypothermic shock were beginning to feel like valid worries. The little raised area I stood on was still threatened by water, only inches away. I had to make a move, or I was going to die, one way or another. Delaying and overthinking wasn't going to work this time.

So: back the way I came.

The water wasn't as cold as it felt earlier. I moved slowly this time. Kept close to the wall and grabbed anything I could get a firm grip on. I made a mental note to drop the theatrics next time and set off the charges once I was topside. Because, obviously, there could very well be another time I'd need to drown a bunch of people to further my self-interests. I almost started laughing, but the laughter died out as a choked gurgle in my throat.

Reunited with the choke point of corpses, I ignored the canoe I'd left behind and continued moving against the much weaker flow of water. I tried my best to ignore the oddly casual feeling of using the occasional corpse to keep momentum. Yet another trauma made redundant after the fifth time I had to do it. Story of my life.

As I moved ahead, there were fewer dead bodies and more detritus. A random frame floated by, empty but followed by other frames, their paintings smudged away. I dodged splintered wood and chunks of concrete for a while before a larger framed painting rammed into my chest with the force of a toddler's punch. I looked down and realized it was in near-pristine condition; the frame's build caused it to float in a way that had kept the canvas out of the water. This was one of Jason's pieces. A scatter of color at each corner framing black and white blobs with realistic human eyes. I was never a fan of this piece, but still, if it came to me, it had purpose. I held onto the portrait and tested its buoyancy. It was agreeable to my bodyweight, so I used it as if it were a pool toy, leaning a little on it to make swimming a bit easier.

There I was: swimming in the filth among the dead and ruined art. Perhaps the one I found not so ruined, but that didn't change the shitty aesthetic of the piece. Beyond the frame's buoyancy, though, there was the fact that I was holding a collector's item. Surely the sale of a painting from a now dead and infamous painter would help supplement any major cash drains in my future.

I laughed to myself, and this time it came out a little stronger, eking its way up a sore throat. My future. At that point, my future was cold concrete and rat shit.

I arrived at a tunnel intersection and was nearly bowled over by a makeshift raft—the remains of two wooden doors haphazardly tied together.

There wasn't much time to react to the hands that pulled me up violently from the water, hung me in the air like laundry, and slammed me down hard against the splintered wood of the raft. The air left me and my vision blurred. Didn't take long for the world to come back to me. Didn't take long to see a face I was hoping remained a memory.

Atticus leered over me. His eyes red-rimmed. A gash over his brow crusted over. His hands wrapped around my throat. His breath ragged as he trembled—if it was from rage or hypothermia, I couldn't tell. He grunted as he squeezed the breath out of me, the way I'd done to Amity. I found myself scratching at him uselessly, hoping for my fingers to find someplace to hook into, some way to damage him enough to break his grip and the silence.

But there would be no words. No screaming.

There was only violence.

Chapter Forty-five

He was trying to kill me. Same way I killed her. Water splashed over us as I struggled, but being wet made it hard for me to get a hold on him. Thankfully, it seemed to make his grip just a tad looser than it could be. That said, I knew better than to kick and scratch. I had a memory of when he told me that was the key to strangulation, to panic the victim, tire them out. A good strangling depended on the victim to be the one that did the real heavy lifting.

Instead, I focused on the task at hand: hurt him enough to make him stop. That big old gash over his eye? That was a good start. Finding that last bit of focus, I reached up and jammed my thumb as hard as I could right into the gummiest bit of the wound. I felt the heat of fresh blood as the flesh reopened. Atticus backed away from me with a roar, his grip loosening enough for me to kick him in the crotch three or four times—as many as needed—and get him the hell away from me.

"You couldn't go and drown like I wanted you to?" I asked, standing up with difficulty. This little raft was built for one.

Atticus sprawled back and held himself up with one hand as he tried to stem the blood flow from blinding him. "You deserve worse than what I was going to give you." He wobbled, unsteady even with the extra stability. The past 48 hours had put him through the ringer. Even if he made it through this sewer apocalypse, an infection would take him out like tinsel in a strong breeze.

"We all deserve worse, you little asshole." I watched him for any sign of movement. There was enough driftwood around to use as a weapon. Hell, that Tasker painting was sitting right at my feet. I propped it upright, waiting for Atticus to come back at me. "We're all playing at being big shots in a literal toilet."

Atticus spit. "There's a difference," he said. "I'm Atticus Garcia. I'm not cosplaying like the rest of you."

I shook my head. "Bullshit. I watched you before, at Silo's. You fight like every last motherfucker I ever seen sloppily struggle with other assholes. And even if you got the edge of, what, having shot more people than me, we're the same down here." I wasn't sure if it was the lack of oxygen, but that made sense to me. We were on even ground now. None of the pageantry or tradition mattered when we were surrounded by corpses and trash. When our bodies were already exhausted from simply trying to survive.

"You *think* you're the real deal," I said. "But the truth is, you're the single worst fucking hitman in all of Brooklyn. I mean, you needed an assistant to help you prepare for shooting people. You needed help with the easy part. How you haven't died or rotted away in a prison cell is all the proof anyone needs that white mediocrity rules the world." I wanted to vomit. Rage. Blood. Everything inside of me. I wanted it out. I wanted the waters to carry all this pain away.

"And you're a parasite. A bug under the rock pretending it's human. Big deal: you helped me. That's all you were good for, Pop: side work. You think you never received opportunities because people held you down? That's more delusion on your part. You never got offered anything because nobody saw enough in you to bother." Atticus wiped his brow and sneered at the blood he saw on the back of his hand. "You're just another spoiled asshole. Nothing unique about that in this city."

"Oh, yeah," I said sarcastically. "Nice job going for the low hanging fruit. I'm spoiled, yeah, wow. How did you come up with such an amazing retort, Atticus? Same place as you got the idea to *leave that fucking skillet behind*?" I snatched Tasker's painting, braced the edge against the bottom of the raft, and used my heel to break a portion of the frame. I picked up a jagged piece of wood and pointed it at Atticus. "You walked around Brooklyn like royalty. You lived the exact life you wanted at the literal expense of lives and then you decided that made you sad, so you figured, *fuck it*; what's the big deal if you fuck over more people, right? That's how it works when you can't bother to see folks for who they are."

"You used and killed Amity for your own ends, Pop. You can't talk like you're blameless."

"I gave up something I cared about."

"Something?" Atticus finally got to his feet. "You can't even call her a person."

"And she was a target for you. But now you don't have a gun, just your weak-ass hands."

Atticus nodded. "You seriously think that piece of wood is going to change a damn thing once I come over there?" He tried standing up, but his legs were fried. The boy was weak as a kitten by this point, the chaos and his attempt to strangle me took the last of his strength out of him.

We could go on like this forever, I realized. Each of us looking to shovel each other's baggage: our rage, our resentment, our insecurities over each other until we were buried alive, choking on our inadequacies. This was enmity, wasn't it? He wasn't mad at me for killing Amity—well, that wasn't the only reason—and I wasn't mad at him for being an asshole to me. Atticus and I saw a lot of what we hated about ourselves in each other.

"I've got one thing going for me you don't," I said.

Atticus snorted.

And I took my shot. I dipped to the side—his blind side—and closed the distance between us. By the time he realized what was happening, I had the sharp end of the wood against his neck. "I didn't give up my momentum, Atticus. You decided to stop moving. You forgot that people like us are fucking sharks. We chase blood, but when we stop moving—"

The impulse was too strong to resist. The anger swallowed me whole, and without a bit of hesitation, I jammed the wood into Atticus Garcia's milky throat. It didn't feel good, it didn't feel bad, it didn't feel like anything—just *something*. It wasn't like ending Amity or Stanley or anyone else. The moment was satisfying and visceral. Terrifying and joyous. I dragged the jagged edge towards the center of his neck as hard as I could. Felt the blood pour out onto my hands, hot and sticky. Watched the bubbles come up from his open throat as air escaped from the wound. The color drained from his face, and Atticus' hands weakly flopped up to my face but dropped back to his sides. Atticus stared into my eyes, his mouth opening and closing; the bubbles still forming in his wound—pop, pop, pop.

Motherfucker still had to try to get the last word in, didn't he?

I kicked him into the waters. I stood up, tossed the piece of wood into the water as well, and wiped my hands clean on my legs.

"When we stop moving, we die, Atticus. We fucking die."

CHAPTER FORTY-SIX

I emerged from a manhole three blocks away from where I'd entered the show. I couldn't tell if I was the source of the smell or if it was coming from elsewhere—like the pile of trash across the street. I felt like I was birthed by the city, caked in its placental discharge.

I stared at a maelstrom of blue and red lights down the block. I could see people wrapped in blankets milling around or sitting on stretchers. There were survivors. That was a good thing, I guessed. Fewer bodies on my head and more people to tell the story. I saw some folks emerge from other manholes. Men and women crying or struggling to crawl out from below the street.

I watched them. "Look at how strong you all are now."

Find the silver lining. That I survived. That anybody else did? That meant we were destined for good things. Maybe great things. In my case, I knew they would be great because I saw what I was capable of.

I saw that I could do whatever was needed to accomplish my goals.

I couldn't risk being recognized, so I walked the opposite way, away from everyone else. Away from the lights. Away from the cops. There was a McDonald's up the way, where I'd told Eddie to wait for me. I didn't have a phone, just a hope that he did as he was told. That he would take me to the closest shower to help me clean the blood off my hands. It was going to take a gallon of mouthwash to get the taste out. I had no idea what I was going to need to do to my poor nose. My throat ached something fierce, and I coughed every couple of steps. It was a deep cough, like something was embedded at the bottom of my lungs.

"Well. That isn't going to be great." I walked a little faster when I felt eyes on me from the surrounding buildings. The lookey-loos were out in force, and hell, couldn't blame them. That many police cruisers and I would be outside in a lawn chair and a bucket of Pop Secret.

Limping on the sidewalk. Smelling like the sewer. Feeling like a turd under someone's boot. Things were heavy. Killed friends. Killed former friends. Maybe wiped out an enemy or ten. But I'd made it out. I made it to see the sun shine down on the dirty sidewalks—not Amity, not Silo, and certainly not Atticus. Guilt wasn't a luxury to afford when the deaths had a point and when that point was to make me a better Poppy—to make me the best version of Poppy Leathers I could be. It was my time to assess my domain for the very first time as its royalty.

Scratch that. Fuck the monarchy. I was the goddamn

boss.

My only real regret at that moment? Maybe I could have chosen a better wetsuit to wear.

There was an Escalade parked at the McDonald's. The horn sounded and the passenger side front door opened. "Miss Leathers," Bill said, and motioned to the rear of the SUV. "We have some clothes for you if you need to change now."

I closed the gap between me and the car and nearly fell into Bill's arms, but I couldn't show weakness. Not now. Not after everything that had happened. "Just take me to Silo—my apartment," I said. "We got a headcount of our people who made it out of the party?"

Bill opened the side door for me. "Not yet. Eddie's got people texting and touching base."

I climbed into the car and gave Eddie in the driver's seat a nod.

He turned to me with a small smile. "Good to see you got out," he said. "I heard about the, eh, Albanian thing. Took the initiative and sent a few people out their way to have a discussion or two."

"Anybody we need to talk to locally?" I asked.

Bill slid into the car and we started moving.

Eddie made a left and cleared his throat. "Nobody I know of. From what I'm hearing, people are agreeable with the current changes—feeling shit out. They're not sure who this Poppy Leathers person is, but would you fuck with someone who took down Silo Jotter and drowned a third of an Albanian drug running ring?"

Damn fucking skippy. "Word travels fast," I said.

"Well, you've got a few boosters." Bill smiled. "You hungry, Miss Leathers?"

"I'll decide that after a shower and three bottles of mouthwash." But it felt wrong to go straight to relaxation. I was buzzing. I did the work, I earned almost everything I wanted, but there was one last thing to do, and it was nipping at the back of my neck like a flea on a dog. "Scratch that. We're going to New Jersey."

"New Jersey?" Eddie asked. "Why?"

"I still have something to do. The first thing on my list. Problem with working backwards is you can't shake that feeling you didn't do anything until the first one's checked off. You know?"

"Then the shower?" Eddie's nose crinkled.

"Then the shower," I said. "And I apologize for the smell. I'll pay for a new car. I don't think this one's going to last much longer with me sitting in it." I stared at my feet. There was a slow throbbing at my toes. That was going to be fun.

"Hey, Eddie?"

"Yes, Miss Leathers?"

"Thank you. The both of you. I don't think I say that enough."

Eddie smiled.

"You're welcome," Bill said.

I closed my eyes and prayed for a micro nap. Tried to

ignore the sound I kept hearing. Those foamy, red bubbles coming from Atticus' throat.

Pop, pop, pop.

Secaucus might have stunk worse than I did.

It didn't appear as if anyone was around. Maybe a bad sign—or maybe that was just New Jersey. My heart sank a little bit as I walked towards the entrance of the backup baby clinic. I saw the front desk was abandoned, and no lights were on. I limped around the side of the building and saw that a few cars were parked nearest the rear. There was a small trucking dock and an open shutter entrance with lights on—a relief, as a storm of disappointment was churning in my gut. Or maybe that was sewer water. Whatever it was, the storm subsided when I saw a young woman with quite the pregnant belly emerge from the entrance, cigarette in hand.

I approached the girl with a finger to my lips. I pointed over the girl's shoulder with my clove. "Frankie?"

The girl smirked. "A dentro, en la officina."

"Gracias, mami," I patted the girl's stomach gently. Her bulge looked fit to kick right back. "Todo esta bien?" My

Spanish was a little off. Consequence of having nobody else to speak the language with anymore.

The girl nodded. "Si."

"Good. It'll stay that way." I walked past the girl and into the shipping area. There was a long hallway inside that led to corner offices on one end and a series of makeshift bedrooms to the other side.

At the end of the passage, there was an open door, light spilling from within. Seemed important enough. I heard the distant twang of Frankie's accent. None of the words, but all of her melody.

Through the door and past the threshold. Still wearing a stinking diving suit. Barefoot. Borrowed a baseball cap from Bill because nobody should have to suffer seeing the complete state of my head.

"As I live and fucking breathe. How long has it been?" Frankie grinned as I walked into her office. She leaned back in her leather executive chair and adjusted her cuffs. "I had this feeling I'd see you again after all the hubbub going around today."

I gave her half a smile. "I was hoping to get another tour."

"Third time's the charm, right?" Frankie's smile faded.

Oh, so we were done pretending. Beautiful. "You piece it together the first time I came with Jason, or when we picked up the babies?"

"Oh, Grace, I knew it was you the moment I saw you." Frankie motioned at me. "Your face looks the same. You haven't aged at all."

Power play with the real name thing. "I very much prefer Miss Leathers now."

"It's a cute name."

"Suits me fine."

Frankie tapped her fingers against her desk. "So, all of this was for what? A hostile takeover?"

"Not entirely. Maybe a management shift," I said. "Truthfully, this shouldn't matter as much anymore. I've got a few other pokers in larger fires." I smiled. "I think this is more of a sentimental thing. A little treat after all I've been through, you know?"

"If you want to find out where your child went, you can simply ask, Poppy." Frankie typed for a moment. "We keep our records from the start."

"Don't need to. I figured all that shit out years ago. Kid's out in Colorado now. Doing damn well. Not a surprise. Also, not a surprise: you keeping those records. Fairly sure the real business ain't so much in selling the babies as touching base after a while to see how invested the new parents are in maintaining confidentiality."

Frankie scoffed sarcastically as she placed a hand on her chest in that Southern way. "Are you suggesting I'm a blackmailer?"

"Suggestions are for the weak."

"I suppose. But if I were you, I'd take great care about what you suggest, assert, or accuse others of."

"Threats are also for pansies." I watched her. She was

comfortable. Too comfortable. There I was, coming off the literal battlefield, and this woman really sat there thinking she had one over on me. As if I hadn't practiced this entire moment in my goddamn head a million times before.

"My threats are and always remain open wounds, sweetheart." Frankie licked her lips. "Especially when they're directed at a troublemaker like you."

"Trouble ain't the half." Enough pontification with people who made the mistake of constantly underestimating me.

We drew our pistols at the same time, but Frankie's rush—and her office chair—gave her an awkward momentum. She bobbed back just an inch and her aim was simply not true. See, me, I was smart enough to square up the moment I walked into that office. I was still hiding that adrenaline high that left my hands steady as high school sweethearts. Three pulls of the trigger. Two to the chest. One to the head. I'll admit going for the chest first was dumb, but it was worth it to see that look of shock on Frankie's face as she realized her life was half over. The bullet to the head ended things.

There was a small part of me that wished she knew how special she was at that moment. That I fully intended this woman would be the last life I'd take with my own hands. I wasn't naïve enough to believe that, but in the moment, it was as romantic as a thought I could have to help pull me across the finish line.

A little treat to myself from myself. Full circle. Poppy Leathers fucking won.

CHAPTER FORTY-EIGHT

I bought Amity's space. Took greasing a few wheels—with a few baseball bats—but I managed a fair price. I bought the whole damn building. Gutted the original store. Decided to make it something new; something in her spirit. Would this piss people off uptown? Probably. Who fucking cared? Let them come for me. I had the biggest stick, and I was more than willing to swing that shit for the fences.

Meat Charcuterie would open for business in late summer. We hired a few phenomenal cheesemakers. Managed to get licenses to house capybaras on site. Added an entire menu of meats selected by artisans of the dry aging craft. It was a natural evolution of what Amity started. A place devoid of the legacy she was chained to, joined with all the things Silo plied into. They never would have accomplished this alive. In death, they would work together. I thought it was a little poetic, but hoped it would be damn profitable.

I sat at the unfinished counter near wine storage. Eddie walked over and leaned in. "Miss Leathers, she's here."

"Send her over," I said.

Milagros DelValle. Striking. Elegant as all hell. She looked like someone carved her out of marble. Her bona fides were impressive. Good education—Seton Hall, like me—strong work background. Afro-Latina—a plus. No priors for assault or anything else. Skirted with the law on a shoplifting charge while she was an undergrad. Her expertise was restaurant management, and I knew the moment I saw her: she'd be perfect to run Meat Charcuterie. She was also a perfect foil to me. A person to begin grooming as a right hand.

Didn't hurt that she didn't ever question the looser aspects of doing business. Not an eyelash bent over odd paperwork or the disappearance of a contractor or ten. She knew damn well what she was involved in and didn't give a fuck.

"How good are you at wordplay?" I asked as she sat down at the counter.

"Do you mean puns? Portmanteau?"

I nodded. "Yes, ma'am."

Milagros shrugged. "I'm okay. Whatever I can't figure out, I'll outsource."

I liked when she admitted to weakness. Milagros wasn't showy or full of herself. She was a professional. Kept a steady head at almost all times. Beat out twelve other candidates who all came shy of her assertiveness, ability to connect with near anyone, and disposition. She had ambition. A person to watch—closely.

I shuffled my papers away and gave Milly my full attention. I didn't call her Milly to her face, but I wished I could. It suited her. "We looking good for open?"

"Excellent, Miss Leathers. Menu's near final and we're beginning to interview support staff. I'm trying not to be overly optimistic in case we hit any unseen obstacles." Milly adjusted her skirt.

I made her nervous. Good.

"Excellent. I'm going to be busy upstate for a few days finalizing the contracts with a few farms. Found a fella who's doing some freaky shit with kale, from what I hear. We'll see how that pans out. What that means, though, is I need you driving this little endeavor on your own. And it ain't like I think you can't handle it."

"I know, Miss Leathers. We should be all set. I can call if anything requires your say-so, though."

"If I got a cellular signal I'll try to get back to you. Who the fuck knows what happens when there's more trees than people? Not my scene, but I need to show my face, you know?" I stood up. "We got your office finished, by the way. Need one favor from you."

"What's that?"

"There's some last-minute stuff for you to go over in there. Follow the directions and we're golden. Bill's going to stick around in case I can't be reached and you need some help, Okay?"

"Sounds great," Milly said.

"Oh, and do me a solid. Eddie's niece has her quinceañera coming up this weekend. Please send something absolutely ludicrous and frilly in his name. I want the man to look good for his family since I'm keeping him away."

"You've got it, Miss Leathers." Milly took some notes.

For a moment, under those fluorescent lights and in her cute outfit, she reminded me of myself when I started with Atticus. All that energy and that determination. She clearly wanted to impress, and I knew that meant she had aspirations. Once upon a time, that would have thrilled me, but I knew better. She was good for two or three years at the most, but it would have to come to an end at some point. I made a mental note to talk with Eddie about her severance. Never a bad thing to plan ahead, especially with someone so charming and hard-working.

I got my things together and left. Eddie drove me back to my apartment where we finished off plans for a complete renovation, tasted a few new cheeses, and checked in with families looking to adopt cute little babies.

Those babies always made me think of Colorado. I'd never been there before. Wondered if I should pick up skiing but couldn't suss out when I'd have the time. Life was too damn busy, and there was a whole cavalcade of management decisions to make and money to grow. I had what I wanted, and I wasn't about to rest on my ass. My arms were finally long enough to box with God.

Or at least give Her the reach around.

ACKNOWLEDGMENTS

Firstly, not a word of this book happens without the guidance of Chuck Pahlaniuk. He's the person who read a short chapter about a hitman at a gun shop and gave me the notes/encouragement to build what would become *POP!*. Will he ever see this? Probably not, but still, it has to be called out.

To my fellow writers and friends, S.A. Cosby, Errick Nunnally, Alex Segura, Hector Acosta, Libby Cudmore, Nik Korpon, Chris Irvin, Ed Aymar, Nick Kolakowski, and the Discord chat—thank you all for helping me keep my craft up and my sanity in place.

To the staff at Ruadán Books and my amazing agent Jon Michael Darga—thank you for having faith in this chaos gremlin of a novel.

To a world and industry that at times works as hard as possible to make writers like me feel unwanted and as if our perspectives mean nothing: I'm still here and I'm still typing away.

And to my family. I can't find the words to express how grateful I am to have people in my life who inspire and support me in ways like you all do. You're with me every key stroke and not a moment goes by that I am doing this for anyone else but you. Thank you.

ABOUT ANGEL LUIS COLÓN

Angel Luis Colón is the author of the award-nominated novels *Hell Chose Me* and *No Happy Endings*, the Blacky Jaguar series of novellas, the award-winning young adult novel *Infested*, the hit middle-grade novel *Minecraft: House of Horrors*, and the short story collection *Meat City on Fire and Other Assorted Debacles*. He has spent time editing flash fiction for websites like *Shotgun Honey* and was the editor of the Latine-focused anthology, *¡Pa'Que Tu lo Sepas!*. He's also had multiple short stories appear in web and print publications, including *Literary Orphans*, *The Molotov Cocktail*, and the legendary crime fiction mag *Thuglit*.

When he's not writing, you'll find him baking bread or enjoying a scotch—mostly at the same time.

COMING SOON

"*Darling* is an unflinching horror novel—an unsettling story about what constitutes true evil."

—Catherine Thureson, *Foreword Reviews*

DARLING

Mercedes M. Yardley

Some things are best kept in the rearview, and Darling, Louisiana, is one of those things. A single mom's return is the haunting cautionary tale of what hell may come in small towns where evil walks tall.

OUT SEPTEMBER 8, 2026